Praise for Michae
The Forbidde

"[An] unforgettable story of love, deceit, and redemption... extraordinary."
—*Library Journal* (starred review)

"Intriguing and entertaining... compulsively readable."
—Daniel Silva, author of *The Unlikely Spy*

"The intrigues of Communist Russia during the last day of the Cold War... Well-paced and exciting, with crisp dialogue, believable setups, and first-rate atmosphere."
—*Kirkus Reviews*

"... a first-rate thriller, a terrifying account of the cruelty, the betrayals, and the countless victims of the Communist machine. This book caught my imagination from the first page to the very last."
—Robert Strauss, last U.S. Ambassador to the Soviet Union, first Ambassador to the Russian Federation

"A grand adventure... fast-moving and terrifying."
—*Boulder Camera*

"Fascinating."
—Robert Harris, author of *Archangel*

"Suspenseful... a lively and readable tale told with extraordinary clarity."
—*Naples* (FL) *Daily News*

"Keeps the reader turning pages late into the night... A thriller with solid meat on some very strong bones."
—*American Way* magazine

"Well-written, attentive... full of compassion for the Russian people, and of pleasure for American readers."
—*Publisher's Weekly*

"This is what every reviewer hopes for when opening a book by a new author. A fine debut."
—*The Boston Globe*

"Fantastic... a major success as a new star, to the joy of readers, has entered the sub-genre with a strong winner."
—Harriet Klausner, *Under the Covers*

"... an exciting read and the author's knowledge of the Russian scene stings clear and cold as a Moscow morning... an extraordinary job... adds a chilling dimension of Soviet reality."
—Jerrold Schecter, author of *The Spy Who Saved the World: How a Soviet Colonel Changed the Course of the Cold War*

"... does for the Soviet Union what Michael Crichton's *Jurassic Park* did for dinosaurs—brings the remote past back to life in all its blood and terror."
—Anthony Olcott, author of *Murder at the Red October*

"... impressive realism... [with] a compelling storyline and a satisfying conclusion. I recommend it."
—*Advocate*, Baton Rouge, LA

"It is a joy to read a thriller that is totally plausible... it is excellent."
—*The Roanoke Times*

Van Gogh's Lover

Michael Hetzer

Pilgrim Trout Books

Copyright © 2025 by Michael Hetzer

All rights reserved.

No portion of this book may be reproduced in any form without written permission from the publisher or author, except as permitted by U.S. copyright law.

ISBN Ebook: 979-8-9927233-1-1
ISBN Paperback: 979-8-9927233-0-4
ISBN Hardback: 979-8-9927233-2-8

Cover design by Richard Ljoenes

This is a work of fiction. The characters, incidents and dialogue are products of the author's imagination and are not construed as real.

Part 1

The Lover

One

Sophie

April 12, 1888
Arles, France

Yellow.

The color hung over the streets of downtown Arles like constellations on a starry night—yellow sun, yellow wheat fields, yellow haystacks, and sulfur-stained stone houses with sunflowers in every window. A fierce wind whipped the scene into delirious motion, swirling dust and paper into the air like vegetables in a boiling soup pot. It was wild and alive and, for the woman standing alone on the street that crystal afternoon, exhilarating.

Sophie von Tessen grinned. She was free!

In the distance, a police whistle blew, rousing her from her celebration. She slipped into the shadows of an alley. Instantly, her mood darkened. She hesitated.

She should not have come this way. The stone façades felt like walls. Sophie hated walls. She had lived too long behind them. She was thirty years old, and it was time to begin her life, for better or worse, no matter what it meant for someone like her. She was never going back.

Whistles screeched again. Nearer now. She fled down the alley. Beside her, the wall opened into a courtyard, and she ducked inside. She pressed her back to the cold stone and waited for the men to pass.

"That way!" the *gendarme* said in French when he was a few feet away. "*Allez!*"

Sophie panted as the pounding of their boots grew fainter. In the courtyard, a chicken strutted toward her. It pecked her toe.

"Ow!" Sophie nudged it away with her foot. "Shoo!"

A woman carrying water came into the courtyard from behind the shed. Their eyes met.

Sophie knew she presented an alarming sight. She wore a gray smock that hung on her like a sack. Her bare feet were black from three days on the run. Her brown hair was wild with neglect.

Sophie pressed her fingers to her lips. "*Non. S'il vous plaît, madam. Non.*"

The woman dropped her bucket. "*Ici*! Here! She is here!"

Sophie fled back out onto the street. The mistral winds of Provence roared in her ears. Across the river, wheat fields danced like kelp in a current.

She needed to get off the road and out of sight. But how?

As if in answer, the street opened before her, and she found herself looking at an enormous Roman coliseum. Two levels of arches with walkways and ramps all around promised hundreds of places to hide.

An angel was guiding her, surely! Every time she was confused about what course to take, the answer presented itself. She had never made it this far before.

She sprinted around the coliseum looking for a way inside, but the structure was contained by a high stone wall. As she circled the coliseum along its ring road, she came upon a man selling jewelry from a cart. He looked her over and then drew a knife. He held it toward her, protecting his wares.

She circled past his blade.

Far off, a police whistle pierced the air. The man smirked at her predicament.

"Pretty necklaces," she remarked and ran on.

She came upon a ramp leading into the coliseum. She went inside and began looking for a place to hide. The coliseum was eerily quiet. A woman and her dog lay beneath a ramp in a makeshift camp. The dog stopped chewing its bone to growl at her.

She went on. She came out into the arena and blinked against the powerful sunlight. A pair of lovers on the top bleachers were too busy kissing to notice her. Down on the arena's dirt plaza, a man wheeled a trash cart. Sophie stole upward, where she hoped to hide under a ramp as the homeless woman and her dog had done.

And that's when she saw that the entrance to the ramp was blocked by a broad-shouldered man with his back to her. He was painting behind his easel. She crept closer, hoping to slip past him. He was deep in concentration and did not hear her.

Sophie caught sight of his canvas and was taken aback by the work in progress. Her pursuers were forgotten. As a girl, Sophie had been taught the basics of watercolor. Of all the silly diversions she was expected to master, painting had been Sophie's favorite. Not that she mastered it. Her paintings were as manic as she was. It wasn't long before Mama took away her brushes.

The painter was working with oils, a medium Sophie admired but which, for some reason, was considered unfit for a girl. He was attempting to paint the arena as it would appear on a busy day when it was filled with spectators to a bullfight. He did not seem happy with the result. He grumbled to himself, and smoked furiously on his pipe.

The wind was giving him trouble. He painted a few strokes and then the wind took his hat. He raced to retrieve it, and then his paint supply basket was blown over. He straightened it and then managed to lay down a few strokes before the cycle repeated. He was like a man in a dream trying not to wake up, despite the relentless caw of a rooster. Sophie was fascinated by him.

A police whistle sounded. He turned toward it, and his face came into view—first a stern, Nordic profile with a blunt nose and elongated chin, then auburn hair, thick eyebrows, deep-set eyes, and a stubbly beard. He had the rugged look of a man who'd lived a hard life.

He saw her. His blue eyes widened in alarm. He thrust his paintbrush toward her, wielding it ridiculously, as though it were a sword.

What an odd man.

Vincent Van Gogh considered how he would defend himself if the woman attacked him. She was half his size, so he had no obvious cause for concern. But even a raccoon could be dangerous if it were rabid, and she certainly had a feral look about her. She was slender with a graceful neck that disappeared into an unruly brown mane that resided atop her head like a living organism. She wore an institutional smock the color of raw wool. She was barefoot. Here, surely, was the reason for the police whistles.

"*Pardonnez-moi*, Monsieur," she said. "I didn't mean to startle you."

Her French was not native, but still better than his.

"May I watch?" she asked, and then plunked herself down on the bleacher without waiting for an answer.

What an odd woman.

He was nervous about turning his back on her, but his canvas beckoned. He was in a fever to capture the scene. Such light! He dabbed his brush on his palette and disappeared into his work. The woman was a memory.

A few minutes later, he was interrupted yet again—this time by the sound of official voices conducting a search.

"It's the *gendarmes*," said Vincent to the woman. "You should probably hide."

She scampered out of the bleachers and plunged into the darkness of the tunnel.

Vincent set down his palette and relit his pipe. He waited. He had his own troubled relationship with the police. Nothing serious. He was new to Arles, having arrived from Paris only a couple of months earlier, but already there were complaints that he frightened the children, that he was often drunk in the streets, and had a short temper. People called him "*le fou roux*," the red-headed madman. Boys threw cabbage heads at him. Not to mention the regrettable incident at Madame Giroux's brothel...

The policeman came up to Vincent.

"*Bonjour*, Monsieur."

"*Bonjour*."

"Have you seen anyone pass by?" he asked. "We are looking for a woman. She escaped from the monastery, St. Paul de Mausole."

"She escaped from a *monastery*?"

"It's an asylum now."

Vincent nodded. "Is she dangerous?"

"One must assume so."

"I haven't seen anyone, but thank you for the warning. I will be vigilant."

The policeman turned to go, but then something occurred to Vincent.

"*Un moment, le gendarme.*"

"*Oui?*"

"I was wondering, is there a reward for her capture?"

Sophie collapsed on the bunk in the Arles city jail and punched the mattress in frustration. The painter had turned her in for a reward of twelve francs! So much for her guardian angel! It led her straight to that devil with a paintbrush. The only reason she wasn't already on her way back to the asylum was that the coachman was drunk. She was being held overnight like a common prisoner until he sobered up.

She crawled beneath the scratchy wool blanket and, sobbing, buried her face in the stained mattress.

She awoke in darkness to a clank in the outer room of the station.

"*Merde!*" a man cursed.

"Shh, you drunken fool!" hissed a girl.

"Where are you taking me?" the man asked.

Sophie sat up. She knew the man's voice. The painter!

"Come on," said the girl. "They keep the women back here."

Through the bars of her cell, Sophie could make out the silhouette of the painter and a girl, perhaps sixteen years old. She wore a bustier and a lacy skirt.

"There she is," said the painter.

The girl looked at Sophie and raised her eyebrows. "Are you sure about this?"

"*Mais oui*! But how will you unlock the door?"

"What's going on?" asked Sophie.

"It's a jailbreak, *ma chérie*!" said the painter.

"Shh! *Le fou roux*!"

The girl climbed onto the cell door, clutching the bars for balance. She invited the painter and Sophie to join her. All three of them now hung on the door.

"Bounce!" she said.

They began to jump up and down in unison. The hinges groaned, and the lock released with a click. The door swung open. They stepped off.

"It's true," the painter said in wonder to the girl. "You are a witch."

He swept her into his arms and kissed her.

The girl pushed him away. "Ach, Vincent, you reek!"

Sophie faced the painter squarely. "You turned me in!"

"*Au contraire*!" he said, his blue eyes glistening in the dim light. "We have outsmarted them! I have twelve francs, and you have your freedom. Vincent Van Gogh is a genius, *non*?"

Sophie followed her rescuers out of the courthouse and up a hill to a cemetery. A full moon etched shadows over the helter-skelter headstones. The only sound was the chirping of cicadas and the haunting *whoo-hoo-hoo* of owls on the hunt. From the vista, the whole of Arles and the French countryside lay bathed in silvery light. Scarlet lamps burned in two buildings along the wharf far below them. The Rhône wove a shimmering, serpentine path to both horizons.

The girl led them to a tomb in the center of the cemetery. It was a small room with a stone coffin at one end, and a window through which moonlight entered. The space gave them protection from the night chill and a place to talk. The clandestine cemetery rendezvous had something of *Huckleberry Finn* to it, Sophie thought. She had just finished reading Mark Twain's latest novel, so it was fresh in her mind.

"We're safe here," said the girl.

Sophie's anger returned with full force. "I want my share of the reward!"

"She has a point," said the girl, who introduced herself as Marie. "Four francs each. It's only fair."

"But that's all I have left!" Vincent protested.

"Because you spent your share on liquor and paint," said Marie. "That's hardly her fault."

Reluctantly, Vincent put the coins in Sophie's hand. She marveled at the weight of them. How long had it been since she held money that was her own? It then occurred to her that she had nowhere to put the coins.

Marie saw the problem and spoke up. "I'll hold them for you," she said.

Vincent watched Marie take the coins and said to Sophie, "You can kiss those goodbye."

"Oh, shut up, you fool," said Marie.

Marie climbed onto the coffin and lay on her side as though she were on a bed. She displayed no respect for the corpse beneath her.

"Now, you must tell us your story," she said to Sophie.

Vincent lit his pipe and stared at her with curiosity. When Sophie didn't answer, Marie turned and dangled her feet and kicked the coffin with her heels.

"I can get you some clothes," said Marie. "But it'll cost you."

"I have money," said Sophie.

"Now I see where this is going," said Vincent. "By the end of the night, the whore will have all the money. Same as always."

Marie winked at Sophie. "He's not as dumb as he looks."

"Now that's settled, who's up for a night swim?" asked Vincent.

Marie's eyes lit up. "*Allez!*"

Vincent led them downhill along a different path leading east, clear of town. They crossed a road and then followed a path that sloped down to the river.

They arrived at a small beach, and Vincent was the first to strip off his clothes and dive in. Marie unclipped her bustier and stepped out of her skirt. Sophie couldn't help but notice her youthful skin. It glowed like polished marble in the moonlight. Vincent also watched her, paralyzed by the sight of the nude girl.

"I must paint you, *mon cœur*!" he said after she slipped below the surface.

"We've been over this. You can't afford me."

Marie waved to Sophie, who stood on the bank. "What are you waiting for?"

Sophie was staring at Vincent. How could she undress with *him* there?

Marie recognized the problem and splashed Vincent. "You dog! *Très impoli*! Give the lady some privacy."

Vincent turned. Sophie stripped and slipped into the river. The feeling left her delirious with joy. She dove beneath the surface and then rose, spitting water. She splashed Marie, who splashed her back. They laughed.

Vincent was excited about something.

"A fish brushed my leg!" he cried. "A big one! I will catch it with my hands."

"You will not," said Marie.

"I will. And when I do, then you will let me paint you."

"If you catch a fish with your bare hands, then yes, Vincent, I will let you paint me."

"Nude, of course."

"Whatever."

Vincent's eyes were glowing now. "Your breasts, I will make them the color of the chestnut blossoms! I have the color on my palette. Oh, what a portrait it will be! I will project all the colors of Provence onto your body. You will be my French angel of spring! Your eyes will be the cobalt blue of the sky. Your hair will be purple wisteria. Your neck will be the ruddy red-brown of the tilled fields. I will make you famous!"

"And what of my bush?" asked Marie.

"Ah," said Vincent. "That I will place at the center of the portrait. It will be blackberry briars to protect the fruit of your womb. When people see the portrait, they will not gaze upon your eyes. *Mais non*! They will look first to your blazing *raison d'être*!"

Sophie's jaw fell. What a notion! The man was crazier than she was.

"Idiot," Marie scoffed.

Vincent began trying to catch his fish. Sophie laughed and kicked water into the air. She had never skinny-dipped before. How could she have known that the bathing costume ruined the experience? She vowed that from then on, she would only ever swim nude. The thought delighted her. She floated on her back, looking up at the moon, and thought about the guardian angel who had guided her here.

"Best night of my life," Sophie said aloud.

Marie looked at Sophie strangely before dunking her and then swimming for shore.

"Come on," she said.

On the beach, Marie went to work on Sophie's hair. She washed it three times using sand for soap. She scrubbed so aggressively that Sophie's scalp ached. She combed the snarls with her fingers. Finally, she tied the wad behind her neck with a ribbon from her dress.

As she worked, Marie carried on a monologue about the other girls in the brothel where she worked. It was called Madame Giroux's White Rose House of Temperance. Marie had only been there a few months, but already had several regulars. A French army base was not far away. The men, she said, were "young, fit, and *fast*."

During this time, Vincent was forgotten. Suddenly, his voice came from the bank.

"*Bonne nuit, mes dames.*"

They turned. He stood on the trail, fully dressed in the same soiled clothes he had been wearing in the arena. He had failed to catch his fish, and now he was leaving. He looked defeated.

"I've got to paint in the morning," he said.

"Uh-huh," said Marie.

"In this wind?" asked Sophie.

"Yes, in this wind!" he barked. The sudden change in his mood was alarming.

He whirled around and collided with a tree. He collapsed at the base of the trunk and sat there. Marie laughed. Vincent hung his head over his lap and sat so long that Sophie wondered if he had fallen asleep.

He found a branch and peeled back the bark to create a point. He pressed the sharp edge into his arm. Blood rose from the wound.

"Vincent!" Sophie cried.

He started, as though surprised to discover he was not alone. He dropped the twig and climbed to his feet, before staggering off into the night.

Two

Jane

Ontario Hills, New York
October 29, 2012

She was awake. But where was she?

She surveyed her surroundings. Metal rails on the bed. A monitor beeping beside her. The faint smell of bleach. A woman in scrubs at the foot of the bed tapping on a tablet.

Okay, a hospital room.

"Excuse me," she called to the woman—or rather, *tried* to call to the woman; for some reason, her vocal cords didn't respond.

Still, she managed to make a noise. The nurse, an elderly woman, jumped as though a spider had fallen on her neck. She raced out of the room calling for a doctor.

Seconds later, a doctor arrived wearing a white lab coat and a look of astonishment.

"What is your name?"

"Ja... Ja... Jane Wa... Ward."

Her voice sounded strange.

The questions went on. *Your birth date? Can you wiggle your toes? Your fingers?*

"Miracle," someone said.

"Where am I?" Jane asked.

By then, the room was filled with doctors and nurses and people in business suits. A man in slippers and a hospital smock wandered in from the hallway pushing his IV stand.

"The hospital," said the doctor.

"What happened?"

A lot of words followed, but Jane heard two. *Accident. Coma.*

"How long?"

"Two weeks," he replied. "What's the last thing you remember?"

Jane thought. "Pulchritudinous."

"Pulchri... what?"

Yeah, the word was new to her, too.

The vocabulary test would account for a quarter of Jane's grade. So Jane decided to walk to school and study on the way.

Jane left her house and started along Maple Street, keeping to the sidewalk. The day was as crisp as a fallen leaf. The air was soaked with the smell of ripe apples. Far overhead, migrating geese honked as they fled the approach of winter.

Jane arrived at Cherry Lane and turned left.

Obfuscate: to make something unclear...

Like using the word "obfuscate," she thought. She continued to Village Grocery, where she bought a copy of *Seventeen*. As of last week, seventeen was her age. The realization pleased her. These days, when she looked in the mirror, she saw a woman. Jane was average height, with brown hair that always wanted to frizz—cue the straightening iron. Jane had a delicate face some might call "sweet." She was learning how to apply makeup to draw attention to her round, brown eyes, and that's how *Seventeen* was going to help. Could she be a feminist and still use makeup?

She continued on.

By the post office, she paused to pet Mrs. Turner's beagle, Sonny. She gave him a Ritz cracker from her lunch bag. He swallowed it whole and wagged his tail for another.

"That's all for now," she laughed.

She went on. The school was in sight now. She felt a tinge of excitement to think that, as a senior, she would never again endure a fall semester at Ontario Hills High School. In a few weeks, she would declare early for NYU, write a killer essay, and get a full scholarship. It was not an unreasonable dream. She was in the running for valedictorian, after all.

Back to work. Just a few more words to go.

Loquacious: talkative...

Then why not just use "talkative"? Sheesh. When Jane was a writer—and someday she would be—she would never use "loquacious." It was so... obfuscatory. She smiled at her cleverness. But was it a word? She would have to look it up when she got to school.

Pulchritudinous: possessing great beauty...

Such a sophisticated word! She considered who might be worthy of such a word. Certainly no one in provincial Ontario Hills. Sophie sprang to mind. Yes, Sophie! Sophie was the woman in a painting her grandmother owned. It was Jane's favorite piece of art in the whole world. Granny Jo knew nothing about the woman besides her name, so they let their imaginations fill in the blanks, inventing the most fascinating stories. Yes, Jane decided, Sophie was pulchritudinous.

Jane stepped off the curb—

"Where are my parents?" Jane asked.

"They're on their way."

Jane became aware of a vase of flowers beside her. A single sunflower surrounded by daisies and carnations. Jane frowned at the arrangement.

"Do you like the flowers?" asked the doctor.

Jane frowned. *What was happening?*

"They're... they're..." she stammered.

"They're what?"

Jane looked away. Then back again. She studied the room. Something was wrong. She didn't even have words for it.

"Jane?" said the doctor with alarm. "The flowers are what?"

"Gray."

"What?"

At that moment, a woman entered the hospital room. Her hair was styled in an updo that had largely unraveled and now fell around her face like hay through the wires of a chicken coop. She wore dark lipstick, and around her neck was a pair of tiger-print reading glasses on a spotted lanyard. There was only one person in Ontario Hills who fit such a description. Jane had given her the lanyard for Mother's Day.

"Mom?"

"I'm here, baby. Momma's here."

The woman pulled Jane into her arms. Jane's nose filled with Chanel No. 5.

Yes, it was her mother.

Had to be.

But...

Jane pulled back and frowned into the woman's face. She knew her mother. Of course she knew her mother—the glasses, the hair, the lipstick, the smell—so why did she not *recognize* her?

Jane surveyed the faces of the doctors and nurses. The *beep-beep* of her heart monitor accelerated. It mingled with a growing buzz in her ears.

"Jane? What is it, baby? What's wrong?"

Jane Ward took a deep breath and screamed.

Twelve years later

The boughs of the ancient white oak tree reached outward beneath the low-hanging clouds of pre-dawn. Five feet away, a man in a hard hat held a chainsaw that rattled and belched smoke. Between him and the tree trunk stood

Hattie Everly, Rebecca Williamson, and Edna Burke. At age seventy-seven, Edna was the youngest of the trio.

Jane stood to the side watching. She wore a camera around her neck and took notes in a narrow notepad.

The man in the hard hat, Evan Holmes, eyed the trio warily.

"Move on out there now, Auntie Edna," he said. "You don't want your gout flarin' up. And I got work to do."

"The devil's work!" Edna screeched. "Go ahead. Saw me in two, you ingrate!"

Jane smiled. Edna was president of Dirt Diggers, the local gardening club, and she was clearly relishing her new role as eco-warrior.

Jane climbed onto Evan's bulldozer for a better view and snapped several pictures. She made sure the oak tree framed the picture; it made the actors in the little standoff appear minuscule beneath the tree's majestic canopy, which covered nearly a quarter-acre of earth.

At that moment, two cars appeared at the edge of the field. They bounced toward the tree over the uneven field. One vehicle had "Sheriff Ontario County" on its door. The other was a black Cadillac Escalade Jane had seen around town ever since the plans for a new shopping center appeared in the records of Ontario Hills Planning and Zoning Department. As editor of the *Ontario Sun News*, it was her job to review those plans each month. When she saw that the plans would require removing the tree, she invited a Ph.D. arborist from the State University of New York at Potsdam to inspect the tree, which he determined to be roughly three hundred and forty years old. It was her lead story in the newspaper, and she dedicated a hefty fifty-two column-inches to it. Next, she interviewed a historian, also from Potsdam. He noted that the tree had stood at the time of the French and Indian War. It was not inconceivable that Colonel George Washington himself may have paused beneath that very tree along with the Iroquois chief, Half King, as they planned their campaign against the French. In her article, Jane dubbed the tree "Half King Oak."

Posters began to appear around town: *Save the Half King Oak*. Jane covered that story, too—who put them up, who printed them, and why it mattered to them. She interviewed Chief Awenasa of the Iroquois tribe about the profound transformation of his people during the years the white oak stood. She covered the tense city council meetings in which the developers defended their plans. She did an extended one-on-one interview with the president of the developers' group. And so it went until they arrived at this moment, in the pre-dawn chill beneath the great oak itself, where the total membership of Dirt Diggers faced off against Evan Holmes and his sputtering chainsaw.

The vehicles stopped and doors flew open. The SUV expelled four men in suits. They wore loafers that sank in the mud up to their argyle socks. Sheriff Marcus Young got out of his cruiser and walked briskly toward Evan. As he passed Jane, he shot her a wink.

"Kill the chainsaw, Evan," he said. "We got an injunction."

Evan turned off the saw. Jane thought he looked relieved. Marcus explained the injunction to the suits and then walked up to Jane.

"Early enough for you?" he said, rolling his eyes.

"They probably thought they'd get the deed done before anyone noticed."

"At which point it would have been too late."

"They should have known better," said Jane. "Those ladies never sleep. I think Hattie might be a vampire."

The sheriff laughed. He gave Jane a brief statement for the newspaper. The tree, he explained, had been declared a historic landmark, a first for New York.

He left, and Jane took a photograph of the victorious ladies of Dirt Diggers. In triumph, they clasped their hands and raised them over their heads like civil rights activists. Jane finished with them and went to the men in suits.

"Good morning!" she said.

"I hope you're happy," said one of the men.

"Just doing my job."

"Hmph."

"We don't have to be enemies," said Jane. "Ontario Hills needs this shopping center."

"You have a funny way of showing it."

Jane closed her pad and put away her pen. "I have an idea how this can work out for everyone. Wanna hear?"

An hour later, Jane arrived back at the one-room office above Cherry Street Liquors that housed the editorial office of the *Ontario Sun News*. She went to her desk and turned on her computer. Her fingers flew as she wrote the piece for the next day's edition. She paused only to check her notes or listen to recordings of interviews on her phone. It was a big story: The developers' group was proposing to rename the shopping plaza "Half King Center." The tree would stand in the parking lot and be maintained by professional arborists from the university, while the plaza's logo would be an elegant white oak. Jane made no mention of where the idea had come from.

When she finished, Jane typed up the week's high school sports scores; the girls' field hockey team had a big win against their cross-county rival. The new honor rolls were out, and Jane typed up the names, all ninety-seven of them, most of which were familiar to her. When she finished, she imported the stories into the layout software, merged them with the ads and finally, wrote headlines to fit the space. When it was done, she emailed the finished edition to the printer. She turned off the light and then went downstairs and out onto the street. It was nearly three o'clock, and she had been at it since before dawn. Though it was April, there was talk of a snowstorm, and Jane could feel its weight in the air. Winter in Upstate New York was like that; it delighted in dispensing one last kick before retiring for the year.

She walked one block to the public library and opened the door.

Her mother was waiting for her behind the checkout desk.

"How did the story go?" her mother asked.

"Good, I think."

"The returns cart is full," her mother said. She grabbed her coat and went out, leaving Jane to run the library.

Assistant Librarian was Jane's main job. Her mother gave her Thursdays off to put the newspaper to bed, but Jane's bills were paid by her civil servant salary. The newspaper barely covered its print costs, much less a salary for a full-time editor.

Not that Jane minded. Though it had never been her plan, she loved being a librarian, particularly at this library. Jane had practically grown up within these painted, cinderblock walls. After school, she would come straight to the library to be with her mother. She played hide-and-seek in the stacks, built book forts, and secretly read novels beyond her years. It all felt perfectly normal.

Jane found the returns cart and pushed it toward the stacks. The usual suspects were behind the computers, reading news and scrolling through Facebook. Young Kip, who lived in a tent behind the high school, sat at Carousel Three. His long hair was freshly washed, and his scruffy beard trimmed. She grimaced; he had obviously used the library's bathroom again. Later, she would have to clean up the mess. Still, she was pleased he was feeling well and flashed a smile at him.

Jane steered the cart toward Home Improvement and began shelving books.

Two hours later, in Landscaping, a voice came from behind her.

"Excuse me, miss. Can you help me find a book?"

Jane turned to face a short, husky man with a full beard. He wore a sport coat and stylish, round glasses.

"Sure. Title?"

"It's called *Breakfast of Champions*."

"Ah, Kurt Vonnegut. Yes, we have a copy. It's in fiction."

She started down the aisle. He followed.

"Have you read it?" he asked.

"A long time ago."

"I hear it's really good."

"It has its fans."

"But not you?"

She shrugged.

After a pause, he went on. "I suppose you think its satire is just fashionable disillusionment."

She stopped. "What did you say?"

The man was grinning at her. He pulled up his sleeve to reveal a small tattoo. It looked like an asterisk.

"Ted?"

"Hi, Jane."

"Oh, my god."

She rushed to hug him. His big arms closed around her, and for a moment she clung to him like a life raft. They parted and she punched his shoulder harder than she intended.

"Ow."

"You monster! What kind of an asshole plays a practical joke on a person with face-blindness?"

He grinned. "The kind of asshole with a tattoo of an asshole on his hand."

She laughed. "Touché."

Ted had gotten the tattoo in high school, right after her accident, as a way for her to recognize him. Getting a small tattoo on one's right hand became a thing at Ontario Hills High School as dozens of classmates did it in solidarity with Jane. In the end, she had to put a stop to it. There were other ways that a person with face-blindness could identify people, ways that didn't involve defiling one's body. As for Ted's asterisk, that was an inside joke. It was from *Breakfast of Champions*—Vonnegut's hand-drawn depiction of an anus. Jane hated the novel, and Ted knew it. Nothing was ever easy with Ted. Still, she loved him for the gesture.

He was shaking his head in wonder. "Jane Ward, as I live and breathe. Shelving books in your mother's library. It's as though not a day has passed in twelve years."

Something about his tone made her stiffen.

In high school, they had been frenemies. When Jane started a creative writing club, Ted Banks was one of only four students to join. They both planned to become journalists. They argued over Vonnegut and Morrison and Angelou. They shared pages from their journals, still in long-hand, and competed for writing prizes, which Jane tended to win. They were both planning to attend NYU after high school and were competing for the same scholarships. They kissed a few times and, once, in the library, he put his hand on her breast. Jane recoiled, for he had done nothing to prepare her for this escalation in their relationship. He apologized immediately and then fled the scene of his crime. For days afterward, he was unable to look her in the eye. Eventually, she persuaded him to put the episode behind him, and their combative friendship resumed more or less as before. She waited—somewhat hopefully—for him to make another romantic advance, but he never did. In college, she heard he came out as gay and was now living with a partner in Paris. They had adopted a girl from Nigeria, who was now in high school and roughly the same age Jane had been when he got to second base with her. Through his partner, an artist, Ted developed an interest in art and went on to write two well-regarded biographies of artists. His books sold well and received favorable reviews. Jane stocked them in her library. Ted was living a life she had once imagined for herself. Their friendly competition had ended long ago. Ted won.

"What brings you here?" she asked.

"Why do you say it like that? Can't it just be to see an old friend?"

Jane blinked at him.

"Okay, you got me. This is going to sound weird. It's about that painting your grandmother owns. The nude."

"*The Lover*? How do you know about that?"

"Are you kidding? You practically forced me to look at it so many times. You were obsessed."

Jane frowned.

"Anyway, something's come up and, well, I think you should see this."

Jane checked the clock. Fifteen minutes to closing.

She went to the utility panel and pulled the plug on the Wi-Fi. Within minutes, the library's few remaining patrons were filing out. Jane held the door for Young Kip and then locked it behind him. She flipped the door sign, switched off the overhead lights, and then went to Periodicals where Ted sat behind his laptop. She sat across from him.

"Have you ever heard of an artist named Francis Firth?" Ted asked over the top of his screen.

Jane shook her head.

"He's Swiss. Post-Impressionist. An amateur who painted from 1901 through the late thirties. He was a goat-herder by profession, if you can believe it. In his spare time, he painted. He never sold a painting. Never tried. Just filled a big room with them."

"That might explain why I've never heard of him."

"It would, except that in the last two decades, his art has become extremely valuable. His family releases just two of his paintings a year from their vault, very unusual, so no one really knows how many of them there actually are. Very hush-hush. Anyway, they opened a gallery in Geneva in the forties, and now they have six mega-art galleries worldwide."

"The Firth Gallery," said Jane.

"You've heard of them."

"I thought they handled modern art."

"They do. Some exciting stuff, too. But it's a tough racket. Brutal. Don't get me started on that."

"What's any of this got to do with Granny Jo's painting?"

"I'm getting to that. As I recall, your grandmother's painting is a portrait of a brown-haired woman in a garden."

"Sophie."

"Sophie," he repeated. "And..."

She shrugged. "That's it."

He scoffed. "Not even a last name?"

"Nope."

"How did Granny Jo acquire it?"

"She inherited it from her father, I think."

"How did he get it?"

Jane felt herself growing impatient with the journalist-style questions. "It's a family painting, Ted," she said.

"Your grandmother must know. I mean, have you ever asked her?"

"About a hundred times! Are you going to tell me what this is about?"

"Pity," he said and cleared his throat. "Okay, so Francis Firth was a landscape painter. Scenes from his life in the Alps. Mountains, waterfalls, game, birds... like that. But every once in a while, he would do a portrait. They were only ever of one person—his wife, Caroline."

Ted turned his laptop to face her.

On the screen was a portrait of a woman seated on a boulder in a stream. A turtle shared the rock with her. The woman had almond-shaped eyes and was grinning mischievously. She had a single flower in her hair.

Jane lurched in her chair as though hit by an electric shock. A buzzing sound filled her head.

"Jane?" said Ted with concern.

She barely heard. She gawked at the image in disbelief.

The woman was Sophie.

The flower was red.

Red!

The sight of the colored flower seized her like a narcotic. The petal pulsed like one of those optical illusions where a static image can seem to move...

"Jane?"

Jane's brain injury had affected a tiny part of her brain called the gyrus, which was responsible for interpreting color and faces. After her accident, she awoke to a gray world where she could no longer recognize faces, not even her own reflection in a mirror. Brain scans of her gyrus were as dark as outer space. But there was one exception to her face blindness and color blindness—her grandmother's painting. It was an oddity about which only her neurologist and Granny Jo knew. Her doctor called it "phantom sight" and compared it to an amputee feeling pain in a lost limb. Jane knew the painting so well that her brain merely "filled in" the absent colors. Jane had always accepted this explanation (what else could it be?)... until now. To see color in this *other* painting was euphoric... and terrifying.

"Jane?"

She tore her eyes from the hallucinogenic poppy and looked into Ted's round face.

"Are you alright?" he mouthed through the roar of the buzzing.

She took a deep breath to compose herself. The effort took all of her strength; she could have stared at that flower for hours. Later, she knew she would. Later. Slowly, the buzzing faded.

"I'm fine," she croaked.

"You're sure?"

She nodded, and after a moment, he seemed to accept this.

"So?" he said.

"So... what?"

"It's the woman in your grandmother's painting!"

"It is?"

"You don't recognize her?"

"Ted, you're forgetting, I'm face-blind."

"Fuck me. Sorry. Well, trust me, it sure looks like her. I was wondering, hoping really, that you could arrange for me to inspect it. We might even want to get a pigment analysis done, X-ray imaging—"

"She got rid of it," said Jane.

"What?" he exclaimed. "Why?"

"Since the accident, I can only see in black and white. And I can't remember faces. Granny Jo put it away so I wouldn't be reminded. Then a few years back, she was having a yard sale and set it on the curb. Some guy gave her twenty bucks."

"Jesus. And you don't know who he was? It could be worth millions."

"No idea."

Ted closed his laptop. "Well, damn."

Jane leaned back in her chair and looked at the man she had once called Teddy Bear. She used her system of non-facial clues to identify him. The beard, the trendy round glasses, the tattoo. She noticed two still-open piercings in his right earlobe. Had he removed the earrings for fear of offending poor, provincial Ontario Hills? Or for fear of offending poor, provincial Jane Ward?

"You came a long way from Paris," said Jane.

"It seemed important."

"You could have sent an email."

He nodded. "True."

Jane narrowed her eyes. "You're doing a book on this Francis Firth, aren't you?"

He smiled sheepishly. "Nothing's settled. My agent says it won't sell. No one outside the art world has heard of him. But I say a good book has the power to change that."

"And you thought a connection to an undiscovered painting would be a good hook."

"Something like that."

Jane looked at her watch. "Damn. I'm late. I have to run."

"Really? I thought we might have dinner."

"Oh, that would have been lovely. But I can't. Family matter."

They went out and Jane locked the library door. Ted stood beside her looking bewildered. It was probably not the way he thought the night would go. He kissed her awkwardly three times on the cheek, and then they walked away in opposite directions. When he was out of sight, Jane ran to her car and leaped in.

Twenty minutes later, she was at Granny Jo's farmhouse, standing before the fireplace, looking up at *The Lover*.

The painting had hung over Granny Jo's mantel for as long as Jane could remember and was as much a part of her world as her yellow bedroom, the public library where her mother worked, and the football teams her father coached each year to mediocrity. The notion that she would set it by the curb was so far-fetched that Jane had to invoke her brain injury to get Ted to accept the lie. Over the years, Jane had learned that she could use her accident to end almost any argument.

The portrait was a nude, which was a lot for a young girl to take in. It burned Jane's young brain on so many levels, it would take a poet to make sense of it. (It burned her brother Davis's brain on precisely one level, which was why Granny Jo had to cover it whenever he was around.) The painting was the subject of many hours of speculation about the alluring woman with the almond-shaped eyes, the artist who so clearly adored her, and the strange word written in the corner where the signature should be: *Amant*. It meant "lover" in French, which was about the most perfect thing that could have been written there.

It showed a beautiful woman seated before a lilac bush in some kind of garden. There was a winding path, a little bench, a poplar tree, and a partial fountain with perching crows. In the background was a hill with a Roman coliseum and a winding river. Storm clouds darkened the horizon, which cast a mood that was incongruous with the idyllic garden and the beautiful woman. As a girl, if Jane could have changed anything about the painting, it would have been those storm clouds. They unnerved her. But as an adult, Jane understood that the clouds were precisely what gave the painting its sense of urgency. The woman's beauty, her very existence in the mean world, was both fragile and precious. Her nudity amplified the sense of peril. Even now, Jane felt an urge to dive into the painting and protect her.

Jane's mind raced as she thought about what Ted Banks had told her.

"Are you alright, Jane?" Granny Jo asked.

"I'm... I'm not sure," said Jane.

She pulled out her laptop and invited Granny Jo to sit beside her at the kitchen table. She googled "Francis Firth artist" and just like that, there she was! Sophie in a field. Sophie on a rock in a stream. Sophie with a poppy in her hair. Sophie in a field of poppies. Sophie at a picnic with poppies. Except that it wasn't Sophie. According to the website, her name was Caroline, the artist's wife.

"Oh, my," said Granny Jo each time Jane scrolled to a new picture.

Jane's heart was racing. It was like seeing someone from your hometown on a street in another state. Artistically, Firth was completely different from the anonymous painter who created *The Lover*. He was closer to Picasso, whom Firth clearly admired. The "Carolines," as the portraits of his wife were called, were bringing huge prices.

"It might not be her," said Granny Jo doubtfully. "It's a painting, after all."

"It's her."

"How can you be so sure?"

Jane pointed to one of the wildflowers in the picture.

"Yellow," she said.

Granny Jo's jaw dropped. "You mean..."

Jane nodded.

Like the painting Ted Banks had shown her in the library, this one was also in color.

Granny Jo fell back in her chair. "Well, butter my biscuit."

Outside, it began to snow, and Jane decided to spend the night at the farm. She took her laptop to bed and opened it beside her. She didn't so much lie on her bed as float above it in a swirling universe of color. She was reminded of that moment in The Wizard of Oz when Dorothy leaves behind the black and white of Kansas for the Technicolor of Munchkinland.

Jane paged through picture after picture. Adding to the mystery, she realized that the only pictures in color were the ones with Sophie in them. Firth's landscapes remained black and white to her. What was so special about Francis Firth that his work had this effect on her sight? Was it related to *The Lover*? Why only the paintings with Sophie in them? Was she getting her eyesight back? Or was she going crazy?

All good questions, to be sure, but Jane could not think too much about them. The color had taken hold of her. She was delirious, as though she were tripping on opium or LSD, though she had never done either. At one point, deep in the wee hours, she came upon a portrait of Sophie with a single poppy in her hair. Jane stared at the poppy, at the rich yet delicate red of the simple flower, and began to sob. She couldn't stop. Tears soaked her pillow. What was happening to her?

Her laptop beeped, warning of low battery. She closed the screen and, in the dark, found a tissue to blow her nose. Her eyes adjusted to the darkness, and that's when she realized light was coming from downstairs. She got up and slipped on a robe. She crept down the steps. Granny Jo sat at the kitchen table talking to herself.

"Gran?"

"You're up."

"I couldn't sleep," said Jane. "Are you okay?"

"I'm fine. I've just been talking to Matthew."

Matthew was Granny Jo's deceased husband. Whenever Granny Jo faced a decision, she would "talk to Matthew," as she put it. Jane often caught her grandmother talking to herself and listening to a reply only she could hear. Jane viewed it as a harmless indulgence from a woman who spent much of her time alone.

"About what?" Jane asked.

"About *The Lover*."

"What about it?"

"Whether I should tell you the truth."

Jane gaped at her. "You always said you didn't know anything other than her name!"

"I said I couldn't say. That's different."

Jane's heart quickened. "Gran, if you know something that might help—"

"It was a gift."

Jane recoiled at this new information. "From whom?"

Granny Jo pointed at the picture. "From her. From Sophie. Sophie du Burgen. She gave it to *my* grandfather. Your great-great-grandfather. John Planter."

Jane's eyes widened. Dr. John Planter was a family legend. He was the first Planter to come to America, and Jane knew his story well. He was born in France as Jean Duplantier. He got his medical degree in Paris and then promptly set sail on a clipper ship for the New World. He was a young doctor eager to see the frontier. He had planned to go to San Francisco but settled in St. Louis instead. He set up a medical practice using the name John Planter.

Almost immediately, he attracted controversy. He insisted on treating *all* patients, including the local Shawnee. Eventually, he married a beautiful Shawnee girl, Aponi. The white settlers tried several times to boycott Doc Planter for his progressivism, but good physicians were rare on the frontier, and he prospered despite the local bigots. Eventually, his youngest son joined him in the practice. Old Doc, as he came to be known, continued to see patients into his eighties until, at last, dementia ended his distinguished sixty-five-year career. His funeral in 1962 was one of the largest St. Louis had ever seen, surpassing any politician's. It drew hundreds of mourners, including a Shawnee chief who conducted a traditional burial. His body was covered with tree bark and then a small wooden house was built over the grave. Prayers were said in Shawnee, English, and his native French.

"He lived above the clinic his whole life," Granny Jo said, retelling parts Jane already knew. She had made up her mind now, and her eyes had become windows to the past.

"My father had a hardware store outside of town. It was pretty far away, so I didn't get to see Old Doc very often. By the time I was old enough to know who he was, he was completely senile. He had stopped speaking. I never heard him utter a word. He would just look at me, and I could see he was trying to work out what was going on. I would bring my dolls and play at his feet. I liked to make up stories about the dolls, and I would tell them out loud in great detail. He would watch and listen. My father said it seemed to calm him, so I felt like I was being useful.

"Then one day, when I was eleven years old, my father picked me up from school and took me to the clinic. There was some plumbing emergency. My uncle, who ran the clinic by then, was useless with those sorts of things. My father took me upstairs to be with Old Doc while he went off to fix the leak. I could hear him downstairs cursing as he did whenever he was working on plumbing. I didn't have my dolls with me, so I wandered up to the attic looking for something to play with. And there, behind an old spinning wheel, I found *The Lover*. I couldn't take my eyes off it. It wasn't just that the woman was nude. It was the way those powerful, masculine brushstrokes had created such a delicate female neck. It took my breath away. You know what I mean."

Jane nodded.

Granny Jo winked. "I know you do. I used to watch you."

"So what happened next?" asked Jane, anxious to move the story along.

"I carried my newfound treasure downstairs as though it were a kitten. I came into the room and Old Doc saw it. And..."

Granny Jo's voice cracked. Tears filled her eyes. She blew her nose into a tissue. It sounded like a trumpet.

"I'm sorry."

"Take your time, Gran."

Granny Jo fiddled with her tissue. "I'll never forget his eyes when he saw it, Jane. Oh, my god! Those empty eyes of his... they just filled up. I don't know how else to say it."

"Wow," Jane breathed.

"He motioned for me to bring it closer. I was a little afraid, but I did anyway. He stared at it for a long time—not with sadness, but with a joy I can only describe as childlike. But that wasn't the most extraordinary thing. Old Doc began to speak! He spoke in French. And for the first time in my life—also the last, as it turned out—I heard the voice of my grandfather."

"'Sophie,' he said. 'Oh, *mon amour.* Why have you left me?' He was talking to the painting."

"He called her 'my love'?"

Granny Jo nodded soberly. "My father returned to the room, and what Old Doc told us that day was a secret he had intended to carry to his grave. Until his dementia betrayed him."

"What secret?"

"That this woman in the painting, Sophie du Burgen, was the love of his life."

Jane and Granny Jo turned to look at the painting. Jane was instantly lost in those magnificent brushstrokes, which at times seemed to swirl like eddies in a rushing stream.

Granny Jo went on. "The story poured out of Old Doc as though it had happened yesterday, not a half-century ago. They met on the ship coming to America, *La Virginie,* out of Marseilles. She suffered from an ailment Old Doc did not name. John treated her aboard the ship, and her health improved. A bond formed. The young doctor was so smitten he abandoned his plan to go to San Francisco. She was bound for St. Louis, so he went there instead. He set up his clinic. Meanwhile, she became a colorful character in a city filled with colorful characters. She befriended the prostitutes at the many brothels of St. Louis, declaring them "my sisters." Word got around that she was skinny-dipping in the Mississippi River with the other working girls. No one quite knew what to make of her.

"She was fascinated by the Shawnee and would ride side-saddle like a proper European lady into wild lands where the few remaining natives still dwelt in teepees and hunted the dwindling bison herds. Later, she took to wearing pants and rode astride. One day she turned up at John's clinic with a Shawnee boy with a broken leg. Doc Planter set the leg, and so began his lifelong service to the Shawnee of Missouri.

"Riverboats enthralled her. She would hang out at the docks to watch them come and go. One day a boat arrived with no one ashore to take the spring line. She offered to help, and in desperation, a young mate threw her a line. She had watched the task done so many times, she knew exactly what to do. When done correctly, it requires little physical strength—simply make a clean catch and then put a wrap on the bollard. The ship's engine did the rest. After the boat came alongside the quay, the bosun would sound a whistle, and Sophie finished the line with a neat cleat hitch. Even seasoned captains couldn't help but be impressed, and none feared trouble when they saw 'the boat girl' on the dock, ready to take their lines.

"But the thing that caused the greatest scandal among the settlers was her painting. She arrived in St. Louis with a nude portrait of herself, which she hung on the wall of her little room above the general store."

"*The Lover?*"

Granny Jo nodded.

"The way he spoke about her, I knew he was completely under her spell. Hopeless. Then, one night after about a year, as he was making plans to marry her, she turned up at his clinic door. It was the night of a thundersnow storm. That's when snow falls with lightning and thunder. Sophie was frantic. She was leaving for Europe the next morning. There was an emergency. She didn't know when she would return.

"John was horrified. He tried to talk her out of it, and when that didn't work, he professed his love and asked her to marry him. But she refused. When John pressed, she blurted out that she loved another man, the only man she could ever love. That ended the discussion.

"And that's when she gave him the nude portrait she had brought with her on *La Virginie*. Sobbing, she put it into John's hand and turned away. He watched her disappear out the door. He never saw her again.

"There, in that little room, it was clear to me, even at my tender age, that Old Doc was mourning her. In a way, I suppose, he was even searching for her."

"So this was all before Aponi?"

"That's right. He went on to marry your great-great-grandmother, Aponi. And I suppose it was out of respect for his wife that he kept the painting—and his feelings—hidden. The secret was supposed to die with him, and that's why my father made me promise that it would die with me."

"And now it will die with me."

Granny Jo smiled. "No need to be so dramatic. I think Old Doc would understand."

Jane leaned back in the wooden chair and stretched her arms. She yawned. The first rays of the new day pierced the gaps in the lace curtains and fell about the room. Jane walked to the window and pushed back the curtain. A foot of snow lay over the farm.

Her phone beeped with a text message. All county services, including the library, were closed due to the storm. It was a snow day.

Jane went to the hearth to build a fire while Granny Jo made bacon and eggs. They ate in front of the fire and talked about what to do next. By the time the breakfast dishes were washed and put away, it had been decided.

"Are you sure, Gran?" Jane asked. "I don't know where this is going to lead."

"Oh, sweetie, it's nice of you to be so concerned with what I think. But I'm so old, the painting'll be yours soon enough."

"Gran—"

"Your brother will get the cuckoo clock, of course," she said. "He always did love that thing." With that, Granny Jo got to her feet. "Now, if you'll excuse me, I need to get my beauty sleep."

"Can I give you a hand?"

Granny Jo waved her arm irritably. "Oh, shush."

Jane watched her grandmother climb the stairs. She winced with every step, her old bones creaking nearly as audibly as the stairs. Jane grimaced and tried to imagine what her childhood would have been like without Granny Jo.

Her name was Josephine, which always came out as "Jofasine" for young Jane, so it was shortened to "Jo," which then became Granny Jo. The name stuck. Granny Jo had been a widow for twenty years. Her husband, Matt Winooski, had died at age fifty-two of a massive heart attack while clearing hay from his baler. Granny Jo found herself alone on four hundred acres of prime farmland with little knowledge of how to make money from it. She was the daughter of a hardware salesman from St. Louis. And while she could fix a leaky faucet, the business of running a profitable farm was not something she could expect to learn from a book. She leased her acreage to a neighbor, which allowed Granny Jo to remain in the farmhouse. The homestead lay along the shores of Lake Ontario, and although it was in the state of New York, it had more in common with rural Canada across the lake than its bustling, never-sleeping namesake to the south.

Through a lucky complication in her parents' schedules, Jane had been required to spend each Thursday afternoon with Granny Jo. Jane would take the school bus to the farm directly from school. She would leap down the steps of the bus, push open the creaky gate, and then dive into the waiting arms of Granny Jo, who met her on the porch. They watched birds, worked in the garden, played Gin Rummy, and had tea parties in French with Granny Jo's gold-leafed tea set until 7:45 p.m. when her father arrived to take her home. For those few hours each week, Jane felt safe, loved, and appreciated.

Jane walked to the window and pushed back the lace. The snow was melting fast. She might be able to open the library for a half-day. Her eye went to the birdhouses atop high posts that surrounded the house. Granny Jo had dozens of birdhouses, each designed for the comfort of a different species. The farm was located in the path of countless migratory birds, and their twice-annual passings provided a cycle of entertainment that was as reliable as the phases of the moon. Young Jane laughed at the way male birds danced for prospective mates and was alarmed by the cruelty they showed competing males. The appearance of eggs in a nest was always a cause to celebrate, but not all chicks survived. There were many solemn burials within the boundaries of that picket fence. Tears were shed, and Jane learned the hard facts about life and death as only a farm could teach them.

Jane frowned at the old birdhouses, which were now crumbling and uninhabitable. These days, birds flew by without stopping. Jane's father had begun discussing Granny Jo's move to a nursing home. The thought of Granny Jo in a nursing home broke her heart, for it was within these walls on Thursday afternoons that Jane received her only taste of unconditional love. How many more times could she expect to pull up in front of the house and see smoke rising from the chimney? Any trip—including this one—could be the last.

Jane plugged in her laptop and navigated to the website for the Firth Gallery in Geneva, Switzerland. The home page noted that the gallery was the official *catalogue raisonné* for the works of the Swiss master. No work could be sold as an authentic Firth without validation from the gallery. Jane clicked a link labeled "Authentication Request."

A form appeared. She filled in the information and then uploaded an image of *The Lover*.

She hit SUBMIT.

The thank-you page was not encouraging.

Your application will be processed in the order it was received. Allow up to six months for us to reply. Do not contact us during that time. WE WILL NOT RESPOND.

Six months?

Jane put another log on the fire and sat back to read the only biography she could find on Francis Firth, a self-published ebook on the gallery's website. The author, it turned out, was Francis Firth's grandson, Gunther—now seventy-five years old, and the founder of the first Firth Gallery. The book was dreadful. It raised more questions than it gave answers. Caroline was barely mentioned. Jane could see why Ted Banks thought the artist deserved a proper biography.

Her phone dinged with an email. Jane gasped when she saw the name of the sender: Gunther Firth.

We are interested in inspecting your painting. When can you bring it to Geneva?

Three

Sophie

The world awoke for Sophie one sound at a time. Her little room had no window, so the accumulating sounds were the only sign that morning had arrived. Two starlings laughed at each other from neighboring trees. A calf bawled for its mother. A grinding *squeak-squeak* from the courtyard told Sophie that someone was drawing water from a well. Downstairs, the rattle of kettles promised breakfast.

Sophie grinned into the blackness. These were the sounds of the first day of her new life. She could not remember ever feeling so content.

The previous day had been a marvel, maybe the best day of her life. A midnight jailbreak, a clandestine meeting in a tomb in a cemetery, skinny-dipping with painters and prostitutes. She stifled a giggle as she relived every precious moment.

After Vincent had staggered away from the beach, Marie took Sophie back to her brothel, Madame Giroux's. Sophie used the last of her reward money to buy a few clothes and then Marie invited Sophie to stay the night. They climbed into the twin bed and lay face-to-face, sharing the only pillow. Sophie was afraid Marie might try to kiss her. If she had, Sophie decided she would pretend Marie's lips belonged to the painter. But, within seconds, Marie was snoring.

Someone knocked on the door. Her room had two doors—one that opened to an interior corridor that led into the house, and another that opened onto a back porch. The knock came from the porch door. Sophie shook Marie, but the girl merely groaned and rolled over. Then came another *rap-rap-rap*, this time more urgent.

Sophie got up and tiptoed to the door. She wore her new shift, one of the garments Marie had sold her with her reward money. Sophie cracked open the door and peered out.

It was the painter Vincent Van Gogh, standing in the morning twilight. He wore yesterday's clothes, a straw hat, and paint-stained trousers with suspenders. On his back, he carried his painting equipment—easel, blank canvas, and a basket with a shoulder strap.

"Thank god," he said when he saw her. "The *gendarmes* are going door-to-door. I think they're looking for you. We have to go."

"Okay. Let me get dressed."

"Hurry!"

Sophie closed the door and tried again to rouse Marie, who responded by throwing a punch at her. Sophie gave up and lit a candle. She found the dress Marie had sold her and began to put it on. It was a summer dress with light fabric and buttons down the front. It was low cut, and with the corset, the tops of her breasts were bare. Sophie had never worn anything like it in her life.

"Is it... decent?" Sophie had asked Marie.

"I wouldn't wear it to church," she'd replied. "But it'll do for around town."

Sophie wished the painter wasn't going to be the first person to see her in it, but she couldn't do anything about that. It was her only dress. She put it on and then dragged a brush through her hair. She was proud of her hair, which was brown with hints of yellow in the right light. It was thick and fell in natural waves. In the family portraits, Sophie's hairstyles were always more elaborate than either of her younger sisters'.

For now, she tied it back with a yellow ribbon and slipped out the door. Vincent surveyed her appearance and nodded. How different she must have looked from their encounter in the coliseum!

Vincent led her to the edge of the courtyard and peered up and down the street. He waved her forward.

Allez!

They slipped along the deserted street toward the edge of Arles as the sun rose over a muddy field. Mist swirled shin-deep over the ground. Sophie turned her face toward the sun and blinked happily. Today promised a new adventure. The pace of this new life was thrilling!

She looked at her escort. He was burdened by his equipment, but you'd never know it. He carried it as though it were an extension of his body. His arms swung freely from broad shoulders joined at his powerful neck. He held a pipe in his mouth, which he puffed just enough to keep lit. Smoke curled around his straw hat and filled her nose with the smell of Father's study.

"You're painting today?" she asked, keeping to French. His German was poor, and they had unconsciously settled on French as their language.

"*Oui*. I was on my way when I saw the *gendarmes*. I hid behind a wall at the Carrel Inn. They woke the innkeeper and demanded to see papers for all the guests. I thought they might go to the brothel next. I had to get you away."

He was so clever! Sophie supposed she should have been frightened about the manhunt, but she was not. She felt safe with the painter, who she imagined knew all the angles.

"Where are we going?"

"I have a friend. He's a painter, too. He has a little house. You can hide there until we figure out what to do with you."

"What about you? What will you do after you drop me at this little house?"

"I'll paint."

"Can I come?"

"No!" he laughed.

"Why not?"

"I just told you. The *gendarmes*."

"Tell them I'm a friend. No one will be suspicious."

"I think you overestimate my sway with the police."

Sophie frowned. "I think you're afraid."

"Afraid?" he scoffed. "Of what?"

"Of what I'll think of your painting."

"Oh, that I already know. You'll hate it."

"Why would you say that?"

"Experience."

They passed a peasant hut with a thatched roof. Smoke from the chimney rose into the morning sky. Sophie smelled potatoes cooking. Her stomach grumbled.

An idea came to her. "What if I can pay you?"

"How? I assume Marie has all your money."

"I'll pay you with my complete honesty."

"Huh?"

Sophie was delighted by her idea. "How often does a person get that? I promise to tell you exactly what I think of your painting. Even if I hate it. That will be my payment for getting to watch you work."

Vincent stopped walking and said, "Do you even know anything about art?"

"No, you don't get to do that," Sophie scolded. "You don't get to tear down my opinion before it is even given. It will be my honest opinion. That's all. So, what do you say?"

"You're a strange girl," he said.

They walked for almost an hour before Vincent found the particular almond tree he wanted to paint. Sophie wondered what was so special about this tree that they had to walk past a hundred others just like it. He set up his easel and began preparing his painting equipment. She sat down on the ground beside him, where she could watch him but not see the canvas. She didn't want to corrupt her opinion by seeing how it was made.

Vincent stared at the almond tree for several minutes, doing nothing but staring. Then he picked up a brush and began mixing paint.

He had a strange tic in his technique. He would tip his head skyward before falling forward at the canvas with his brush. He was like a human pendulum, swinging away from the canvas before crashing into it. Sophie was fascinated.

After several hours, he took a break. He sat down on a stool and pulled out a paper and pencil. Sophie didn't realize he had a stool. Why hadn't he offered it to her?

He began to write.

"What are you doing?" she asked.

He looked up, seemingly surprised to find her there.

"Writing a letter to my brother in Paris."

"You won't tell him about me, will you?"

"Maybe. Why?"

"You can't ever tell anyone about me," she said fiercely. "Ever."

"Why?"

"Just promise."

"Okay."

"I'm serious!"

"I promise, okay. I know how to keep a secret."

"That's good," she said. "So few people do. Now, what's for lunch? I'm starving!"

The question seemed to puzzle him. "Lunch?"

"You must have something to eat inside that basket of yours."

"Just paints and turpentine."

"But that's crazy! Why wouldn't you throw in some fruit or bread or something?"

"I usually just smoke. I didn't know I would be having company."

He went back to writing his letter.

Sophie got up and wandered off in the direction they had come. At the base of a fence post, she spotted a patch of early wild strawberries and began to pick them. She took great care to only select the ripest ones. She piled them into the hem of her dress. A little further along the fence, she found some wild asparagas and garlic. She stole several spinach leaves from the farmer's field, then set them all by a brook under a shade tree. She pulled two pieces of loose bark from one of the old trees and sat down beside the stream. She removed the tops of the strawberries and cleaned everything in the water. She set it out in the sun to dry. While she waited, she spotted a patch of poppies in bloom, so she picked the reddest blossom and put it in her hair. She piled everything back into the hem of her dress and returned to Vincent. He had finished his letter and was now working again on his painting. He gave no sign that he was aware of her.

She knelt and dumped everything into a pile. Using the tree bark as plates, she assembled two salads. She arranged the berries and vegetables neatly, and made sure she gave Vincent the bigger salad.

"Lunch!" she announced.

He looked up from his easel. "I'm not hungry."

"Vincent!" she scolded. "Don't be rude. I made this for you."

He looked like a man being shaken awake from a dream. The lines around his eyes faded. His awareness shifted from the two-dimensional world of the canvas to the little picnic at his feet. His gaze fell on the flower in her hair.

"Okay," he said. "The paint could use more drying time, anyway."

He sat down across from her. He put a strawberry in his mouth and then piled in two more without swallowing the first.

"Slow down!" she said. "Taste your food. It took me an hour to make it."

He did as she asked. She noticed he closed his eyes as he put each bite into his mouth. She smiled.

"So?" she asked. "How is it?"

"It's good. Really good."

"I'm glad you like it."

She began to eat, too.

"You know a lot about nature?" he asked.

"I can tell you that your almond tree is a Berre almond tree. Its common name is 'princess almond.' It's native to this part of France."

"Princess almond," he repeated, then pointed at her hair. "I like your flower."

"It's a poppy. There's a field of them right over there."

"Perhaps I'll paint there tomorrow."

"Perhaps I'll come."

He shrugged.

"I like watching you paint," she said. "Would you like to know why?"

"Okay."

"I get to look at you. We never get to just look at a person, do we? 'Don't stare!' we're told. 'It's rude.' But while you were painting, I got to look at you."

"And you liked that?" he asked.

"I did."

Vincent leaned back on his hands. "It seems a little unfair."

Sophie laughed. "Oh? Would you like to look at me?"

"Maybe I would," he said.

"Then look," she said. She fell back into a flamboyant pose, flipping her hair. "I give you permission."

Their eyes met and Vincent wore an expression so serious, she burst out laughing. "Not like that, silly. You can't look me in the *eye*! That *is* rude! I'll look over there at your almond tree while I eat my salad. You can look at me for as long as you like."

"Okay."

She stared at the tree and ate her salad. After a while, she could tell Vincent had finished his lunch. She snuck a peek at him. His eyes were still on her.

"I want to paint your portrait," he said.

She shook her head. "No."

"Why?"

"I hate having my portrait done."

"You've had a portrait done before?"

"Many times."

"Seriously?"

"Is that so hard to believe?"

"Well, yes. Portraits are expensive."

That was true. She had forgotten about that.

"I have a hard time sitting still," she said.

He chuckled. "That I *can* believe."

Sophie didn't appreciate being the object of his joke, but she was too happy to let it spoil her mood. She went on eating her salad.

"You can't stay in Arles," Vincent said. "They'll catch you."

"I know."

"Where will you go?"

She crawled beside him and put her lips beside his ear.

"Missouri," she whispered.

She pronounced the strange name slowly, syllable by syllable. Until then, she had only ever read the word. "I want to see the Miss... iss... ippi River. Don't you just love those names? They're so exotic!"

"Where is Missouri?"

"The American frontier. I read about it in Mark Twain. Have you read him?"

"No."

"Oh, you must! He's so clever! And the way he describes America! I just know I'll be happy there. I've had enough of this dusty old Old World. Haven't you?"

"Sometimes," he said in a way that made her feel she had touched a nerve. "How will you get there?"

This sudden turn to practical matters caused Sophie to sit up and frown. "That's a problem. Do you know anything about ships?"

"Not really. I have a friend, Paul Gauguin, who worked his way across the Atlantic in the engine room of a cargo ship. I've often thought about trying something like that. He's a painter, too. He says there are too many painters in Paris, all painting the same scenes. He's right, of course. And now his work is selling, and mine isn't. That's why I came here."

"Are you saying I could work for my passage?"

Vincent grimaced. "No. Paul's a big man. Bigger than me. I don't think that would work for you."

"No, I wouldn't think so."

"You'll need to buy a ticket. You need money."

"I have money," she said. She lifted the leather string around her neck. Out of her cleavage, she pulled a gold pendant, bejeweled with emeralds and rubies.

"*Mon Dieu!*" Vincent exclaimed. "Is that... real?"

"Of course it's real."

"It can't be! It looks like it belongs to a queen! Where did you get it?"

"It's mine."

"Be serious. Did you steal it?"

"What a thing to say!" she said. "It's mine. Oma gave it to me."

Sophie recalled that day. It was twelve years ago, the last time she had been home before coming to the asylum at St. Remy for good. Her parents had gotten so old. Father was bald. His head was as shiny as the Kaiser's helmet. Mother was frail and slept whole days in bed with the drapes drawn. Her younger brother, Eduard, wore his military uniform day and night. He looked so grown up. Her twin sisters didn't know her. Sophie was a stranger to her family. It was Sophie's eighteenth birthday, and everyone had forgotten—except for Oma. After dinner, Oma invited Sophie to her bedroom and pulled the necklace out of a leather pouch.

"For you," she said.

"Me? Oh, it's so beautiful, Oma!"

"It's a monstrosity," she growled in her raspy voice. "But the day may come when you need money. Now, your parents…"

She broke into a fit of coughing.

Sophie patted her back. "Are you alright, Oma?"

"Don't worry about me, dear," she said when the fit ended. "Now, what was I saying?"

"My parents."

"Right. You must not tell your parents about this gift. They would not approve. That's a very special necklace. They will want it to go to one of the twins. But it belongs to you, by rights. You are the eldest."

"Okay."

Oma began coughing again and waved for Sophie to leave.

When Sophie reached the door, Oma said, "Happy birthday, my dearest Sophie."

"Thanks, Oma."

Sitting in the Arles field, Vincent looked shaken by the sight of the necklace.

"You would sell it?"

"If I have to. I was thinking that a jewelry shop might give me some money."

"You can't sell it like this!" exclaimed Vincent. "Not whole! You have to break it down."

"I do?"

Vincent laughed.

Sophie felt her face flush. He thought she was stupid. She knew she wasn't, but it was embarrassing how little she knew of how the world worked. Vincent understood the world. By the look of him, he had lived a hard life. He knew things. She had lived most of her life surrounded by walls.

"My brother is an art dealer. He might know someone. I could ask—"

"No! He can't know about me. About this."

"You can trust him."

"No!" she shouted. Vincent's laughter had made her angry. She didn't want to be angry. She had been having such a wonderful day.

Suddenly, a familiar sound reached her ears. Her head whirled toward the fence where she had picked the strawberries.

"Shh, do you hear that?"

The bird sang again, and she broke out laughing. "Do you know what that is, Vincent? It's a citril finch!"

She whistled and waited for a reply. "They migrate thousands of miles a year. This very bird could have perched atop the buttresses of Notre-Dame or the Tower of London. Think about that. Perhaps I'll fly away with him now. That would solve everything! Let me ask."

She whistled again and then waited for the bird to reply. Suddenly, Vincent's hand was on hers. His touch broke the spell. She turned to him. He was frowning.

"You're not a finch, Sophie. You can't just fly away from here."

She pulled her hand away. "I know that."

"Maybe..."

"Maybe... what?"

"Maybe the asylum isn't such a bad place for you."

"How could you say such a thing?" She began to sob. "I'm never going back to that place. I... I would rather die."

"Don't say that."

"It's true."

She waited for him to comfort her, but he just sat woodenly looking at her. He seemed unnerved by her change of mood. She was, too. She hadn't realized until that moment how exhausted she was from her escape and flight from St. Paul's. Three days on the run. Starving. Cold. Sleeping in haystacks. The *gendarmes* with their horrible, horrible whistles. And all the while having no concrete idea how to get to America—just her necklace and a sense that she was being guided by a shimmering angel.

Slowly, Sophie regained her composure using a trick she learned at the asylum from Dr. Peyron. She listened to the birds and identified each species by its song—nightingale, finch, warbler, crow, hawk. As she began to feel better, she saw how long the shadows had grown. She sat upright and wiped her tears.

"Oh, no!" she said. "I've interfered with your work. I always do this!"

"It's okay."

"No! You have to finish. I promised to give you my honest opinion, and a deal's a deal, right?"

Vincent nodded. He got up and walked to his unfinished canvas. He stood there a long time. He studied it as though it belonged to someone else, and he was rethinking every decision. Vincent picked up his brush and, as Sophie watched from the ground, he disappeared into the canvas.

No walls in his world.

Sophie closed her eyes. The turmoil of her emotions left her feeling spent. She took a deep breath and savored the pollen-soaked air. Bees hummed from all directions. The sun warmed her skin, especially the virgin skin at the top of her breasts. A gentle breeze washed over her. She felt it lift her off the ground. It carried her swirling into the sky, where she soared with the citril finches...

She awoke to a man's voice above her.

"Time to go."

She opened her eyes. Vincent stood over her. He looked exhausted.

"Oh," she said, getting her bearings. She rubbed her eyes and looked around. The sun was low. It was late.

"I dozed off."

He nodded.

"You're finished?" she asked.

"Yes."

"Can I see?"

He motioned for her to go to the easel.

She got up to see his painting.

What she saw was beyond shocking. She had expected to find a pretty picture of almond blossoms in spring. She figured she would make a few kind remarks and that would be the end of it. But this... this was a *tour de force*, as subversive as it was ambitious. As a girl, Sophie's governess had taken her to most of Europe's major museums, and in all those visits Sophie had never seen anything like Van Gogh's almond blossoms. Everything was exaggerated for effect—the color choices were brazen; the angles of the branches were unnaturally sharp; the ripeness of the blossoms practically oozed with nectar. She put her face next to the canvas to see how the effect was created. But it was not a trick. It was just a bunch of brush strokes. He hadn't even tried to conceal them. There was madness to it, a reflection of...

Then it hit her.

"You put me in it," she said.

He nodded. "I think, yes, I may have. A little bit."

He offered no apology.

She considered Vincent anew. Who was this man who could create such a thing?

"You don't like it?" he asked.

She cleared the lump from her throat. "I would give ten years of my life to make one thing as beautiful as this."

He blinked at her. His gaze fell to her lips, and she knew he had the urge to kiss her. But time passed, and he didn't move.

"Aren't you going to kiss me?" she asked.

"May I?"

"Yes."

He took a step toward her, suddenly looking much larger than before. Her heart raced. He stopped in front of her and then lowered his lips to hers. She tilted back her head and let him kiss her.

The kiss was surprisingly delicate. When she sensed he was about to try again, she took a step back.

"That's enough," she teased. "*Amant.*"

Lover.

Four

Jane

Jane Ward had two simple tasks that morning.

Be still.

Look at the images.

She lay on her back in an MRI tube watching pictures pass by on a screen mere inches from her face. It was like watching a manic slideshow while sealed in a deafening coffin that *whirred* and *rattled* and *thumped* with each new image. And such images! A serene beach, a child about to fall from a cliff, a man with a huge tumor on his neck, *The Mona Lisa*, maggots on a carcass, a sunset over mountains, a ship about to be capsized by a huge wave...

For Jane, the images were all in black and white, *except* for the fourteen portraits of Caroline Firth that had been inserted into the sequence. These pictures shone in vivid color.

After a half-hour, a voice called over a microphone.

"Okay, we're done."

An hour later, Jane and her neurologist, Dr. Claire Harris, sat in her office looking at the brain scans. Dr. Harris had been Jane's physician since she first woke up from her accident, and she was the only person besides Granny Jo she dared to trust with her secret.

Marching across the laptop screen were dozens of pictures of her brain. The images varied slightly depending upon what image she had been viewing at that moment. The machine was called a Functional MRI and revealed brain activity through heat and blood flow. Jane knew it well; this was hardly her first trip into "the coffin."

Jane was able to locate her dead gyrus in every picture. It was as dark as ever. What was happening?

Dr. Harris grouped the scans of Jane looking at "The Carolines."

"Notice anything?" she asked.

Jane studied them for a while and then pointed at a dot near the center of the left lobe. It glowed white in every case.

"What's that?" she asked.

"That's your amygdala. It's used for emotional responses. Look at this."

She showed her another brain scan.

"This is you looking at the picture of the child at the cliff."

"It's bright white."

"And that's what I'd expect. You had an emotional response—fear, alarm—to the image. But for these other paintings, these ones by Francis Firth, the amygdala shouldn't be active. But as you can see, it's blazing away."

"So what does it mean?"

"It means your brain has rewired itself to see color using the amygdala."

"It can do that?"

Dr. Harris nodded. "It's called 'neuroplasticity.' The brain has a remarkable ability to heal itself. It's important to remember that your eyes and your optic nerve are perfectly fine. They were undamaged from your accident. They're still carrying signals to your brain. They're just not being received at the other end."

"But why only with these pictures by Francis Firth?"

Dr. Harris looked at the pictures and chewed on her lip. "All I can confidently say from these scans is that your brain is activating the amygdala in a very specific way when you see these paintings, and only when you see these paintings."

She sat back and rolled her nails thoughtfully on the desktop. "With your permission, I'd like to send these to someone. His name's Dr. Ravi Das. He's a specialist at MIT. He has some fancy equipment that uses AI to link images to brain activity. He's actually succeeded in using AI to create an image from the brain activity. Actually *reading* the brain. Really advanced stuff. He might have some thoughts on what's going on here."

"Sure."

"Would it be okay for him to call you?"

"I'll be in Geneva."

Dr. Harris sighed. "You're determined to go ahead with this trip?"

"I leave tomorrow."

When Jane Ward fastened her seatbelt at the start of the flight to Geneva, it was the first time in her life to do so. Jane's finely honed system of facial cues was manageable only within the bubble of Ontario Hills. Outside the bubble was a horror film of masked strangers, which tended to discourage travel. Over the years, she had made a few attempts. Each fall, there was a library convention in Manhattan, and once, Jane got up the courage to go. She saw a Broadway show and took the boat to Ellis Island to learn how immigration records were kept. She lost track of her guide and got scolded for failing to stay with the group. She never went again. Meanwhile, Davis had wanted her to visit him in Washington D.C. where he was working as an FBI agent. She kept promising to go but then she always found some excuse to cancel. Jane's dream of traveling the world had ended the moment she awoke from her accident unable to recognize faces.

In recent years, especially after taking over the newspaper, she had even managed to convince herself it was for the best. Jane was not unhappy. She had a place to go on Christmas and Thanksgiving. She was content working in the library. She ran two book clubs. Circulation at the paper had doubled since she'd taken over. Her physical therapist, Donnie, doubled as a competent lover. Sure, it bothered her that he read her newspaper for the horoscope and kept a weight bench in the middle of his living room. He didn't even pretend they were exclusive. It wasn't great, but it was *controlled*, and that had to be enough. And it was enough, that is, until that night she lay in bed sobbing at Francis Firth's *Caroline in Field of Poppies*. Her tears were a river that swept away the half-life she had built in Ontario Hills. It left a void to be filled. But with what?

Her parents had been against the trip. *What do you hope to gain?*

Davis offered to go in her place. *International travel can be tricky.*

Her therapist suggested she schedule an extra session. *I'd like to explore why it is so important to you.*

At least Donnie had been constructive—he gave her exercises she could do on the long flight and a goodie bag of Kale chips.

Granny Jo was the only one in favor of the trip, and even loaned her two thousand dollars for expenses. The night before she left, Granny Jo removed *The Lover* from the wall and placed it in Jane's hands. Jane was surprised at how light it was; it weighed no more than a book. But the hole it left in the wall was a thousand miles deep.

"Take good care of our girl," said Granny Jo.

Jane booked an Airbnb not far from the Firth Gallery. She would have to share a bathroom, but it was cheap, and hotel rooms in Geneva cost a week's salary. She did splurge for a window seat on the plane, and bought a leather art case for *The Lover*. Lastly, she wrote an email to Gunther Firth.

Dear Mr. Firth,

Thank you for your swift reply to my application for authentication of my painting. I will be in Geneva next Thursday and look forward to showing it to you.

His reply came almost immediately.

7 p.m. at the gallery. Bring the painting, sans frame.

On the plane, Jane listened carefully to the flight attendant's safety presentation. She located the nearest exit door which was, indeed, behind her. She felt beneath her seat for the life vest she would require "in the unlikely event of a water landing." As the plane began to move, she looked out the window and tried to quell her butterflies.

All around her, passengers put on headphones and picked their movies. But movies were a problem for Jane. She was unable to keep the characters straight. Who was the villain? Who was the hero? It was all very frustrating. Books suffered from no such defect, which was yet another reason being a librarian was the perfect profession for her. It was a logic Jane recognized not long after her accident. After high school, she enrolled in Ontario Community College and earned a bachelor's degree in Library Science. She got a job in the Ontario

Hills Public Library. When her mother retired, Jane would take over. There was a sense of destiny to it.

Jane cradled the portfolio that contained *The Lover* and thought about Caroline Firth. Gunther Firth's biography claimed Francis met Caroline at an art exhibition in Zurich in 1901, eleven years after Sophie gave *The Lover* to Doc Planter in St. Louis. They were married a year later. Jane reasoned that somewhere there must exist a marriage certificate from 1902 bearing the name Francis Firth. That document would give Caroline's maiden name. From there, Jane could trace backward for a link with Doc Planter's Sophie.

One perk of being a librarian was having access to highly specialized digital databases. So Jane purchased Wi-Fi access on the plane and began reading handwritten, French-language church records of births, deaths, and marriages. The archives were scans—images essentially—which meant they could not be searched except by reading each document individually. It was a massive undertaking, so daunting that few people would even consider it.

Jane's plane touched down at Geneva Airport at seven a.m. on the day of her appointment. She cleared immigration and customs without a hitch, and collected her luggage from baggage claim. There, a man in a tweed jacket started a conversation with her, and so she introduced herself. He frowned and moved away. She realized he must have been the person sitting beside her on the flight; his coat concealed the plaid shirt that had been her cue. But the embarrassment couldn't dampen her mood. Her brain was buzzing with the excitement of her first trip to Europe.

Jane walked past the airport taxi stand to find a city bus to Geneva. She dragged her roller bag the last half-mile over the brick streets to reach her flat. It was too early to check into her room, but her hostess allowed Jane to leave her bag with the art case that held *The Lover*. Jane's meeting at the Firth Gallery was not for another eight or so hours, so she went back outside and made her way up the long hill from the river to the center of Geneva's Old Town.

On Place du Bourg-de-Four, she found a sidewalk café with an awning beside a fountain. It looked like a postcard. She ordered tea and an éclair and then sat among the smokers watching people go by. She had her waiter take a picture, which she emailed to her parents, brother, and Granny Jo with the subject line: *Switzerland!*

Jane had intended to climb to the belfry of St. Pierre Cathedral—a must-do, according to her guidebook. But jet lag kicked in like a drug. When she finally made it back to the Airbnb and her little room, all she could do was face-plant fully dressed onto the twin bed. She awoke sometime later, undressed, and crawled under the sheets.

She awoke to her alarm going off. It was time for her meeting.

The Firth Gallery was located in a restored Art Deco house in the heart of Geneva's cultural district, fifteen minutes' walk from Jane's flat. Jane arrived on time and climbed the steps to the door. A sign read "Closed" in German, French, and Italian, but as Jane approached, the door swung open.

She went inside, and there they were—three generations of Firths. Jane knew them by their respective ages. Gunther, the grandfather and author of the biography of Francis, was bald with two tufts of gray hair on each side of his head. Gunther's son, Otto, was the genius who took the family business to the pinnacle of the art world. He wore a suit, designer glasses, and a striped bow tie that matched his pocket square. The third person was Otto's son, Tomas. He was pudgy with a narrow nose and close-set eyes that gave him a weaselly appearance. He wore a t-shirt with a superhero emblem; Jane couldn't say which. He had a diamond stud earring in his left ear and a tattoo sleeve that ended at his knuckles. An enormous gold watch encircled his fat wrist.

The men deferred to Otto, who made introductions.

When he finished, Jane spoke to Gunther. "I read your book."

"Then we owe you an apology," said Tomas with a laugh.

Gunther showed no reaction. Jane sensed it was an overused ice-breaker. Otto pointed at her art case. "Is that it?"

"Yes."

"Let's have a look then, shall we?"

A click came from behind her. Jane turned. Gunther had bolted the door.

Otto led them through the gallery to a back room. He opened the case and placed *The Lover* on an easel. He and Gunther exchanged a glance. Jane could not read its meaning.

They began to speak to each other in German.

Tomas slid beside her.

"First time in Geneva?" he asked in passable English.

Jane couldn't take her eyes off the men as they examined Granny Jo's painting.

"Uh-huh."

"Are you looking forward to dinner?"

"Dinner?"

"Of course. Wait, Gunther didn't tell you?"

Tomas spoke to his grandfather in German, and then shook his head in disgust.

"The old bugger forgot. Still. You like fondue?"

The two men had turned the painting around and were discussing water stains on the canvas. Jane had seen them for the first time when Granny Jo removed the painting from the wall.

"Fondue? Sure. I had it once."

He laughed. "Not like this. I know a place—"

"What are they talking about?" Jane asked, cutting him off.

Tomas listened a moment and then said, "Just technical stuff. The painting was damaged at some point."

"I know."

"Do you know how?"

"No."

"Anyway, about the restaurant... it's called Portia's."

Otto turned the painting around again and was holding some sort of device over the surface. It looked like a blow-dryer with a tiny screen. He pointed it at the lilac bush and then studied the screen. He hit a button, and repeated the process in another location.

"Bruker Tracer," said Tomas. "Analyzes pigments. Helps with dating."

This went on for a while, with Tomas chattering away and Jane half-listening. Gunther was standing to the side while his son worked.

"Do you think I could talk to your grandfather?" Jane asked Tomas.

Tomas called out for him, and Jane found herself face-to-face with perhaps the only man alive who had known Caroline Firth.

"Hi, Mr. Firth," said Jane. "I'm very excited to meet you. The woman in my painting, she's been like family to my grandmother and me."

Gunther grunted.

"I have some questions," Jane went on. "Would that be okay?"

He shrugged. Tomas chuckled at Gunther's rudeness.

Jane had thought a lot about her next question. "Did Caroline ever make a trip to America?"

"America?" he snorted.

"This would have been about 1888."

"Certainly not."

"What about a chronic ailment? Something that would require medical attention?"

Gunther looked at her as though she were mad. Jane decided to try a gentler tack.

"Okay. What about her tastes? What books did your grandmother like to read?"

"She didn't read."

"Excuse me?"

"Caroline was illiterate."

Jane gaped at him. "By illiterate, you mean..."

"Caroline never learned to read."

Jane was stunned. According to Old Doc, the reason Sophie chose St. Louis was her love of Mark Twain.

While Jane considered what this meant, Otto summoned Gunther. He began pointing at several places in the painting, and seemed excited.

"What's going on?" Jane asked.

"There's a *pentimento*," said Otto.

"What's that?"

"A paint-over. It's Italian for 'regret.' Artists will do it if they don't like a hand or a tree, but sometimes they'll do it to a whole canvas. Have you had this X-rayed?"

"No."

He and Gunther exchanged looks.

"We can take care of that for you," said Otto.

"Okay. How would that work?"

"It won't cost you a thing," said Otto. "You would sign a release and we would run the tests."

"So we would do that right now?"

"Oh, no. We don't have the equipment here. I have someone in Zurich. It'll just take a few days."

"You mean *leave* the painting?"

"Yes."

"With you?"

"Yes."

Jane looked at the three men. Something felt off. She couldn't put her finger on it. She recalled an article she had read in the online blog, *ArtNet* complaining about the Firth Gallery's lack of transparency with its catalog of Firth originals.

Secretive. Impenetrable. Like a mafia.

"I'm sorry but I can't sign a release," she said.

"Why not?"

"It's not my painting."

"What!" Otto exclaimed.

"It's my grandmother's. I'm just helping her."

"You never told me that," said Gunther.

"I'm sorry. I didn't know it mattered."

"She's right," said Otto. "She can't sign a release if she doesn't have ownership. It would be unenforceable."

He turned to Jane with a blank expression. "Thank you, Mademoiselle Ward, for showing it to us."

"Wait. That's it?"

He nodded soberly.

"But what about the woman? Do you think she could be Caroline?"

"No. The painting's too old. Late nineteenth century. There are red lake pigments. See here?" He pointed to the lilacs. "See the fading? Purple to blue? That's typical of the geranium lake pigments. They fell out of use by the turn of the century, a decade *before* Francis began to paint. It's practically a time stamp. Caroline would have been a child when this was painted. The artistic style isn't even close to my grandfather's. And, of course, the signatures don't match. Shall I go on?"

"Signature? You mean title, no?"

He shook his head. "Signature. *Amant*—it's funny."

"*Amant*," Gunther snorted.

Jane flushed. "I never said it was a Firth. I don't care about that. It's not for sale, anyway. I'm merely asking if you think that's Caroline in the picture."

"How could it be?" asked Otto. "Now, if you'll excuse me. I have a flight to Singapore I must catch. I do hope you have some time to enjoy Geneva. I recommend the watch-making museum. *Bonne nuit.*"

He disappeared through a back door. Gunther followed.

Jane stared after them.

What the hell just happened?

Dinner with Tomas was as dull as it was long. He had never read a novel, and as far as Jane could tell, he didn't seem interested in art except as a means to make money. He surfed and traveled to places "that threw bombs," whatever the hell that meant. He owned a speedboat he kept on the lake. When Jane asked him to name his favorite artist, he replied, "Leonardo da Vinci, duh." At one point during the meal, he took a phone call. Jane escaped to the ladies' room. When she returned, she sat down heavily and bumped the table, nearly spilling her glass.

"Sorry."

"Are you alright?" he asked.

"I'd like to go. I'm feeling pretty tired."

He nodded sympathetically. "Jet lag."

He paid the bill, and they went outside. Jane stumbled as she navigated the revolving door. Tomas caught her before she fell on top of her art case.

"Whoa, there," he said. "Here, let me help you." He reached for the portfolio. "Let me carry that for you."

She hugged it to her chest. "I got it."

They walked on. She allowed him to support her. She had hoped the fresh air would revive her, but the heaviness in her legs was getting worse.

"Is it much farther?" she asked.

"Not far."

It was surprisingly dark for being in the center of a major city. The only light came from a few scattered oil-burning lamps that flickered in the chill air of mid-April.

The bells of the cathedral began to chime. She stopped walking and wavered on her feet. Her ears buzzed. She looked up at him.

His round face wore an expression of entitlement Jane had loathed from the moment they strolled past the queue at the front of the restaurant. He was Prince of the Art World. He owned a speedboat on Lac Léman. He drove an Aston Martin and went to Cannes. He was Tomas Fucking Firth. Who was she, anyway? Some hick from a place no one had ever heard of. A *librarian*.

Each clap of the church bell reverberated behind her forehead. Tomas's smile grew and grew until it was the toothless, Seussian sneer of *The Grinch Who Stole Christmas*. Jane blinked to clear the hallucination, and then frowned at Tomas.

"You drugged me," she said.

The Geneva police report would show that Jane Ward and Tomas Firth entered her apartment off Place Franz-Liszt on April 14 at 10:07 p.m. Video footage from a jewelry store across the street confirmed the time and showed that neither of them were carrying a leather portfolio case.

The initial statement was taken the following evening by Detective Lieutenant Martina Delgato. It was in French.

DELGATO: After you left the restaurant, what do you remember?

WARD: We were outside. It was dark. It was cold. He was helping me get back to my flat.

DELGATO: Helping? I've seen the video. You two looked cozy.

WARD: It wasn't like that. I may have accused him of drugging me. I'm not sure.

DELGATO: That's quite a thing to say. How do you know you weren't drunk?

WARD: I don't think I was.

DELGATO: The dinner receipt shows two bottles of wine. Is that normal for you?

WARD: No.

DELGATO: Perhaps you have a high tolerance?

WARD: I don't think so. He kept filling my glass.

DELGATO: And you kept drinking.

WARD: It was good.

DELGATO: Château Margaux. Five hundred francs per bottle. I'm sure it was. Why is your French so good, by the way? I thought Americans only spoke English.

WARD: My grandmother has French ancestry. I studied in college, and Quebec isn't far. Now, can we talk about my painting?

DELGATO: Okay. When did you discover it was missing?

WARD: This morning, I mean, afternoon. I woke up at three o'clock. I looked everywhere. It was gone.

DELGATO: And then you came here.

WARD: No. First I retraced my steps back to the restaurant. I talked to the hostess. She remembered me, but she knew nothing about my art case.

DELGATO: The video from outside Portia's Café confirms you had a leather case when you left. So you got separated from it somewhere between the restaurant and your flat.

WARD: We didn't get "separated." He *stole* it! His family wanted it, I'm telling you. They tried to get me to sign it over. When I refused, he took it."

Jane was doing her best to hold herself together, but inside she was dying. Granny Jo's painting! It was a nightmare!

"Something about it scared them," said Jane. "I don't know what. Just ask them. Ask Tomas."

"Oh, I will."

"You will?"

"Of course. These are serious charges."

Martina turned off the recorder and rolled her chair around the desk.

"Listen to me carefully, Jane. The Firths are one of the most prominent families in Geneva. Money, power, friends in high places." She paused. "But I don't give a shit about any of that. We're going to get to the bottom of this. I promise."

Jane felt her eyes fill with tears.

"Now, where are you staying tonight?" asked Martina.

Jane wiped her eyes. "I don't know. My room is rented. I don't have much money. It might be a park bench."

"That would be illegal," said Martina. "This is Switzerland, not San Francisco. Let me make some calls. I'm sure we can find something."

Across the room, a male detective was trying to get Martina's attention.

"Excuse me," she said and got up. Jane watched as the detectives talked for a minute. They kept looking toward Jane. When Martina came back, she looked troubled.

"A few more questions," said Martina. "You were with Otto Firth last night?"

"Yes."

"At the gallery?"

"Yes. I told you."

"And what time was this?"

"Seven o'clock."

"How long were you there?"

"About a half-hour, I suppose."

"And from there, you and Tomas left on foot for Portia's Café?"

"Yes."

"And what about Otto? When did he leave?"

"Right before. He and Gunther left together."

"Where?"

"I don't know. They went out through a back door."

"And you didn't see him after that?"

"No. What's going on?"

Martina closed her pad. "There's been a development. Otto Firth is dead."

The news of Otto's death was everywhere. Speculation was rampant. Heart attack. Overdose. Murder. Mafia connections gone bad. No theory was too outlandish.

Jane's father wanted her to get on the next flight home. Her mother told her to listen to her father (a first). Davis suggested she get a lawyer. But the call she dreaded most was to Granny Jo.

"But you're alright?" Granny Jo asked after Jane told her what happened.

"No, I'm *not* alright! Your painting!"

"He didn't..."

Oh, that.

"No, Gran. He didn't. They did a test."

"Good. Now, listen, I'm sure you're upset. You think you let me down and all that nonsense."

"I did!"

"You could never do that, Janey. You're my brave girl."

"Mom and Dad want me to come home."

"I know."

"Should I?"

Granny Jo paused. "You know what I do when I can't decide? I ask myself, 'What would Sophie do?'"

Jane moved into a spare room with the detective's mother. Jane was the last person to see Otto Firth alive, and the detective wanted to keep her close until they had a report from the coroner. That was fine with Jane. She wasn't going anywhere without her painting.

She spent her days at the Bibliothèque de Genève, huddled in a cubicle researching the Firths. In the evenings, she scanned archives for the elusive marriage certificate.

On the first day after Otto's death, Ted Banks called. Jane winced when she saw his caller ID on her phone.

"So, I'm writing an item for an online blog about Otto's death," Ted began, "and imagine my surprise when I read that a key witness is an American librarian named Jane Ward."

"Yeah."

"Who claimed to have been drugged and robbed by Tomas Firth."

"I can explain..."

"No need. I was a dick that day in the library. I wouldn't have confided in me either."

After a long pause, he laughed. "Thank you for not arguing with me. I'm so sorry about the painting. I knew Tomas Firth was a creep, but this... I had no idea he was capable of something like this. Did he tell you about his speedboat?"

"Before we got our menus."

"Putz."

"So you believe me?"

"Of course."

They talked for a half-hour. The next day, Ted Banks's article in *ArtNet* contained a sentence about Otto's planned trip to Singapore. Jane flushed when she read it. She had let that fact slip. She needed to stop thinking of him as "Teddy Bear" from the creative writing club. When he called the next day, she was ready.

"What do you think's going to happen to the Firth galleries now that Otto's gone?"

"Wow, what a great question. Otto was a genius, the whole package—smart, savvy, a visionary, exquisite taste. Tomas can't fill his shoes. I doubt Gunther would even try. Normally, I'd say they'd bring in a talented manager, but the Firths are different."

"What drove Otto?" Jane asked.

"What drives any man? Power. Money."

"But he already had that. All he had to do was keep selling his Francis Firth paintings out of the vault. I read he was bleeding money on his modern art."

"That's true. It can take decades to build the career of a single artist, and he was funding dozens."

"Why? Why the need for these alternative revenue streams?"

Ted was quiet a moment.

"You're suggesting the Firth vault is not as full of family paintings as they let on?"

"I just think there's something a little frantic about his business strategy."

On the fifth day following the death of Otto Firth, Detective Delgato appeared at Jane's cubicle in the library. Jane recognized the detective by her eyebrows, of all things. They were fabulously bushy, and the left eyebrow had a vertical line through it from a scar. Jane was a fan of scars.

"There you are!" she said. "You wouldn't believe what I had to go through to get up here. It's like the Kremlin."

Jane smiled. "Johan?"

Johan was head of the Bibliothèque de Genève. He and his team had become Jane's allies in her research. Together, they had done in a few days what would have taken a month working alone.

Martina nodded.

"They're like the Politburo! Are they librarians or bouncers?"

"They're just protecting me."

"From what?"

"Outsiders," Jane laughed.

"Hey, I'm Swiss, remember? *You're* the outsider."

"Library before country," said Jane. "We're a cult. We look out for each other."

The detective surveyed Jane's cubicle and frowned. It was strewn with books, photocopies, scans, and notepads.

"You're not working on the Firth case, I hope."

"Just educating myself."

Martina squinted at her. "Stay out of this, Jane."

"Why are you here, Detective? Have you recovered my painting?"

"Not yet. But I wanted to let you know you are free to go. I mean, you always were, but I won't keep you any longer. I would appreciate it if you kept me apprised of your whereabouts—"

"The coroner's report is in?" asked Jane.

"Yes."

"Otto Firth killed himself."

Martina nodded. "How'd you know?"

Jane shrugged.

"I suppose you'll leave Geneva now?" asked Martina.

"Soon. There's just one more thing I need to do."

The funeral for Otto Firth was held at Holy Trinity Church in downtown Geneva. The event drew hundreds of mourners from around the world, including celebrities, billionaires, and politicians.

Jane sat in the back wearing a black dress she had bought for the occasion. The tributes were pretty much what Jane expected: "brilliant businessman"; "a friend to artists"; "devoted husband and father"; "pillar of the community."

Afterward, a receiving line formed in front of the open casket. Organ music played from enormous pipes at the rear of the church. Mourners offered solemn platitudes to the Firth family. The smell of burning paraffin filled her nostrils. Jane slid into the line.

When she reached Otto's widow and his daughter, she offered her condolences. They thanked her and then turned to the next woman. Jane stepped to her left and found herself face-to-face with a man in a black suit with his hands crossed in front of him. He wore a huge gold watch over the fringe of a sleeve tattoo.

Tomas saw her, and his eyes widened.

"*You*," he hissed.

"I have something for you," she said.

She reached into her pocket. He stepped back defensively. She withdrew a folded sheet of paper and held it out to him. It showed two pictures side by side. On the left was a painting by Francis Firth, *Seven Birches at Dawn*. In the background, barely visible, Jane had circled a small church set against a wall of granite. Beside the painting, Jane placed a color photograph of a chapel that looked identical. It, too, was set against a granite wall.

"What's this?"

"Give it to Gunther. He'll know."

Tomas took the paper and started to wad it up. She grabbed his wrist and squeezed. He looked around for someone to notice. He tried to pull free, but she held firm.

"I know it was you," she hissed. "I know you drugged me. I know you stole my painting."

"Let go."

Jane went on. "I know your family is lying about Caroline…"

"Crazy bitch."

"And maybe about Francis, too. I don't know why. Not yet. But I will find out the truth. And when I do, I will tell everyone. I'll write a fucking book about it."

The receiving line had begun to pile up behind her. The woman beside her was frowning.

Jane released his hand. He massaged his wrist and stared at her wide-eyed.

"My condolences on your loss," she said.

As she turned, her eye fell on the bald head of Gunther Firth, who had been watching the exchange. She bowed her head.

"Burgen," she mouthed.

His eyes flashed. She turned and marched down the aisle, out the door, and into the cold drizzle of the dreary morning. She climbed into the Range Rover she had rented thanks to a fresh infusion of cash from Granny Jo.

Ahead, the Alps rose like stone giants.

Five

Jane

To get there, you take the E-79 out of Geneva. Morning traffic is bumper-to-bumper along the shores of Lac Léman, past the condo stacks that cling to the hillsides, past the ten-million-dollar chalets and the hundred-million-dollar castles until, at length, you veer east into the mountains and begin a climb that goes on for three harrowing hours. At first, you are part of a slow-moving parade of coaches, camper vans, cyclists with a death wish, and convertible Lamborghinis of day-trippers with plaid caps and perfect teeth. Then, one by one, they arrive at their scenic overlooks, campgrounds, and B&Bs. But you climb on, taking fork after fork, each road narrower than the last, up one valley and the next, each cozier than the last, until you are joined by a river whose roar you hear long before you ever see it. And when you do finally see it, the road has shrunk to a single lane of cracking asphalt sandwiched between sheer cliffs with no guardrails and no shoulder. You wonder how you would turn around if you needed to, and perhaps you *will* need to because you may be lost and you have not seen another car for a half-hour—about the same time you lost the signal on your GPS and cell phone. And with a sick feeling, you realize you actually *miss* the congestion of the E-79.

And that's how, on a drizzly afternoon in late April, Jane Ward arrived on the same remote stretch of road as an old man with a cane.

She was distracted by a bird that had nearly struck her windshield. It was sparrow-sized and darted like a bat. Jane thought it might be a common swift.

They had chimney swifts in Ontario Hills, and a pair nested each year at Granny Jo's. Jane eased off the gas for a better look. It stayed just in front of her, matching her speed as she climbed the mountain road.

Swifts were remarkable birds. They stayed aloft for ten months straight—eating, sleeping, and mating without ever touching the ground. The only exception to their airborne existence was during the nesting season. Even then, swifts were unable to perch. They had to build their nests on vertical surfaces so that when they were ready to take flight they could fall with outstretched wings. They were monogamous, and the pair that nested under Granny Jo's eaves was the same couple every year. Their arrival was always a cause for celebration.

Jane drove slowly up the road, marveling at the bird. Suddenly, it dove left and perched atop a boulder.

Perched!

Jane gasped.

She looked back at the road, and her windshield was filled with an old man leaning on a cane.

Oh, my god!

She slammed on the brakes. The vehicle screeched to a stop. The man seemed unaware of her. He stood transfixed, staring at something on the edge of the road.

Jane put the car in park and ran to him.

"I'm so sorry! Are you alright?"

He muttered something in German.

"Monsieur?"

"The parking brake," he said in perfect French.

"What?"

He waved in the direction of her car. "Did you set it?"

"Damn!"

She raced back to the car. It took her a while to locate the brake in the rental. When she returned, the man was still standing in the road in a trance. She went to his side.

"Monsieur—"

He grabbed her arm and pointed.

"Do you see that?"

She followed his gaze to the bird on the boulder.

"You mean the swift?" she asked.

"You see it, too!"

"It's the reason I nearly hit you. I was watching the bird instead of the road—"

"What color is its throat?" he asked urgently.

"What?"

"Its throat. Please. My eyes are not so good these days."

The plumage of a common swift is unremarkable, and from a distance of twenty feet without binoculars, what could Jane expect to see but a smallish, gray-brown bird with an ivory face? Jane's color-blindness was beside the point. She took a step toward it, then another and another. It had its back to her, and seemed content with its panoramic view of the valley.

Jane's foot crunched a pebble and the bird turned. Its beak and chest came into view.

"What do you see?" the old man asked.

She frowned. Birds were identified by behavior as much as appearance, and this bird's behavior was beyond strange. A swift, which never perched, now stood before her as though posing for a picture. While she considered this incongruity, the clouds parted, and sunlight began to walk up the valley. When it reached the bird, its plumage came alive.

"That's odd," she said.

Protruding from the bird's neck was a feather that didn't lie with the rest.

"What?" the old man asked.

"There's a feather there. It looks almost..."

"What?"

"Gold."

She heard a noise behind her and turned.

The old man lay on the ground unconscious.

Jane raced to his side, crying out, "Monsieur!"

His eyes fluttered open. "What happened?"

"You fainted."

He blinked and seemed to consider this information. "Nonsense. I've never fainted in my life. Now, Mademoiselle, help me up."

Jane held his arm as he climbed to his feet. She picked up his cane and handed it to him. He took it and then dusted himself off. His thin, gray hair was tousled and flapped like a flag in the wind. He ironed it back into place in a dignified way. He looked toward the boulder.

The swift was still there. Still watching.

At that moment, an enormous black pickup truck roared to a stop behind Jane's SUV. The sound flushed the swift, which dove from the backside of the boulder and disappeared without a sound.

A tall thirty-something man in a sleeveless shirt leaped out of the truck and rushed toward them. The man carried a walkie-talkie and spoke into it.

"I found him!" he said in French. "He's on Laurel Ridge!"

The man passed Jane without a glance. Jane, who was always on the lookout for tattoos, noticed one on the man's arm. A bird.

"Opa!" he cried. "We've been looking all over for you!"

From the walkie-talkie, Jane heard a woman asking for information.

"Are you alright, Opa?" the young man asked.

"Such a fuss," groaned the old man.

The young man put his lips to the walkie-talkie. "He's fine, Oma. Tell Brigitte to call off the search."

He turned to Jane. "I'm Max. This is my grandfather, Klaus."

"*Bonjour.* I'm Jane."

"What happened here?" he asked.

Jane raced through her visual cues. Tall, with a slightly hunched posture, as though embarrassed by his height. Thirty-ish. Dark, thick hair. Squinty eyes like Clint Eastwood. Or was that a frown?

"I came around the corner, and he was just standing in the road."

"Not the road," Max said to Jane, "the driveway."

He pointed to the side of a chalet several hundred feet up the drive.

"Oh... Oh, god. I'm sorry. I'm so lost—"

"You're looking for Burgen, I presume."

"That's right!"

"You missed the turn. It's about a kilometer back. You'll see a waterfall on your left, then a small sign on your right pointing down a gravel road to the village."

Jane looked down the narrow lane and tried to imagine how she'd turn the car around. He seemed to read her mind.

"There's a place to turn ahead. Just keep going straight and you can loop back this way."

Jane got in her car and drove on. Max followed in his truck with his grandfather.

She reached the loop and gawked at the chalet as she circled the driveway. The chalet, it turned out, wasn't just any chalet. It was Chalet von Tessen, the landmark she had been admiring for the last thirty minutes. It was an Alpine landmark and the subject of many *"BONJOUR FROM THE ALPS!"* postcards she had seen in gift shops in Geneva.

It towered over the valley, seemingly bolted to a vertical cliff. It was sprawling, with two wings connected to a central, three-story tower. The style was of a Swiss chalet with intricate lattices and painted shutters. It struck Jane as incongruous since the essence of the Swiss chalet was simplicity, and there was nothing simple about Chalet von Tessen. Jane had come across it in her research on Burgen. It had been built as a hunting lodge in the mid-nineteenth century by Baron Rudolph von Tessen III, the so-called Banker of Leipzig. As far as Jane could tell, it was still a private residence, though there had been no information about the owner.

Jane looped past the house and started back down the mountain in the direction she had come. This time she spotted the sign marking her turn. It was, just as Max had said, located near a small waterfall.

The sign had an arrow that pointed along a gravel track with the words *"Auberge de la Vallée des Géants."*

The Valley of the Giants Hotel.

Jane spun the wheel and started down the gravel road. Ten minutes later, she stopped in a parking lot outside the village of Burgen.

Sophie du Burgen meant, literally, Sophie of Burgen.

Could it be this simple?

Burgen was an Alpine village nestled at the bottom of a natural bowl of green pastures that rose in all directions. It lay on the southern edge of any map of Switzerland. You could go no further without arriving in Italy. Granite peaks surrounded the valley like stone giants, giving the valley its name. Several dozen stone houses poured down the eastern hillside toward a church. Streams roared down from the heights to meet at a junction above the village on their way to Lac Léman a hundred miles away, and nine thousand feet below the place where Jane stood.

People had been coming to this valley for as long as men had ventured into the high passes of the Alps. They were traders mostly, plying their wares to the fishermen of the Italian peninsula. In recent years, retreating glaciers uncovered many of these Bronze Age traders still dressed in their animal skins with undigested strawberries in their bellies. Later, during the Dark Ages, Burgen became a refuge for the upper classes fleeing plagues in the cities. By the early twentieth century, Burgen found new life as a community of farmers and devout Christians who tended goats, grew plots for their subsistence, and worshipped a Calvinist form of Protestantism. Then began a slow decline. The lure of the cities drew away young people who were Burgen's future. Throughout the Alps, hundreds of such villages were becoming ghost towns almost overnight. All that remained to show they had once been places of note were a few ivy-covered stone walls and neat cemeteries tended by the ever-dwindling number of descendants who remembered or cared. Still, Burgen managed to cling to its existence, precarious as that may be.

Jane left the parking lot and made her way down the slope into town. The "streets" were not streets at all, but walkways that preceded the invention of the automobile. As she came into the village, she realized Burgen was not the picture-postcard place it had appeared from the road. A third of the buildings were vacant and deteriorating. In one place, a wall had fallen across her path, and she had to detour around it.

Before long, she arrived at a lavishly restored cottage and went inside. A bell clanged, and a pretty young girl looked up from her desk.

"Madame Jane Ward," she said. "We've been expecting you."

She checked her in, grabbed a key, and then led her back through the door. "Your cottage is this way."

They went outside and began to walk through the village in the direction of the river. The girl introduced herself as Brigitte. She was studying tourism at the University of Geneva. Her grandparents lived in Burgen, and she was spending the summer with them while interning at the Valley of the Giants Hotel. It was not a normal hotel; it was an *auberge diffuso,* Italian for "scattered hotel." They were becoming quite popular in the Alps. Vacant properties in a dying village were acquired and then restored so that guests could live among the locals, giving tourists an authentic Alpine experience. It served the dual purpose of rescuing villages by repurposing them as tourist destinations.

Brigitte chattered on in this way while Jane admired the mountains, which seemed so close she could touch them.

"It's so beautiful here," said Jane.

"Ah, yes. We may not have museums and restaurants, but we have other compensations. You can go fly-fishing, climbing, horseback riding, hang-gliding, or even wingsuiting if that's your thing. Just let me know ahead of time. The guides have to drive up from Geneva."

"Thank you, but I won't be needing a guide."

"May I ask, what brings you to Burgen?"

"I'm a birder."

"A what?"

"A birder. My life list stands at two seventy-five. I'm hoping to spot a wall-creeper, a bearded vulture, maybe a snow finch—though it's a bit late in the season for them."

Jane had googled all this in Geneva in case she needed a cover story (though she wouldn't have minded seeing a wallcreeper).

"Well, that's a first," said Brigitte. "We certainly have plenty of birds. I can't say I know much about them, though."

Jane quickly changed the subject. "Are you learning much on your internship?"

"Loads. The owner is a visionary. He lives up there in the chalet." She pointed to the sprawling chalet whose driveway Jane had used to turn around.

"You met him on the drive up, I believe."

"I did?"

"He said you almost hit Klaus with your car. Is that true? He called to let me know you were on your way. That's how I knew. Sorry about that tiny sign at the turn. I keep telling him we need to get a proper sign, but we're just a small operation. Four cottages. There were supposed to be twelve by now, but..." She shrugged. "Anyway, we're adding four more cottages next year, plus a new generator, and, hopefully, a convenience store. You'll see the contractors working. We have a bunkhouse where they sleep. They're a good bunch, mostly. They can be a bit boorish, I'll warn you now. They can't help themselves. If any of them cause you trouble, let me know."

Brigitte halted in front of an immaculate stone cottage. "Here we are!"

Stepping into the cottage was like stepping back in time. Oil lamps. No phone. No TV. Handmade furniture, a twin bed with a straw mattress, sooted walls, and ancient beams. Jane was mesmerized. It had hot and cold running water, in-floor heating, handmade wool carpets, and a general coziness that reminded Jane of Thursdays with Granny Jo. It even smelled like Granny Jo's... minus the cookies.

"We're going for authenticity," said Brigitte. "But just between us, I think we go too far sometimes. If you don't want to use the oil lamps, there are electric lights in the closet and receptacles all around. Let me know if you don't like the straw mattress." She wrinkled her nose. "Most people don't. I can get you a foam one. I have a few extras we keep for the contractors."

She explained about the meal plan, the thermostat, and how to use the radio to contact the front desk, and gave a few tips about getting around the village.

"In the valley, we live by the sun. You'll see. Everyone's up at dawn and in their beds just after dark. We call sunset 'Burgen's Midnight.'" She laughed. "You'll get used to it. Will you be wanting a fire?"

"That would be great. If you just point me to the woodpile—"

Brigitte shook her head. "I'll have someone come to light it for you. Wildfire Code." She turned to go but then stopped. "Oh, one thing. I don't have a checkout date for you."

"I'm not sure how long this is going to take. It depends on the birds. Is that a problem?"

"We have a group of climbers arriving next week. I can give you the cottage till then."

"That should be long enough."

Brigitte left. Jane opened her suitcase, grabbed a sheet of paper, and went outside.

The steeple of Burgen's church rose into the clear sky. She studied the paper. It was the same paper she had given Tomas at the funeral. It showed Francis Firth's painting of seven birch trees in a field. In the distance, a church steeple stood before a granite wall.

Jane compared the picture with her view of the church. The angle was wrong. And she was too close.

She started up the hill over the stone street. She passed an elderly woman carrying a basket of flowers. Two grizzled old men sat on a porch, hunched over a game of dominos, hand-rolled cigarettes dangling from their lips. Somewhere in the distance, a lamb was bawling. A chill breeze blew down from the heights. No one seemed to notice her.

Jane walked on, checking over her shoulder, walking backward at times as she tried to bring the granite wall and the steeple into the correct alignment. She found a dirt trail heading out of town in the correct direction and took it. She crossed a pasture to a gate and climbed over. Then another pasture and another gate. On she went.

The sun was standing on the peaks as she came at last to the spot on a hillside that seemed to match Francis Firth's painting. The birches were gone, replaced by mountain laurels and pines. The laurels blocked her view of the church. Was this the place, a century ago, Francis Firth had set up his easel? She shrugged. There must have been a hundred places in the Alps that looked like this one. If Sophie's last name hadn't been du Burgen, Jane would not have bothered coming to investigate. Back in Geneva, she had been stunned to learn of the existence of a Swiss village with that name. She discovered it by chance on the website for the *auberge diffuso*.

"*Travel back in time in the Valley of the Giants.*"

As Jane had breezed through the pictures on the website, she realized the church looked like the one in Firth's painting, *Seven Birches at Dawn*.

On the hillside, Jane studied the painting again. Francis's focus was on a stand of birches, not the distant church. The silvery bark of the trees was weathered and fraying like peeling wallpaper. He had exaggerated the angles to give each tree a distinct personality, as though they were seven weary soldiers who had stopped for a rest. And there was something else. The artist had painted the roots *above ground*. It gave the picture an unsettling quality. Jane traced the roots and realized they connected each tree to the next. Were the trees separate entities, or simply the visible part of something greater? The more she looked at the painting, the more it impressed her. Francis Firth was no mere craftsman. This was an ambitious work that involved the viewer. No wonder the prices for Firths were skyrocketing!

With the sun now behind the mountains, Jane felt an urgency to get back. Getting caught out here after dark, with the vertical cliffs and strewn boulders (and predators, no doubt), seemed like a bad idea.

After a half-hour, she found her feet once again on Burgen's stone street. She walked down the slope until the air swelled with the smell of fresh bread. Her stomach rumbled, and it occurred to her that she hadn't eaten since before the funeral. She detoured up the main street and arrived at a cottage with a hand-carved sign over the door between two hanging flower pots.

Elsa's Kitchen.

Jane knew about it from the website. Elsa Brucker was Burgen's cook and, according to the website, the village's most important citizen. The middle-aged widow supported herself by transforming her home kitchen into a diner that served three meals a day, seven days a week for locals and guests alike. She cooked in the same kitchen where she had raised her three children and fed her husband until his death from cancer.

Several tables were set up on the walkway. A group of men dressed in outdoor gear were drinking schnapps and talking loudly. Fishermen from the city, Jane supposed. At a long table, eight men in work clothes sat hunched over bowls of stew. These must be the contractors Brigitte had warned her about.

Jane sat down at an empty table and before she could wonder how to order, a bowl of stew and a bread basket appeared before her. She turned to see who had served her, but the woman was already heading inside.

Jane took a bite and paused. It was delicious! Everything was fresh and filled with flavor—lamb, carrots, green beans, and potatoes. In no time, she was mopping the bowl with bread. She felt almost giddy.

At the other table, the workers had finished their meals, too, and were drinking beers and laughing. Among them, a stocky man with dark hair was looking at her.

"I guess you liked it," he called out. That stopped the conversation at his table. The men all looked at her.

"Is it like this every night?" Jane laughed.

"It's the only reason we work here," said one of the other men.

"It sure isn't for the nightlife," said another. He said something in Italian, and they all laughed.

They stood up and then wished her good night, one by one, with a chorus of "*bonne nuit*s" and "*ciao*s."

The stocky man came to her table. Jane squirmed. These were the sort of interactions that gave her trouble.

"Hi, I'm Pauli from Rome."

"Jane Ward," she said. "From the United States."

She offered her hand.

He kissed it. "*Enchanté.*"

She made a list of cues in case they met again, which in the tiny village seemed likely.

He released her hand and smiled pleasantly. "You had a good walk?"

"Walk?"

"Yes, I was working just over there," he said, pointing to one of the cottages, "and I saw you climb the far hill."

"It was lovely."

"You like to walk?"

One of the men called across the street. "Hey, Pauli. Leave the *regazza* be."

Another called out, "Yeah, Romeo. Time to go."

Pauli rolled his eyes. "Wives."

Jane laughed.

"See you around, Jane Ward from America!"

Jane spent the next hour in her cabin studying the paintings of Francis Firth on her laptop, which she'd downloaded ahead of time. Gunther's biography claimed that Francis had painted in a village called St. Séverine's Parish, which was located one hundred and fifty miles west. Could that be a lie? If so, why?

It occurred to Jane that the paintings themselves contained the best clue. If she could find places in his paintings that were unique to Burgen, then she could show that at least that part of the story was a lie. Her plan was simple—walk around Burgen trying to find places that matched up with the paintings.

She decided to begin with river scenes. While trees change, rock formations in the stream were more likely to endure the passing of time.

She found a painting called *Turtle Rock*. It showed a sloping rock with a strange hump in the middle. It looked like a turtle. Atop the rock were four turtles. Francis had used the location for another one of his paintings, a portrait of Caroline with a poppy in her hair. The rock was distinctive. If she could find it here—

Someone knocked on the door. Jane glanced out the window. The darkness was absolute. Who could it be? Surely not Pauli...

"Who's there?" she asked through the door.

"Maintenance, Mademoiselle. You wanted a fire?"

Jane pulled open the door to face a tall man with dark hair. He stood on the stoop wearing a tool belt and a headlamp, which he switched off the moment she opened the door. He carried a crate filled with wood, kindling, and old-fashioned baffles.

"May I?" he said.

"Of course. Come in."

He went right to work, deliberately and with great economy. He began by checking the flue, going so far as to reach up the chimney to make sure the handle was in the correct position. The kindling was cut in precise lengths that stacked easily. After a bit of kindling fell, he retrieved it and set it back in place to create a perfect stack. Next, he lit a match and then gently fanned the flames with his baffles. In less than a minute, a perfect fire was roaring. Jane felt like applauding.

"Well done," she said.

"I'll leave a few logs for you to keep it going."

"Thank you."

"If you don't mind, I'd like to take a look at your water heater."

"Of course."

He went to the bathroom and pulled a power drill from his tool belt.

Jane stood at the door.

"My name is Jane."

His brow furrowed. "Yes, I know."

Jane's guard went up. She was familiar with this puzzled reaction; she got it a lot. He had expected her to know him. She went back over her day. Was he one of the contractors? Possibly. Definitely not Pauli. Max from the road? She knew Max only by his tattoo, which was currently concealed beneath his shirt.

Jane leaned against the wall and admired his large, powerful hands. The man removed a half-dozen screws and then shook his head in disgust at what he saw. He got a different tool and adjusted the setting. He put it all back together and stood up.

"That should do it," he said.

"Thanks."

"I want to thank you for helping my grandfather on the road today. He told me what happened. That was scary. He's never wandered that far before."

Jane relaxed. It *was* Max.

He went to the hearth and poked the fire, even though it was burning well.

"You said something to Klaus," he said. "I suspect he misunderstood, but now he's pretty worked up about it. I'm going to need your help to straighten it out."

"What do you mean?"

"I think you know what I mean."

"No, I don't."

"About the bird."

"What about the bird?"

"You told Klaus you saw a common swift with a gold feather. Are you going to deny it?"

"Why would I deny it? We both saw it."

"A swift with a gold feather? Seriously?"

Max's hunched-over posture was gone. He hovered a full head above her. His eyes narrowed to slits.

"It's what I saw," she said.

Max's gaze fell on Jane's computer screen with the picture of the turtles on the rock. He looked at it a moment and then lifted his gaze.

"He's ninety-two years old, Jane. He's got some fanciful ideas that go back to... well, *way* back. You shouldn't feed his fairy tales. It's not nice."

"How so?"

"You really don't know?"

Jane sighed. "I'm getting a little tired of this. It's been a long day."

He rolled back his sleeve to reveal his tattoo. It showed a common swift perched on a cliff. On its throat was a gold star.

"It's the von Tessen family crest," he said.

Six

Sophie

A brothel is a prison with bows on the walls. Others didn't see it—not the girls, and certainly not Vincent. But Sophie knew a thing or two about walls.

She was living at Madame Giroux's, hiding out until Vincent could arrange her escape to America. Nine girls lived with Sophie and Madame Giroux within those gilded walls. In their free time, the girls didn't stray far from the brothel, so everyone was close. They stayed away from the public places of Arles, where they suffered cold judgment from the good citizens—even if many of these same good citizens could be found in the brothel after dark. Madame Giroux's was one of six brothels in Arles that served the soldiers of the nearby military garrison, and business was good.

Vincent Van Gogh had taken Sophie's necklace to Madame Giroux the day she showed it to him. Together, the three conspirators formulated a plan. Madame Giroux, who had the cold business acumen of John D. Rockefeller in the body of a prostitute, knew a jeweler in Marseilles who could discreetly break down the necklace into separate gemstones of tradeable size. The gold would be further melted down into ingots that could be used as currency for tickets on the ship and other needs for Sophie's passage to America. Sophie would sell the gemstones when she got to New York. Vincent assured her that this cloven treasure would be enough to get her to St. Louis with plenty of money left over. Everything would be ready in one month.

One month!

Sophie was bursting with nervous energy—which made it torture to stay hidden behind the walls of Madame Giroux's, as she had been instructed. The streets were dangerous. Chief Constable Michel Rivoli had taken her escape from his prison as a personal humiliation. Making matters worse, a physician from the asylum had arrived in Arles to help with the manhunt. This was a lot of interest for one non-violent escapee. But Madame Giroux was too dazzled by the necklace and the sizeable commission she was about to receive to care where it came from. She was the perfect accomplice. Vincent was so clever!

Sophie came through the door of her room to find three of the girls—Marie, Anna, and Pauline—on her bed, taking turns learning to smoke a pipe. The room reeked. Anna was coughing while the others laughed.

Marie looked up when Sophie entered. Through the haze, she gave Sophie a look of warning and said, "Madame is looking for you."

"Someone's in trouble," Anna teased.

Pauline took her turn on the pipe and blew a smoke ring into the air. Anna fanned it with her hand.

"Hey!" Pauline shouted while the others giggled.

Sophie left the girls to look for Madame, whom she found in her office. Madame Giroux was a middle-aged woman who still carried a reflection of her former beauty, though it had hardened into something that was now cynical. She turned her cold stare on Sophie.

"You stupid little bitch!"

"*Pardon?*"

"You went for a *walk*? Are you daft? You brought the *gendarmes* to my door! My business! You must be mad!"

Madame Giroux's words stung, especially the last bit. But Sophie had not escaped one asylum to join another. This arrangement was suffocating her.

"You were seen!" Madame went on. "The constable just left. He wanted to know if I had a new girl in my employ. The only reason he isn't tearing this place apart right now is that I have a special relationship with him."

"I am *not* one of your girls," said Sophie. "I can do as I please."

"*Mon Dieu*," she breathed. "You're as crazy as that painter." With that, Madame snapped her fingers and shouted, "Willetta!"

A young girl, perhaps twelve years old, came running in from the salon.

"*Oui*, Madame?"

"Is Marie still with the young lieutenant?"

"*Non*, Madame. He finished. She's in her room now."

"Good. Bring her here."

"*Oui*, Madame."

Willetta fled back through the salon.

"Listen to me, Sophie, you will stay inside these walls until I say otherwise. Do you understand? If you can't follow these rules, then our deal is over. I don't need this aggravation."

"Why hasn't Vincent come to see me?" Sophie demanded.

Madame gaped at her. "Are you simple?"

"I want to see him."

"Monsieur Van Gogh is banned from Madame Giroux's."

"By whom?"

"Me!"

"Why?"

Madame continued to gape at her. Sophie glared back.

Marie appeared in the doorway. "*Oui*, Madame?"

"I'm putting you in charge of your... roommate. If she leaves the premises, I'll have both of your hides. *Comprenez-vous?*"

Marie nodded.

Madame Giroux cocked her head at Marie. "Have you been smoking, girl?"

"No, Madame."

"You reek!"

"It was the lieutenant, Madame," Marie lied. "His pipe was like a fucking chimney."

Madame looked hard at Marie, but the girl didn't flinch. Sophie was impressed. Marie was an excellent liar.

"Don't you ever let me catch you."

"Never."

"Now go! Both of you!"

Sophie spent the rest of the day trying to honor her bargain with Madame Giroux. She helped Rosetta peel potatoes. She read a book she found in the parlor, but it was terrible, all about war and human cruelty. The heroes looked like cowards to her, always doing what they were told, no matter what they thought about it. She put it down. She wondered what Vincent Van Gogh was doing, what he was painting, and how the painting was turning out. She had been helpful to him with the almond blossoms, she was sure of it. Maybe she could help again. Maybe he needed her.

The next morning, Sophie awoke in her bed before dawn. Marie snored beside her. Sophie lit a candle and slipped out from under the covers. She crept to the placard and began to get dressed. The corset clipped in front, so she needed no help to put it on. When she finished, her gaze fell on the bed. Marie was watching her.

"*Bon matin*," said Sophie.

"Where are you going?"

Sophie put her finger to her lips. "To see Vincent."

Marie's eyes grew wide, and she pulled herself up in bed. "That's not a good idea. You heard Madame."

"I *have* to see him."

Sophie fastened the final clasp on her corset, and pulled on the dress. She straightened the folds and faced Marie.

"Why is Vincent banned from Madame Giroux's?"

"You should stay away from him," said Marie.

"Tell me."

Marie sighed. "He came one day, not long after he arrived in Arles. He wanted to do portraits of the girls. Not nude or anything. Just whores in their off-hours. He did a few sketches of me. For some reason, he was fascinated with Rosetta—you know, the fat girl who works in the kitchen. He did a bunch of sketches of her. She loved it. They were terrible, childish drawings. You've seen his work; the man has no talent. But what the hell, it relieved the boredom. Then Madame found out about it and insisted he pay."

Marie shook her head in wonder. "Vincent went completely crazy. He lectured Madame on art and modeling and *égalité*—like Madame would care about any of *that*. He was out of his mind, yelling and pounding his fist at the injustice of... of everything."

Marie shrugged, but her eyes were glowing. "Monsieur Van Gogh is not exactly stable, you may have noticed."

"So that's when Madame banned him?"

Marie shook her head. "It got worse. I've never seen Madame so angry. People don't argue with her. It just isn't done. Her face was as red as a cherry. She snatched his sketches and threw them into the fire."

"*Mon Dieu!*"

"Then Vincent did the craziest thing. He went to the hearth and pulled the burning paper right out of the flames. I mean, he calmly stuck his hand right into the fire! It must have been so painful, but he didn't blink. I think that scared Madame, and she is not a woman who scares easily. She sent Willetta to bring the constable. I grabbed Vincent by the sleeve and pulled him out of there. He would have gone to prison for sure. Madame and the constable are on special terms."

"You were a good friend, Marie."

Marie thought about that. "Vincent is... amusing." She beat the back of her head against the wall. "Ach, I get so bored here! Who would have thought the life of a whore would be so fucking *dull*? But Vincent is never dull. Being with him is like fucking a stick of dynamite."

Sophie ignored the disgusting imagery. "So, you've been with him?"

"As a lover, you mean?" Marie laughed. "Lord, no! He has no money!"

Sophie finished dressing and put her hand on the door to leave.

"Sophie," said Marie, who had been watching her the whole time.

"Yes?"

"Vincent can be a sweetheart. I don't want you to think I'm some kind of stone-cold bitch."

"I don't think that."

Marie smiled sweetly. For an instant, Sophie saw her as an ordinary teenager sitting up in bed.

"People aren't nice to him," said Marie.

"What do you mean?"

"I've seen things. People pretending to be Vincent's friend, then stealing his paint as a joke. One time, this kid put a snake in his basket. Girls flirt with him, get him excited, and then run away calling him names. They call him *le fou roux*. I'm glad you're being a friend to him. He needs one."

"Go back to sleep," said Sophie.

Marie slid back under the blanket and dug her ear into the pillow.

"If Madame catches you," said Marie, "I was asleep when you left."

Sophie found Vincent outside his yellow house. She waited behind the corner, then stepped out as he was leaving.

"Sophie!" he cried. "What the hell?"

She stuck out her bottom lip. "You're not happy to see me."

"Of course I am, but... What are you doing here? It's not safe. You could be seen."

"I can't stay in that place another day."

"It's just for a little while, Sophie. Be reasonable."

Sophie hated those two words. Why were people always throwing them at her?

"The streets are empty. We'll go to the countryside. You can paint there. I'll stay out of sight. Who's going to see me?"

Vincent sighed. "I may know a place. Let me grab some food. We'll have a picnic."

He ducked back into the house, leaving Sophie to stand alone outside. She looked around anxiously. Why hadn't he invited her in?

He reappeared and said, "Okay, let's go. Quickly!"

They hurried along the dirt road heading out of town. To the east, the sky glowed with the approach of dawn. To the west, the brightest stars still clung to nighttime. Smoke trails wiggled into the sky from chimneys. Sophie drank in the smell. It reminded her of home when their kitchen maid, Ingrid, would stoke the breakfast fire and pretend to listen to young Sophie as she prattled on about her ponies or something wonderful she had read in a book, or a dream, or a nightmare, or whatever else was occupying her mind that morning.

"So, *Amant*, have you been thinking about me?" asked Sophie.

Vincent flashed a guilty smile.

"I want today to be perfect," said Sophie.

"I should warn you," said Vincent. "I tend to mess things up."

"Me, too," she said and took his hand. She could have skipped, she was so happy. But Vincent was burdened with painting supplies. He looked like an ox on its way to market.

They came upon a woman setting up a fruit stand on the roadside. Vincent bought two oranges and handed one to Sophie. She brought it to her nose like a flower. The citrus smell was electric.

On the ground, the vendor's infant daughter played in a stand of wheat stalks. Vincent put the orange in her hand. She giggled and pressed it to her chest.

Vincent stood fascinated as he watched the little girl roll the orange over in her hands. He spoke with the woman and then handed her a coin. He began to set up his easel.

"Here?" asked Sophie. She looked around. They were on the side of the road within sight of the town. It didn't feel safe.

Vincent didn't answer. He was in it.

Vincent Van Gogh was happy with his portrait of the child. Her flushed, pudgy cheeks were as fresh as the orange she held. Who could help but smile at it? He might even sell this one. He decided he would use more props in his portraits—like Gauguin's native women with their flowers and exotic fruits. He would have to ask Theo about it in his next letter.

At some point, he realized that the little girl had disappeared. She must have gotten bored and wandered off. No matter. He painted from memory now. All that remained was to paint a background to support the subject. The downward viewpoint of the painting meant it contained no sky, just wheat stretching to the four edges of the canvas. He threw himself into filling the space with wheat as yellow as Sophie's hair in sunlight...

Sophie!

He looked around. She was gone. He set down his brush and palette and went to the vendor to ask where Sophie had gone. She motioned toward the house. He hurried along the dirt walkway and cursed himself for neglecting Sophie. Why did he always have to ruin everything?

The house was two stories of gray stone with a thatched roof. There was a single window on the upper level. No glass, of course. All around, chickens pecked at the ground. A goat was tied to a post. The air smelled of hay and manure.

He called through the doorway, "*Bonjour?*"

"In here, Vincent," Sophie replied.

He found her seated on the dirt floor surrounded by three children, one of whom was the little girl from his portrait. Sophie was playing a game that used the orange as a ball. They would clap hands with the person beside them, and the orange would be tossed to another player. Then the game would continue. Vincent didn't know the game.

She grinned at him.

"I'm sorry," he said.

"For what?"

"For abandoning you."

"Don't be silly. You were working. Besides, we're having a wonderful time, aren't we?" she asked of the children, who replied with nods all around. "Now, Monsieur Van Gogh, you must meet my new friends."

Sophie introduced the children, including the youngest, Annette, who was the girl from the painting. Vincent joined the game "Clap Goes the Orange," which was something Sophie had invented. Sophie taught him the rules, and in no time, he was dubbed "The Unbeatable Monsieur Red Beard." Everyone laughed as, time and again, Vincent held the orange at the winning moment.

The game felt like a dream to Vincent. He was not invited into people's homes. He scared them. He was *le fou roux*. When he first entered this house, the grandmother frowned and challenged Sophie about him. But Sophie vouched for him in a way that was disarming, and so Vincent found himself welcomed into the fold.

Sophie was a marvel. For too long, Vincent had been living a solitary life. Entire days passed when he spoke only to his waiter at dinner. He no longer entertained naïve notions about the romance of the lonely artist. He was sick with loneliness. He dreamed of turning Arles into an artists' commune of the south, with his yellow house as the artists' accommodation. The idea, though farfetched, burned in his mind like a lighthouse over a dark sea. It filled him with hope that his present misery was temporary.

As the oldest of six (one of whom predeceased him), it hadn't always been so for Vincent Van Gogh. He had grown up in a house filled with voices. At times, the commotion of his childhood home had been too much, and he would escape into the fields of Holland to capture beetles and worms for his collection. He loved bird nests, and his first sketches were of them. His father was a minister who preached that God spoke to men in many languages, and one of them was nature. It was a person's duty to learn all of God's languages. Lately, Vincent had been thinking about that a lot.

On Sundays, the family would go to church to hear Father's sermon. It was the low point of the week. But even as young Vincent squirmed in the pew beside his brothers and sisters, he recognized the satisfaction of being a Van Gogh among Van Goghs.

Of course, he had driven them all away. He was the problem child of the family. Anna wouldn't even talk to him anymore. His sister blamed Vincent for his father's stroke. And perhaps she was right about that. Their arguments had been fierce. Father had tried twice to have Vincent committed to an asylum. The year before Father's death, Vincent had refused to attend his father's Christmas service. Why? He couldn't even remember now, but the row had been so ferocious Anna asked Vincent to leave. He never saw his father again.

Why did he always have to be so much trouble? When Vincent looked back, he saw that his illness had been with him even when he was out collecting beetles by the stream with such fierce focus. What mattered most to Vincent—what always mattered most to Vincent—was whatever thing was in front of him at that moment. It was like today; he had wanted to spend the day in the fields painting, and perhaps stealing kisses from Sophie. But once he saw the little girl—Annette—with the orange, Sophie had ceased to exist. His mind was like a painting: White-hot within the borders of the canvas, but outside the frame... nothing.

Inside the hut, the grandmother returned to break up the game. The children groaned, and little Annette cried. But the old woman was resolute; there were chores to be done, naps to be taken. The children said *au revoir* and made Vincent and Sophie promise to return to play.

Vincent resisted the urge to suggest that he paint the entire family. He sensed it would corrupt the moment. He was rewarded for his restraint with a hug and a peck on the cheek from Annette before she scampered away to take her nap.

As Vincent walked beside Sophie along the path from the house, he stopped and turned to her.

"Did an angel send you?" he asked.

Sophie was delighted by Vincent's question. Lately, she had been wondering the same thing about Vincent. Without his help, she would be starving and sleeping in haystacks without any hope of reaching America. He acted like it was nothing. It was everything!

Vincent asked her if she wanted to go back to Madame Giroux's.

"But we haven't had our picnic!"

He smiled and then led her to a livestock pond not far away. It was surrounded by a grove of poplar trees and there was a small beach. It was out of sight of the road with shade and water in which to dip her feet. It was perfect!

Sophie was looking for a place to sit when Vincent held up his hand and said, "Wait!"

He set down his equipment and leaned Annette's portrait against the easel. He walked to a fallen tree and began tugging wildly at a large artery. It broke, and he fell backward. He sprang back to his feet. He squatted to lift the branch.

"Vincent, no!" said Sophie. "It's too much."

But it was too late. Vincent hoisted the enormous log onto his shoulder and carried it, legs trembling, to their little beach. He dropped it on the ground. It landed with a heavy thump.

"Your chair, Mademoiselle," he said, his face red with exertion.

Sophie sat on the log and watched him set up the picnic. He hummed two bars of some tune over and over. He behaved as though carrying the log was nothing, but Sophie recognized it for what it was—a symptom of mania. Highs and lows. She knew it well. Vincent had underestimated the log's weight; she had seen the shocked look on his face the moment he realized his miscalculation. Then he summoned the strength to lift it anyway. He was powerfully built, but it was too heavy. Even for him.

She watched his focus turn to building a fire. He began gathering anything he imagined might burn—pinecones, dried grass, moss. It was more fuel than was needed for ten fires. He stacked it all carelessly, without skill, into an unventilated lump at the center of their beach. It was obvious to Sophie that Vincent had never built a fire in his life. She kept quiet, for he was utterly absorbed by his task. He lit a match and held it to the kindling. When the fire didn't catch, he lit another match. And another, and another until he arrived at the last match. His focus was absolute. All that existed was the match, the pile of kindling, and the picture in his mind of a perfect fire.

"Vincent," she said gently. "I don't need a fire."

He started at her voice. "No?"

"The day is warm enough, don't you think?"

"Fine. I'll save this last match for my pipe."

Without another thought, he abandoned the unlit mound of wood and laid out the food. The picnic was extravagant, with two-day-old croissants from the *boulangerie*. They stole sideways glances at each other as they ate.

A gust of wind carved a swirling pattern in the wheat.

"Did you see that?" Vincent asked.

"The wind?"

He nodded enthusiastically. "Wind is visible in the wheat. The wheat makes the invisible visible."

Sophie watched him fall into thought. She left him alone. He was imagining a painting.

When they finished eating, Sophie asked to see Vincent's painting of Annette.

He got up and set it in front of her. The paint was still wet, and glistened in the shifting shadows. She smiled at the awkward, unskilled drawing. The girl's eyes were off-center, and her ears were too low on her head. But somehow it didn't matter. The portrait radiated his enthusiasm for the subject.

"I knew it would be good," she said. "You like children."

"I scare them."

Sophie continued to study the painting. "Am I here anywhere?"

He smiled and pointed at the wheat. "It's the color of your hair. I call it 'Sophie Yellow.'"

"My hair is brown."

"Not when the light hits it."

Sophie was considering this when her eye caught movement from the direction of the road. A man was coming toward them. Vincent saw him, too.

"Lie down now against the tree!" he said. "Now! Pretend you are posing!"

Sophie crawled to the tree and sat with her back against it. She raised one leg and put her hand behind her head to throw out her chest.

Vincent stood and waved to the man. "*Bonjour!*"

"You're on my land!" the man shouted as he came under the trees. He wore overalls and a large straw hat. He stole a glance at Sophie.

"It's a lovely spot," said Vincent. "My name is Vincent Van Gogh. I'm a painter."

Vincent put out his hand. The man ignored it.

"I know who you are." He spat at Vincent's feet. "*Le fou roux.*"

Sophie's anger flashed. "That's not nice!"

"It's okay, Adele," said Vincent. He winked at the man and said, "My model."

"He's being rude!" said Sophie.

"Model, you say?" said the farmer.

"That's right. We were just doing a portrait."

"I've never seen her in Arles before."

"That's because you're an upstanding citizen," said Vincent. "She's a whore from Madame Giroux's. I don't suppose you frequent that district."

"Certainly not!"

"I hired her for some poses. I thought the pond was a good spot."

The farmer chuckled and looked at Sophie with fresh interest. "Poses, huh?"

"Poses, yes!" Sophie snapped.

"She's a firecracker, that one," clucked the farmer. "Uh, how come she's got her clothes on?"

"I couldn't afford the nude."

Sophie felt her face flush at the way they were talking about her—as though she weren't even there.

"Whores," sighed the farmer, shaking his head. "Monsieur, the reason I am asking is the *gendarmes* are hunting for a woman who escaped from the nuthouse up in St. Remy."

"I heard. And you thought Adele was her?"

He looked her up and down. Sophie glared at him.

"She fits the description."

The farmer continued staring at Sophie. He spat on the ground. Suddenly, his eye caught sight of the portrait of little Annette.

"Hey, what kind of game are you playing?" he said. "That's a child. Not a woman."

Sophie's heart skipped a beat, but Vincent remained calm.

"That? It's something I worked on this morning. Before Adele arrived."

The farmer squinted at him, filled with suspicion. "I don't believe you. Where's this painting of her?"

"Do you know anything about art, Monsieur?"

"I know about goats."

"I see. Well, understand, portraits begin with sketches. You sketch, then you paint."

"I think you're a liar."

"Shall I show you the sketches?"

Vincent went to his basket. Sophie half-expected him to pull out a knife and stab the man. But his hand came out with a sketchbook. He opened a page and handed the book to the farmer. Sophie couldn't see what was there. The farmer compared what he saw with Sophie. He turned page after page, looking back and forth between her and the sketchbook.

"My wife won't approve of having no whore on our property," he said.

His eyes lingered on Sophie's breasts. She snapped, "If you look any harder, I'm going to have to charge you."

The farmer couldn't help but laugh, and handed the book back to Vincent.

"Yeah, a firecracker for sure."

Sophie glared at the farmer until he turned away. "You best pack up your things and go now before the wife catches you. You don't want that kind of trouble, believe you me."

The farmer took a last look at Sophie and then walked back through the field. Vincent closed the sketchbook and walked to his basket to put it away.

"What's in the book?" Sophie asked.

"Nothing."

"Not 'nothing.' Show me."

"No."

She lunged for the book, and they played tug-of-war for several seconds before he let it go.

She turned her back to him and opened it, flipping through the pages. There were dozens of sketches of fields and cottages and trees in bloom. There was a close-up sketch of a grasshopper. Then, suddenly, there was a sketch of her. She was asleep in the tall grass.

"You did this on the day you painted the almond blossoms," she said. "While I was asleep."

He didn't answer.

She turned the page. There were more sketches of her. Pages and pages of them. These were imagined poses. Sophie in a chair. Sophie on a haystack. Sophie's face up close with her lips exaggerated. She turned another page to find a sketch of herself lying on a bed nude. She was posed on her side with her hand supporting her head. Her breasts were enlarged and lay like raindrops across her chest. Her nipples were small and hard. She was looking directly at the artist. Her eyes were shiny and inviting.

"What is this?" she asked.

"Sophie, I'm sorry. I know I shouldn't have. It's wrong. I'm sorry."

She closed the book and handed it back to him. She was in shock.

"We should go now," she said.

They didn't speak as he packed up his equipment and his portrait of Annette. They walked in silence through the wheat field. Vincent looked miserable.

Sophie's mind raced. The sketches stunned her to the core. Were they art or pornography? Was he using them for self-gratification?

They reached the road and turned toward Arles.

"Vincent?"

"Yes."

"I want you to destroy those sketches of me."

"Of course."

"And then I want you to do a proper portrait of me," she said. "Like the one you described to Marie that night in the river. I will be nude, and you will project the French countryside onto my body. 'A canvas in a canvas,' your angel of spring, as you said. Can you do that for me?"

Vincent swallowed hard.

"Yes, Sophie," he said. "I can do that."

Seven

Jane

Jane Ward stood on the isolated riverbank, stripped, and then slid into the water. The feeling was incredible. She had never skinny-dipped before. Her impulse to do so was a surprise even to herself. She had been feeling overheated from her long, fruitless walk and then thought, W*hat would Sophie do?* Granny Jo had started it, and now it was a mantra for listening to her inner voice.

Over the last seven days, Jane had walked nearly fifty miles along the unnamed rivers of the Valley of the Giants. She found no turtle-shaped rock, nor any other scene to confirm that Francis Firth had once painted here.

In the river, the current was trying to carry Jane away, so she swam to a rock in the center of the stream and held on. She looked back at her pile of clothes on the bank and allowed herself to savor the sensation of the water flowing past her naked body. Every nerve in her skin tingled. It was thrilling!

She was only able to skinny-dip because, for once, Pauli wasn't with her. The contractor she had met the first day often joined her for her walks, to the point she had begun to worry he was neglecting his work. He had become a friend and an enthusiastic participant in her quest. He didn't know the full scope of her purpose, but it was enough for him to know she was looking for what she had come to call the "Rosetta Scene" which would connect Francis Firth to Burgen.

Pauli was a contractor from Rome who installed the heated floor she admired so much in her cabin. He didn't share Jane's connection with the outdoors, and could be so distracted by the sound of his own voice, a bear crossing their path wouldn't have interrupted his running monologue.

Jane had not forgotten Brigitte's warning about the contractors, but Pauli was different from the others. He was married and spoke constantly about his beautiful wife and their baby daughter in Rome. He was in Burgen to save enough money to open his own flooring business back home with his brother.

It was his second season in Burgen, and his knowledge of the people was invaluable. With a quick laugh and his terrible French, he could disarm even the most suspicious Burgener. Jane had already interviewed a half-dozen Burgeners, thanks to Pauli, though none of them had heard of Francis Firth.

Jane had not spoken to Max von Tessen since that night when he revealed the extraordinary coincidence of the von Tessen family crest. For the first few days, she had seen him around the village. But then a young girl had appeared at the chalet, and the only time Jane saw Max was in the pastures above Burgen—Max on his jet-black horse, and the little girl on a spotted pony trailing behind.

Jane finished her swim and followed the smell of Elsa's Kitchen through the village. Swimming always made her hungry, and she had skipped breakfast to get an early start. Along the way, she passed a cottage being renovated. Three men were on the roof working in the hot sun. One of the men was cutting slate tile with a power saw, while the other two set the tiles. The cutter was shirtless but wore overalls, a backward baseball cap, and safety goggles. He finished his cut and turned off the saw. Slowly, the dust cleared, and she spotted Max's tattoo.

Jane sat on a stone wall to watch him work. Max's face was covered with a mixture of dust and sweat that had formed a paste. He shouted something to one of the men. He turned, and for an instant, their eyes met. Jane nodded. He hit the switch on his saw, and it roared back to life. Jane rose and moved on.

Elsa's Kitchen was packed for lunch. From the corner, two middle-aged women were motioning to her frantically. "Mademoiselle Ward! *Venez ici*! *Ici*!"

Jane didn't know them, but it was clear they were not to be refused. She went to their table and sat down. Instantly, she was swept into a maelstrom of banter and gossip that tested Jane's French. The women couldn't have been more different. Bernadette was a large woman with a powerful presence to match, whereas Rochelle was barely five feet tall and demure. Even now, she was holding her coffee cup with a pinky extended. They had one thing in common, though—they were both married to shepherds who were gone most days and some nights. Each of them had a brood of grown children—Jane lost count—but like all the members of Burgen's younger generation, they had moved away. One of Rochelle's sons was working in New York as a bartender, and Rochelle wanted to know if Jane knew him.

"I'm from Upstate," said Jane.

Rochelle looked at her blankly.

"No, I haven't had the pleasure," Jane said.

Rochelle clucked. "Pity."

Elsa put a plate of stew and bread in front of Jane, and then went back to her stove. The women watched as Jane devoured the stew and mopped up the last of the gravy with her bread.

"I like a healthy appetite," said Bernadette.

"That's never been your problem," said Rochelle.

Bernadette ignored that. "I saw you watching Max," she said.

Jane felt the room go still.

"He was working on the roof," Jane said.

"Yes, he was," said Bernadette.

"It must be hot up there," said Rochelle. "I suppose that's why he doesn't wear a shirt?"

Jane flushed.

"Are you married, dear?" asked Rochelle.

"No."

"Mm-hmm."

At that moment, Pauli arrived at the table out of breath. He had found a place he believed was the Rosetta Scene. It was an overlook along a path to Chalet von Tessen. There was a flat rock and an outcrop with a view of the entire Valley of the Giants.

"I know that spot," said Elsa. "That path is treacherous. Be careful."

"I've walked it many times," said Pauli. "She'll be safe with me."

Jane excused herself from lunch, and together they set out, with Pauli leading the way.

"What is Max von Tessen doing on the roof?" Jane asked him.

"One of the roofers quit, and they're way behind. Max is helping out."

"You can't help?"

"I do floors."

"But—"

Pauli sighed, exasperated. "Do you want to see the overlook or not?"

"Of course."

Pauli led on, and that's when Jane noticed the clouds slipping over the peaks. Weather in the Valley of the Giants could change by the minute. One instant the sky was clear, and the next, clouds descended like an avalanche. At times, the fog was so thick that it felt dangerous for Jane to even walk from her cottage to Elsa's Kitchen.

Pauli saw the clouds and cursed. "*Miseria!*"

"Maybe we should turn back?"

"You'll be safe," he said. "You're with me. I could find the way blindfolded."

As they left Burgen for the trailhead, they seemed to pass through a door. The sun vanished into a fog. The Alps were gone, along with the meadows, the river, and most of Burgen. The temperature plummeted, and the air dripped with moisture. It soaked Jane's clothes and coated her skin. She could see no further than a few steps ahead of her.

"Pauli..."

"I know what you're thinking. Trust me. I've taken this path dozens of times. The vista is worth it."

Vista?

And indeed, Pauli was an excellent guide. He led them unerringly through the fog across a meadow to a little gate. They went through. He fastened the gate behind them, and they began to climb. The fog thickened.

Pauli was uncharacteristically quiet. Normally, he filled the silence with jovial chatter.

"Maybe we should turn back," said Jane.

"Almost there."

"But we won't be able to see anything."

"It'll clear. This is just a passing cloud. You'll see."

About halfway up, they came to a switchback, and Pauli pointed ahead along a side path.

"This way."

Jane hesitated. "Are you sure?"

He held out his hand. "Come, *ma chérie*. You won't regret it."

He had never used a term of endearment before.

They left the main trail and followed the small spur along a downward slope. After a few hundred feet, it ended at a ledge with a stone bench.

He sat down and patted for her to sit beside him. "Have a rest."

Jane sat down. They stared blankly into the fog. It was ridiculous.

"I told you I'd get us here," he said.

"Pauli, we can't see."

"It'll pass."

"I don't think so."

"It will."

"Maybe we could try again tomorrow."

"But you're leaving. You need to relax, Jane. You've been working so hard."

He put his arm around her.

She stood up.

"What's wrong?"

"I want to go back now."

He stood up to face her. She became aware of his size. He was not tall, but he was stocky with thick arms bulked from years of laying heavy floor tiles and pavers.

"But why?" he asked.

"I just do."

"Why?"

"I don't like this fog."

"You're safe," he cooed. "You're with me."

"I want to go."

"Soon."

Her heart was racing now. "Please, Pauli. We've had such a good friendship. I'm grateful for everything. Don't ruin it now."

"You're the one ruining it. Don't be like this."

He took a step toward her.

She turned and started back in the direction they had come.

"Hey, be careful!" he shouted after her. "You don't know where you're going."

"Then show me!" she cried. She could hear the fear in her voice. He must have heard it, too.

Suddenly, his hand was on her shoulder.

She reacted instinctively. She grabbed Pauli's hand and then twisted his wrist so that the arm was forced back against the joint. He went down on his knees. She held him there, pinning his thumb against his wrist.

"Ow! Hey! What are you doing? Stop that!"

Jane had learned the maneuver from her brother. "Everyone should know a little self-defense," Davis had said at the time. "Women, especially."

"Let me go!" said Pauli.

Jane released him. He scrambled to his feet and massaged his wrist.

"Why did you do that?" he asked, looking hurt.

"I want to go."

"I don't understand. I thought we were getting along so well."

Jane's mind was racing. He was not giving up.

What were her options? She didn't dare brave the path alone—either by going forward or back. She'd fall to her death. And that was assuming she could get away from Pauli in the first place. She couldn't remain, either. The fog could last through the night. She'd freeze to death. Pauli had chosen his spot well. She wondered if there had ever been a Rosetta Scene at all—

A voice broke through her thoughts.

"What's going on here?"

They turned. It was Max, sitting atop his black horse.

"Boss!" said Pauli in shock. "Uh, nothing. I was just escorting Mademoiselle Ward back to her cottage."

The horse stomped impatiently. Max spoke to it in German, and it stilled.

"You seem to have strayed from the path," Max observed.

"I was just showing her the view."

Max gazed into the impenetrable fog. He turned to Jane.

"Mademoiselle, would you like me to take you up to the chalet?"

She nodded.

"Pauli, I'll see you back at the bunkhouse."

Pauli shot Jane a wounded look and then started back along the path. A few seconds later, he disappeared into the fog.

Max held out his hand. "Grab on."

She grabbed hold, and he swung her onto the saddle behind him.

"Hold tight," he said, and she put her hands around his waist.

He clucked, and they started up the trail. Jane tightened her grip. They reached the main trail and began to climb. She could barely see the ground below them. It seemed to Jane they were moving through a vacant universe. All that existed was Max's body in front of her and the powerful beast beneath them. Max spoke gently to the horse in German. The only other sound was the crunching of stone and the snorts of the horse as it labored to carry them up the slope. Jane knew that one false step would send them tumbling into the abyss, but strangely, she felt no fear. It was exhilarating.

After ten minutes or so, Max broke his silence.

"Hold tight," he said. "This last part gets steep."

She pressed her chest against his back and squeezed.

The horse lunged several times as it made the final climb. Then, quite suddenly, they stood on the flat lawn of the chalet, the outline of the building visible in the mist. The ride was over.

He dismounted and held out his hands to her. She slid into his arms. He set her gently on the grass, and they stood facing each other for a moment.

He pointed to a side door of the chalet. "Just through that door is the kitchen. Agatha—that's our cook—is there now. Tell her what happened. She'll take you to a fire and give you some tea. You're shivering. I'll be along shortly."

He climbed back onto his horse.

"Wait, you're going back *down*?" she asked.

It was beyond belief! Before she could say another word, he clucked and started down the path. He disappeared into the mist. She could still hear the beat of the horse's hooves, but after a few seconds, that faded, too. She stood looking at the place where he had been. It was as though the cloud had swallowed him up.

The next morning, Jane arrived as usual for breakfast at Elsa's Kitchen to find the workers in a state of excitement.

"Pauli left last night," said one of the men. "Packed up and caught a ride to Geneva. Took all his tools. Everything. Max must've fired him."

"I wonder what he did," said another man.

While everyone began to speculate, Jane grabbed her pastry and returned to her cottage. It was her final day in Burgen.

Poor Pauli! Was he fired because of her?

A knock on the door saved her from this spiraling train of thought. She pulled open the door, half-expecting to see Pauli on the stoop with his infectious smile.

But it was Max. The little girl was beside him. She was about seven years old with brown hair escaping from her riding helmet.

"*Bonjour*, Mademoiselle Ward," said Max.

"*Bonjour*."

"I thought I'd come by to check on you."

"You already did that," she said. "Twice!"

The previous day, he had driven her back to Burgen from the chalet and then insisted on escorting her to her cottage. He built a fire and made tea. Later, he returned with a plate of food from Elsa's Kitchen and a copy of *The Count of Monte Cristo*.

That night beside the fire, Jane opened Max's book and saw, to her astonishment, it was a first edition—probably worth a hundred thousand dollars in excellent condition. But this copy wasn't "excellent." It wasn't even "fair." Pages were dog-eared, the spine was broken, and notes in French were written in the margins.

On the stoop of Jane's cottage, Max's daughter was looking up at the adults impatiently. "Tell her, Papa. We're here to invite you to go riding!"

Jane noticed the black horse and speckled pony tied to the post by the street.

"Allow me to introduce my daughter," said Max. "This is Mademoiselle Sydney von Tessen."

"*Enchantée*. A ride?" said Jane doubtfully. "Where?"

"It's a secret!" said Sydney, clearly delighted by the prospect of adventure.

Jane looked at the horse. "So I would ride…"

"Pillion," said Max.

"I don't know that word."

"Double. I'm sorry, Jane, I don't have another horse for you. Just Lela."

"Her name is Lela?"

"It means 'dark beauty,'" said Sydney. "Like *Black Beauty*. I read the book. It's fantastic!"

"I read it, too, when I was about your age," said Jane.

"It made me cry."

"Me, too," said Jane.

Jane squinted at Lela, who was happily munching grass. "Are we going far?"

"We'll be making several stops," said Max. "Elsa packed us lunch."

Jane looked down at herself. She was dressed for a hike—shorts and a sports bra. It was her last day, and she had a notion of taking a final skinny-dip.

"Do I need to wear anything special?"

"Just this," he said, holding up a helmet.

"You have to wear a helmet," said Sydney. "It's a rule."

"What about you?" Jane asked Max, who wore a black cowboy hat.

"Oh, he doesn't need to," Sydney explained matter-of-factly. "His head is harder than any helmet."

Jane went inside to put a shirt over her sports bra and then came back out. Max sat Jane in front of him on the saddle. When she asked about the change from the previous day, he replied, "I thought it might be more fun for you. A much better view than my backside."

Sydney giggled.

They started through the village with Max in the lead and Sydney close behind. The shoes of the horses *clip-clopped* on the stone walkways. Villagers waved as they passed. It was obvious to Jane that they liked Max. He greeted them by name and often with thoughtful remarks: "How is your knee?" or, "Your tomatoes look ready to burst," or, "Will your mother be here for Bonfire Day?"

"What's that?" Jane asked.

"That's just what we call Burgen Day. We have it on the first fair weekend in September. We have a big bonfire, so everyone just calls it 'Bonfire Day.' I'm sorry you'll miss it. I understand you're leaving us tomorrow."

"Yes."

"So you spotted all your birds, then?"

"You know about that?"

"It's a small place, Jane."

They entered a dirt trail. The *clip-clop* of Lela's hooves was replaced by a soothing *thump*. Jane swayed to the rhythm of the horse's gait. Max held the reins in one hand in front of her. His other arm rested at his side.

"So, you offer this service to all your hotel guests?"

"No."

By the stream, they stopped to greet three guests with fly-fishing rods. Max made a few suggestions about where to fish, and then wished them luck. He clucked and Lela carried them away.

A few minutes later, they arrived at a cottage with two women knitting on the front porch. Max reined Lela to a halt.

"*Bonjour* Madame Martin. Madame Bouché."

Jane realized she was looking at Rochelle and Bernadette from Elsa's Kitchen.

"We're having tea this afternoon at the chalet, and we were wondering if you two ladies could join us."

"At the chalet, you say?" asked Rochelle.

"Four o'clock?" said Max.

Rochelle and Bernadette exchanged nods.

"I'll send a driver."

The women went back to their knitting. As they rode away, Jane looked back. The women were now on their feet, talking excitedly.

Lela carried them to a wide, shallow area of the stream and started across. The horse kicked up water that spritzed Jane's bare ankles. Behind them, Sydney was squealing as her pony stomped at the water as if trying to dig a hole in the liquid. Midstream, Lela stopped and dropped her head to drink. Jane held tight to the horse's wiry mane and leaned back against Max's chest. Max closed his arms around her to keep her from tumbling over the horse's neck. Lela finished drinking and then splashed to the opposite bank.

"Grab hold," said Max.

He clucked and Lela lunged up the bank. Sydney and her pony followed, and Jane heard her laughing.

By this time, Jane's face was sore from grinning. It was thrilling to be traveling in this way. She thought of all the miles she walked along the river. How much faster it would have been on horseback! Jane always wished she'd learned to ride.

"You like to ride, I guess," said Jane.

"I do. And you like books," he said.

Max must have seen her reading alone in Elsa's Kitchen when there was no one to talk to.

"Well, I'm a librarian," said Jane.

"Oh, we have the most amazing library!" said Sydney. "It's a whole room of nothing but books!"

Jane laughed at Sydney's description.

Sydney went on. "I would show it to you, but Opa won't let anyone but family go in there. It's a rule."

"Books are private," said Jane.

"That's what Opa says!" Sydney replied. "Plus, sometimes people borrow books and don't return them."

"Oh, I hate that," said Jane.

"So does he."

Max laughed. "He certainly does."

"Papa, can we run?" asked Sydney.

"Would you like that, Jane?" Max asked her.

"Okay."

Max's arms closed around her as he took the reins in both hands.

"Hold tight!"

She dug her hands into the mane.

He clucked at the horse, and they were off. It was like flying. Behind her, she could hear Sydney crying, "Whoo-hoo!"

Max answered Sydney, "Whoo-hoo!"

Jane joined them, crying out, "Whoo-hoo! Whoo-hooooo."

They reached the far end of the meadow. Max reined Lela, and they slowed to a stop. Sydney came beside them on her pony. Both animals were panting with huge, rattling blasts of air.

"Are you okay?" Max asked.

Jane nodded.

"Did you see me go?" cried Sydney. "Yara was trying to keep up with Lela! I thought I was going to fall."

"But you didn't," said Max.

"No!"

"Good. Now, come. We're almost there."

They left the meadow and rejoined the trail that followed the riverbank. A few minutes later, they came to a bend in the river. Max stopped and dismounted. He held out his hands to help Jane off the horse. The ground was muddy where he stood, so he carried her a short distance to a flat stone.

"This is it," he said and set her down effortlessly.

She looked around. It was a pretty spot, to be sure, but there was nothing particularly noteworthy about it. The river made a sharp bend, which created a deep pool. There was an oddly shaped boulder, like an egg with a spine on top…

A chill ran down her spine.

"Oh, my god," she said.

It was the scene from Francis Firth's painting, *Turtle Rock*. It was unmistakable! Same rock, same fallen tree, same bend in the river. There were even two turtles on the rock!

"I saw the painting on your laptop that first night when I lit your fire," said Max. "I knew what it was. Then Pauli told me what you were doing. I googled 'Francis Firth' and went through his paintings. I recognized most of the landscapes at once."

"*Most*? There are *others*?"

In all, Max showed her seven more scenes that morning that could have only been painted in the Valley of the Giants.

Jane was in shock. The scenes proved that Gunther Firth had been lying in his book. The paintings were done in Burgen, not St. Séverine Parish!

Why would he lie about that?

Afterward, Max took them back to the same meadow where they had run the horses. He laid out a blanket and then the picnic. The horses grazed beside them as they ate egg salad sandwiches on Elsa's homemade bread. Max filled Jane's water bottle from the stream. It was so cold that Jane got brain freeze. She didn't know the French word for "brain freeze," so all she could do was wave her hand and make a dumb face.

Sydney giggled and said, "Look, Papa, poor Jane has *céphalée de la crème glacée*."

An ice-cream headache.

They finished eating, and Sydney left to pick flowers for her tea party.

"This is so helpful, Max. I don't know what to say. Thank you so much."

"These places I've shown you, Jane, they're not places a casual visitor would know about. Growing up, I spent all my summers here. I fished from Turtle Rock many times. There are always turtles there. It's actually called Turtle Rock. To know that, to know these places, you would have to know the valley very well."

"So you're saying Francis Firth wasn't just a visitor? You're saying he was a Burgener?"

"I'd be surprised if he weren't."

"But you've never heard of him?"

He shook his head. "There have never been any Firths in Burgen as far as I know." Max took an apple from the bag. "Want one?"

Jane shook her head. He took a bite and then sat back to watch Sydney.

"Can I ask you something?" asked Jane.

"Sure."

"Yesterday, in the fog, you didn't just happen by on Lela, did you?"

"No."

"So, you suspected something?"

He nodded. "I saw you leave town with Pauli, and I was... concerned. I asked Elsa about it, and she told me where you were going."

"So you saddled up your horse and came after us?"

He nodded.

"Pauli never actually did anything, you know," she said.

"I know. If he had, we'd be having a whole different conversation."

"Still, I'd hate to think you fired him because of me."

"I fired Pauli because of Pauli. He wasn't coping. As I said before, the valley isn't for everyone. It wasn't for Pauli. Besides, I'm sure you could have handled him yourself. That was a pretty impressive move you put on him."

"You saw that?"

"I didn't want to just assume you needed saving."

At that moment, Sydney squealed. The little girl had become distracted by a butterfly. She was trying to get it to perch on her finger.

"She sure seems to love it here," said Jane.

Max leaned back and the edge of his tattoo came into view. He watched Jane's eye go to it.

"I think I owe you an apology for the way I acted that night in your cottage," he said. "I'm sorry."

"It's okay. The next morning I called an ornithologist at the University of Geneva about the swift."

He smiled. "Really? What did he say?"

"Apparently, if a swift is injured, it has been known to perch while it recovers. The strange feather could have been the result of an attack of some kind. And to be perfectly honest, I'm not one hundred percent sure the feather was gold. I had a strong impression it was, but I can't know for sure. I'm color-blind."

"Oh."

"Sorry I didn't tell you that night. I should have. But you kinda backed me into a corner, and I got belligerent, I guess. I can tell Klaus if you think it will help."

"Thanks, but I don't think anything's going to change his mind."

"About what?"

"You."

"Me?"

Max shook his head. "Klaus is on a first-name basis with every chipmunk that ever buried a nut in the Valley of the Giants. You have to understand, he's lived his entire adult life in the valley. He never went into the family business. At the time, they dismissed him as the black sheep, but there might be a little more to it. There's a history of mental illness in the family. I think he may have gotten a touch of that. The family sent him to the chalet as a kind of house sitter, but really, he and Ursula—that's his wife—became like the babysitters for the whole valley. Klaus sees meaning in everything. And I think because..."

Max winced.

"Is he sick?" asked Jane.

Max nodded solemnly. "His heart. The doctors can't believe he's still alive. It's the reason I'm up here this summer. I took a sabbatical from my engineering firm in Geneva to help Ursula. This will be his last summer in the valley. I know he's fretting about who will take over as caretaker, and I'm sure he was waiting for some kind of sign."

Jane gasped. "You mean the swift?"

He nodded. "That bird you both saw... for him, that was *huge*."

"Gosh, I'm sorry. I didn't mean to... trigger him like that."

He shrugged. "You saw what you saw."

"So you believe me now?"

"I do."

His gaze was remarkably direct.

Jane shifted and said, "May I ask, what's the significance of the family crest?"

"Ah, now that's a family legend," he said. "You sure you want to hear this?"

Jane nodded.

Max tossed away his apple core and moved closer to Jane. His hand rested an inch from hers.

"Okay. So Eduard von Tessen—that's Klaus's grandfather—was hiking with his sister in The Crags. That's right up there." He pointed to a patch of boulders below one of the stone giants. "This would have been in the mid-nineteenth century. The story goes that, in the narrow part of The Crags, they spotted a swift perched on a boulder above them. His sister was convinced the bird was injured and insisted they hike up to see. She practically dragged him up there. When they got close, they saw it had a gold feather on its throat. It flew away, and then they heard a loud rumble like a freight train."

"A landslide?"

He nodded. "It swept over the very place they had been hiking. They would have been killed for sure. The bird saved them."

Jane thought about that. "Give some credit to the sister."

"Anyway, that's the legend. Later, Eduard changed the family crest. It used to be a dragon." Max shook his head. "Stupid."

"Could the story be true?"

"No. Eduard's sisters were younger twins, and let's just say they were not the type to be caught dead in The Crags if the family history is to be believed. They were debutante-types. Married at sixteen. Pregnant the same year."

They sat a while watching Sydney play with the butterflies. For Jane, the scene was in black and white, and she wished with a fervor she had not indulged in years that she could see colors. Then it hit her—maybe there was a way. Dozens of paintings by Francis Firth celebrated pastures like this. With a trick of the mind, perhaps she could superimpose the colors of his paintings onto the scene before her. The medium-gray flowers… those were certainly yellow daffodils. And the delicate light grays, she had seen them as cream-colored splotches on dozens of his paintings. The clusters of dark gray were surely red poppies. The pasture was pale green, of course, the granite rocks were shades of gray (that was easy), and the sky was a special shade of icy cobalt that Francis liked to use. Element by element, Jane painted the scene in her mind until... she saw it! It wasn't the same as seeing, but it was the closest she had come since her accident.

Max must have been watching her, because he said, "Are you alright?"

She nodded and then cleared her throat. "I guess you figured out I'm not a birder."

"I did. What is this, some kind of research project?"

His question was conversational, and Jane could have easily deflected it. But in the end, she told him everything. What difference did it make? She was leaving the next day. She'd never see him or the valley again. She began with her accident, and ended with Otto Firth's funeral. When she finished, she was keenly aware she had been talking for nearly a half-hour. During that time, Sydney had moved on from butterflies to grasshoppers, and was now back to picking flowers.

"Sorry for rambling on," Jane said.

"Tell me about this face-blindness," Max said. "What's that like?"

"Oh, wow," she said. She had not expected that question. "It's called prosopagnosia. Some pretty famous people have had it. Jane Goodall, the chimp lady, for one. Oliver Sachs, the neurosurgeon. He wrote a lot about it. Every time I see a face, even my reflection, it belongs to a stranger. On the flight here, I tried to watch a movie. James Bond. I mean, how hard could that be to follow? Good guy wears a tux, bad guys have scars and kill people. But then there was a scene where the villain was in a tux, and Bond was killing people too, and I got so confused. I had to turn it off." She laughed. "I guess that's why I'm a librarian."

"You sure cope well. I would never have known if you hadn't told me."

"It's a trick. I use a system of cues. Like for you... the next time I see you, you'll be a tall man, slightly hunched over with a tattoo. Tattoos are the best. I love tattoos." Jane flushed. "Sorry. I shouldn't—"

"It's fine. My tattoo was... controversial, shall I say. Bankers don't get tattoos, which was kinda the point. It's good to know it serves a purpose other than youthful rebellion. Go on. What about Brigitte?"

"Blonde. Finishes people's sentences. Tinted contacts. Smells like a cosmetics counter."

He laughed. "That's true!"

"I use associations, too. Large old woman with petite old woman equals Bernadette and Rochelle. Plus, Bernadette has a lower voice than yours."

"It sounds exhausting."

"You have no idea. That's why I live in my hometown. I need a place that's small and not too hectic. Like Ontario Hills."

"How's Burgen working out?"

"Not bad. It's small, of course, and the population is elderly. Older people are easier, I find. They develop distinguishing marks—wrinkles, scars, and gray hair. Young people, especially young girls, all look alike to me. Last week I was in Geneva, and I was like a cat in a car, just..." She bared her teeth and raised her hands like claws. "You know, I'm sure people in wheelchairs dream of a world with ramps. Blind people must wish for all books to be in braille. In my dream world, everyone would wear a name tag."

She laughed. Max regarded her thoughtfully. His dark eyes were slits as he squinted in the afternoon sun.

"It took courage for you to get on that plane," he said.

His observation took her aback, and for several seconds they stared at each other in silence. Suddenly, Sydney was beside them with her bouquet. She thrust it at Jane.

"Look!"

"Oh, my, those are beautiful!" Jane exclaimed.

"I have daisies, heather... and what is this, Papa?" Sydney asked, pointing to a simple, dark-shaded flower.

Max answered, "It's called 'monkeyflower.' Watch."

He touched a petal, and the flower closed.

Sydney's eyes widened, and she tried it herself on another flower. It closed, too. She now regarded her bouquet as though it were magic.

"I'm ready for my tea party," said Sydney. "You're coming too, right, Jane?"

Jane arrived last. Brigitte dropped her off in the driveway, and Sydney used both hands to pull her into the house.

"I found her!" Sydney announced.

Jane stood in a marble foyer. Ahead of her was a wooden staircase with an elegant, carved banister. To her right was a sitting room, laid out for a tea party. On a cozy table atop a lace tablecloth were salmon tea sandwiches on three-tier stands, freshly baked *macarons* in assorted pastel colors, and a dainty porcelain tea set with matching pitchers for milk and sugar. At the center of it all stood Sydney's bouquet.

At Sydney's announcement, everyone looked up. Jane stiffened. It was the sort of situation she studiously avoided—six women and three men, all strangers in her eyes. Then she saw something that took her breath away. Everyone wore a name tag! Even Sydney had one on her tea dress.

Sydney handed a name tag to Jane.

"Here's yours," she said. "We're wearing these today."

"Jane Ward" was written in Sharpie in block letters. Jane smoothed the sticker onto her shirt.

She quickly read the other names—Max stood with Reverend Jacques Barbeau at the fireplace. Judging by the way Jacques was holding out his hands, he was talking about a fish. Jane had met Burgen's summer chaplain a few times along the stream, where he could be found fly-casting in deep concentration. He was in his early seventies, but still able to walk miles to reach the perfect fishing spot in the river. The two women setting the table were Ursula and Agatha. Agatha was the cook who had given Jane tea the previous day after Max's rescue. Her hair was styled as though she had come directly from the beauty parlor; Jane could not imagine how that effect had been achieved. Ursula buzzed around the table in a way that suggested excitement to be hosting her great-granddaughter's party. She had short gray hair and oversized glasses that magnified her eyes. She bore an air of authority. When she exchanged glances with Agatha, Jane sensed an enormous amount of information being transferred.

In the foyer, Bernadette and Rochelle were discussing the rug upon which they stood. Rochelle's eyes glowed in approval at the elegance of the gathering.

Bernadette's stiff, hulking form suggested she would have been more comfortable back home pulling a plow through her field. But Jane had never seen the two women more than a few feet apart, so if Rochelle was coming, then by god, so was Bernadette. Across the room, Klaus von Tessen stood alone, leaning on his cane and stroking his Dumbledore beard. His gaze was fixed on Jane. She nodded at him, and he nodded back.

For Jane, the sensation of entering a room and recognizing the people assembled was overwhelming. It was like a deaf person suddenly being able to hear. She had forgotten what it was like. Her eyes flooded with tears. She caught Max's eye over the chaplain's shoulder and mouthed, "Thank you."

Tea parties, Jane learned, were a daily event at Chalet von Tessen while Sydney held court. The opulent table presented an amusing contrast to the chalet's eclectic interior, which seemed to have a bit of everything. Remnants of the original nineteenth-century hunting lodge were evident in the paneled walls, wood beams, and plank flooring. An enormous chandelier composed of deer antlers was suspended from the ceiling. The fireplace was large enough for an NBA center to stand up in. But over these masculine bones lay a skin of something more recent and delicate. The furnishings were modern and made of floral fabrics, which softened the room's rugged look. Window treatments matched them, and throw pillows tied it all together. It was an elegant room, but not standoffish—the kind of room that invited you to grab a book and curl up on the sofa.

Agatha finished pinwheeling the *macarons* and summoned everyone to the table. They sat in seats assigned to them by name cards.

"Now *this* is a proper tea party," proclaimed Sydney, and everyone laughed.

Reverend Barbeau said the blessing, and the party began. Manners were elaborate and formal. Sydney regaled everyone with the tale of their morning ride and picnic. She showed them how the monkeyflower closed when touched.

Rochelle was talking to Sydney. "On your ride, you must have passed through my south gate. I don't suppose your father told you about the time I had to rescue him from it?"

Max groaned.

"*Rescue* him?" said Sydney.

"That's right. He was about your age. I was in my kitchen, and I heard this terrible wailing sound from across the meadow. I thought it must be a sheep giving birth, but we had none in that condition."

"You mean having a baby lamb inside her belly?" asked Sydney.

"We say 'full.' But yes, that's right. Anyway, I put on my mud boots and went out to see. I found young Max there with his finger caught in the gate, screaming like the Grim Reaper was about to take him."

"Did you open the gate for him?" asked Sydney.

"I couldn't. The way the gate swung, the hinge would have closed further on his hand no matter which way I swung it. He was in a pickle, for sure."

Sydney's eyes were saucers. "What did you do?"

"I sent one of the dogs to get Henri from the high pasture so he could get his tools and remove the gate by its hinges. I sat with Maxi while we set him free. To distract him from the pain, I asked him where he was going so early in the morning. Guess what he said."

"What?" asked Sydney.

"Italy."

Ursula clucked.

"Italy!" Sydney exclaimed, giggling.

"That's right. Your nine-year-old father was going to hike over the mountains to Italy. He got the idea from some book."

"It was *White Fang*," said Max. "Jack London."

"That's Alaska," Jane pointed out.

"Italy seemed more realistic," he said.

"I like these stories!" said Sydney.

That was all the encouragement Bernadette needed. "Remember the time you stepped on the nest of yellowjackets, Max?"

"No."

"Don't let him fool you, Sydney. He remembers. They chased him clear to the river! Poor lad, he leaped in without realizing it was spring. He nearly got swept over the waterfall. How long did you spend on that rock crying for help?"

"I wasn't crying," Max said defensively. "I was cold. And it was overnight."

"He hates bees to this day," said Bernadette. "He may look like a brave man, your papa, but just wait till a bee appears. He starts jumping and swatting like a little girl."

Sydney was giggling.

Klaus's raspy voice cut through the laughter.

"Mademoiselle Ward, I hear you're a librarian."

"Yes."

"Would you like to see our library?" asked Klaus.

Ursula gasped audibly.

Sydney turned to her dad and whispered, "What about the rule, Papa?"

The library was beyond belief. Jane had often gawked at pictures of the world's great private libraries, and this one certainly belonged to such esteemed company.

It was octagonal with eight full walls of books rising upward to a two-story atrium. A skylight in a vaulted ceiling provided natural light for reading. On the second floor was a catwalk for access to the upper stacks. A spiral staircase in one corner beckoned to the upper level.

Sydney and Max joined Jane and Klaus in the library. The others remained in the parlor.

"See, I told you!" cried Sydney. "It's a whole room of nothing but books!"

Jane was speechless. She walked past the shelves in a near-hypnotic state.

And such books! Leather bound, gold leafed, one after another, sandwiched between trade paperbacks, modern bestsellers, mass market paperbacks, and back issues of *Paris Match*, *Der Spiegel*, and *The Economist*. She'd never seen anything like it. The bedstand of any true reader could be expected to contain an odd collection like this, but here was a whole room of it! Jane now understood her first edition of *The Count of Monte Cristo*—Max had simply plucked it from a shelf.

In the center of the room were two armchairs with a single reading light and table. On the table, a book lay open with the spine up. Jane winced. It pained her to see a book treated in this way. She walked to see what it was.

Nana. Émile Zola. First edition.

Jane closed the book and set it on the table.

"Well?" asked Klaus. "What do you think?"

Jane sat. "I'm home. I'm never leaving."

Klaus smiled and sat beside her.

Sydney wanted ice cream, so Max led her away. Jane barely noticed. She was in a dream.

"So?" said Klaus. "Which book are you going to take?"

"*Borrow*, you mean."

"I assumed that was understood."

Jane walked to the spiral staircase. Klaus watched from his chair.

"May I go up?" she asked.

"Please. It has been ages since I was able to go up there."

She climbed the staircase to arrive on the catwalk. She walked past the shelves, pulling down books, inspecting them, and putting them back. Many of the older editions contained a small flower on the title page.

"What's with these flowers?" she called down to Klaus.

"Markers of some kind. One for each read, I figure. They're in hundreds of books. It's a forget-me-not. I assume that's not a coincidence."

"They're damaging the paper. You ever think of removing them?"

"Never."

Jane spotted a long shelf dedicated to leather-bound copies of Mark Twain. Recalling that Sophie had gone to Missouri because of her love for Twain, Jane went for a closer look.

"Excellent collection of Mark Twain," she said.

"Someone was a fan. You'll find multiple petals in every copy."

Jane began opening books one by one. It was true. Each contained several petals.

Jane pulled down *Life on the Mississippi*, a lesser work by Twain that she had never read. Four petals were tucked into the title page, along with an inscription.

To Sophie,

Thanks for setting me straight. Sometimes, literature does *save lives.*

Your Servant,

Samuel Clemens (Mark Twain)

The book seemed to gain a hundred pounds in her hands.

"Did you find something?" Klaus called up to her.

Jane carried her treasure back downstairs to Klaus. She set the book in his hands and opened it to the inscription. He glanced at it.

"Yes, I know." He grinned. "Mark Twain."

"Who's Sophie?"

He shrugged.

"How did the book get here?"

"It was here when I arrived. The library dates back to 1860. I'm old, but not *that* old."

Jane's heart was racing. She dug her phone out of her pocket and showed him *The Lover*.

"That's quite a painting," he said.

The nudity was distracting, so Jane pinched the screen to zoom in on Sophie's face.

"The woman's name is Sophie," she said. "Does she look familiar to you?"

He squinted at the image and asked, "Where did you get this?"

"It belongs to my grandmother."

"In New York?"

"Yes."

He sat back heavily and regarded her strangely. "May I ask, how did your grandmother get it?"

"A woman named Sophie du Burgen gave it to *her* grandfather."

"du Burgen?"

"Yes."

"Like our village?"

Jane nodded and put the phone back in her pocket.

"When was this?"

"April 9, 1890."

"That's very specific."

Jane had found a newspaper clipping in the *St. Louis Daily Record*. It gave an account of a thundersnow storm of "terrifying power, the likes of which no white man or savage could recall."

"I've done my research," she said.

"So it seems."

Klaus set the book on the table and stroked his long, gray beard. His deep-set eyes regarded her fiercely.

"Tell me one thing, why do you care? It's so long ago. What difference does it make?"

Jane thought about that. She had come to the valley from Otto Firth's funeral determined to expose the Firths as frauds and get *The Lover* back from them. She was angry and wanted revenge. Her threat to write a book was not empty, either. Perhaps the story of the Firth Gallery's corruption would make a good book. Ted Banks had thought there was a story. What if she got there first? But since she'd come to the valley, her quest had evolved. Perhaps, she thought, there were *two* stories to be told. One was an art mystery about the Firth Gallery—fraud, theft, and corruption on a massive scale. The other story was about Sophie, a woman Jane found herself drawn to ever since Granny Jo told her Old Doc's tale. What happened to her? Somehow, Sophie never got her due.

Of the two stories, Jane had no doubt which she preferred to tell.

"I suppose it's because Sophie was remarkable at a time when women weren't allowed to be remarkable," said Jane. "Her story was robbed from her. I think I would like to give it back."

Klaus lifted his cane and rose from his chair.

"Come with me," he said.

The portrait room of Chalet von Tessen had been built as a ballroom, but it found more practical use in displaying family portraits.

"We don't have many formal balls around here anymore," said Max with a smirk.

"We never did," said Klaus.

He had led Jane back to the salon where he invited everyone to accompany him to the portrait room. Reverend Barbeau had to prepare his sermon and excused himself. The remainder of the party wove through a back hallway to emerge into a large room that was little more than a big, empty space lit by a single chandelier. Its purpose was to provide wall space for dozens of portraits on three tiers that climbed to a twelve-foot ceiling. Jane could discern no obvious order in the way the paintings were hung. Seventeenth-century portraits were shown beside modern family photographs. Jane, who by profession and nature was attuned to indexing systems, could make no sense of it.

Klaus explained that the East Wing of the chalet had been built by "Old Rudy," as he called his great-grandfather, Rudolph von Tessen III. He was trying to lure one of the Austrian Habsburg emperors to the chalet, and the three-thousand-square-foot hunting lodge he had completed the previous year wasn't adequate for the purpose. He commissioned an addition that more than doubled its size, adding sleeping quarters for staff, a banquet hall, and a ballroom. He never succeeded in luring the emperor, nor did it matter because along came Kaiser Wilhelm I, and there ceased to be an emperor. Old Rudy found himself with a money pit in the Alps he used once a year. He declared it "cursed." And for him, it was. He died at the chalet in perfect health at age fifty-seven after being thrown from his horse. At the time, he was one of the richest men in Europe.

"It happened right out there on the lawn," said Max. "Almost in the exact spot, Jane, where I let you off Lela yesterday."

By then, the group had gathered around Klaus. They were staring up at a portrait of Old Rudy with his family, a son in military uniform and twin daughters in shimmering gowns, pearl necklaces, and elbow-high gloves—debutantes on the cusp of society.

"He *died*?" asked Sydney in horror. "Was he wearing his helmet?"

"No, Sydney," said Ursula with exaggerated seriousness. "He was not."

Sydney nodded as though that explained everything.

Jane said, "How interesting it must be to have your family woven into history."

"The Leipzig Archives keep wanting to send someone here to go through the basement," said Max. "They think there could be some papers of historical significance. Opa won't let them near it."

Klaus grunted.

"It's a mess!" said Ursula. "Boxes upon boxes. And we do have a few skeletons in the von Tessen closet—isn't that right, Klaus?"

The remark struck Jane as odd. In Geneva, there was a statue of Eduard von Tessen that celebrated his role in resisting the rise of the Nazis at considerable loss to his fortune. During the war, he fled from Germany to Switzerland, where he rebuilt his bank as a haven for Jews.

"We can't have a stranger digging around in all that," said Ursula. "Who knows what they'll find?"

Jane pointed to the painting. "Which one's Eduard?"

Klaus pointed at the boy. "That's him. Rudy's only son. My grandfather."

"He was always so kind to the Burgeners," said Bernadette. "Mama said he treated us like family. He built the schoolhouse, hired a teacher from Geneva—"

"Dorina," said Rochelle.

"Yes, Dorina, God bless her. He commissioned our church, and even paid for the pastor."

"Eduard built the church," said Jane. She had been trying to determine how Burgen came to have such a magnificent one. "Were the von Tessens very religious?"

"Not particularly," said Max. "It's a bit of a family mystery."

Sydney's voice called out from across the room. "Look, here he is again!"

Sydney stood below another portrait of Rudolph with his family. In this portrait, the family was much younger. Rudolph stood tall and square, in the prime of life. His wife was a rosy-cheeked beauty. She gazed lovingly upon her children as they gathered around a spaniel. Eduard, who must have been on the cusp of puberty, was focused on the dog, while the twin girls in ringlets stared into the distance with placid, empty expressions.

With Sydney's help, they found five more portraits of Old Rudy with his family, each painted at a different time in their lives. Ursula explained that the von Tessens once owned seven houses throughout Europe, and each portrait was commissioned for a different house. As those properties were sold over the years, the portraits found their way back to the only remaining family property from that era—the chalet.

"Look!" exclaimed Sydney. "It's me!"

The group had stopped in front of a photograph of Max with Sydney and her mother. The family appeared to be on vacation in a place with white stucco buildings and sandy beaches. They stood on a balcony overlooking the sea. Sydney's mother wore a broad-brimmed hat with a ribbon that even Jane could see was the same shade as the water.

"Of course it's you," said Ursula. "You're a von Tessen. Did you think you wouldn't be here?"

"My mama is very pretty," said Sydney with pride.

"Yes," said Ursula, "she is."

They all stood a moment admiring the picture.

Klaus said, "I brought Mademoiselle Ward here because there's a picture I think she will find interesting."

Klaus stepped backward to reveal a framed cover of a French-language business magazine. It showed a woman in a business suit leaning against a desk, arms folded powerfully. Behind her was a panoramic view of Geneva and the Alps. The headline was in French: "*Ne Croise Pas La Vipère*"—Don't Cross the Viper.

The woman was Sophie's doppelgänger. A chill ran down Jane's spine.

"Opa," Max asked, "why would Jane be interested in this?"

Klaus's eyes twinkled. "Show them."

Jane's hand trembled as she retrieved her phone and pulled up her image of *The Lover*. She zoomed in so that only Sophie's face was visible. She held it beside the magazine cover.

"It's Aunt Hannah!" cried Sydney.

"Who?" Jane asked.

Max replied, "My sister. The Viper."

Two women, one hundred and fifty years apart, bore a resemblance so striking everyone was stricken silent. The almond-shaped eyes were the obvious shared trait, perhaps because the artist had devoted so much effort to rendering them as windows to a restless, inquisitive soul. But other features were evident, too—a full upper lip, high eyebrows, heart-shaped face, and slightly oversized ears. It was also true that both women were strikingly beautiful.

Ursula's voice pierced the silence. "What's going on here?"

Max intervened defensively, "Mademoiselle Ward is tracking down the origin of a family painting. It was stolen—"

"I thought she was here for the birds," snapped Ursula.

"Uh, well, she is, kinda," Max said. "But—"

"I lied," said Jane.

Bernadette clucked.

"Oh, my. Oh, my," Rochelle repeated.

Ursula glared at her.

"I'm sorry," said Jane.

"Max, can you see that Mademoiselle Ward gets back safely to her cottage," said Ursula.

And just like that, the tea party was over.

Jane and Max drove in silence down the mountain.

"She's just very protective of Klaus," Max explained, clearing the air. "Especially now."

"I know. I get it."

At the parking lot, Max wanted to walk her to the cottage, but Jane refused. They stood beside the car and said goodbye.

"When's your flight?" he asked.

"It's a night flight. I figure I need to be on the road by noon. Maybe I'll catch one more lunch at Elsa's Kitchen."

"*Zopf.*"

Jane smiled. "Yum."

Max drove off, and Jane watched his car climb back up the road. Her gaze lifted to Chalet von Tessen. Clouds scraped the peaks behind it. She had a powerful premonition that within its walls her answer lay hidden, even if she wasn't entirely sure of the question.

She felt adrift and realized with shame she was looking forward to the flight home the next day, to getting back to her apartment above the hardware store. Jane would sleep on her foam mattress (not straw!) and, after a good night's sleep, she would rise early, make coffee in her Keurig, fill her Yeti mug, and then go downstairs. If the weather was nice, she would walk to work. She knew every crack in the sidewalks. The streets would be quiet, except for a few shopkeepers and school bus drivers. She would arrive at her library, insert the key, and turn the lock. *Click-clack-clunk*, three turns, such sweet music! An hour would remain before opening. She would use the time to catch up on the news and then wander the stacks looking for something out of place—just her and fifty-two thousand, four hundred books. At lunch, she would walk to the *Ontario Sun News* office and begin getting Friday's edition ready. There had been no newspaper for three weeks. She needed to do a follow-up piece on the Half King shopping center. Surely, there had been some movement in that story. The high school was scheduled to name its Teacher of the Year, and Jane would do the profile. In the evening, Granny Jo would be expecting her. Jane thought of that deep hole over the fireplace where *The Lover* had hung, and an icy grip seized her heart. She felt sick.

What could she possibly hope to accomplish by staying? The Firths were too rich, too powerful, too well-connected. She was twice a fool—once for losing the painting, twice for thinking she could get it back.

The sun was still high over the valley, so Jane decided to take a final walk along the river. As she stepped off the road onto the trail, she spotted the chaplain in his waders and floppy hat. She smiled. Jacques must have fibbed about needing to work on his sermon. She couldn't blame him. It struck her as above and beyond the call of duty to have attended the tea party in the first place.

"*Bonjour*, Jacques," she said.

"*Bonjour.*"

"Mind if I tag along?"

"Please."

He led her along a path on the riverbank. The air was misty from the churning river. They chatted amiably over the roar of the cascading water.

They came to a ditch with a small stream feeding into the river. Jacques scampered over the rocks to show her the way, and then watched her follow.

"You've got good balance," he said. "Alas, mine isn't what it once was."

As they walked, he told her what he knew about the church. After it was built in the late eighteen hundreds by Eduard von Tessen, it was deeded to the diocese, along with a stipend for a summer pastor, but nothing for upkeep. "It's more than you might think," he added with dismay.

They continued along the path. The sun was sinking fast. A nightingale sang joyfully.

Jacques halted suddenly, raising his hand like a soldier on patrol signaling his platoon. "Here's the place."

He set down his wicker basket on the bank and crept toward the stream. He stared into the water for several seconds.

"See that?" he asked.

"No."

"There!" He pointed and clucked with excitement. "A four-pounder."

He took a fly from his basket and tied it onto his line.

Jane started to ask a question, but he put his finger to his lips again.

"Does the name du Burgen mean anything to you?" she said softly.

"No."

"What about Firth?"

"No. Why?"

"Nothing."

He finished his knot and got to his feet.

He waded a few feet into the stream and then cast his fly expertly to the center. She watched with interest. She had never actually witnessed a person fly-fishing.

His concentration was fierce. Cast and wait. Reel and repeat. After several casts without a bite, he waded back to shore and opened his basket. He began rummaging. It was filled with flies, reels, spare lines, pliers, and many other things whose purpose she couldn't guess at.

"A lot of equipment to catch a fish," she observed.

"You have no idea," he said. He found a different fly and began to tie it onto his line.

"You said you're only here in the summer?" she asked.

"That's right. I'm in residence from May to October. You wouldn't want to be caught up here once the snow starts. They say you can walk from rooftop to rooftop on the drifts. Max has a giant snowcat he uses to keep the roads open. Without that, I'm not sure anyone would be reckless enough to live here year-round."

The chaplain looked up from his lure. "To tell you the truth I don't know how long there will even be a Burgen. Take a look around. This place is one defeat from death. I have my stipend, but what's the sense of preaching to an empty church? This hotel you're staying in, this *auberge diffuso*... it's Klaus's last desperate gamble to save the place. Everyone says he's nuts."

"They can work. I've seen stories online."

"I hope you're right. I'd hate to lose this gig."

Jacques got up and waded back into the river. He cast his new fly, it landed, and instantly the water exploded.

He fought the fish for a full minute before he brought it, exhausted, beside his boots. He scooped it up and carried it to the bank, where he set about removing the hook. Jane stood over him, watching the fish's gills flap vainly in the air.

He removed the hook and then returned to the stream. He lowered the fish into the water with both hands. The fish was either too exhausted or incredulous that it was being set free, for it just floated in his hands, waving its tail ever so slightly in the current. Jacques stirred water onto its gills, which he explained would revive it.

"Watch."

Suddenly, with a flip of the tail, the fish was gone.

Jacques wiped his hands on his pants and they both sat in silence for a while, listening to the churning river and trying to see their fish moving in the depths. It occurred to Jane that the chaplain was saying a prayer. He turned to her and flashed a grin.

"Did you just say a prayer for the fish?" Jane asked.

"Well, not exactly," he laughed. "I thanked God for his magnificent creation. The fish is part of that creation, right? As is this glorious afternoon, and it is glorious, is it not?"

Jane looked around with satisfaction. He was right. The day was glorious.

In the boughs that overhung the river, two birds began singing in notes so pure it was like musical harmony.

"What is that?" Jane asked.

"Citril finches," he said. "They come here every summer to nest and mate."

"It's like music."

He nodded. "Around here, they have a name for their song. They call it 'La chanson de Sophie.'"

Sophie's Song.

An hour later, Jane stood on the front stoop of Chalet von Tessen. She had driven up in her SUV even as thunder rumbled, and the air didn't so much rain as weep moisture.

The chalet's door had a brass knocker shaped like a wolf. Jane pulled it back and rapped it three times. The sun slipped behind the stone giants and the temperature dropped instantly.

Agatha answered and then closed the door to get Ursula. It began to rain, so that by the time Ursula pulled open the door, Jane was soaked.

"What do you want?" Ursula snapped.

Jane had to raise her voice to speak over the rain.

"The archivist from Leipzig, the one who wants to archive the records in your basement—is his name Dr. Reinhold Schmidt?"

Ursula frowned. "Maybe."

"If it is, he'll never give up. I did a course in college on the care of sensitive documents. We used his textbook. His stubbornness is world-renowned."

"I fail to see what this has to do—"

"Let me archive the records in your basement," said Jane.

"What?"

"I'm asking you to hire me."

Ursula scoffed. "Why would I hire a liar?"

"Because I have a degree in Library Science, and I can convince Dr. Schmidt to let me. Because, unlike one of his interns, I will be discreet. And because we both want the same thing."

"What's that?"

"To find out who Sophie is."

Lightning flashed, and a thunderclap followed immediately. Ursula jumped, but Jane barely noticed.

"Oh for heaven's sake, come out of the weather," said Ursula.

Jane stepped onto the marble floor and stood dripping in front of Ursula von Tessen.

"Today in the portrait room, we both saw the same thing," said Jane. "Your granddaughter Hannah is the spitting image of the woman I know as Sophie du Burgen. du Burgen, like the village. There's a book in your library with the name Sophie written in it; Klaus knew all about it.

"Max told me the legend behind the von Tessen crest. It was Eduard von Tessen's sister who saw the injured swift and dragged him out of harm's way. *Sister.* The timeline suggests this sister should be in those family portraits. Why isn't she? She's the skeleton in your closet, isn't she?"

Ursula glared at her.

"In Burgen, do you know what they call the songs of citril finches?" Jane asked.

"Sophie's Song."

Jane nodded. "Sophie is in this valley, Madame von Tessen. She's in the library, she's in your family crest, she's in the birdsong, and I believe she's in those records in your basement. Can you afford to have just *anyone* digging around? Eduard has a legacy to maintain. Your family's reputation, your bank's prestige, it's all built on that. You can't have them pulling down his statue in von Tessen Square like it's Russia. Or Virginia. No, it has to be me. Hire me."

"No, Mademoiselle. I cannot. This is a bad time. My husband is very sick—"

Klaus's voice came from the top of the stairs.

"It's why the swift chose her."

Ursula glared at Jane and then raced to help her husband down the stairs. Klaus was out of breath when he reached Jane.

"Good lord! This poor girl is soaked clean through. Let's get her into some dry clothes."

"Mademoiselle was just leaving," said Ursula.

"No, she isn't," said Klaus. "Not yet."

He stood a moment gathering his breath and regarding Jane with curiosity.

"You wanted to know why that book was in the library?" he said.

"Klaus—" said Ursula.

"I'll tell you why," he went on. "It's because I don't burn books!"

"Monsieur?" said Jane.

He stroked his beard. "Yes, I know Sophie well. For three decades, Sophie lived in the servants' quarters at Chalet von Tessen. She appeared not long after Old Rudy passed—in the late eighteen hundreds or thereabouts. Officially, she was *la gardienne du maison*, but in truth, she was more like a permanent guest.

"There is no 'family mystery'—as my grandson said—about why Eduard built the church and the school and the English Garden with the private chapel on the main property. It was for her. Sophie was Eduard's mistress. That's right, Eduard had a mistress! Or at least, that's what I believed until today when you showed up with that picture of her. Now I don't know what to think. Why does my granddaughter look so much like her?"

A thought burst into Jane's head. "But how do you know what *your* Sophie looked like? Are there other pictures?"

"You get right to it, don't you? Good. I like that. No, Jane. There are no more pictures. There were. Once, the chalet was filled with them. But that was before I burned them."

The year was 1953. World War II was over, the Cold War was in full swing, Germany was divided, and Geneva's beloved banker, Eduard von Tessen, was dead.

His grandfather's passing wore heavily on ten-year-old Klaus, more than any of those other events. But that was about to change. A month after his grandfather's funeral, he awoke in bed in Geneva to find his father standing over him.

"Wake up, Klaus," Henri said.

"What is it?" he asked groggily.

"I need your help with something. Quick-quick."

From the start, Klaus knew something was off. His father always called him by his full name, "Nicholas," never Klaus, which was what his grandfather had called him. Henri was a small-minded man, obsessed with work, who barely acknowledged his children. A task like waking his son would ordinarily have been delegated to his mother. To see his father leaning over his bed was alarming indeed. Klaus got dressed quickly and went downstairs.

"We're going to the chalet," Henri said. "There are a few things I need to take care of now that your grandfather is gone." And then he added mysteriously, "I think it will be good for you."

Klaus was happy to be going to the chalet. It was his summer playground, a happy place where his parents, for a few months, left behind the stodgy world of banking for the open-air freedom of the outdoors. Klaus had a horse in the stables there. His name was Charlie after his favorite actor, Charlie Chaplin.

They got into his Mercedes-Benz and set off. Henri had bought the car the previous year as a petty revenge on his father who was boycotting Mercedes because of their ties to the Nazis. Henri von Tessen was prone to pettiness. He had grown up in the shadow of a man beloved for his stance against Nazism—St. Eduard, they called him. From the safety of Swiss neutrality, Eduard had rebuilt the bank as a haven for Jewish wealth. Business flourished, but he could take no pride in the success—the reason for it was too monstrous. Eduard's funeral had drawn hundreds of admirers from as far away as New York and Tel Aviv.

Henri followed his father into the family business, but they fought constantly about the direction of the bank—not in front of Klaus, of course. But over the years, he overheard enough to know that Henri did not approve of Eduard's business decisions.

"Are we running a bank or a charity?" he heard his father fume.

Three hours after setting out from Geneva, Henri brought the car to a stop in front of the chalet. It was a strange moment for Klaus. Their arrival was not as joyous as he had expected. It was the first time he had come here since Eduard's death. To think that Opa wasn't there to greet them filled him with sadness. The chalet, once his happy place, had become a somber monument to what he had lost.

"Why are we here, Papa?"

"I think it's important you know the truth about your opa. You need to know who he *really* was."

In the den of the chalet, Jane watched Max rise to poke a log on the fire. Max had put Sydney to bed and joined them. Klaus wanted everyone to hear what he had to say. Jane wore a dry robe and sat with her legs curled beneath her body. Somewhere, Agatha was drying her wet clothes. Ursula sat beside her husband, studying his face.

Jane sipped her tea and listened, hypnotized, to Klaus's story.

"Reverend Barbeau met us on the lawn—not Jacques, whom you know, but his father, Rolf. My father led us to a portrait in the parlor. It was the woman from your grandmother's painting. Sophie. I knew her well; she was in portraits throughout the house. Over the years, I asked who she was. 'A distant relative,' was all I was ever told.

"And that's when my father told us both about Sophie. She was Eduard's mistress! He had kept her for decades in his love nest outside Burgen! I was flabbergasted. He made me promise to never tell my oma. 'It would break her heart,' he said.

"He instructed us to scour the house for every portrait of her, as well as anything else that looked like it could be traced back to her. We were to remove all evidence of her. I think he would have burned down the chapel and torn up the English Garden if Reverend Barbeau hadn't been there."

Jane stared at Klaus in wonder. He had seemed to Jane to be indefatigable, but now he looked distraught.

Ursula patted his hand.

Klaus smiled at her and went on. "I felt a little bad, even at the time. The paintings were beautiful, and so was the woman. I had seen her my entire life, so she was linked to my happiest childhood memories. But that day I was driven by outrage at the idea that Eduard had kept these paintings on display, even as his wife unwittingly lived beneath them. It was horrifying! I threw myself headlong into the mission of purging Sophie once and for all from the chalet.

"We were like the Gestapo. We went room by room through the entire chalet—it took hours—until we had everything connected to her piled up on the front lawn. Besides dozens of paintings, there were blankets she may have knitted, even an embroidered footstool she may or may not have embroidered—who really knew? I was aware of the Mark Twain book in the library with her name in it. My father didn't know about the book, of course; he wasn't one for novels. I wanted to read the book someday, and besides, burning books just felt wrong to me. So I didn't add *Life on the Mississippi* to the pile.

"And what a pile it was! Ten feet high, at least. We stood marveling at it. Then Reverend Barbeau went off to the maintenance shed to find matches and a gas can."

"Oh, my god," said Jane.

Klaus nodded in shame. "It was terrible. And I would be punished for it, too. As we drove away, I realized I hadn't visited my horse. I hadn't seen Charlie." The old man shook his head at the memory. "He was such a goofball, that horse. He loved to roll in the dirt like a dog. I'd wash him, getting him looking so handsome—'handsome boy,' I would say. Then I'd let him loose, and the first thing he'd do was roll and roll until he was coated with this layer of dirt and mud. It was ridiculous! But he looked so happy afterward, I couldn't be mad at him for it."

He paused a moment to compose himself.

"I never saw Charlie again. It was three years before I returned to the chalet. Henri hated the place. By then, Charlie was gone. I don't know what happened to him, even to this day. It was my punishment, you see, for what I did that day with my father. Forgetting to see Charlie, missing my chance to say goodbye, to rub that big, beautiful nose one last time..."

Klaus's voice cracked. A tear slid down his weathered cheek and disappeared into his beard.

No one spoke. A log on the fire shifted. Somewhere, a grandfather clock counted out the seconds, *tick-tick-tick*.

Klaus went on. "As the years passed, I realized that my father's true mission that day had been to forever alter my opinion of Eduard von Tessen. It worked. After that, and *because* of that, I thought I understood my father a little better. He had spent his life being compared to a great man. People looked right past him to Eduard. Poor Papa couldn't tell anyone about Sophie without hurting his family and his business. Eduard had made my father an accomplice in his lie. Papa kept his father's secret. I admired him for that. Until today. Until you showed up with that picture, and I saw what everyone else saw—Sophie was the spitting image of my granddaughter. There could be only one explanation: Sophie was not a mistress. She was a von Tessen! Everything I thought I knew about that woman, about my father, about my grandfather having a mistress—it all got turned upside down."

"What happened to Sophie?" Jane asked.

"I don't know. She was long gone by that day, that's all I can say."

"And the artist? Who painted all those portraits of her?"

"They were signed 'Francis,' that's all I know."

"Francis Firth?" said Jane.

"No. Just 'Francis.'"

"You're sure?"

Klaus nodded. "Why?"

"Nothing. Sorry. Go on."

He sighed. "What my grandson told you is true. I'm unwell. Dying."

Ursula let out an involuntary whimper, and now Klaus took his turn to comfort her.

"Jane, before I die, I should very much like to know the truth about Sophie. It would give me peace. Do you think you can do it?"

Jane looked at Max for guidance, but he appeared to be in shock over his opa's revelations. She turned to Klaus and Ursula.

"I'm a librarian," said Jane. "Finding out things—that's my superpower. But..."

"But what?"

"I can't guarantee you'll like what I find."

Eight

Vincent

Vincent arrived home to find a man in a top hat outside his door, smoking a pipe. Vincent paused when he saw him. He was in no mood for talk. Vincent was tired and deeply embarrassed about Sophie's discovery of the sketches he had made of her. He had already ripped them up and thrown them in the Rhône.

But it was too late to avoid the man. Vincent went to the door.

"Monsieur Van Gogh?"

"Yes?"

He took in the sight of the equipment Vincent was carrying. "You're a painter?"

"I am."

"Marvelous! They didn't tell me."

"They?"

"Sorry. My name is Dr. Theophile Peyron. I am a physician at St. Paul de Mausole."

He offered his hand, and they shook.

"The asylum?" asked Vincent.

"That's right. Constable Rivoli gave me your name and your very nice postman told me where I could find you. I hope that's okay. You collected the reward for Sophie Alt's capture, I believe."

Vincent nodded.

"I wonder, can I trouble you for a few minutes of your time? I have a couple of questions."

"Just let me unload my supplies."

Vincent opened the door and invited Peyron inside. Crates and garbage mingled with dishes, canvases, and painting supplies scattered from wall to wall.

Peyron looked around. "Are you moving, Monsieur Van Gogh?"

"I'm sort of in the middle of a renovation."

He put down his equipment. Against the wall, he stood the portrait of Annette holding the orange.

"You did that?" asked Peyron.

"This morning."

Peyron nodded. "Hm."

"Do you know anything about art, Doctor?"

"No. But I have found it therapeutic for some of our patients. We have a beautiful garden. They paint there whenever the weather is good."

Vincent nodded. It sounded nice. "I can't *not* paint. It keeps me sane." Suddenly he realized who he was talking to and added hastily, "I'm speaking as a non-professional, of course. It was just a figure of speech—"

"It's fine, Monsieur Van Gogh. I understood that, yes."

Vincent pointed at a crate. "I don't have any furniture yet, but you can sit there."

Peyron sat and looked around. "It's a lot of space. You're doing a renovation, you say?"

"Yes. It will be an artists' commune eventually. If I ever get it done."

Vincent sat down facing the doctor and lit his pipe. He inhaled deeply. He shut his eyes and drifted away on the rush of tobacco smoke in his lungs. After a minute, Peyron spoke.

"I like a pipe, too, though I am finding it strangely addictive. I can't seem to stop."

"What can I do for you, Doctor?"

"Right. You probably heard that Sophie Alt escaped from her jail cell the same night she was arrested."

Vincent nodded. Though he had never heard Sophie call herself by the name "Alt"—but that was what was in the papers and posters. Sophie used "du Burgen." He sensed it was an alias, something she had made up after her escape.

"It's all over town," he said. "Big news."

"It's imperative that I find her."

"And you think I can help?"

"Heavens no! We'll leave the manhunt to Constable Rivoli. He seems competent enough—aside from his porous jail, that is."

"Then I'm confused."

"I'm trying to get a sense of Sophie's mental state. How was she when you saw her?"

"How *was* she?"

"Did she seem agitated? Depressed? Irrational?"

Vincent took another puff of his pipe. "Just normal, I guess. We only spoke for a few minutes."

"About what?"

"Art. I was painting, and she wanted to watch."

"With the *gendarmes* chasing her?"

Vincent shrugged.

Dr. Peyron nodded solemnly. "That sounds like Sophie."

"Is she dangerous?"

"Only to herself. In the nine years she has been with us at St. Paul, she has attempted suicide four times."

Vincent lowered his pipe. "What's wrong with her?"

"The diagnosis is *melancholia*, but that only covers part of it. Sophie goes through significant mood swings. When she's up, like now, she believes she can do anything."

"Like what?"

Peyron shrugged. "Like once we found her on the high roof of the monastery walking the peak like a circus act. She was going to jump to the next building. One of the orderlies had to go out on the roof to stop her, or I think she would have tried to fly. Another time, we found her planning to escape to Paris to join the Moulin Rouge as a dancer."

"Wow."

"Lately, she has been saying she wants to move to Missouri."

"Missouri!"

The doctor waved his hand dismissively. "It's something she read. It doesn't matter." Peyron sighed and shook his head.

To Vincent, the doctor's concern appeared genuine. "She was normal when I saw her," he said.

"I know. That's the tragedy of it, Monsieur Van Gogh. Sophie is such a dear person. She's on a high now. But when she crashes…"

He shook his head.

"What?"

"We must find her before that happens."

Nine

Sophie

From the moment Sophie heard about "the living paintings show," she knew she had to be a part of it. Madame Giroux's signature event saw the brothel's salon converted into a makeshift theater, where the girls acted out scenes from famous paintings. Men in suits bought tickets and sat in chairs in the dark. Everyone pitched in with props and costumes. What fun!

As the big day approached, the brothel was buzzing with excitement. Sophie was swept into it. She had often imagined being an actress on stage. Here was her chance!

Madame Giroux was against it, of course. She was against anything that meant Sophie would leave her room.

"Parading about on a stage in plain sight... it's out of the question," she huffed. "I mean, really!"

The next day, Sophie complained about it to Vincent. He was painting outdoors on the banks of a stream where peasants fished and loaded water into buckets. He was using a device he had built called a "perspective frame" that helped him capture the busy scene. Sophie was fascinated and tried to ask him about it, but he snapped at her. He apologized immediately, but she could see that his concentration was especially fierce. She grimaced. The incident with the sketches hung over them like a dark cloud. After that day, a chagrined Vincent had become more reserved than before. She missed the old Vincent with his feverish enthusiasms. He had not even brought up the subject of the nude portrait he had promised, yet surely he had not forgotten.

She waited for a break to tell him about the living paintings show. To her surprise, when she told him about it, he was fascinated. She supposed he had heard about it from his friends at the tavern, and now Sophie was able to give him all the backstage gossip that the men wouldn't otherwise know. He smoked and listened intently.

After lunch, Vincent went back to his painting. She lay on her back and practiced identifying birdsong.

"Has Madame picked the paintings yet?" Vincent asked suddenly.

The question surprised her. When Vincent was painting, his focus was absolute.

"I don't know," Sophie replied. "She has an art book."

"A book," he said thoughtfully, then went back to his painting.

That evening, as Sophie lay in her room listening to the laughter downstairs, Marie burst in. Her face was still flushed from wine and flirting with customers.

"Madame wants you. She's in the kitchen."

"Now?"

Marie snorted as though the question were nonsensical. "She said to get dressed and use the back stairs. There are men here."

Now what?

Sophie put on her only dress and crept barefoot down the back stairway. She came into the kitchen to find Madame Giroux seated at Rosetta's prep table. To her shock, Vincent was beside her. They were looking at a book.

"Marie said you wanted to see me," said Sophie.

"Monsieur Van Gogh may be a scoundrel, but his knowledge of erotic art is quite impressive," said Madame Giroux.

Sophie's eye went to Vincent. He winked at her.

"We have just been going over the selection for the living paintings show, and, well, I think we have a part for you after all."

Sophie was cast as the sultan in *Picking the Favorite* by Giulio Rosati. She would wear a Turkish robe, a white turban, and a fake beard. No one would recognize her.

Sophie should have guessed that Vincent would be familiar with such a painting, given his interest in lurid subjects. It showed a Turkish sultan at the moment he enters his harem to choose his woman for the night. The concubines lounged in a large, carpeted room in various stages of undress. One woman bathed nude from a brass bowl. Others were eating. Some women were vying for the sultan's eye, while others hid. All the women were beautiful.

"So we stage these paintings?" Sophie asked Willetta the next day. For all Sophie's enthusiasm about the show, she hadn't bothered to learn the extent of what was expected of the performers.

Willetta nodded. "Every Saturday night during tourist season. It's Madame's trademark."

On the night of the performance, Sophie was in the kitchen with the other girls. They were performing five paintings in total. Sophie's painting would be the finale. The girls came and went from the kitchen to make costume changes. Madame directed the scene changes, then took a position at the back of the theater to narrate the story of each painting. The pace of activity was dizzying. Sophie felt as though she were backstage at the Moulin Rouge.

Sophie could hear the applause of the men after each painting. She was sick with nerves. The house was packed.

Willetta fitted her beard, then took out a charcoal stick, mixed it with cream, and began to paint her face to give her skin a dark tone. When she finished, Sophie looked at her reflection. A Turkish man stared back at her.

"Let's see you, girl," said Madame.

Sophie turned and the girls broke out laughing.

"Oh, pick me, pick me, Sultan!" begged Marie, hands clasped.

Pauline traced her finger down Sophie's chest. "Sultan is sooo handsome. He will not be sorry if he picks me. The things I will do—"

"That's enough!" Madame snapped.

"Who's getting picked, Madame?" Marie asked. "You never said."

"Annette will be 'The Favorite.'"

The others groaned.

Annette was the newest addition to the brothel, a native Algerian who looked more like the Turkish women in Rosati's fanciful painting than the other French girls.

"Oh, shut up," said Madame. "Annette will be the shy girl from the picture. The sultan will pick her as the favorite. It will play well."

"Wait," said Sophie in horror as the implication of the conversation hit her. "So we don't just *pose*?"

"Of course not," Marie scoffed. "What's the fun in that?"

"We play the scene," said Pauline.

"I can't do that!" said Sophie.

"Don't be ridiculous," said Madame. She turned to Willetta. "It's time to take the art book to the men. Let them pass it around and get a good look at it. We want them drooling over what's to come."

"Drooling," said Marie with a giggle.

A knot twisted in Sophie's stomach.

"The sultan's the best part," Marie told Sophie, sensing her nervousness. "It'll be fun. Inspect the girls one by one. You'll be great!"

"And don't rush it," said Madame.

"Poor Sultan can't make up his mind," cooed Marie.

Regina, who was nude, cupped her breasts. "So many pretty girls to choose from."

"Hush!" said Madame.

She turned to Sophie. "You must behave as though the girls are your property. Be sure to touch each of them as you ponder your choice."

"What?"

"Just light caresses," said Madame. "As though you're touching a bolt of fabric at the shop. Really, what's the big deal? You *wanted* this."

Sophie nodded.

"Go to Annette last, then take her hand and lead her back through the audience. The men will love it."

Sophie gulped.

"This is how we earn our living," said Madame. "You understand that?"

"It gets the men so worked up," Pauline explained. "They completely forget about the cost! They forget they have wives who are going to kill them when they figure out the money is gone. Ha! After the show, the men will only care about one thing: To be sultans, too, and pick *their* favorite."

"They won't want to sleep with me?" Sophie asked.

"With the sultan?" Madame exclaimed. "What kind of a place do you think this is?"

"Well, there was the one time—" Pauline teased.

"Enough!" barked Madame. "It's time to take your marks. Now go!"

Sophie didn't move.

"What's wrong with you?" Madame asked.

"Is Vincent here?" Sophie asked.

"Of course not."

"I need him to be here."

"Why?"

"I... I can't do this without him. Please."

Madame clenched her jaw, but she saw something in Sophie's eyes that made her give in. "Fine. I'll send Willetta to the tavern. I'm sure that's where he'll be. Now go to your mark!"

Sophie couldn't help but be impressed at how Madame Giroux had transformed the brothel's salon into a theater. In place of the hearth was a stage. A dressing curtain served as a stage curtain. About twenty men sat shoulder to shoulder on chairs and sofas that had been moved from throughout the brothel. The men were dressed in suits and top hats as though they were at the opera. Several soldiers wore their uniforms. They sipped brandy and waited for the show to begin. Sophie had never seen so many men at Madame Giroux's. It was a sellout.

The girls went behind the curtain to take their positions. Madame led Sophie through the audience to a position at the rear of the room. She spotted Vincent in a chair at the back. Their eyes met, and he nodded with encouragement.

She felt a little better. If Vincent thought she could do it, then maybe she could.

Willetta extinguished two of the oil lamps. The room dimmed and the men fell quiet. Madame stood before the closed curtain and spoke grandly.

"Welcome to the finale of the living paintings show!"

Polite applause followed.

"This evening we present a new painting to the show: *Picking the Favorite* by Giulio Rosati. You have all seen the picture, no?"

Sophie watched the men's heads nod.

Madame cleared her throat and lowered her voice to affect the tone of a narrator of a play.

"Sultan will not sleep alone," she boomed. "He has his own harem, after all. If you had a harem, would you sleep alone?"

"Never!" shouted one of the soldiers, and everyone laughed.

"Of course not," said Madame, who was laying it on thick. "But with so many concubines to choose from, who will he pick? Who will be..." She paused for dramatic effect. "... the favorite?"

Madame nodded at Willetta, who pulled back the curtain. The men's eyes went wide at the scene. The painting had come to life! Even the props were correct. There was a wash basin, a potted palm tree, a gold tray covered with teacups, and four beautiful girls posed as they were in the painting.

The men turned to Sophie. She felt herself blush.

"Go!" Madame hissed, nudging her forward.

Sophie moved woodenly toward the stage, weaving past the men. She forgot to look down, and her foot caught the leg of a stool. She stumbled. Someone laughed.

She reached the stage, where Regina was standing nude at the front. She was playing the eager concubine, squirming provocatively as the sultan approached.

Sophie glanced back across the salon at Madame. She motioned for her to go on. Sophie's gaze fell on the men. Their eyes glowed. The scene was pure male fantasy—Madame Giroux certainly knew her business.

Sophie surveyed Regina's body by looking up, then down, then back up again. Sophie brushed back her hair and then lifted Regina's face by her chin. Madame went on.

"Sweet Regina. So eager to please. And so capable of doing so! How could Sultan not choose her for his bed? But wait..."

Sophie understood that this was her cue to move to the next girl. Pauline was topless and bathing with a sponge she dipped into a basin at her feet. She drew the laden sponge to her neck and squeezed it. Water slipped over her curves and dropped into a puddle at her feet.

"Smell me," Pauline whispered.

Sophie pretended to sniff her.

Madame continued. "Look! Sultan is drawn to the charms of Pauline. Of course he is! Pauline takes such good care of herself, does she not? She does it for Sultan. Surely his appreciation will include an invitation to his bed. But wait..."

Next up was Marie, who sat at Pauline's feet, helping her to bathe. Sophie knelt beside her.

Madame went on. "It appears Sultan is distracted by the youthful beauty of his beloved Marie. Look at those ripe breasts!"

"Touch me," whispered Marie.

"What?"

"Please."

Sophie traced the shape of Marie's breast beneath her corset. Sophie was aware that Vincent was watching, and her face flushed with embarrassment.

Madame went on. "Oh, yes, see how he wants her? But wait... who is that trying to hide behind Marie?"

Sophie stood and walked to where Annette sat. The black girl was fully dressed, a shimmering veil concealing her face.

"It is Annette, Sultan's newest concubine," said Madame. "A princess from his Algerian conquest. Poor Annette is shy. But she cannot hide from Sultan."

Sophie thought about her next move—to take Annette's hand and lead her to the kitchen. Suddenly, an idea flew into her head. Sophie put her lips to Annette's ear.

"Slap me," Sophie whispered.

Annette looked at her in shock.

"Slap me, then run."

A faint smile formed on Annette's lips, followed by a hard slap to Sophie's cheek. Her beard dislodged, and Sophie quickly pushed it back in place. Annette rose and fled through the audience to the kitchen.

No one moved. The room was silent. Then someone whistled, and everyone burst into laughter. More whistles. Wild applause.

Sophie fled the stage after Annette. She passed a dumbstruck Madame Giroux and then joined Annette in the kitchen. They hugged and jumped up and down in excitement.

Back in the theater, the men were stomping and yelling, "*Encore! Encore!*"

Willetta was wide-eyed. "They're going crazy," she said.

Madame's head appeared in the doorway. "Get back out there, girls! Take your bows!"

Sophie and Annette walked triumphantly back through the audience to join hands with the rest of the cast. They bowed dramatically, while the men applauded.

A half-hour later, as Sophie lay in bed, she could still hear the applause in her head. Madame Giroux was no doubt taking credit for a record night. Downstairs, the familiar pattern of the brothel was already in full swing. The living paintings show, after all, was merely a prelude to the main business. Money changed hands. Men and women escaped to private rooms. Madame Giroux filled her cash box.

Sophie stared up into the darkness and giggled. Life outside walls was thrilling beyond her wildest dreams! How much she had missed! So many lost years! But she would not dwell on that. She was happy now. Her whole life lay before her, and she would make the most of every second. Anything was possible! She imagined herself as an actress on stage in New York. Sold-out theaters. Rave reviews. Standing ovations. Americans had a new theater district called Broadway. She could visit there when she got to New York in a month.

A month.

A shadow fell over Sophie's sparkle. It was as though a bird had momentarily passed in front of the sun.

The flicker was quickly forgotten, and Sophie resumed her fantasy of acting on the Broadway stage. But somehow, the applause was not as loud. Some of the seats were empty.

Ten

Vincent

In the week that followed the living paintings show, Vincent Van Gogh failed to notice the small changes in Sophie. One day, she overslept. Another time, she broke into tears because she had accidentally squished a ladybug. She no longer closed her eyes when she tasted her food. She had become argumentative.

Vincent only recognized these signs in hindsight. At the time, it seemed to him that the pattern of their days had picked up where it left off. Vincent painted and Sophie kept him company. Provence was drenched in a blazing light that ignited the colors of the countryside as if everything was lit from within. Vincent was frantic to capture it. Sophie brought lunch that Rosetta made secretly for them. Sophie would insist that Vincent eat, no matter how fervently he protested. While he rested, they lay in each other's arms watching clouds. He listened as she named the birds that were migrating through Provence. She listened to his stories about working as an art dealer in London, as a missionary in Belgium, and as a painter in Paris. It was bliss.

On the fourth day, she arrived with a bar of soap and a towel. But it wasn't for her.

"I thought you would want to bathe," she said, motioning toward the stream.

He was painting. "No, thank you."

"It will feel good."

He drew a line of paint on the canvas. "Not now."

"You reek, Vincent!" she cried out in frustration.

He turned from his painting. "Huh?"

"You stink! I can't stand it! I absolutely will not kiss you again until you have bathed!"

Without a word, Vincent put down his brushes, stripped, and dove into the river. She passed him the soap, and he scrubbed himself from head to toe. When he finished, he walked to where she sat on the bank.

"That was fantastic!" he said, grinning.

She held up a razor. "Now the beard."

She held a small mirror while he shaved. When he was done, she rubbed his face with her hand. She smiled.

"Much better."

She kissed him and, with their lips pressed, pulled him to the ground beside her. They kissed for a long time and, afterward, lay in each other's arms listening to the birds.

"Did you know St. Francis once preached to birds?" asked Sophie. "He's my favorite saint. Do you know about him?"

"Of course I do. Catholic nonsense."

Sophie sat up. "Don't do that."

"Do what?"

"Belittle things."

"I'm not."

"You are. You shouldn't make fun of things you don't understand."

"You honestly believe Francis of Assisi could talk to birds?"

"I don't know. And neither do you. Maybe he tried. I can love him for trying, can't I? And what difference does it make? It's a lovely thought. Honestly, Vincent, sometimes you make me so angry!"

"Come here, " he said, reaching up to pull her to him.

She pushed him away. "No! I'm really mad at you right now!"

Vincent sighed and became aware of the canvas on his easel. But for once, he didn't feel like painting. He decided to change the subject.

"I spoke with Madame Giroux yesterday," said Vincent. "Still nothing from the jeweler. She better not be screwing us."

"You shouldn't be so hard on Madame," said Sophie.

"Why not?"

"It's not nice."

"She's a nightmare. She'd sell her own child for an edge—"

"STOP!"

Sophie's cry carried as far as the little bridge where peasants were drawing water from the stream. Their heads turned toward them for a moment. A dog barked.

Vincent was baffled by her reaction. He waited for her to continue.

"Madame carries a tremendous burden, Vincent. You have no idea. So many people depend on her. I wonder how she does it."

"Madame can take care of herself," snorted Vincent.

Tears filled Sophie's eyes. "I love them all so much, Vincent. Annette is so sweet. She's smart, too. She could do anything! And Pauline—she pretends to be tough, but it's just an act. I caught her feeding a litter of kittens in the barn. She denied it, of course. And Regina... oh, she is so pretty. She lets me brush her hair and tells me about all the men who are in love with her. Such stories! If I were a man, I'd be in love with her, too! And Marie..."

Sophie's lip quivered.

"When I left the room this morning, she was still sleeping. I kissed her forehead. She smiled like a little girl. Oh, Vincent, I can't bear to see her lose that innocence. Why is the world so hard?"

"I don't know."

"What does God say about it?"

"God?" he exclaimed.

Suddenly Vincent was nine years old, sitting in his father's church. Theo was on their mother's lap. Old Dorus was at the pulpit, thundering on from James—sin and corruption.

"God says the world is broken," said Vincent.

"Yes, that's it! It's broken! So broken! Marie says she's nineteen years old, but I don't believe it. I think she might be fifteen."

Vincent nodded solemnly. "I think so, too."

"And men *buy* her." Sophie's eyes grew wide. "*You* buy her!"

Vincent recoiled. "Me?"

"You're a *man*!"

"I've never been with Marie!"

"But you've been with others! The only reason you haven't been with Marie is you can't afford her!"

Vincent hesitated. For nearly a year, he had lived with a prostitute named Syren and her baby. He hadn't loved her, but he cared about her. He saw how prostitution corrupted her. When she went back to that life, Vincent was heartbroken.

"Sophie—"

"Don't deny it!"

"Sophie, I'm with you now."

"You are?"

"Of course. Look how we take care of each other."

She sniffled. "We do, don't we?"

"You make sure I eat, bathe, shave. You even washed my trousers the other day."

"I couldn't get the paint out."

"You give me your honest opinion about my art."

"I love your art," she said fiercely. "You are a great painter, Vincent. You will be famous someday. Your work will hang in museums."

He loved her conviction, but she knew nothing about what it took for a painting to be on permanent display in a museum. He would have been happy with a few sales to pay back a fraction of what he owed Theo. Their partnership had turned into outright charity. It was embarrassing. Who cared about museums?

"You are my angel, Sophie." He kissed her. "I will..."

He stopped himself.

"Will... what?"

"Nothing."

"Say it."

Vincent had almost said, "I will be lost when you go." He stopped himself. Sophie needed to leave Arles. She couldn't stay. But when he thought of his life going back to the way it was before Sophie—the oppressive, inescapable loneliness—a sadness broke over him like an ocean wave. The only consolation was that, back in Paris, Theo was talking to Paul Gauguin about joining Vincent in Arles. It was such a brilliant idea! Vincent had written a long letter to Paul about the scenery. Such light! Vincent was certain they would get along fabulously.

"Vincent?" Sophie asked, looking worried.

Her expression brought a lump to his throat.

"I'm sorry for what I said about St. Francis," said Vincent. "I don't believe in saints, it's true, but if I had to have a favorite saint, it would be Francis, of course. The patron saint of all the creatures."

"Right!" Sophie exclaimed, falling into Vincent's arms.

A sudden gust of wind sent Vincent's canvas flying from the easel. It rolled end-over-end, pinwheeling for the stream. He jumped up to chase after it. When he returned, Sophie had dried her tears and was grinning at him. Her mood swings were truly unnerving.

"What?"

"It's a west wind," she cooed.

He turned his face into the gathering breeze. She was right. The wind had shifted.

"Rain tomorrow," she said. Her almond-shaped eyes glistened flirtatiously. "Good day for a portrait."

Vincent gulped. She was alluding to the nude portrait he had promised to do of her.

"Remember, you can't use our real names," she said. "You promised. No one must ever know about us."

Sophie had never revealed the reason for the secrecy surrounding her identity, but he didn't care. She was here. What else mattered? Sometimes Vincent *did* believe an angel must have sent her...

Or a saint.

He winked at her. "I'll sign it after my new, favorite saint."

She aimed a teasing look at him. It hit him like a horse's kick. *Dear God*, he prayed, *grant me the skill to capture her as she is now!*

Sophie stretched out her leg and threw back her head in a dramatic pose. "I'm all yours, *Francis*."

Eleven

Constable Rivoli

"The woman has disappeared."

Constable Rivoli sat behind his desk in his office on Place de Libertine in Arles and glared at the young deputy. Until that moment, he had been able to hide his frustration. But the word "disappeared" changed that. It hovered in the air over Deputy Corbin like a cloud of shit.

The case of Sophie Alt was certainly a puzzle. The woman's escape from the locked cell, followed by her ability to elude capture, was unprecedented in the constable's twenty-two years as Chief of Police. It was a blight on his reputation and an affront to his pride. The previous day, a cartoon had appeared in *L'Arlésien* lampooning him personally. It showed a rotund Rivoli handing a key to a female prisoner through the bars of her cell. The caption read: "Mademoiselle, do you mind holding these while I take a nap?"

After three weeks of door-to-door searches, thousands of flyers distributed, a dozen volunteers deputized, and a respectable reward offered, how was it possible that his deputy's conclusion was that she'd disappeared?

Rivoli tapped his fingertips together and repeated the offending phrase. "Disappeared."

Corbin nodded solemnly. Beside him, the constable's other deputy smiled faintly. Deputy Moreau was far too wily to use such a vague word in an official report to the boss.

"I'm afraid so."

"So she's magical then?" asked Rivoli.

"What?"

"She's a witch? Is that what you're telling me, Deputy? Sophie Alt is a witch?"

"No, sir."

"She has some other magical power, then? A secret potion?"

"She's not magical."

"So how did she 'disappear'? I can't do that. Can *you* do that, Corbin?"

"It's a figure of speech."

Rivoli stood suddenly, slamming his desk chair against the wall that held his service awards, hunting trophies, and a standard-issue portrait of French president Sadi Carnot. Rivoli put his hands on his desk and leaned over the men.

"You came highly recommended, Deputy. The consensus at the academy was that you were on the fast track to Police Chief. Could that be an error?"

"I don't believe so, sir."

"A figure of speech has no place in an official police report."

"I see your point, sir. My mistake."

Rivoli sat down heavily.

"She's probably in Paris by now," said Moreau. "Or London."

"Then show me how she got there," said Rivoli. "Was it by train?"

Corbin shook his head. "Seventeen females matching her description bought tickets to Paris since her escape. We've identified them all. I even checked tickets going south. Nothing. Sophie Alt did not buy a ticket at the train station in Arles. Of that I am sure."

"Could she have taken a carriage?"

"With what money?"

"Walked?"

"In inmate scrubs? It's a miracle she got as far as Arles."

"Stole a horse?"

"All horses, mules, and donkeys are accounted for."

"So she must still be here."

Moreau weighed in. "We've checked everywhere. We've shown that sketch Dr. Peyron gave us to every local and tourist in Arles. Nothing. The trail's gone cold."

This was good police work, and the constable knew it. Rivoli couldn't fault his deputies, and he was not a man who laid blame on others. He was the chief of a leaky jail. He grabbed the station logbook and got to his feet.

"Come with me."

He led the two deputies through the station to Cell B. He went inside and closed the door.

"Now, lock it."

Corbin inserted the iron key and turned the lock three times. Rivoli tugged at the bars. The door held.

"How did she do it?" he asked through the bars. "How did Sophie Alt escape from a locked cell in the middle of the night?"

Neither deputy spoke.

Rivoli opened the logbook and read.

6:15 p.m.: Inmate locked in. Cell B.

"This is your handwriting, Corbin?"

"Yes, sir."

Rivoli went on.

7:30 p.m.: Inmate served dinner.

"What did she have?" Rivoli asked.

"A little bread," said Corbin. "Some dried fish from the tavern."

"Did you unlock the door to serve it?"

Corbin shook his head. "I slid the tray under the door."

Rivoli returned to the log.

10 p.m.: Retrieved tray. Inmate requested water.

"You brought her a mug of water?"

"I did."

"Was the mug here the next morning?"

"It was."

Rivoli rubbed his chin. "But not Sophie Alt. Hm. The final entry says, '*Ten-thirty p.m.: Bed check.*' Then you went home?"

"Yes, sir."

He pointed to a note in the book. "What is this?"

Corbin flushed. "It says she was crying, sir. I believe she was crying, yes, poor thing. I made a note of it."

Moreau scoffed, but Rivoli held up his hand to silence him before he could mock the sensitive young deputy. Rivoli looked around at the stone walls and the iron bars. "How did she do it—this crying girl? How did she get out?"

"Someone let her out," said Corbin.

"Impossible," said Moreau. "You and the chief have the only keys. Even I don't have a set."

"Could she have gotten a hold of the key somehow?" asked Rivoli.

"Not mine," said Corbin. "I had it with me all night."

"As did I," said Rivoli. He sat on the edge of the cot and tapped the logbook against his knee. "What are we missing?"

They fell into thought. Outside on the street, someone shouted to a carriage driver to watch where he was going. In the distance, a train whistle blew, and a dog barked.

Corbin broke the silence. "Chief, can I see that logbook?"

Rivoli passed it to his deputy through the bars. Corbin leafed back through the pages.

"What is it?" Rivoli asked.

Corbin stopped at a page and pointed. "Here. I've been wondering about this for a while." He continued to hold his finger on the entry. "In May, we locked up a whore from Madame Giroux's."

Moreau chuckled. "Yeah, I remember. She threw horse manure on a tourist. Drunk as a sailor she was. A little powder keg, that one. Scratched my face. I gave her back as much, and more."

Corbin shot him a sharp look and then returned to the book. "It says here she was locked in Cell B at ten p.m. on May 14. Same cell."

"Sounds right," said Moreau. "We always use Cell B for females."

"She was released the next morning at eight a.m."

"So?" said Moreau.

"So May 15 is my birthday," said Corbin. "I took the day off. But I forgot to leave my keys at the station. The constable arrived at noon, as usual, I suppose."

"Sounds right."

"So, Deputy Moreau, how did you release your prisoner at eight a.m. without a key?"

Moreau stared at him.

Rivoli walked to the bars. "Deputy, how did you open the cell?"

Moreau's eyes darted around. "Pardon?"

"Corbin had one set of keys," said Rivoli. "I had the other. How did you release the prisoner without a key?"

"Well, sir, you see, she was due to be released at eight a.m.," Moreau stammered. "I... I couldn't keep her longer without an order from the judge, and you know how he hates to be disturbed before ten o'clock—"

"Deputy!" boomed Rivoli. "How did you open the cell without a key?"

Moreau gazed at his boots. "The latch bolt on the door, sir. It's too short."

"Show me," said Rivoli.

Moreau climbed onto the door's cross rail. He jumped up and down. On the third bounce, the lock popped, and the door swung open.

A stunned silence fell over the men. Rivoli's heart was racing.

"Who knows about this?" he asked.

"No one!" Moreau exclaimed. "That's why I figured it didn't matter."

"Not 'no one,'" said Rivoli. "There's one person who knows."

He turned to Corbin, who read from the logbook.

Marie Elaine Anastasia La Tarte, age 19, formerly of Marseille, currently residing and working at Madame Giroux's White Rose House of Temperance.

"I think we have our accomplice," said Rivoli.

Twelve

Sophie

The day of Sophie's portrait arrived with a drumroll of faraway thunder. Sophie lay in bed for an hour listening as the rumble gave way to booms and then to sharp claps.

She got up, lit a candle, and then stood a moment over Marie, watching her snore. She bent to kiss her forehead as she did each morning. On impulse, Sophie pressed her lips against Marie's. The girl's lips were soft and full—like kissing a sponge. They were so unlike Vincent's. His lips were thin and ringed by whiskers. And while his lips certainly had their appeal, Sophie could see why men wanted to kiss Marie. For a moment, Marie's snoring changed pitch and then went on as before.

Sophie set the candle on her dresser and put on her clothes. She grabbed her hairbrush and bows and then swiped Marie's makeup from the top drawer. She gathered it all into her arms and then slipped outside.

From the veranda, the storm was visible as a featureless, black horizon rising in the west. Bursts of heat lightning danced silently within the clouds. The air was drunk with the smell of an approaching storm.

Sophie went down the stairs and onto the street in the direction of Vincent's house.

Her head was in a fog. She had been unable to sleep. When she did doze off, she was visited by wild, shifting dreams that left her exhausted. It was better not to sleep at all.

She walked along the riverbank, glancing back at the storm as though it were chasing her. A gray dog trotted up to her. It was wet from foraging on the riverbank.

"*Bon matin*," she said, trying to sound cheery.

"They're coming," the dog said.

"What?"

The dog stared at her. Its eyes glowed red like embers at the bottom of a fire.

"*He's* coming."

Sophie backed away from the animal. She turned and fled in the direction of Vincent's house. She dropped one of her bows but didn't bother to pick it up. Vincent's house came into sight, and she broke into a sprint.

Thirteen

Vincent

Sophie arrived at the yellow house wide-eyed and out of breath, but Vincent barely noticed. He was too busy chasing his own demons.

For starters, he had spent the morning scraping the paint off his failed attempt at a religious painting of Jesus in an olive orchard. How he had struggled with it! He had painted Christ in vivid yellow and blue. There was a red angel, blue-green foliage, and a yellow sky.

He had a good reason for destroying it. The only thing he liked about the painting was its yellow sky. The rest looked like Paul Gauguin on a bad day. A painting of such importance needed a model. Painting from memory never worked for him. He had tried so many times. How much easier it would be than lugging his equipment around in every kind of weather! Still, scraping the image of Jesus Christ from a painting—even an image he had put there with his own hand—had unnerved the minister's son. He could easily imagine the rumble of the approaching storm as the footsteps of avenging angels—or worse, his father.

He had no intention of using the restored canvas for Sophie's portrait. The activity was intended to distract him from a problem more vexing than the destruction of a painting of Christ. How could Vincent paint Sophie without revealing his lust for her? His feelings always showed in his work. It was his curse. Her nude would reveal him to be a dilettante using art to get between a woman's legs. A disgrace! Worse, he was betraying his brother's faith in him as a mature artist.

Two impieties in a single morning.

So when Sophie burst into his house that morning looking like somebody was chasing her, Vincent Van Gogh barely noticed. He invited her inside and then led her upstairs to his bedroom.

Vincent set the canvas on his easel and went through his preparatory ritual. How would he go on? He was trapped.

"You look so serious," she said from beside the window.

"Sorry."

"No, I like it," she said.

He finished cleaning a brush and went on to the next, even though he didn't need to. He was stalling.

"I borrowed some makeup from Marie," said Sophie. "You want me to—"

"It's not going to be that kind of portrait."

"Can I at least fix my hair?"

"No."

She accepted his commands. She had such faith in him. Would her faith remain after she saw the finished portrait? He could not paint her without revealing his lust. It would be like the sketches all over again. Impiety number three. What a day!

Sophie called his name.

"Vincent, how's this?"

He looked up.

She was nude. She had posed herself kneeling turned partially away from him. She looked back at him with a glistening gaze that was playful yet vulnerable.

He froze.

Oh God, help me.

But it wasn't God who saved Vincent. It was Willetta.

He painted through the day and was still painting when the errand girl arrived at the door of the yellow house drenched to the bone and panting from the long run from the brothel. The storm had turned the streets into rivers. Shutters banged with every gust.

"Madame Giroux sent me," Willetta said, her eyes wide. "Marie has been arrested!"

As Vincent listened to Willetta's news, he was roused from his artistic trance. Marie was in Rivoli's jail. Madame Giroux and Constable Rivoli had argued so fiercely the whole brothel heard it. Madame left for several hours—no one knew where. When she returned, she dispatched Willetta to bring Vincent to the brothel.

Vincent put it together. The constable figured out that Marie was involved in Sophie's escape and confronted Madame at the brothel. They argued, and Madame rushed to Marseilles to retrieve Sophie's dismantled necklace.

How much time did they have before the constable showed up at Vincent's door? Hours? Minutes?

"The constable seems to think Marie was an accomplice in the escape of that lunatic from jail," Willetta said breathlessly. "Do you think it's true?"

Sophie appeared behind Vincent. She had put on her clothes.

"Shame on Madame for sending you out in this weather," said Sophie.

"What are you doing here?" Willetta asked.

"Modeling," Sophie replied. "I'll make some tea."

"Tea?" Willetta exclaimed. "*Quoi*? *Non*! Vincent must come *immédiatement*!"

At that moment, a burst of lightning flickered, followed instantly by a powerful explosion.

"That was close," said Sophie anxiously.

"I'll get my coat," said Vincent.

She grabbed his arm. "Don't go!"

Vincent regarded her curiously. She looked petrified. Why? It was just a storm.

"I have to," he said. "Marie's been arrested."

"Marie?"

He removed her grip from his arm and then pulled on his coat. She mumbled in German. He pulled open the door and flashed her a smile.

"You'll be safe here," he said. "I'll be right back." He winked. "To finish the portrait."

She nodded, momentarily reassured by the existence of the half-finished portrait. As Vincent looked back at Sophie from the doorway of his house, a premonition swept over him that the portrait would not be finished, and the thunderbolts were, as feared, footsteps.

He set aside the thought and, with Willetta at his side, plunged into the storm.

"This is outrageous!" Vincent fumed.

Madame Giroux looked across her little desk with an expression he recalled from the time she had burned his sketchbook.

Doing business with Madame Giroux was never going to be easy, and the sudden arrest of Marie had only made things worse. Still, Vincent had spent hours working out the logistics of Sophie's journey to America, counting every expense, writing letters, and mail-ordering transportation schedules on two continents. The deconstructed necklace would cover everything with money left over for Sophie to set up a new life in Missouri. He had assured her of that. So now he was horrified when Madame handed him a purse with less than half of what he expected.

The number of rubies had shrunk from seven to three. The four emeralds were missing altogether. The number of gold ingots was half of what she promised. The jeweler, Madame claimed, had taken an increased commission for the "expedited service." It was a lie. Madame was also using Sophie's reckless behavior during her stay at the brothel as a pretense to increase her commission above the agreed-upon amount.

What she presented to Vincent was enough to get Sophie to St. Louis. No more. She would arrive destitute, without even money to return. It was a disaster!

Vincent felt his blood rise. Madame was a thief! This was the moment when normally he would fly into one of his rages. The room went red around him. But then he thought about Sophie's faith in him, and the red world came into focus. He could not indulge this temper. Not this time.

His hands trembled as he pulled his pipe from his pocket and put it in his mouth. A little tobacco remained in the bowl, and it looked dry enough. He struck a match and puffed five times until he heard the tobacco crackle. He shook out the match and dropped it in Madame's ashtray.

Madame watched his sideshow with amusement. Clearly, she believed she held all the cards. What Madame didn't know was that Vincent had worked for five years as an art dealer in London. Nothing in the art world ever sold for the listed price. Plus, he was Dutch, and haggling was practically a national sport. Vincent would come out on top this time. For Sophie's sake.

Madame Giroux never knew what hit her. Vincent told her he was withdrawing from the deal and pretended to walk out of the room. She called him back with a partial refund. He sat down and reminded her that fencing stolen jewelry was a crime. Who would seriously believe she thought the necklace belonged to an escaped lunatic? Madame pulled several more emeralds from her desk drawer. Vincent suggested that harboring a fugitive could create problems for her with the constable—*if* someone were to report it. That did it. Madame produced the last of the missing emeralds, adding two more rubies and all of the missing ingots.

Vincent made a mental calculation. Yes, it was enough. He put the loot in the purse and then stuffed it in his pants.

"What about Marie?" he asked.

Madame scoffed. "Rivoli has no proof. Just some half-baked theory about a faulty lock. He's trying to scare her into confessing to something." She snorted. "That girl is indestructible. By tomorrow, she'll have everyone in that place in love with her."

"You'll make sure she gets her cut?" asked Vincent.

Madame clucked with irritation. "Go on now, get out of here! And use the back door."

He glanced at the clock on the mantel. Eleven o'clock. He had been gone for two hours!

He got to his feet.

"I don't want to see either of you here ever again," she said.

Vincent made his way through the downpour to the yellow house. Lightning flashed continuously. He used it to light his way.

When he arrived home, the house was dark. He came through the door.

"Sophie!" he called out into the darkness.

Had she gone to bed? He lit a candle and went upstairs to his room.

The bed was empty.

The painting was gone.

So was Sophie.

Where would she go?

Think, Vincent. Think!

The brothel was the obvious place, but he would have passed her on the way. So where?

There was nowhere else!

Something must have spooked her. Was it the storm? Was it something else?

He became aware of a scratching sound at the door downstairs.

Sophie?

He raced downstairs and pulled open the door. A shaggy gray dog looked up at him.

Vincent was about to slam the door when a thought struck him. Sophie had arrived that morning acting as though she were fleeing something. The impression was so powerful, he had glanced up the road in the direction she had come from. But the street was empty except for this dog.

Had it come to the door while he was gone? Could the dog have spooked her somehow?

Vincent knew the dog. Everyone did. They called her Rhônetta because she lived on the riverbank...

The riverbank!

He heard Dr. Peyron's voice in his mind—*She's on a high now. But when she crashes... We must find her before that happens.*

Vincent grabbed his coat and ran out into the teeth of the storm. He sprinted along the dark street leading away from Place de Libertine. He drove his legs to run faster. He sensed that every second could have consequences.

He reached the fork that led to the riverbank and turned down the long slope. The rain had turned the path into a river in its own right. He nearly slipped in the mud as the slope steepened toward the river's edge. The ground leveled onto the beach where they had skinny-dipped that first night. In the mud, mangled and torn, lay his portrait of Sophie. From out of the bushes, Rhônetta appeared. She looked at Vincent and wagged her tail.

"Where is she, girl?" Vincent asked.

The dog turned toward the river.

"Sophie!" Vincent called into the darkness.

Lightning flashed and, for an instant, illuminated the surface of the river. About fifty feet from the shore, an object drifted in the current.

His heart stopped.

Another flicker of lightning. The object was a body.

"Sophie!" he cried, diving into the river. He swam blindly in the general direction of the body. Another flicker, and he saw it again. Closer now. He adjusted course and, with a few strokes, came alongside. The body was a woman. She floated face down in a yellow dress. Vincent knew the dress. With dread, he rolled her over.

It was Sophie. She was unconscious.

He shook her. "Sophie! Wake up!"

She didn't move. He put his arm around her chest and began swimming back to shore.

He felt something slip from his pants. He knew at once what it was—the purse with Sophie's money. It was now at the bottom of the muddy river.

There was no time to think about that now. He swam on. He reached the beach and pulled her limp body into the mud. He brushed her hair from her face.

"Sophie! Wake up! Sophie!"

He shook her, but there was no response. Her skin was the color of a callus.

He buried his face in her chest. "I'm sorry, Sophie," he sobbed. "I shouldn't have left. Why did I leave? I'm sorry. I'm so sorry."

Vincent raised his eyes skyward and blinked into the falling rain. "Please God, don't take this woman. My own life means nothing now. Please just let her see the Mississippi River."

The mention of the Mississippi reminded Vincent of something Sophie had once said about a scene from her favorite author, Mark Twain. She loved retelling his stories. In the scene, a boy was lying unconscious on a beach from having drowned. His friend knelt over him and then somehow brought him back to life.

How? Vincent thought. How had his friend saved him?

Vincent rolled Sophie onto her side. Water spilled from her gaping mouth. He began patting her back, harder and harder. Suddenly, she convulsed and then coughed. Her face flushed with a rush of blood.

"Sophie! Oh, my god. Sophie!"

She coughed again and her eyes fluttered open.

"Vincent?" she said.

He pulled her into his arms and rocked her.

"Oh, thank God. Thank God."

Sophie was too weak to walk, so Vincent scooped her up to carry her home. She held on to his neck as he cradled her, not speaking, simply looking into his eyes as though she couldn't believe she was seeing him.

He ignored the mounting ache in his arms as he carried her through the rain along the empty streets to his door, then upstairs, where, dripping, he placed her on his bed. He removed her wet clothes and then wrapped her in a dry blanket. She continued to watch him with eyes that observed him from somewhere far, far away.

"Rest now, Sophie," he said. "You're safe now. I'm here. I won't leave you."

She blinked at him. "Why don't they love me?"

"Who?" asked Vincent.

She closed her eyes and fell asleep. Vincent sat beside her on the bed watching the blanket rise and fall over her chest. He allowed himself to relax. She was out of danger.

But for how long?

The situation was dire. Vincent had lost Sophie's money. The purse was at the bottom of the river. She couldn't afford to leave Arles without it. Nor could she stay. Constable Rivoli and Dr. Peyron were looking for her. How long before they arrived at Vincent's door? He was shocked they weren't here already. But those were minor concerns compared to Sophie's health. She was unfit to travel. Was the whole idea of going to Missouri merely a delusion of her illness? Peyron had said as much.

He watched her lips move as she dreamed. He arranged her blanket. He thought about her love for birds and their unique songs; her brutally earnest critiques of his work; and her childlike joy at the simplest things. A ladybug landing on her arm could fill her with happiness for an hour.

Was Sophie her illness?

He wondered if they were drawn to each other because each saw the same defect in the other, even if that defect was also their superpower. It certainly served Vincent now, for he saw what most people could not see, maybe even Peyron: Sophie's dive in the river was not a suicide attempt. She had more desire to live than anyone he had ever met. Vincent knew only too well that a mind gripped by dark thoughts formed its own twisted logic; it could make the unthinkable look reasonable.

Vincent is not coming back... Peyron will take me to the asylum... Destroy the evidence... The portrait must be destroyed... find peace at the bottom of the Rhône.

Vincent watched her sleep. Her beauty brought a lump to his throat, and he thought about his promise to God. He would never paint again if it meant she would live one more day.

By dawn, the storm had passed. Sophie continued to sleep. Vincent waited. He knew what he had to do.

At nine o'clock precisely, Vincent heard his postman, Joseph Roulin, splashing up the muddy street to his door. His bearded friend was whistling some folk tune, as he always did. Vincent stuck his head out his window and called down. Could he go to Hôtel Arles at once and summon Dr. Peyron?

"Why, Vincent? What has happened?"

"Tell him it's a medical emergency."

Vincent watched from the doorway as Dr. Peyron knelt beside Sophie and took her hand. Suddenly, he felt like an outsider.

"How do you feel, Sophie?" Peyron asked.

Sophie's face turned toward the voice. "Dr. Peyron?"

"I'm here."

"I want to go home," she said.

"Of course."

He prepared a hypodermic needle. Vincent had never seen one before and was alarmed. He stepped forward.

"Is that necessary?" he asked.

"Sedate, then evaluate," said Peyron.

Peyron jabbed the needle in Sophie's arm. Vincent winced, but not Sophie. She let out a deep sigh as the drug took effect.

"How do you feel now?" he asked her.

She smiled at him.

"In the garden, your lilac bush is in bloom," Peyron told her.

"I want to see it," she replied.

"You will."

Peyron took out a pencil and notebook. He turned to Vincent. "Now, Monsieur, you must tell me everything."

Constable Rivoli arrived with his two deputies. He was not interested in making arrests. The escapee had been captured and was now in the custody of the asylum's chief of staff. Rivoli's reputation was restored. The whore, Marie, would be released having confessed to nothing. Madame Giroux's ridiculous claim that she didn't know Sophie was a fugitive would be accepted as the truth; Madame was a better ally than an enemy. The painter, Vincent Van Gogh, was guilty of aiding and abetting the fugitive in Arles, but in the end, he had come forward. That counted for something.

The constable and his deputies closed their notepads and marched out of the yellow house for good.

Vincent watched as Dr. Peyron and his carriage driver moved Sophie onto a stretcher. They set her on the floor beside Vincent. The driver went downstairs to get the carriage ready.

"Poor Sophie," said Vincent. "What's wrong with her?"

"I wish I knew. Believe me, Monsieur Van Gogh, I'd love nothing more than to see Sophie live a normal life. It's just not possible. I tried to tell you that."

"I didn't see. I'm sorry. I wish there was something I could do."

Peyron thought for a moment. "She loves getting letters. And her family doesn't write."

Vincent started. "Her *family?*"

"I can't talk about that."

"I'll write every day," said Vincent.

"Every day is not necessary."

"Every day," said Vincent.

"Excellent," said Peyron, looking pleased. "She'll love that."

Sophie's eyes were open. She was listening.

"Are you ready to go home now, Sophie?" Peyron asked.

Vincent said to Peyron, "Can I say goodbye to her, Doctor?"

Peyron nodded and said to Sophie, "I'll be downstairs."

Vincent listened as Peyron went down the stairs. Vincent took Sophie's hand into his.

"I'm sorry, Sophie," said Vincent.

"No, *I'm* sorry," she said.

"For what?"

"For the river. For your beautiful painting..."

"Shh. I'll make a new one."

"You saved my life."

He smiled. "Actually, it was Mark Twain." He told her how he had remembered her story and then repeated the procedure on the riverbank.

"Mark Twain," she said, sounding pleased.

Vincent could hear Peyron downstairs giving instructions to the carriage driver.

"Peyron seems like a good man," said Vincent.

"You're a good man," Sophie replied.

"I love you, Sophie."

"I love you, Vincent Van Gogh."

"What can I do for you, Sophie? Tell me."

"You told Peyron you would write to me."

"I will. Every day."

She closed her eyes wearily. "In your letters, Vincent, don't just tell me the same things you tell your brother—all art and theories and money. When you write to me, let it be about the birds and the other animals. Write about the clouds and the insects and the flowers. Tell me about all the crazy characters you meet in Arles. Tell me that you love me, Vincent. Don't leave that out." She opened her eyes. "Can you do that?"

He gulped. "I will."

"Good," she said wearily. "Now, I'm ready to go home."

Vincent called Peyron, and the three men carried Sophie on her stretcher down the stairs and put her into the carriage. The streets were ankle-deep with mud from the storm. The carriage was drawn by two horses that splashed impatiently in the puddles. Peyron kicked the mud from his boots and got in beside her. He shouted to the driver, and they began to move. The driver did a U-turn and then headed north toward St. Remy.

Vincent stood watching the carriage shrink and then disappear over a ridge. Sophie was gone.

He went back inside his empty house, not even bothering to close the door behind him. On the floor, Sophie's clothes from the river lay in a wet heap. It was the dress and corset she had worn all month, her only outfit, the one she bought from Marie the night they swam naked in the Rhône. He stared at the frock for a long time, paralyzed by emptiness.

Sophie's last words echoed in his head. The men had just finished loading her into the carriage when her eyes found Vincent.

"I would have liked to see Missouri," she said.

In his house, Vincent sat down on the edge of a crate and wept.

Part 2

Starry Night

Fourteen

Jane

Jane Ward found the letters in a wooden crate behind a file cabinet in Chalet von Tessen's basement. They were love letters.

My Dearest Soph,

I was out before sunrise today and the citril finches were singing. I cannot hear their song without thinking of you and that strawberry salad you made for us. You served it on plates of tree bark and then scolded me for eating too fast. It was our first picnic together. Our first kiss...

Love Always

The letters were bound with string tied in a neat bow with a flower petal pressed on top. They were written in French with a charcoal pencil. Jane chose another at random.

My Dearest Soph,

Sorry for the wet spots on the paper. No, they're not tears. I decided to dive again into the river looking for your purse. I didn't find it, of course, but what a great excuse for a swim. You always seem close when I'm there...

Love Always

The letters were one half of a conversation that took place between Soph (Sophie?) and her lover.

My Dearest Soph,

That's such exciting news about the flamingos. I saw them, too! They passed right overhead! It made me wonder if they were from the same flock—your flamingos and mine—and for a while you didn't seem so far away. But you're never closer than when I'm writing to you. I pretend you are sitting beside me and I'm telling you these things. My pencil becomes my lips. I feel less lonely...

Love Always

Who was the author? Jane kept expecting to find some clue that would tell her who he was, but it was as though he was deliberately concealing his identity.

My Dearest Soph,

I saw Marie today on the street. She sends her love. We had a good laugh about the time you played Sultan in The Living Paintings Show. *Madame still stages it that way. Can you believe it? I told her Madame should be paying you royalties...*

Love Always

Jane gathered up the letters and headed upstairs. She had promised Ursula to show her anything of a personal nature, and this certainly qualified.

She felt her way along the dim corridor toward the stairs. The basement of Chalet von Tessen was not truly a basement; it was more like a cave existing under the house. The illusion that the chalet hung from the cliff was created through a clever design by Rudolph III's nineteenth-century engineer. A natural ledge in the face of the cliff was entirely filled by the house and grounds. This made it appear from below that the house was bolted to the cliff. But the truth was evident in the spaces under the house. The natural ledge upon which the chalet was built was not perfectly level, which created voids. In places, the caves provided standing room; in others, it was necessary to walk hunched over. In the remotest corners, crawling was required. Jane had nothing to do with those places.

A cave is fine for storing food and wine, but a worse environment could not have been devised for the von Tessen archives! The optimal humidity for storage of books and archival documents is 35 percent, and Jane's moisture meter read 95 percent! Her first decision was to move everything up to the portrait room where the records would be safe, and she could work more comfortably. When the job was complete, the significant records could be sent to the Leipzig Archives, while the rest could be placed in a suitable storage vault—preferably off-property. From what Jane had seen of the underside of Chalet von Tessen, it was a tinderbox of retrofitted electric wires, closed-off gas lines, and the persistent smell of rotten eggs.

Ursula gave Jane a second-floor room in the back hallway. There was a bed, a table, a cupboard, and a chair with a good light where Jane could read. From her window, Jane looked past the English Garden and the private chapel that occupied the yard to the broad valley with the stone giants watching over. She rose every morning and checked the weather from her window. It was more reliable than the best weather app.

She ate her meals with the others as though she were a family member. Agatha did the cooking. Ursula looked after Sydney whenever Max was working in Burgen. Once a week, a crew of maids arrived to clean and deliver the food order. A maintenance man came up from Geneva when he was needed for repairs, which was constant. Max pitched in when he could, but was often needed in Burgen. Agatha made weekly trips to Geneva for all other supplies. Occasionally, Jane went with her.

Each evening, when all her work was done and the house fell still, Jane would turn on her laptop and page through The Carolines of Francis Firth. The portraits spanned a quarter-century, yet Caroline never aged.

Jane wondered if Caroline had died young. Had Francis Firth, in his grief, inserted her into his work as he remembered her, permanently fixed in radiant youth? It was a sobering thought.

The work went on. By day, Jane catalogued the von Tessen archives. The rest of the time was her own. When the weather was good she walked the grounds, soaking in the chalet's command of the valley; when the weather was poor, she browsed the library.

In the early weeks, she saw little of Max. If he wasn't working in Burgen, then he was spending time with Sydney, or caring for the horses, or making some repair at the chalet, or in his office hunched over the bills and ledgers of Klaus's big project. As time wore on, however, he seemed more present. He would appear at her side, sometimes with Sydney, sometimes alone. In the library, they would wander the shelves together, pulling down books they had read and discussing them. He was nowhere near as well-read as Klaus, who was the best-read man Jane had ever met. But still, Max had spent his childhood summers in the chalet, and when the weather was bad there was little to do but read. He was a fan of horror and mystery, and she supposed he was responsible for the mass market paperbacks by Stephen King and John Grisham sprinkled throughout the library.

One day, Jane pulled down a copy of *Jane Eyre*.

It was a game they played: "Read it? Never read it?"

"Read it," Max said.

Jane laughed. "What? Really? Why?"

Max shrugged. "I was fourteen. I was hoping for some insight into girls."

"You're kidding."

"I think it was an important book for me," he said slowly. "Before *Jane Eyre*, I don't think I ever considered the possibility that girls might want as much out of life as boys."

Jane waited for him to laugh, but he wasn't joking. It struck her as an astonishing confession. She tried to imagine a fourteen-year-old boy alone in the library of his grandparents' chalet trying to learn about girls by reading *Jane Eyre*.

"You had a sister," said Jane.

"I rest my case," he said.

"I was named after Jane Eyre, you know," said Jane. "My mother denies it, of course. But for some librarians, Jane Eyre is practically a patron saint."

"Why does your mother deny it?" Max asked.

Jane recoiled. Max had an unnerving habit of zeroing in on her offhanded remarks. She searched his face to see if he was mocking her somehow, but his dark eyes regarded her earnestly. He waited.

The thing about an unhappy childhood is that you don't recognize it as such. At best, you sense that something is off. Young Jane never wondered why her parents didn't show affection to each other or their children. There were no hugs; no kisses; no hand-holding; and even smiles were dispensed frugally. The family didn't eat together. Food was left warming on the stove or spread out in takeout bags. Everyone grabbed what they wanted and took it to their private corners. Her brother, Davis, ate while playing video games. Her mother had a tray for eating in bed. Jane rarely saw her father eat; he was forever "grabbing a bite" who knew where. Jane ate with whatever book she had plucked that day from her mother's library and tried not to spill food on the pages. Sure, there were moments when this cold truce was shattered by a slammed door and the sound of her mother crying. But things would quickly return to their former condition, and Jane had no cause to question it.

"Well, I was not exactly planned," said Jane. "My parents were both still in college. My mother wanted to be a book editor for one of the big publishing houses in New York. My father was playing Minor League baseball with a shot at the Majors. Then I came along. Mom took the job at the library. Dad became a high school coach and chemistry teacher. I think they just never forgave each other. Or me."

"Okay, but what's that got to do with denying the source of your name?"

"When I was born, there must have been an instant when my mother was happy. It lasted just enough to name me after her literary hero. Then reality set in. By then it was too late. I had the name. She couldn't exactly change it. It was easier to deny its source."

Max took *Jane Eyre* from her hand. He slid it into place on the shelf.

"A person can raise a child *and* be a book editor," he said.

In the dark corridor beneath the house, Jane clutched her box of love letters and hurried toward the stairs as fast as she dared. Gaslights had once lit the space, but they were disconnected long ago. Max ran a long extension cord to the "records room" for Jane's use, but the entire length of the corridor to the stairs was lit by a single electric bulb suspended by its wire. Drafts caused the bulb to swing, and shadows danced over the uneven earthen walls, dangling pipes, electrical wires, and spider webs. The whole effect was creepy, and Jane was always glad to reach the stairs and climb up into the house.

She arrived in the kitchen to find Agatha alone at the stove. Max was in Burgen helping the men lay floor tiles, while Ursula and Sydney were at a playdate in a neighboring village.

"We feel the little girl is spending too much time with adults," said Agatha. "She's becoming..."

"Precocious?" Jane offered.

"I was going to say 'spoiled.'"

Jane took the letters into the portrait room to read. The big room was now Jane's office. She had a desk, a comfortable chair, and eleven file cabinets. There was also a top-of-the-line document scanner, a label maker, and stacks of hanging folders and file boxes.

Klaus had pronounced her new office "impressive," but Jane saw only disorder. For her, disorder always needed to be conquered with order. It was an itch she experienced the moment she saw the stacks of papers in the dank basement, the same itch she had felt every day she worked in the library in Ontario Hills. She didn't say that to Klaus, though. He'd think she was just some weird librarian from Hicksville, USA—which she supposed she was.

In the portrait room, Jane put the love letters on her desk and walked the perimeter looking at the pictures. These sober faces in paint had begun to come to life thanks to the yellowing papers Jane found in the basement. She paused beneath a portrait of Rudolph III with his family.

Here was his dashing son, Eduard, in military dress. He would become an important figure in the failed resistance to the rise of Hitler. Beside him were the twin daughters, Adriana and Zelia, with their trendy French names, A to Z.

From the start, Jane's focus was on Rudolph III. Granny Jo's picture showed Sophie in her late twenties, meaning Sophie would have been born in the early 1860s. This made her too old to be the vixen in The Carolines of Francis Firth, but that was a separate matter. If Sophie were indeed a von Tessen, then she must be the daughter of Rudolph III, elder sister to Eduard and the twins. But Jane could find no evidence of it. A two-volume history of the von Tessen family—commissioned by Rudolph III before he entered politics—was exhaustive to a fault. Ursula and Max both referred to it as "The Big Book." There were pages upon pages listing the family genealogy. The "begetting" was worthy of Genesis. This information was sandwiched between lofty commentary extolling the significance of the von Tessens to German history, if not *all* history. An appendix contained family trees emphasizing intersections with Habsburg royalty. The family Bible, likewise, had no mention of Sophie. Max studied the book and noted that several pages were missing. If Old Rudy had rewritten his family history to exclude a firstborn daughter, he could not have allowed any evidence that might refute his version. Perhaps Sophie had existed somewhere in those missing pages.

Jane's eyes moved over the portrait. The twins took after their father, poor things. It would be unfair to call them homely, but even the portrait artist could not transform them into beauties without perjuring himself. If Sophie were a bastard, then why did she take after her mother's side of the family?

In the portrait, a spaniel lay at the twins' feet. It was looking happily toward a burgundy drapery, as though the drapery itself were a friend. It was a strange artistic decision by the painter, and Jane stepped forward for a closer look. But then the grandfather clock in the parlor began to chime.

Two o'clock! She was frittering away the afternoon! Dr. Schmidt was expecting her first report in a week, and she hadn't yet finished her initial sort. She went back to her desk and sat down to read.

The letters were a delight! They were written simply but with the kind of specific observations the best writers always managed to find. He had an artist's eye for significance in the smallest things, and the letters hooked her. One letter ended, and Jane immediately reached for the next. And as she read on, a disquiet began to weigh on her. Between the declarations of love, cringe-inducing lust, and touching recollections of a month spent in the south of France, she could feel a tragedy brewing like storm clouds darkening the horizon. The lovers didn't seem to see it. He wrote of their mutual loneliness, despair, and illness as though they were being led somewhere neither wanted to go. Jane found some letters downright chilling.

My Dearest Soph,

I'm so relieved to hear you're feeling better. This latest episode was scary. When I didn't hear from you, I was ready to get on a train. Thank god your letter came! I wish you were here, my love. How I long to touch you! To feel your lips! To breathe

the lavender of your hair! But at times like these, I am reminded why you are there. You are in a place where you are safe. Get well, my little finch.

Love Always

Jane pored over the elegant French script, letter by letter, with mounting dread.

My Dearest Soph,

Why have you stopped writing? I am so lost without our connection. I lean on it more and more each day. I can't seem to remember your face the way I once could. I find myself wondering, were you ever real? Did I dream you? I am so lost, my love. Nothing is working out the way I planned. I think about the terrible night of the storm, and I hear voices calling from the deep. Something is wrong with me...

Love Always

With two letters to go, Max arrived to tell her dinner would be at seven p.m. She barely heard him over the knell of that final sentence.

Something is wrong with me...

"A special dish in your honor," Max said mysteriously, and said no more.

Jane set the last two letters aside and watched Max breeze out of the room. He was heading out to the barn to clean stalls, then shower, then spend time with Sydney reading and playing games before retiring to his office to prepare the latest financial reports for the hotel. He was a man in constant motion. Jane marveled at his energy. He got up every day knowing who he was, where he belonged, and what he wanted to accomplish. What must it be like to be him? she wondered. She was content with her situation, but she was also aware that it would all come to an end the moment she finished the archives. She estimated she would be done at the end of summer. Max suggested she remain at the chalet through Bonfire Night, the Burgen Day festival in September that would also be the end of Sydney's summer. It was as good a deadline as any. But the only real deadline Jane cared about was Klaus's. She had made a promise to him.

Dinner was being served in the kitchen, not the usual dining room. For Sydney, this amounted to an adventure. Max, Klaus, and Ursula were already seated when Jane slid beside them. Agatha set plates in front of them. Jane looked down in wonder.

"Cheeseburgers!" Agatha announced with pride. "And French fries with… with…"

"Ketchup," said Jane.

"*Oui*!" exclaimed Agatha. "Ketchup! *C'est ça*! So, how does it look?"

Jane laughed. "Wonderful. My god, I haven't had a hamburger since… I can't remember."

Burgen's cuisine was heavy on stews, interspersed with fried trout and catfish. By the time Jane picked up her hamburger, Max's was half gone.

"Slow down there, Maxi!" said Agatha.

He swallowed heavily and said, "Delicious!"

"American culture at its finest," said Jane, taking a bite.

Klaus was using a knife and fork.

"That's not how you do it, Opa!" Sydney laughed.

"It's how Opa does it," said Klaus.

Max finished his burger and slid his plate at Agatha. "Another?"

He got up to get beers from the refrigerator, popped the caps, and set them out for everyone. Klaus reached for one, but Ursula moved it out of reach.

"Dammit, woman," he growled.

They talked easily as they ate. Max shared a story from his day. Two of his men liked to play practical jokes, and Max had been on the receiving end of the last one. Now it was his turn.

"For the last three days, I've been putting fish heads from Elsa's Kitchen on this one particular rock by the river. Every day at noon. It doesn't take long for birds to figure out that sort of thing, and sure enough by day three at noon on the dot, they were circling. So I sent these two guys to that rock for their lunch. I told them I wanted to talk to them about something. 'Start without me,' I said, 'I'll be along shortly.'"

He began to laugh. "They sat down, and instantly, I mean the second their butts hit the rock, the birds descended. There were so many birds they nearly carried the men away with them!"

He was laughing so hard now, he had to put down his beer.

"What did they do?" asked Jane.

"They got off that rock as fast as they could, minus their lunches. It was like a horror movie. I was standing on the road pointing at them and laughing. They knew they'd been set up."

"Won't they try to get even?" Jane asked.

"They'll try."

Sydney finished and left to feed her pony, while Ursula reported on Sydney's playdate. It hadn't gone well. The two girls fought over what games to play, what books to read, what television shows to watch… pretty much everything. They even got into an argument at lunch about whose piece of chocolate cake was bigger.

Ursula was glaring at Max.

"What?" said Max.

"You know what."

"You think I've spoiled her," said Max.

"You *have* spoiled her," Ursula said flatly. "Pony rides and tea parties? Really!" She snorted. "The child needs chores. She needs to hear 'no' once in a while. She's running wild."

Jane stayed quiet, but she found herself enjoying the banter. She thought about how her family always ate meals separately. Certainly, neither she nor her brother could have been accused of being spoiled. To her parents, they had been invisible.

Suddenly, Max became aware of Jane. "Sorry. A little family drama."

"It's okay."

Max got to his feet. "I need to check on Lela. You can come along if you like."

"Sure."

Max found her a raincoat and rubber boots only two sizes too big. She put them on, and they went outside.

It was dark, and the fog was heavy. Jane had to shuffle in her oversized boots. Max slowed his pace to match hers.

She felt flushed from the beer, so the wet air on her skin was refreshing. Her senses hummed like an electric wire on a humid day. Chickens clucked in a coop outside the kitchen door. A lamb baaed from a hillside in the distance.

She could smell the barn somewhere ahead of her—the sweetness of hay mixed with earth and manure—long before she saw it. But mostly, she was conscious of Max beside her left shoulder. She was intensely aware of his breathing. And her own.

The barn appeared, and Max pulled open the heavy sliding door. He switched on a light, and the barn came to life. Lela's big black head protruded through the opening of her stall. She let out a snort as they came near. Max lifted the latch, and they stepped into the stall. Lela pressed her head against Max's chest. He rubbed her long face and cooed to her in German.

This ritual greeting was so intimate, Jane felt embarrassed to be watching.

"Now let's have a look," he said.

"Is something wrong?" Jane asked.

"I'm not sure. She was rubbing on the fence post in Burgen all day. That's not normal."

Jane petted the horse's snout while Max began his examination. He slid his hand over every inch of Lela's body, caressing down one leg and then up the next, along her back, and so on, until Jane found herself envying the horse. Max relied on feel and her subtle responses to his touch to assess her condition. When his hand neared one of Lela's hooves, she raised her leg.

"Uh-oh," he said.

"What is it?" she asked.

"Have a look."

On the back of Lela's leg was a patch of dry skin. The horse had rubbed it raw, probably on the fence post.

"It's called 'sweet itch,'" he said, shaking his head. "From the *moucheron*."

"The what?"

"It's a kind of biting fly. They're bad this year. I have a spray from the vet, but this damn fog washes it right off."

He got an ointment from a drawer and applied it to the rash.

"Will she be alright?" Jane asked.

"Give her a few days. She'll be fine."

After that, Jane helped him turn on the water to the hose to fill Lela's water trough. Max shoveled manure into a pail and then used a pitchfork to spread fresh straw from the loft.

He closed the door and repeated the process with Yara.

"Horses are a lot of work," Jane said when they finished.

He closed the pony's stall door and stroked its snout through the window.

"It's not work," he said.

He put a horse treat in Jane's hand and let her feed it to the pony. It left a slime she wiped on her blue jeans.

They went back outside. Max switched off the light and pulled the barn door closed. They stood a moment in the foggy darkness listening to the clucking chickens and the steady *chirp-chirp* of summer crickets.

"Are you tired, Jane?" Max asked.

Jane had never felt more awake.

"Not really," she said.

"Would you like a tour of the house?"

Jane nodded, and side by side they walked back to the kitchen door.

And that was how, an hour later in a windowless room in the East Wing, Jane discovered *Portrait in Winter*.

Years later, in her bestseller, *Van Gogh's Lover*, Jane would write about that moment.

My heart stopped in shock when I realized what it was. I heard a sound and turned to see. But it was me, gasping, for I was looking at a thing that could not exist and yet somehow did.

Fifteen

Sophie

St. Remy, France
May 8, 1889

Sophie von Tessen tiptoed down a dark, open-air corridor of the asylum of St. Paul de Mausole. It was two o'clock in the morning, and the converted monastery was quiet except for the distant wails of a patient everyone called The Corporal. Thirty years ago, he had been a French soldier in the Second Opium War. Since then, he suffered nightmares and terrible flashbacks. When he was lucid, Sophie would sit in the garden and listen to his stories of China—the raging rivers, the magnificent palaces, and the exotic people who were as rugged as their land. The Corporal's nightmares would pass shortly, she knew. They always did. Then he would fall back to sleep, weeping and muttering, *"Je suis désolé,"* to the families he had slaughtered in the fulfillment of his duty.

Such were the rhythms of St. Paul de Mausole.

Sophie moved like a ghost through the asylum. Her feet were bare, and the stones of the floor were still warm from the afternoon sun. She knew every brick from her many years as an inmate. She climbed a staircase to a walkway and then dropped down onto the wide wall that separated the male and female wings. Female inmates were not allowed in the male quarters, and until that night, she had never violated that rule.

She held out her hands for balance as she walked along the top of the wall. She reached a tree, climbed into the branches, and slid down into the courtyard of the male wing. She crossed the courtyard, keeping to the dirt—the gravel walkway would have made noise. She entered the open corridor and followed it to the end.

She found Vincent Van Gogh asleep in the first bed inside the door. He had not yet been assigned a room, so he was in the shared dormitory, where beds were only separated by a curtain. Moonlight slipped through the bars of the three windows that lined the south wall, and he appeared as a lump on the bed with his back to her. He lay in a fetal position. She knelt on the floor beside him and studied the back of his head. Around her, she could hear the snoring of the other men.

Her heart was racing. He was here!

A year had passed since those four incredible weeks in Arles, the best of her life. Then came the daily march of Vincent's letters, one per day without fail, just as he promised. "My Dearest Soph"—oh, how she learned to love those words! When the weather was good, Sophie would carry the latest envelope into the garden to sit on the bench beside her lilac bush. At other times, she would read by candlelight in her room. She kept the letters in a box and sometimes pulled them out at random, trying to recapture the excitement of the initial reading.

After her breakdown in Arles, Sophie had recovered to find the first twenty letters from Vincent. Twenty! How they saved her! Dr. Peyron seemed to recognize this and made a point of informing her of the daily arrival of every letter.

She never read a letter less than five times. Vincent was such a clever writer! As she read, she could hear his voice behind the words. And with his voice, she felt his breath on her neck, his lips on hers. He kept his promise by leaving them all unsigned and devoid of incriminating details.

Recently, she had begun rereading his letters for a different reason. A storm was coming, and the letters foretold his advancing illness. The last one left no doubt.

She touched his shoulder.

"Vincent," she whispered. "Wake up."

Sixteen

Vincent

Sophie's voice came to Vincent Van Gogh in a dream. That in itself was not unusual; she was a regular fixture there. But something was different this time. He rolled over and opened his eyes. She knelt beside him, a silhouette framed in silvery moonlight.

"Sophie?"

"Vincent."

He sat up.

"It's you," he marveled.

She laid her head on his lap. He stroked her hair.

She took his calloused hand and placed it against the delicate skin of her cheek, savoring its coarseness. She loved his big hands.

"Dr. Peyron said I wasn't allowed to see you," he said.

"I know."

"He said it could—"

She put her finger to his lips. "Shh. I don't want to talk about Peyron now."

She lit a candle. Her eyes flitted over his face, then settled on the left side of his head, where he had cut off his ear. Only a small bit of the lobe remained. She reached out her hand.

He recoiled. "What are you doing?"

"Shh."

She touched the scar and massaged it gently. "It's smooth. Like a fingernail."

She put her lips to his ear and kissed it.

"How could you do that?" he asked. "It's disgusting!"

"It's beautiful," she said.

"Aren't you going to ask why I did it? That's what everyone wants to know."

"Oh, Vincent. I know why."

He pulled her into his arms as though she were a life preserver in the ocean. They kissed and then, as if by magic, he knew they had come full circle. They were right back where they left off in Arles before her breakdown. His heart swelled as he looked at her in the moonlight. Her hair fell around both their faces. Her flowery smell and the caress of her hair on his beard brought back the energy of the previous summer. He felt as though he had stepped into one of his paintings.

"I have to go soon," said Sophie. "The sisters will be making bed checks. But first, quickly, tell me about your paintings. What are you working on now?"

Vincent thought for a moment. "Well, I saw a peculiar moth yesterday. He landed right there on that sill. It was black and gray, tinged with cloudy white, and had the vaguest shadowing of olive green."

She smiled at his painter's description. "That's a death's-head moth. They come for two weeks every May."

"I just had to draw it. I pinned it to a bit of canvas and—"

"Wait, you *killed* it?"

"Yes."

"You killed the moth?" she asked incredulously.

Vincent sensed a change in her mood. He froze.

"No," she said. "No. No. Vincent, no. You must never do that."

"How else could I draw it?"

"You killed a moth," she said in disbelief.

"I won't do it again."

"Promise?" she asked.

"You have my word."

"You do keep your promises, don't you, Vincent?"

"I try."

The cloud passed from her face as quickly as it appeared. "Go on then, tell me more about your work. I missed hearing about it. You left it out of your letters."

"Because you told me to. It was damn hard!"

"It was supposed to be. It was good for you, I think."

She paused. "I have another challenge for you, if you're up for it."

"Okay."

"There's a lilac bush in the outer garden. You'll have to get special permission from Peyron to go there. Tell him I wrote to you about it in one of my letters, and you'd like to paint it. He'll believe that. He knows it's in bloom right now. It's a special place for me. There's a winding walkway, a tree, and a little bench. It's where I read your letters, Vincent. Will you paint it for me?"

"Of course."

"And no more killing things, Vincent. Even to paint them."

"I promise."

"Good. I will come again tomorrow night. We will make our plans."

"What plans?"

She smiled mysteriously and said, "I'm so happy you're here, Vincent. It's not so bad here, you'll see. You will be happy here."

They kissed, and Sophie left. Vincent blew out the candle and lay back on his bed.

Though he was overjoyed to see Sophie, he wondered what she meant by "our plans." Furthermore, he had no intention of being "happy here." What nonsense! St. Paul de Mausole was a hospital, not a home. His only plan was to get well enough to return to Arles and resume his work.

Did she understand that?

Sophie had changed.

At first, Vincent thought the perception might be an echo of his breakdown. Perhaps he was altered, and the changes he saw in her were reflections of changes in himself. But no, as they carried on a series of secret liaisons—in the gardens, on the lawn, and in the tower—he became convinced that the asylum was sucking the life out of her. By returning to St. Paul de Mausole, she had traded a quick death in the river for a slow death behind the hospital's walls. What part did he play in this? He had once asked Sophie if she were an angel. Had she been sent to test him?

"Do you believe God tests us?" Vincent asked Dr. Peyron one day.

"We are tested, yes," he replied. "By God? I do not know. What do you think?"

"I think I failed," Vincent replied.

He *had* failed Sophie. Summoning Dr. Peyron to his house to take her away had been cowardly. The specter of his guilt now overshadowed his meetings with Sophie. His paintings, always a reflection of his mood, were lately clouded by these dark thoughts. Once, in a fit of guilt, he had painted stars as swirling vortexes threatening to crush a delicate, sleeping village. The decision to alter the stars from benign dots to monsters of the night had come to him in an instant. His hand now moved to forces lurking behind conscious thought—the same forces, *the same hand*, that had cut off his ear. The situation terrified him.

Meanwhile, life in the asylum found a rhythm. Dr. Peyron prescribed hydrotherapy for Vincent, which meant spending several hours a week restrained in a tub of cold water.

"Cold alters the brain chemistry," said Peyron. "You'll find it invigorates and clarifies."

And it did... for a while. After each session, Vincent was on a high of heightened awareness, like a plunge in a cold river. Afterward, he couldn't wait to get behind his easel. He was painting well, too—instinctually, as he had done when he was at his best in Arles. He began to believe he was strong enough to return to the yellow house for a few days. He had left a mess in his wake. His canvases were in piles and needed to be packed and shipped to Theo in Paris. There was furniture to be stored and debts to be settled. He and Peyron began to work out the logistics of a two-day supervised trip to Arles.

Meanwhile, Sophie had devised an ingenious way of arranging their forbidden liaisons. She told Peyron she missed corresponding with Vincent. She thought the letters were good for her mental health. Peyron offered to carry letters between them during his rounds. Sophie was delighted at the irony of using as a courier the man who had barred their relationship! After a decade as a patient in St. Remy, Sophie was a master of bending the asylum to her wishes.

The place functioned as a complex clock, as predictable in its movements as a swinging pendulum, and Sophie knew every cog and gear. Sometimes she arranged for them to meet at first light near the courtyard's sundial when the shifts were changing. The nuns of the night shift met in the cloister for tea while everyone else slept, which left the lawn unsupervised. At other times, when the weather was good, they met in the outer garden so that Vincent could paint his vistas. A local man escorted Vincent on these outings. Sophie would creep into one of the holly bushes nearby and wait. On his breaks, if no one was around, Vincent would come to sit with her.

But of all their meeting places, their favorite was the tower. They met at night when everyone was asleep. Sophie lay in Vincent's arms, and they talked. Vincent described his latest painting. Sometimes he brought a letter from Theo and read it to her. Sophie told him about the assortment of characters who populated the asylum—patients, nuns, and doctors. It was like Arles again, but instead of an open sky above them, they looked up at the underside of the pyramidal roof. With his eyes, Vincent traced the cracks in the plaster ceiling and came to know them like old friends. Sometimes they simply fell asleep. Other times they would kiss until it was time to go back to their rooms.

It was during one of these liaisons that Sophie asked Vincent if he would like to make love to her.

"It's all I've wanted since the first time I met you."

"Well, then," she said, her eyes glistening like a river under moonlight.

Vincent hesitated.

"What's wrong?" she asked. "You don't want me?"

"Are you...?"

"Am I what?"

"An angel?"

"What?"

"I need you to tell me. I don't trust my mind anymore."

"I'm not an angel, Vincent. Trust me."

"If you're not an angel, then why can't I tell anyone about you?"

The shine went out of her eyes. She looked around as though someone might be listening.

"Because I don't exist," she said.

And then she told him. She was Baroness Sophie von Tessen, the "mad daughter" of Baron Rudolph von Tessen III, one of the wealthiest men in Europe. Her family tree contained names like Habsburg and Romanov.

"I was nine years old the first time they sent me away. I missed my family, my dogs, and my pony, but the asylum wasn't so bad. It was a half-day coach ride from the barony near Leipzig, and they visited me on weekends. One time, Mama brought the twins, which was so much fun. Then I was moved to another asylum, this one further away. Then another and another, always further away than the last one. The visits stopped. That was the pattern.

"Twelve years ago was the last time I went home. I had just turned eighteen and everyone forgot my birthday—except for Oma. That's when she gave me the necklace I showed you. I walked through the rooms where I had played as a little girl, and it seemed to me that my memories belonged to someone else. Maybe I had read them in a book. No one knew me—not the twins, not the staff, not even the dog, which growled at me. I was a ghost."

She paused. "But that wasn't the worst thing. I was wandering the halls when I came upon a wall of family portraits. Of course, I wasn't in any of the recent ones. But then I found several older ones that were familiar. I had memories of sitting for them. But I wasn't in any of them. I was gone."

Up until that moment, Sophie had told her story matter-of-factly, but now tears filled her eyes.

"They got rid of me," she said. "They'd brought in a painter and had my image removed from the portraits. I couldn't believe it. I walked closer to the portrait and held out my candle for a better look. I was able to find a few strands of my hair that had remained in the picture. In another portrait, a part of my hand was still visible beside our dog, Schatze."

Vincent felt his anger rise. "My god."

"It's okay," she said, patting his hand. "I want you to know, I don't blame them. They're my family, and I love them, Vincent. Those were dangerous times in Prussia for politicians and bankers—and Father was both! They couldn't afford to let the world see any vulnerability. That's what I was. A liability. They had an obligation to protect their other children. And I was a bad daughter."

"I'm sure you weren't."

"Oh, I was, Vincent. I was so bad. Willful and disobedient, and so reckless. I would have these tantrums..." She shook her head. "When I was fourteen, I came home during one of my good spells and began an affair with a thirty-five-year-old gardener. The man was married! Father sent the gardener away, and in a fit, I threw myself out of a second-floor window. I landed in a big bush. That was the only reason I didn't die that day. I think when my dear oma died of a stroke a few years after my last visit, it was because of me..."

Sophie's voice cracked. Vincent tried to hug her, but she pushed him away.

"That day, when I saw those painted-over portraits, I knew my duty, the one thing I could do for them. To protect them, I would need to cease to exist." She leaned back on her hands. "But how does one cease to exist? I couldn't just kill myself, could I? There would be an inquest, newspaper stories most likely, and then everyone would be reminded very publicly of the troublesome fact of my existence. And because of the sin of suicide, I couldn't have been buried in the family plot. That was the only thing I still wanted for myself as a von Tessen—to be buried in that beautiful valley in the Alps, in this little place called Burgen. My father has a chalet there. So, somehow, I needed to disappear and then outlive them all so that my death did not trace back to them. So I went to Papa and told him I wanted to come here to St. Remy. I had heard about the asylum, that it was peaceful and in a beautiful part of France with good weather. I told him I thought it could cure me, but that wasn't the reason. I knew it would put me far from the intrigues of the barony. Papa was only too happy to oblige."

"Did they at least write to you?"

"They sent money every year to cover the cost of my care. In the first few years, Papa added a little note with news from home. But after a while, there was just the check."

Vincent was horrified. He, too, lived a solitary life. He relied on letters to stay connected to his far-flung family and friends. There were days when he seemed to spend as much time writing as he did painting. He could not imagine living as he did without daily visits from the postman. His best friend in Arles was the postman. That was no coincidence. Vincent had even done several portraits of him.

"I'm so sorry, Soph."

"So now you know, Vincent. I'm not an angel."

He kissed her. "I think maybe you are an angel."

"No, Vincent. I'm not. I'm just a girl."

Seventeen

Jane

Jane held on to Max's arm as they pressed deeper into the dark of the chalet's East Wing. Max's flashlight beam fell upon door after door along a long corridor. This was part of the annex Rudolph von Tessen III had commissioned in 1847 when he decided his new chalet was not grand enough for the emperor.

"Servants' quarters," Max said. "Not much to see here."

It was an hour after their cheeseburger dinner and the tour of the chalet was nearly complete. Jane didn't want it to end, so she suggested he show her the East Wing even though Klaus had switched off the power to that portion of the house. The wiring was over a century old, and he was worried about a fire. Many of the fixtures were converted oil lamps with antique knob-and-tube connections, and rewiring the entire wing would have cost over half a million euros, so he pulled the plug on it, literally—plunging the entire wing back to its former nineteenth-century darkness.

Max grabbed a flashlight, and together they entered the wing through a dark corridor at the back of the library.

They stuck their heads into one room after another. Max opened a door and then traced his beam in an arc over the empty room. Then they backed out into the corridor to repeat the process on the next door.

The corridor was getting drafty, and Jane shivered.

"You're cold," he said.

"No, I'm not."

"You're shivering!"

"I'm fine, really."

A strange groan, like air whistling in a soda bottle, came from the end of the corridor.

"What's that?" she asked.

He sighed. "That's our ghost."

"You have a ghost?" asked Jane.

He led her to the last door on the right. He put his hand on the knob.

"Now watch," he said.

He pushed open the door, and a blast of icy air blew back Jane's hair. In the same instant, the groaning stopped.

"We scared him off," said Max. "He's quite shy."

"What just happened?"

"There's some kind of draft in this room. It comes from the catacombs under the plank floor, I think. In certain conditions, air whistles through gaps and makes that pitch you heard. When you open the door, the sound always stops."

"Weird."

"You can imagine the stories," he said. "You've probably heard about our curse."

Jane nodded. Burgeners were only too happy to tell her about the curse that plagued Chalet von Tessen. Even Pauli had mentioned it once, perhaps hoping to add a bit of local color.

Max seemed to lose his humor. "This whole business of a ghost and a curse, it's not something to be taken lightly. People are dead. In the eighties, there was a wrongful death lawsuit against my grandparents from the family of a maid who went over the East Cliff. I wasn't born yet, but it's a sore point with Oma. The maid was a friend. Agatha's predecessor, now that I think about it."

"Why does this door have a lock on it? None of the others do."

"I don't know. I never noticed."

"Shine the light inside," she said.

He painted an arc over the room. The light caught something on the wall.

"Go back. What's that?"

"Just an old portrait," he said.

"Why isn't it with the others?"

"It's not family. It belonged to one of the staff. The person who lived here, probably."

Jane asked for the flashlight so she could have a closer look.

It was a family portrait done in oils. It showed a young man in military dress standing grandly beside his seated, rosy-cheeked teenage bride. They were in a drawing room with a little fireplace and blue porcelain tiles all around. It was winter, and the window seemed to invite the snowy Alps into the room. Far in the distance, at the bottom of the valley, was a village.

"Is that..."

"Burgen," said Max.

"Where's the chapel?"

"This must have been done before it was built."

Jane pointed to the blue tiles by the fireplace. "That's your drawing room."

"It is. The view out the window... I know it well."

The conclusion came to both of them at once.

Max said, "So these two people must be Old Rudy and Margaret. My god, look how young they are!"

But Jane couldn't reply. On Margaret's lap sat a little girl.

"Who's that?" Jane asked, pointing to the little girl.

She was about five years old with ringlets in her hair. Her mother looked at her with adoration. Even Rudolph seemed swollen with pride at the perfection of his progeny.

There was a long silence. Jane didn't breathe.

"You don't think..." Max trailed off.

"We need to get this back to the house."

Max took the painting off the wall and handed it to Jane. They made their way down the dark corridor, through the library, and out into the foyer.

They came into the portrait room and stopped. It was exactly as she had left it before dinner. The love letters were stacked neatly on her desk. Her label maker lay beside the letters she had found. A file drawer was half-open with a folder sprawled across the top.

Max removed one of the portraits from the wall and hung *Portrait in Winter* in its place. They stood side by side looking at it. Who was the little girl?

"Maybe she died?" offered Jane.

"There's nothing in the family history about it," said Max. "Eduard was the firstborn."

"Maybe she was a niece? Or a neighbor?"

"Maybe," said Max doubtfully. "But sitting with them for a portrait? That's unlikely. Portraits were a big deal."

Jane studied the shape of the eyes and the face. "It could be her."

"But if this is Sophie, and she didn't die, then why isn't she in any of the other family portraits?" asked Max. "It makes no sense."

"Wait," said Jane. "I have an idea."

She explained it to Max, and they went right to work. The idea was simple: Take down every picture of Rudolph III and those of his immediate clan, and then arrange them chronologically on one wall. *Portrait in Winter* would be inserted into the sequence.

It was more difficult than Jane would have thought. These were oil paintings, after all, not photographs. Portraitists took liberties with their work to enhance the subjects' appearances, and not all painters possessed equal skill. Making matters worse, most of Rudolph III's portraits were on the top tier and could only be reached by ladder. Max went off to find one, which attracted Klaus and Ursula to the project. Soon, they, too, were swept into the task.

"Why are all the Rudys on the top tier?" Max complained.

"Because I put them there," said Ursula, "where I didn't have to look at them."

The placement that had puzzled Jane for weeks suddenly made sense. The paintings Ursula wanted to look at, she kept close. She banished Old Rudy to Siberia, which in this case meant near the ceiling.

It took over an hour, but in the end, the four of them stood before a parade of family portraits marching across the wall. It was like having a time machine.

Walk forward, and the people aged. Walk back, and they got younger. There were fifteen portraits in all—Rudolph III on a white horse posed like Napoleon Bonaparte; Margaret as a young girl in a boat holding a parasol; the family with the happy spaniel; a half-dozen family portraits with Eduard and the twins getting steadily older; four solo portraits of an idealized Rudolph with various game he had killed—bucks, pheasants, a black bear, rabbits—even a wolf.

"He was quite the Buffalo Bill," remarked Jane.

"The chalet was his *Jagdschloss*," said Klaus. "The valley is filled with game. That antler chandelier in the parlor? He didn't buy that at some store. Those are his trophies."

"There must be a hundred antlers in that thing!" Jane exclaimed.

Klaus laughed. "Did you think they were fake?"

"I preferred not to think about it, thank you," she replied.

Portrait in Winter was inserted into the sequence. Viewed in this way—squeezed between Margaret's wedding portrait and a family picture with infant Eduard in a skirt on his mother's lap—there could be no doubt Rudolph III and Margaret were posing with the mysterious five-year-old girl.

"Is that the picture from the haunted room?" Agatha asked.

"If you mean the drafty room, then yes," said Max.

"Oh, my," said Agatha. She fingered her pearl necklace.

Max asked, "Agatha, is that why this portrait was never moved with the others?"

"Maids won't go in there," said Agatha.

"Because of this curse nonsense?" Max asked.

"I go in twice a year to clean," said Ursula. "The portrait has been there for as long as I can remember. It never occurred to me to take it down. I didn't know what it was."

"Look at the way Margaret is looking at her," said Jane. "That's a mother's gaze."

"Okay, so she must have died," said Max. "It was hushed up because the whole thing was so traumatic to Margaret."

"That would be in the records," said Jane. "The Big Book clearly shows Eduard as the firstborn."

A silence fell over them as they considered this puzzle. Jane found herself drawn again to the spaniel in the portrait with Eduard and the twins. The dog was looking happily in the direction of a burgundy drape. Why?

"Does this drapery look strange to you?" Jane asked.

They crowded around.

"It's not attached to anything," said Max.

"It's just floating there," said Klaus. "Odd. What's it even doing there?"

Jane asked Max for his flashlight and shone it at the spaniel's belly, where the drape lay over the dog's paw.

"What's that?"

They all squinted.

"It looks like a fingertip," said Max.

She turned the painting on edge and shone the light along the length. An image rose from the surface. A hidden image.

"Oh, my god."

"What is it?" asked Max.

"It's a *pentimento*."

"*Penti*-what?"

Jane had learned the word from Otto Firth on the night of his death.

"*Pentimento*—it's a paint-over," said Jane.

She held the painting on the edge so Max could see. "See the way the paint rises right where that weird drapery is placed?"

"Like a little hill."

"A hill of paint over paint."

Max found a magnifying glass, and they began examining all the other family portraits for similar hidden features. After an hour of inspection, the conclusion was as evident as it was horrifying: Every family portrait through 1868 carried the *pentimento* image of an older sibling to Eduard and the twins.

"So they painted over her?" said Ursula. "I don't understand."

"The bastard erased her," said Klaus. "His own daughter."

"All but this one," said Max. "They must have missed it. After 1868, they must have stopped having her sit. No more need for the paint-over. She would have been about ten."

Jane walked back to *Portrait in Winter* and looked into the eyes of the little girl.

"It's her," said Jane. "It's Sophie."

"How did it get into the haunted room?" asked Klaus.

"Don't you get it?" said Jane, her voice trembling. "Sophie *hung* it there. That little room with the lock on the door, the one you call 'haunted,' that was *Sophie's room*."

Ursula's hand went to her mouth in horror.

Jane could barely breathe. It *was* horrifying. Sophie von Tessen, after so many years in exile, was home. Her father was dead. Her mother was morphine addicted and living in Leipzig. Her sisters were married with children and firmly embedded in Leipzig society. Her brother, Eduard, was off at war. Sophie wandered the big old house alone, looking for some connection between herself and her family. But Old Rudy had been thorough. He erased her from the portraits and tore the incriminating pages from the family bible. Then one day, Sophie stumbled upon a forgotten portrait. She would have been old enough to remember sitting for it. A happy time. So she dusted it off and hung it above her bed. For the rest of her life, it was the first thing she saw every morning and the last thing she saw every night.

Jane looked deeply into Sophie's face—the playful eyes, and the infectious smile.

"She forgave them," said Jane. "Somehow, she found it in her heart to forgive them."

Eighteen

Vincent

After a month in the asylum, Peyron agreed to allow Vincent to return to Arles for two days to put his affairs in order. Vincent owed money to several people, including his landlord, who was holding his paintings hostage until the debt was settled. The paintings needed to be packed for shipment to Theo in Paris. Joseph Roulin had offered to do it—he was a postman, after all—but Vincent didn't trust anyone to do it right. Plus, there were people in Arles, like Roulin, he wanted to see. They were friends, and he had left without saying goodbye.

On the day before he departed from the asylum, Vincent was painting in a remote corner of the sprawling garden. The skies were a crystal blue, and the mistral was blowing as it had done throughout Sophie's four weeks in Arles the previous year. Sophie reclined in the grass nearby watching the clouds race by with a look of bliss. She had instructed Vincent in her latest letter to set up his easel at the garden's east corner behind a bush. They would be unseen by orderlies until lunch. Vincent was pleased to find a stand of cypress trees bending under the gale. He pondered for a long time about how to capture the wild movement of the trees in a static painting. He abandoned his interest in making an accurate drawing and concentrated instead on the technical challenge of capturing motion in a frozen image. Sophie's voice broke through his trance.

"The crows will arrive soon," she said.

"Hm."

"They perch in rows on the walls," she went on. "Hundreds and hundreds of them. Wait till you see!"

He lifted his brush from the canvas.

"I thought you didn't like walls," he said.

"What?"

"You told me you were done with walls. 'Never again,' that's what you said."

The easy smile left her face. "What a thing to say."

"I'm just quoting your words."

"I need to be here. You of all people should understand that."

"What about Missouri?"

"What about it?" she asked warily.

"You don't want to see it anymore?"

"Don't be cruel, Vincent. What is this? Where is this coming from? We were having such a nice morning, and you're leaving for Arles tomorrow. Why are you ruining this?"

"You are so much more than this, Sophie."

She got to her feet and put her hands on her hips. "You're being quarrelsome, and I don't know if I can be around you."

"Can you answer my question?"

"What question?"

"Missouri! Do you still want to go there? Have you forgotten about the Indians and the buffalo and the Mississippi and Mark Twain? Do you remember any of it?"

"Stop this!"

"Answer me," he said gently. "And I'll stop."

"You're being a... a bully!" she said, sobbing, and then fled in the direction of the asylum.

The next morning, as he prepared to leave for Arles, Peyron delivered Sophie's daily letter. It contained two words.

I remember.

Vincent thought about those words on the train to Arles. It was not out of meanness that he had asked Sophie about Missouri. Her answer shaped what he would do next.

Years ago, Vincent had written to his brother, "Love is the best and noblest thing in the human heart, especially when it is tested by life as gold is tested by fire."

It was time for Vincent to find out if he believed his own words.

The next day, Vincent found himself walking alone along the main street in Arles, grinning happily at the people he passed, and thinking how fine it was to be home. Dr. Peyron had left to check into a hotel, which gave Vincent time to run his secret errand.

An elderly couple with whom Vincent had often exchanged greetings approached from the opposite direction. As he prepared to tip his hat, they crossed the street to avoid him.

He was still puzzling over the encounter when he arrived at the door to Madame Giroux's. He went inside. A wide-eyed Willetta greeted him. He told her he would like to see Madame. She rushed away.

The girls in the salon whispered to each other and gawked at him. He was like a person who enters a party to find conversations halted and realizes it's because everyone had been talking about him. Marie asked awkwardly how he was feeling, and then disappeared as soon as he gave his answer.

Willetta returned to inform him that Madame would see him. He entered her office and sat down.

"I never expected to see *you* again," Madame said across her desk. Her gaze was drawn toward his missing ear.

"I have a favor to ask," he said.

She snorted. "What did I tell you the last time you were here? I never wanted to see you here again."

"It's not for me. It's for Sophie."

Madame squinted at him. "You've seen her?"

He nodded. "We're both at St. Paul de Mausole."

"How is she?"

"She's better," he said with a shrug. "And worse."

"She's a dear girl."

"I'm in love with her."

Madame's expression didn't change. "You really are crazy, aren't you?"

"For loving her?"

"What do men know about love?" she huffed. "Every week I get another man in here whimpering about how he is in love with one of my girls. It's sickening. It's a full-time job with Marie's customers. That girl is a fucking spider web. I wish I had a dozen of her."

"I'm not whimpering," said Vincent.

Madame sat back in her chair, looking thoughtful. "So what's this favor?"

He laid out his request. When he finished, she nodded and said, "I must say, you surprise me."

"So you'll do it?"

"I will."

Vincent's heart raced. "Excellent! I'm in Arles until the day after tomorrow. It must be done by then."

"I'll have Willetta bring everything to the yellow house before then," said Madame.

"Good. A doctor is traveling with me. Peyron is his name. Willetta must deal only with me. She shouldn't speak to him. That's important."

Madame looked bored. "You may go now."

Vincent rose.

"Oh, and Vincent?"

"Yes?"

"Thanks for not whimpering."

Vincent walked back through the streets in the direction of the yellow house where he would meet Dr. Peyron. His happiness at being home was extinguished by a mounting realization that people were either avoiding him or were disgusted by the sight of him. With every averted gaze and unnecessary street-crossing, a rage welled up.

How dare they?

At least *le fou roux*, for all the mocking he endured, was a player in the town's pageant of characters. Now he was nobody. Worse than nobody. He was a man in exile. He was expected to stay away. Until that moment, Vincent had entertained the idea that he could pick up where he left off in Arles. Now he saw the truth: Arles was closed to him. His dream of building a thriving art commune here was dead. No one wanted him in Arles.

A woman on the sidewalk herded her children out of Vincent's path as though he were a monster that might eat them. As he passed, Vincent bent toward them and roared like a beast. They screamed and fled.

Vincent was not walking on the sidewalk anymore. He was hovering above it, suspended on a carpet of pure rage.

A man Vincent knew from the tavern approached. He stared at Vincent's ear with a mixture of curiosity and disgust. Vincent pulled off his hat and pushed his ear into the man's face.

"Want a better look?" Vincent sneered.

The man pushed Vincent. "Freak!"

Vincent shoved him back. The man's heels caught a plank on the sidewalk, and he fell backward into the street. He landed hard.

Vincent didn't stick around to see if he was hurt. He passed a barrel of peanuts and pulled it over. Peanuts spilled out into the street. He kicked at another barrel, but this one was filled with something heavy, and his foot exploded in pain. He cursed and hopped on one foot. He hobbled across the dirt street in the direction of the yellow house. He passed a pile of horse manure and picked it up. He had intended to throw it at something or someone, but instead, he prepared to stuff it into his mouth.

He turned, and that's when he saw Dr. Peyron.

Nineteen

Tomas

Tomas Firth stood outside St. Séverine Parish Church, waiting for his grandfather to catch up. He had a vague sense that he should be helping Gunther up the stairs—it's what Otto would have done—but Tomas wasn't sure how to go about it. Besides, Gunther made no secret about how he felt about Tomas.

"I never liked you," Gunther had told him at his father's funeral. "You're a punk."

"Whatever, Grandpa."

"But I'm going to need you now, and that's just how it is."

That was good enough for Tomas. Where was it written you had to like the people in your family? So Tomas stood outside the church door and let Gunther drag his old bones up the stairs by the railing.

A plaque hung on the wall of the church. He stepped closer to read it. It was in French, which presented a challenge. He spoke German and preferred English as his second language. All the best stuff was in English. Still, he got the gist of what the plaque said.

For eight hundred years, the ground beneath the church had been sacred. There was a cave nearby in the limestone. For a century, it had been a magnet for medieval hermits who wanted to live a life of prayer and deprivation. The greatest of these hermits was Séverine. Every day, no matter the weather, he made the steep climb down to the lake to share his latest vision with the townsfolk, who repaid him with a meal. After his death, a shrine was built on the site of his cave. This drew more admirers, which led to the construction of a small chapel and then a bigger chapel until, at length, Séverine was canonized by the pope, and the present church was built by the Vatican to serve the community of French Catholics who had grown up in the parish that bore his name—St. Séverine Parish, Switzerland.

Earlier that day, on the long drive from Geneva, Gunther told Tomas a family secret: Francis Firth had worked for the church in St. Séverine Parish as a caretaker, not as a goat-herder. He did dabble in art, but ink, not paint, was his medium—the demands of a brush being too bold for his timid nature. He was a pious man and used his skills, such as they were, to copy religious scenes from art books he had collected. Gunther still had Francis's drawings in a box in the gallery's vault.

Like any good lie, Gunther's contained an element of truth.

Tomas finished reading the plaque and turned to take in the view that must have delighted old Séverine as he sat alone fasting in his cave and inventing his latest vision to be swapped for food. The whole of Lac Léman was laid out before him. At the western end of the lake lay the city of Geneva, and even from this distance, Tomas could see the steeples of the Old Town, the sailboats stacked against the waterfront, and the water jet throwing spray into the air like a geyser.

St. Séverine must be the patron saint of liars, thought Tomas with satisfaction. Trading stories for food and being sainted for it! Brilliant! Still, the Firths had upped even the old hermit's gambit, had they not? No bread and water for Tomas. These next two paintings were estimated to sell for over ten million dollars each. They had come here today to St. Séverine Parish to meet the man who delivered them. Gunther called him, The Courier.

Gunther arrived at the top of the stairs beside Tomas, gasping for air.

"Jesus, Grandpa, are you alright?" Tomas asked. "You look like you're about to croak."

Gunther pushed open the door and went inside. The church was empty. He dipped his finger in a basin and drew a cross in the air. They sat in a pew midway back from the altar and waited.

This was a big day for Tomas. He was being let in on the secret of the family business. He felt like the son of a mafia boss being "made." His father's suicide had been a blow for everyone, but the world was expecting two new paintings by Francis Firth, and judging by the way those church stairs had nearly killed Gunther, Tomas was the art world's only hope.

The date was August 1, Swiss National Day, a holiday the Swiss celebrated by being outdoors, not visiting dark churches. It was perfect.

"So how does this work?" Tomas asked.

"*Shh.*"

Tomas's eyes adjusted to the darkness. It was a cozy church once you got over the mildewed smell. Fading frescoes covered the walls. One fresco showed a bearded man in a cave praying before a gold icon. Light rays from heaven illuminated a halo over his head. Séverine. Candles burned and flickered around the edges of the room. Along one wall were three confessional booths. As Tomas watched, he saw the curtain move slightly on the first of them.

"Is that him?" asked Tomas.

"*Shh,*" said Gunther. He leaned close. "August first. One o'clock. Booth One. Got it?"

Tomas repeated the information and asked, "So he's on the other side of the curtain *right now*?"

Gunther nodded.

"Who is he?"

"That's not important."

"How does he get access to the booth? Is he a priest or something?"

"*Shh.* Now we wait for the church bells."

"This is some real Jason Bourne shit, Grandpa."

"Jason who?"

At that moment, the bell chimed the hour. Gunther stood.

Tomas got up, too.

"What are you doing?" asked Gunther.

"The booth—"

"Two people can't go into the confessional! Are you daft?"

"But—"

"Wait."

"But—"

"Sit! Down!"

Tomas fell back onto the pew. Gunther disappeared behind the curtain.

It was insane! How could Gunther allow the entire business to depend on one anonymous man in a booth? What if he got sick? What if he died? It was bad business, that's what it was.

Tomas got up and stood beside the booth. He heard voices.

"... impossible," said the stranger. "I tried."

"Try harder," said Gunther. "You've been paid."

"I know. I'm sorry. It's just too dangerous right now. The American—they've got her working at the chalet. She's showing everyone that picture."

"She doesn't have the painting anymore. We have it."

"She has it in her phone. She's asking questions. She's got people thinking about things in a new light."

Tomas stiffened. They were talking about The American. He should have taken care of her that night in Geneva when he had the chance. His father was dead because of her.

Tomas pulled back the curtain. The man inside was dressed in a black robe with a hood pulled around his head. He turned in surprise, and their eyes met.

"What the hell?" said the man.

"Hey," said Tomas. "Let me handle the bitch."

Twenty

Jane

Jane awoke to the sound of laughter outside her window. She got up to investigate.

Max and Sydney were at the stables. A woman was with them. She was tall and dressed in an elegant suit. Sydney was showing off her pony. The woman reached to pet its nose. It jerked its head, and they all laughed.

Jane recognized the woman. Her picture was in the portrait room. Holiday in Greece. Sydney's mom. Collette.

Collette said something, and Max laughed. He put his hand on Collette's waist.

Jane stepped back from the window. She dressed quickly, grabbed her packed suitcase, and headed down the hallway for a back staircase.

Collette's visit was long planned. Sydney had been counting the days. Agatha had a special menu planned (Collette was vegan). Ursula and Klaus had assigned Collette a guest room in the forward portion of the house (Jane was in the back). Even Reverend Jacques Barbeau promised a sermon on Sunday in honor of their guest.

Jane didn't know what to make of all the fuss, but she decided she would not stick around to find out. The notion of a road trip had been percolating for weeks. Jane needed to follow up on leads from the archives. There were personal matters as well. Jane would probably have left sooner if not for her innate fear of travel. Collette's visit was the kick in the pants Jane needed.

The previous day, she told Max about her plans to leave the valley.

"How long will you be?" he asked.

"Four days."

"That's a shame," he said. "You'll miss Collette. Sydney will be disappointed you won't get to meet her."

Jane circled the chalet through the English Garden to avoid being seen from the barn. She climbed into her SUV and started down the mountain.

Her first stop was the Geneva Police Station. Detective Martina Delgato greeted her warmly, and even presented her with a Swiss roll baked by her mother—Jane's host in the spring.

Jane updated Martina on everything she had learned.

"The Firths are lying," said Jane. "Now, I have the proof."

"The hell you do," Martina scoffed. "You have some paintings that look like scenes in Burgen. So what? You have no motive. Why would the Firths bother to lie about where their ancestor painted? And what does any of this have to do with the theft of *your* painting, which isn't even by Firth?"

Jane was peeved to have been shot down so thoroughly. What made it worse was that Martina was right.

"What do *you* have?" Jane asked.

"We're working on some leads. It's an open case, I assure you."

Jane left Martina and drove to the library. Working with Johan and his team, it took less than an hour to verify the essence of what Pauli had told her about Chalet von Tessen's alleged curse. In the span of sixty years, three women had fallen to their deaths from the chalet's East Cliff.

The first to die was Mary Jenkins of Geneva in 1942. She had been a maid at the chalet for four years at the time of her death. She was described by her co-workers as a "pious woman" who was returning from prayer at the chalet's Garden Chapel when "she went crazy and leaped to her death."

The next to die came ten years later. Anna Hoffman had escaped the Nazi invasion of Budapest to seek work in neutral Switzerland. She was a skilled gardener and had been working in the English Garden when she disappeared.

Her body was found the next day at the bottom of the East Cliff. Like the others, she had been alone at the time of her death.

The third victim, Marie Van Der Berg of The Netherlands, had been the personal assistant to Ursula von Tessen. She vanished on a July morning during her daily stroll of the grounds. Her body, too, was found at the bottom of the East Cliff.

Each story referred to the curse. Journalists borrowed whole paragraphs from past stories, which had a cumulative effect. The oldest of the articles mentioned what it called "recurring bouts of winter madness long known to Burgeners" and "a figure dressed all in black seen moving through the grounds at night."

Some Burgeners even attributed Rudolph III's death to the ghost having spooked his horse. It was nonsense, of course, all of it—but the East Cliff was real enough. Jane passed by there often on her walks. It was a particularly treacherous part of the property with a vertical fall of over a thousand feet to a thicket of jagged rocks. She had seen old pictures of the cliffs in the news clippings. An apple barrel served as a bench. The barrel was still there. Even now, Jane couldn't bring herself to sit on it. The place unnerved her.

Jane printed out the news clips and thanked her fellow librarians. They offered to take her out for fondue (not Portia's), but she had a three-hour drive to her next stop and wanted to arrive before dark.

They didn't ask where she was heading, and she didn't offer. She was not ready to talk about it.

For Jane, the final love letter had been the breakthrough.

My Dearest Soph,

Where have you gone?

For a long time after you left, I was still able to find you. I visited the family with the orange tree and played that game you invented with the children. I heard you in the children's laughter. I swam in our water hole and let the molecules that had touched you touch me. They were like delicate fingers. Later, I sunned myself on the beach, and I found one of your footprints in the sand. I sat beside it for an hour smoking my pipe. We had a whole conversation! Did you hear? Later, a flock of citril finches sang messages carried from you across the mountains.

You were still here, my love. I just had to look a little harder.

But lately, you are not in any of the usual places. The voices of the citrils sound like any other bird. They no longer whisper your messages. The family with the orange tree chased me away like a stray dog. They threatened to call the gendarmes. The river no longer contains your molecules; the current has swept you away. In the sand, the only footprints are my own.

I am working so hard now. I wish you could see. The work is so good. I know I'm not supposed to write about that. But all I have now is my work. It is my shovel. I use it to fill a hole that grows beneath me. No matter how hard I shovel, the hole does not fill. I cannot pause for even a moment lest the ground collapse, and I fall in. So I work, and I work, and I work, and I work, and I work, and I work. And I am getting so tired.

I need to rest in a safe place. So I have decided to take your advice after all. I will come to you. I only hope you will recognize me, for I am not the man you first met at the coliseum.

Jane had stared a long time at the final word. There was a coliseum in Granny Jo's painting. She opened her laptop and began poring over pictures of Roman coliseums from England to Africa to the Middle East, trying to identify the one in *The Lover*. But what she learned was that all Roman coliseums looked pretty much alike. She wrote an email to the author of a book on Roman architecture and attached a picture of the coliseum in Granny Jo's painting. His reply came the same day.

Arles.

Her heart stopped.

Arles. 1888. A man suffering from overwork. A man having a breakdown. A man needing rest...

Jane drove out of Geneva, heading west. A half-hour later, she passed a road sign.

"Welcome to France."

Jane Ward might have been concerned about the man following her if there had been anything remotely threatening about him. He was plump and stood barely five feet two inches tall. He wore a large-billed safari hat with a string tied under his chin. A camera with a long lens dangled from his neck. His shirt was stained with sweat from walking in the summer heat.

She had seen him the first time on the banks of the Rhône in the precise spot where Van Gogh had painted *Starry Night over the Rhône*. A little sign marked the location. Later she saw him in the crowd at the coliseum where Van Gogh had painted *Les Arènes*. And there he was again on the grounds of the Arles hospital, where Van Gogh had painted *The Courtyard of the Hospital in Arles*.

Jane stood in the alley facing Café Van Gogh, the site of *Café Terrace at Night*, when he approached her.

"Goghpie?" he said.

"Excuse me?"

He smiled pleasantly. "Van Gogh groupie? We call ourselves Goghpies."

Jane had never heard the expression and laughed harder than she intended.

The man pulled off his safari hat to reveal a shiny bald crown. He put out his hand.

"Alan Silver of London."

They shook.

"Jane Ward of Ontario Hills, New York."

"First time to Arles?"

"As a matter of fact, yes."

"I come every year," he said. "It's my guilty pleasure. My wife and kids don't get it. They're in Marseilles right now." He rolled his eyes. "Beaches."

Jane nodded.

"I noticed you were hitting all the hot spots."

"I've been trying."

"Have you been to St. Remy?" he asked.

"Tomorrow."

"Oh, you'll love it! Arles has changed a lot since 1888. The yellow house isn't even there anymore. Nazis! But in St. Remy, the asylum has been preserved. To walk in Van Gogh's footsteps, to stand in the place where he painted *Starry Night*—it always gets me."

Jane was sure it would. Just being out of the chalet was thrilling enough. In two months at Chalet von Tessen, she had made just one trip to Geneva, a quick run to get the equipment she needed for her office. The contractors in Burgen made weekly excursions, finding any excuse to rejoin what they called "the outside world." She had thought the expression peculiar, but now that she was in Arles, she understood what they meant. She felt like Rip Van Winkle, shaking off a long sleep and wandering out into another world.

She and Alan stood in front of a sign that had been placed where Van Gogh had once placed his easel. She compared the café scene with the painting on the sign. The effect was delightful.

He watched her. "You like that one?"

"It's one of my favorites."

"Mine too. 'Here you have a night picture without any black in it.'"

Jane frowned. "What's that?"

"Vincent. In a letter. He described the sky as 'spangled with stars.'"

His voice cracked with emotion, and he fell silent.

"Good word, 'spangled,'" said Jane.

Alan cleared his throat. "*Beschimmeld* in the original Dutch. Have you read the letters?"

"No. Just *Lust for Life*."

Jane had re-read the Irving Stone novelization of Van Gogh immediately after discovering the love letters.

Alan wrinkled up his nose. "You should read the letters. You can, of course, read Penguin, but I recommend Bulfinch."

"What's that?"

"Penguin is abridged. Bulfinch is complete. Three hardbound volumes."

"Three volumes!" she exclaimed. "How many letters did he write?"

"Nine hundred and three surviving. Most were to his brother, Theo, but he wrote to other artists and family members, too. That's where 'spangled' comes from. A letter to his sister, Willemien. September 14, 1888. Number six hundred and seventy-eight in the catalog."

Jane smiled. So here was a real Goghpie.

"Alan, I was about to sit down to dinner. Would you like to join me?"

Alan was a banker, a weekend sailor, a father, an amateur painter... and a Goghpie. He had traveled the world to see original Van Gogh paintings wherever they were on display—Amsterdam, of course, where the two largest collections existed, plus Paris, New York, Switzerland, and Russia. He believed the Tokyo *Sunflowers* was a forgery, but he went to Japan anyway, "just in case," he said, grinning.

"There's no substitute for standing before the actual painting," he said.

Alan told her how he had walked in "Van Gogh's Footsteps," a walking route across four countries that re-created the journey of the painter's life as it moved from The Netherlands, through England, Belgium, and various locations in France.

"Of course, I was younger then and in better shape," he said, clapping his belly.

Recently, he returned from a trip to the U.S., where he visited art museums in eight cities.

At Yale University, he saw *Café Terrace at Night* for the first time. His voice dropped to a whisper as he spoke of the experience.

They ate slowly, and the conversation was easy.

"I have something to confess," said Jane. "I have trouble with Van Gogh. He's known for his use of color, but I'm color-blind."

Alan frowned. "Really?"

"I had an accident when I was a teenager."

Alan put down his fork and pulled out his phone. He dropped a black-and-white filter over *Café Terrace at Night* and then turned his phone to show her the image.

"This is what you see?"

"Yes."

He stared at the image. "Wow."

"What?"

"I can't tell you how many times I've wished I could go back in time and see these paintings for the first time. That first punch, you know? Now, here it is! Thank you, Jane Ward!"

He continued to look at the phone.

"What do you see?" Jane asked.

"I see a dozen technical problems beautifully solved—perspective, composition, movement, mood. Bravo! But that's not enough for him, is it? What does he do? He risks the whole enterprise by blotching the sky with those enormous, swirling stars. Without those stars, what is the painting? Just another pretty scene of a café at night, and there are about a billion of them. How did he think to do that? *Did* he think to do that?"

"Did he?"

Alan smiled. "Are you asking me?"

"I am."

He set down the phone.

"Okay," he began, and she sensed it was not the first time he had visited this question. "There's an idea out there that Van Gogh worked by gut instinct. He experienced the world in this unique and intense way, and he was able to translate it into these paintings."

Alan scrunched up his face. "To some extent, I suppose that's true. It's certainly romantic in a made-for-TV-movie kind of way. But I don't buy it. Vincent Van Gogh was extremely well-educated in art. His uncle was the most successful art dealer in The Netherlands."

"Uncle Cent."

"That's right. He even bought some of Vincent's early paintings to help him get started. So much for the legend that he only sold one painting in his lifetime. Ha! Did you know Vincent's cousin was married to Anton Mauve?"

"He gave him art lessons, I think."

"He did, for as long as the two could get along—three whole weeks."

Jane laughed.

Alan shook his head. "Vincent himself was an art dealer in London for six years. And of course, there was his brother. Not only was Theo an art dealer in Paris, but he was also the patron saint of the Impressionists, arranging exhibitions and selling their work out of a back room at Goupil's. He practically discovered Gauguin. Thanks to Theo, Vincent was on a first-name basis with most of the Impressionist painters of that time. So the idea that Vincent was some folk artist who picked up a brush one day and discovered he had a knack for painting is ridiculous."

Alan paused, overcome with emotion from a thought he hadn't yet expressed. "He was, first of all, just a man searching for his place in the world. People forget that. He had that Dutch work ethic but no direction. Honestly, I don't think he particularly cared to be a painter. If the ministry hadn't rejected him, he'd have lived happily as the worst chaplain in The Netherlands. That would have been his happy ending, I think. A wife and a little church with a tolerant flock. He might have lived longer, too."

Alan looked down at his empty plate.

"But then we would never have met," said Jane.

The waiter came to clear away their plates. That broke the spell. Alan blew his nose into a paper napkin.

"I'm sorry," he said, grinning sheepishly.

"For what?"

"Going on like that. In my family, Vincent Van Gogh is 'the V word.' As in, 'Never say the V word around Dad.' At parties, my wife can silence me from across the room by making a 'V' sign like Mr. Spock—and it's not because she wants me to 'live long and prosper.'"

They laughed.

A lull fell over their conversation. Jane saw her opening. "You mentioned his nine hundred letters—"

"That's just what we have. There are also two hundred and ninety lost letters."

"How do they know that?"

"Indirect evidence, mentions in other letters… like that."

"Where are the letters kept? The originals, I mean."

"Most are in the Van Gogh Museum in Amsterdam. Fourteen are in private hands and are unavailable for scholarly study. Tossers!"

"What about digital scans?"

"Of course. They're online, on the website. Vincent used to draw pictures in his letters, so they're worth a look."

"So I can just go to the website and download them?" Jane asked in disbelief.

"They're in French and Dutch, so I can't read them. But yes."

"High resolution?"

"Yes. The museum uses crowd-sourcing for scholarship."

Jane thought aloud. "Hypothetically, Alan, what if someone found one of these 'lost letters'?"

"My god. It would be seismic. But they'd better have their ducks in a row. We Goghpies may seem like a harmless lot, but try to pull one over on us, and we'll eat you for lunch."

"I'll keep that in mind."

"Excuse me?"

"Nothing. What about finding a lost painting?"

"Oh, they find a new one every so often. When Vincent died, most of his paintings were with his brother, but plenty of others were scattered across four countries. He was infamous for using them to settle bar tabs and hotel bills. Years later, one of his paintings was found being used as a wall for a chicken coop."

Jane's eye went to the poster of *Café Terrace at Night*. "You never answered my question about the spangled stars. Did he know what he was doing?"

Alan chuckled. "I didn't, did I?" He shrugged. "In the end, I think Vincent Van Gogh did what every artist does—he creates something that amuses himself and then hopes others feel the same. And I think those spangled stars amused him very much. Of course, there's the other theory."

"What's that?"

"That he really did see a sky of spangled stars."

"Let's hope not, for his sake," said Jane.

"Amen to that."

They finished dinner and stood up to go their separate ways—Jane to her hotel room, Alan back to his family in Marseilles.

"So, you're off to St. Remy tomorrow?" Alan asked.

"First thing."

"It's a beach day for me," Alan said with a heavy sigh. "God, I hate the beach."

Monastery St. Paul de Mausole was a Roman homage to stone—stone walls, stone arches, stone fences, and stone walkways laid out in a sprawling four-acre campus at the edge of the village of St. Remy. It was here that Vincent Van Gogh came after he cut off his ear, and the good people of Arles signed a petition to have him banished as a public menace. He lived and painted in the asylum for a year before deciding to try once again to live in the outside world. Seventy-three days later, he fired a bullet into his stomach.

Jane checked into her hotel and then began the short walk to the asylum. Though autumn was scratching at the door back in Burgen, here in Provence, the air still carried the scent of summer. Birds sang and bees buzzed over the wildflowers. Jane marveled at the contrast.

She walked through the arch of the monastery and bought a ticket. Half of the asylum was now given over to a shrine to its most famous patient. The other half was a working hospital specializing in the use of art in the treatment of mental illness. It was, of course, off-limits to the public.

At precisely two o'clock, a polite art student welcomed Jane and seven other visitors to a tour. They began with Vincent's room—a surprisingly cozy space with curtains on the window, a bed, a chair, and a table. The window had bars. The room adjoined his private studio. Next, they were shown to the "hydrotherapy room" where, twice a week, Vincent was locked in a bathtub of cold water—the only "modern" treatment he received at the asylum.

Unfortunately, none of it was authentic. Vincent's actual room and studio were in the working portion of the hospital, as was the walled garden where he had completed dozens of paintings.

After the tour, the group was deposited in the gift shop, where they were invited to purchase the requisite *Starry Night* mugs, t-shirts, and fuzzy socks. Jane contemplated a Van Gogh bobblehead as she considered her next step.

The Lover showed Sophie kneeling before a lilac bush. The bush looked eerily similar to *Lilac Bush* by Van Gogh, which had been painted shortly after his arrival at the asylum. The painting hung in the State Hermitage Museum in St. Petersburg. It showed an enormous lilac bush in full bloom beside a curving dirt path and a brick wall. *The Lover* had been painted from a different angle and contained some new elements. Besides the bush and the curving walkway, there was a stone bench, a poplar tree, and, in the background, what looked like a bit of a fountain with crows perched on it.

Jane's idea was to do what she had done in Burgen—find the location where the easel had been placed to see if *The Lover* had been painted on the grounds of the asylum. The trouble was, those places were closed to the public.

Jane picked up the bobblehead and a copy of Van Gogh's collected letters—Penguin edition—and went to the register. While the cashier rang up the purchase, Jane asked, "Is there a way to see the walled garden?"

"Afraid not. It's closed to the public."

"What about a private tour? I'm trying to see all the locations where Van Gogh painted."

"Goghpie?"

Jane nodded.

The woman shot a look of pity at Jane and said, "Sorry. Not possible. I've worked here for two years, and I've never seen it. There's nothing to see, anyway, aside from the patients, of course."

Jane took her bag and walked back outside. She studied the long wall and metal gate that led into the hospital. How would she get inside?

—Climb the wall?

Not likely. It was ten feet high!

—Pose as a visitor?

Who would she say she was visiting? Did they even permit visitors?

—Pose as a prospective patient?

She was no Bob Woodward. And was she prepared to invent an illness? Was that even ethical? Besides, she doubted they would give her a tour. It was a hospital, after all, not a spa.

As she stood considering her predicament, a couple passed by carrying a watercolor painting. It showed a small fountain surrounded by irises.

A thought struck her.

"That's lovely," said Jane. "Where did you get it?"

"The gift shop," said the woman. "The patients in the hospital do them. Some of them are quite nice."

Jane went back to the gift shop and found a display of art done by the hospital patients. None showed exactly the view she was after, but it gave her an idea.

Maybe Jane didn't have to enter the facility to see the gardens. Maybe the gardens would come to her.

Dr. Pierre Dupont sat across his desk, reading Jane's business card. He frowned.

"The *Ontario Sun News*? Never heard of it," he growled.

"It's in New York."

He leaned back in his desk chair and eyed her over the top of his MacBook. They sat in a stone-walled room that had presumably once been a patient's quarters. Track lighting illuminated framed works of modern art.

"Nothing by Van Gogh?" Jane remarked.

He smiled indulgently. "We get plenty of that out there. How can I help you…" He checked the business card. "Mademoiselle Ward?"

"I'm doing a piece about art therapy. This seemed like a good place to start."

"It's our focus, yes."

Jane proceeded to ask a string of questions about art therapy, things she had learned from a quick review of their website and an article in *ArtNews*. She wrote his answers in a reporter's notepad.

"That's all for now," she said. "Thank you so much. You've been most helpful."

"You'll send me a copy when it's published," he said. "We like to keep track."

"Of course. I was wondering, could I see some examples of the art?"

"We have some for sale in the gift shop."

"Yes, I saw that. It's rather limited."

"Well, we do make a scan of every picture," he said thoughtfully. "For the patient files, you understand. Those are private, of course. But many of our patients sign releases. They're hoping to sell something in the gift shop. I don't see why you couldn't have a look at those. There must be thousands of them. How many do you want?"

"As many as you can give me."

He shrugged and picked up Jane's business card. "Is this email good?"

"Yes."

He turned to his computer and began to type. After a minute, Jane felt the phone in her pocket buzz.

"I sent you a link to a catalog," he said.

"How many are there?"

He looked at his screen and read. "Fourteen thousand, seven hundred and nine."

"That'll do," said Jane.

The next morning, Jane checked out of her room in St. Remy, loaded up her car, and headed north. Six hours later, she reached the outskirts of Paris. An hour after that, she pulled into a parking spot at *L'Institut Polytechnique de Paris* and turned off the engine.

On the campus, Jane had to ask directions three times to find the Computer Sciences building. From there, she followed signs to the fifth-floor lab labeled "Neural Network Research." A keypad and screen were mounted beside the door. Jane opened a bar code on her phone and held it to the screen. The door clicked. She pulled it open.

A man working behind a terminal on a roller cart looked up.

"Jane Ward!" he cried. "We meet at last!"

Dr. Ravi Das rose to greet her. Jane thought he looked like an Indian Carl Sagan from the seventies. His hair was long and youthful. He wore jeans and a t-shirt with a long quote that read "Love is that condition in which the happiness of another person is essential to your own."

He smiled broadly and put out his hand.

"Dr. Das," said Jane.

"Ravi, please."

Jane had been communicating with Ravi ever since Dr. Claire Harris had done the MRI back in New York.

Jane pointed at his shirt. "I grok it."

He laughed. "You've read *Stranger in a Strange Land*? I'm in love! Marry me, Jane Ward!"

Jane laughed. She had read the book twice—once before her injury, and once after. It was a completely different book the second time. The story of a human raised on Mars seeking acceptance on Earth struck a chord that left her trembling.

The computer lab was a cross between a space shuttle cockpit and a scene from *Alien*. It was packed with equipment racks, one after another, row upon row. The equipment had no covers so their guts were exposed. They glowed and pulsed and hummed all at the same time. Jane felt as though she were inside a living organism.

"What is all this?" Jane asked, forced to shout over the noise.

"Just some of our toys. Yours is a most interesting case, Jane. We've been running AI simulations on both sides of the Atlantic. But before we get to that, tell me what's going on. You said you have some news for me."

"That's right."

He pointed to a rolling desk chair, and she sat down.

"I've begun to see color in the real world," she said. "Just like you said would happen. Not just in paintings."

"Wow. Tell me about that."

The first time was three weeks earlier. She got out of bed and walked to the window to check the weather as she did each morning. In the distance, along one hillside, a patch of poppies shone red. She looked away and then back again to see if she was imagining it. But the color remained, like the girl in the red coat in *Schindler's List*. It was unnerving. Unlike with a painting, she could not simply close her laptop. This was *real*.

"Poppies?" said Ravi. "Like in Firth's paintings?"

"You think that's significant?"

"Go on."

The next time was August 1, Swiss National Day. Sydney wore a red-and-white ribbon to mark the occasion. Jane saw the red. She could barely take her eyes off it. She stalked Sydney through the house and halfway to the barn just to keep looking at that red ribbon.

Ravi nodded. "So also red. Go on."

As summer slipped toward autumn, these little moments of color appeared more frequently. A backpacker's *green* tent. A *blue* bluebird. A *yellow* haystack. Jane spent less time looking at The Carolines on her laptop and more time looking at the world itself. These bursts of color were precious gifts to be sought out and cherished. It made Jane newly alert to the world. She hadn't read a book in weeks. Out of habit, she would bring a book to the bench on the lawn, but then not open it. She marveled at the splendor of the Valley of the Giants. Even when she could find no color, she became attuned to things she would not have noticed before. The rippling of reflected clouds in a puddle as a breeze passed, the way the position of wildflowers on a hillside was not random at all but a mirror of the patterns of sunlight and shadow that preceded their appearance. One day, she had even dared to sit on the apple barrel beside the East Cliff. She spent a half-hour studying the scarring patterns in the boulders that lay at the bottom. Jane used her mind to raise the fallen boulders to their former positions, mere inches from where she sat. The vision was beautiful and violent at the same time. Jane felt she must be seeing the world the way an artist does: First as a whole and then in its constituent parts.

"Fucking awesome," said Ravi when she finished. "Just fucking awesome!"

But Jane would have given it all back for a working gyrus.

"So this is neuroplasticity?" Jane asked. "My gyrus is repairing itself?"

He shook his head. "Nope. Your gyrus is as dead as disco."

"So, I don't understand. How is this happening?"

"You're asking the wrong question, Jane. You should be asking, why are we meeting in a computer lab?"

"Okay. Why?"

"Because in a perfect world, I would just open you up and dissect your brain. But since that would also kill you, I thought I should look for another way."

"Thanks."

He nodded soberly. "So that leaves a digital simulation. Which means supercomputers and AI." He held out his arms grandly. "Welcome to *L'Institut Polytechnique's* AI laboratory. We have a reciprocal relationship with MIT."

Jane looked around at the open machines and exposed wires. "It's... impressive."

"Without data, it's just an expensive space heater. It needs data, lots of it, specifically high-resolution scans of The Carolines. So we contacted the Firth Gallery and, boy, were you right about those guys. What a bunch of fondue-eating, name-dropping, pretentious little shit-faced, lying assholes!"

"I couldn't have said it better myself."

"In the end, we got the scans, but Jesus, what the hell is their problem?"

"Good question."

"Anyway, I gave the AI the digital equivalent of your brain injury. Like you, it could only see in black and white. Then I let it look at the paintings, and your low-resolution image of *The Lover*." He stepped aside. "Have a look at what the AI is seeing."

She looked at his computer screen. It showed *Picnic with Poppies*—a portrait of Caroline in a field of poppies.

The image was in black and white, except for the red of the poppies.

"Red," said Jane.

"You could have knocked me over with a paper sock. By looking at *The Lover*, it figured out the poppies in Firth's painting were red."

"How?"

He shrugged. "That's the thing about AI, Jane. We don't know. We gave the AI a bunch of data and a goal—see color. The AI figured it out, same as your brain did. We're digging into the logs for clues. It appears the AI is finding markers in the black-and-white images that signal certain colors. It's a whole new way of seeing."

Jane must have looked confused, so Ravi went on. "You are using your amygdala to see, Jane. As a neurologist, I would have said that's impossible. The amygdala is as different from a gyrus as a hand is from a foot. But if a person loses their hands, they can learn to use their feet for certain tasks. That's the best way I can explain it. Your brain isn't healing itself. It has found a Plan B."

"So will I recover completely?"

"It's possible."

Jane asked, "But why only some paintings? Why only the painting by *Amant* or Francis Firth?"

Ravi frowned. "Any chance they were painted by the same person?"

"No."

"You're sure?"

"Positive. They lived decades apart."

He sighed. "It's a pity we don't have a high-resolution scan of *The Lover*. It was stolen, you say?"

Jane nodded.

"That painting holds the key. I don't think we can go much farther without it. Whatever your amygdala learned about seeing color by employing these particular markers, it learned during your childhood by looking at that painting. If you ever get it back, I hope you'll let me know. I'll add it to the simulations, and we might get some real answers."

"Unless I agree to be dissected."

"Unless that, of course," he said. "So Jane, first time in Paris?"

"That's right."

"Off to the Eiffel Tower, I suppose?"

"Musée d'Orsay. I've never seen an actual Van Gogh in person. I thought I'd have a look."

Ravi gaped at her. "Van Gogh? Jane, you're color-blind."

"Gee, Ravi, thanks for reminding me. Somehow, I keep forgetting."

Jane's Excellent Road Trip (as she had come to think of it) ended at four o'clock the next day when she arrived at Chalet von Tessen. She sat a moment behind the wheel, listening to the ticking of her cooling engine, and savoring the satisfaction of coming home to a place that wasn't technically home.

On the way to the kitchen door, she passed a Citroën sedan with rental plates parked at the front door. Who was the visitor?

She came through the kitchen door. Agatha was at the stove.

"That smells good," said Jane.

"You have a visitor," Agatha replied.

"What?"

"A man. In the parlor. He says you invited him." Agatha's disapproval was evident.

Jane set down her suitcase by the back staircase and went to the parlor. Beside the fireplace, in roughly the same place where *Portrait in Winter* had been painted, sat a burly, bearded man. He was chatting with Ursula. He stood up when Jane entered.

"Hi, Jane."

Jane noted the tattoo of an asterisk on his hand. Her jaw fell.

"Ted?"

Jane led Ted Banks through the house to the kitchen and out the side door. She walked quickly. She didn't want him stopping to comment on the library, the antler chandelier, the giant fireplace, the hand-carved banisters, or anything else that might capture his insatiable curiosity.

Outside, they passed the chicken coop. Sydney was in the cage playing with one of the chickens. She looked up as they passed. Feathers clung to her hair.

They walked across the lawn toward the cliff. Ted tried to speak to her, but she shushed him. She needed to think. The landscape poured down from the mountaintops in a spectacle of lush green fields and stands of blooming trees and wildflowers. Near the cliff, she stopped and turned.

"What are you doing here?"

"Are you kidding? Your email!"

"I didn't ask you to come *in person*. I signed an NDA! If this got out, they could sue—"

"I'm doing the book, Jane."

Jane recoiled. "What?"

He grinned. "You sure know how to write an email, I'll give you that. I showed it to my publisher, and she agreed to the book. Together with what happened last week at Sotheby's, the timing couldn't be better."

"What happened at Sotheby's?"

"You didn't hear? *Sunset on Lone Aspen* sold for ten million."

Jane gasped. The painting was one of Francis Firth's best Cubist landscapes, an homage to Picasso, his idol, that was worthy of the master himself. She had spent hours looking at it. An aspen tree stood alone in a pasture as the last rays of day illuminated its yellow autumn foliage. The peculiar Cubist rendering deconstructed the tree, making it a symbol for everything that is beautiful but which must someday wither. If Firth had stopped there, then the painting would have been a downer. But Firth went further. He gave the old tree one last moment of glory, letting it shine under the setting sun.

"It's out of control. The pressure on the Firths to change their selling pattern will be enormous. At first, two paintings per year seemed silly, then it looked brilliant because it was driving up the prices. But now? Investors are going to demand to know what's in the vault. How can you invest in something so valuable without knowing its scarcity? And..." He paused. "I've written to Gunther for permission to see the vault."

"Gunther? Why?"

"Why?" he exclaimed. "The contents of that vault just became one of the great mysteries of the art world. There may be an opportunity here."

"I suppose it wouldn't hurt book sales either."

"Which helps us both. I'm not saying they would be so careless as to let me glimpse *The Lover*, assuming it's in the vault, but they're going to have to do something, especially with the death of Otto. Everyone knows Tomas isn't up to taking over the empire."

Jane's head was spinning.

"Anyway, lots of work to do right here in Burgen. I need to establish that he lived here, not St. Séverine Parish as you seem to have discovered."

Seemed?

"That would prove Gunther's a liar. But why? I talked to the chaplain this morning—"

"Jacques Barbeau."

"That's the guy. He says there are loads of documents in the church's basement. Births, deaths, christenings, marriages... if the Firths were ever here, there will be a record of it."

Jane wondered why she hadn't thought of that.

"And if there isn't," he went on, "that means something, too. Then there's the old schoolhouse, probably worth checking that out. Could be some records there. And I'll need to revisit all the places you found where Francis Firth painted—not that I don't believe you, of course. Oh, and thanks to the pretty blonde at the front desk, I have arranged an interview in Geneva this weekend with the woman who is officially the oldest Burgener."

"Dorina Dubois."

"You know her?"

"Of her."

Jane shook her head in wonder. She had awakened a bloodhound.

"She's in a nursing home," Ted went on. "But apparently her mind's as sharp as ever. There could be something there." He paused. "But..."

"But what?"

He spotted the bench by the cliff.

"Can we sit?"

They walked to the bench and sat. Jane never tired of the view. A herd of sheep was grazing in one of the high pastures. Far below, a hawk screeched and circled.

"I am blown away by your work here," said Ted. "Your instincts... How you put Burgen together with Francis Firth, I can't imagine. How did you, by the way? It wasn't in your notes."

She shrugged.

"Okay, don't tell me then. But I have to ask on behalf of my publisher, and also for myself: Why don't you just write the book yourself? Why give it to me? You know my work. It's a bit of art connoisseurship, a dash of biography, and, hopefully, it all adds up to a good read. I've never done anything like this. This is big. And..."

"What?"

"Of the two of us, we both know you are the better writer."

Jane smiled. "Thanks for that, Ted. But I'm working on a different book."

He nodded with approval. "About time. What is it about—if I may ask?"

"No," she said. "You may not."

The next morning, Jane arrived in the portrait room to find a middle-aged woman in an artist's smock. She introduced herself as Greta Reisen, an art restorer from Berlin. Klaus had hired her to restore the family portraits to their original condition before Sophie had been painted over. Jane watched in wonder as the poor woman worked with a Q-tip and a jeweler's magnifier to remove the outer layer of paint atom by atom. An entire trash can was already filled with swabs. The room reeked of acetone.

Greta held out a face mask.

"Here," she said without removing her eyes from her work. "You're going to need this."

Jane put it on and opened her laptop. She navigated to the website of the Van Gogh Museum. She found a link to the high-resolution scans of his letters. She chose one from 1888 when he would have been in Arles, and then downloaded it. She printed it out and then held Van Gogh's letter beside a love letter from the basement.

The handwriting was identical. Even the type of charcoal pencil was a match. Jane collapsed into her chair.

In the corner, Greta went on scraping.

Now what?

Alan Silver's voice entered her head.

We Goghpies may seem like a harmless lot, but try to pull one over on us, and we'll eat you for lunch.

Jane texted her brother, Davis, at the FBI.

—*Hey, bro. Do you have a handwriting analysis guy?*

He replied with a laughing emoji.

—I'm going to email you something. Can you have your guys take a look at it?

Jane used the scanner to digitize a love letter and then emailed it along with the Van Gogh letter she had downloaded. She didn't tell Davis who the author might be. She wasn't ready, not by a mile.

With that task done, Jane opened the link from Dr. Pierre Dupont. She began paging through the artwork made by his patients. Jane quickly realized it was going to be more difficult than she had hoped. The art was strange and rooted in internal demons. Some of it was violent; most of it was childish. Bugs and clouds. Blood and skeletons. Stick figures. Jane clicked on. She clicked so fast that the images became a blur.

After several hours and two cups of coffee, something went by that made her stop. She clicked back and gaped at a sketch made with draftsman-like skill. It showed the walled garden from the same angle as *The Lover*.

Jane positioned the two images side by side on her screen. The lilac bush was gone. It was now a berm with an herb garden and a statue of a turtle. But to the right of the berm, everything lined up with *The Lover*. The curve of the path swept in exactly the same arc. The bench with the chipped leg was there. The leg was still chipped! The stone she had seen in the background, it turned out, wasn't a fountain as she had supposed. It was a bit of the asylum wall. On it, seven crows were perched.

Jane studied the image in wonder. It was as though she had stepped inside *The Lover*.

There was no doubt now. *Amant* had painted Sophie in the walled garden of St. Paul du Mausole. But did that necessarily mean—

A voice broke through her thoughts.

"Jane?"

She turned. Max stood in the doorway, looking grim.

"I need you to come to the den."

"Sure. Let me just finish up—"

"You need to come now."

Jane took off her mask and closed the laptop. He led her to the den, where Klaus and Ursula were seated with a forty-year-old woman in an expensive business suit. She looked familiar.

"Jane, this is my sister, Hannah."

Jane gulped. This was the woman from the business magazine cover—"Don't Cross The Viper."

"Nice to meet you," said Jane.

"Please sit, Jane," said Klaus. "Hannah has come up this morning from Geneva to talk to you."

"If this is about Ted Banks, I can explain."

Hannah handed Jane a piece of paper.

"What's this?"

"It's a petition," Hannah said. "You're being sued."

"Oh, come on!" said Max. "That isn't necessary."

Jane looked around. Max was sticking up for her, but Ursula looked cold, and Klaus regarded her warily.

"You are aware that you signed an NDA?" Hannah asked.

Jane nodded.

"And do you deny involving the author and journalist, Ted Banks, currently residing in Paris, but originally from Ontario Hills, New York, in the confidential work you are doing here at the chalet?"

"No," said Jane.

Ursula glared at her.

"I'm sure you had a good reason, Jane," Klaus said gently. "Can you tell us why?"

Max broke in. "She doesn't have to. I already know why. She told me everything weeks ago."

Max repeated Jane's story as she had told him the day of their picnic. Jane resisted jumping in. It seemed better if it came from him.

When he finished, Jane said, "There's more."

"Go on," said Hannah.

Jane left nothing out—not because it might have been the only way out of her predicament (it probably was), but because they needed to know. The Firths were unpredictable, dangerous even, and Jane had threatened them. How would they react when the truth began to come out? Hannah also needed to know about the love letters Jane had found. If Jane was right about them, then the letters could be worth millions.

So she told them everything. She started with her road trip and ended with her discoveries that morning in the handwriting samples and the sketch of the walled garden in the asylum in St. Remy. She even told them about Dr. Ravi Das and Jane's partial recovery of her sight since coming to the valley.

When she finished, everyone sat silently absorbing the new information. Ursula looked shaken at the reminder of the death of Agatha's predecessor on the East Cliff. Klaus and Max were looking at her in wonder. Hannah appeared unfazed.

"I'm sorry," said Jane. "I didn't tell you this because at first I wasn't sure, and I suppose I was trying to protect you. But I'm sorry. I should—"

"Oh, fuck that!" said Hannah.

Hannah took the petition from Jane's lap and tore it down the middle.

"About these letters you found. We're going to need to get them removed from this fire trap of a house. I'll take them with me when I head back to Geneva in a few minutes. The family safe in Geneva will do for now, but I'll get them moved to a safe deposit box at the bank. As for the Firths, we've crossed paths a few times over the years. Otto was tolerable, but I wouldn't give a half-franc for the rest of them. Nothing would make me happier than to see them exposed as frauds. I hope your friend, Ted, can send them straight to the jail. Geneva will be better for it."

"He needs a place to stay in Burgen," said Jane. "He's been commuting from Geneva every day."

They turned to Max.

"The hotel is booked up," he said. "I suppose I could put him on a cot in the contractor's barracks."

"I'm sure that'll do," said Jane.

"Whatever," said Hannah. "Now, about this painting of yours. You say the Firths asked you to bring it to Geneva and then the grandson, uh..."

"Tomas."

"... stole it when you wouldn't relinquish possession."

"That's right."

"And then Otto killed himself. Hm. How fascinating."

Hannah's eyes were glowing. It occurred to Jane that she was enjoying herself.

"Something about that painting must have *really* spooked them," said Hannah.

"It's the woman," said Jane. "There's a connection between Sophie and Caroline Firth."

"What connection?"

"I'm working on it."

Hannah stood. "Don't let me hold you up. Now, Jane, lead me to these letters."

Twenty-One

Sophie

Sophie snatched Vincent's letter from Peyron and clutched it to her breast. Ten days had passed since his last letter. She hadn't seen him since the morning in the garden when he had asked her if she had forgotten about Missouri. All Peyron would say was that Vincent had a breakdown in Arles. He was locked in his room for his safety. Sophie knew this meant he might even be in a straitjacket. She longed to go to him. She could comfort him as no one could. It was infuriating that she was not allowed to see him!

While Peyron droned on with his usual banal questions about her health, Sophie cradled Vincent's unopened letter like a living creature. What did it say? She answered Peyron in monosyllables, eager to hurry him along, but it seemed like hours passed before he left.

The door closed behind him, and Sophie tore open the letter.

My Dearest Soph,

I'm sorry I haven't written. I hope you haven't been too worried. I have been ill. Arles was tough. I am better now.

I need to see you. It is important. Meet me in the tower. Tonight. Two o'clock.

Oh, how the day crawled! Sophie checked the garden's sundial constantly. At one point, she was convinced the sun was moving *backward*! Would evening *ever* come?

When it did, she lay in bed listening to the sounds of the asylum at night. These sounds marked the hour, and she counted their passing like the tolling of a clock. First, the wails of The Corporal with his nightmare; then the heavy boots of Sister Melanie patrolling the north corridor; then the *hoot-hoot* of a pair of tawny owls who had taken up residence in an old olive tree outside the south wall. Tawny owls mated for life. Sophie couldn't wait to tell Vincent about it. Next came the *clank* of Sister Melanie's keys as she turned the locks of the doors of the patients under confinement.

And then, at last, came the sound she had been waiting for. A distant train whistle. It was the night train to Paris, passing Gare de St. Remy. That event fixed the exact time to the official railroad schedule—1:47 a.m.

Sister Melanie used the whistle, too, Sophie knew. It signaled her last bed check before going to the chapel to meet Sister Yuliya, a fellow orderly who was also her lover.

Sophie rose from her bed and fixed her hair in the mirror. She stuck her head out the door and looked both ways to make sure the hall was clear. She tiptoed barefoot along the corridor to the tower steps and climbed. The stairs hugged the four walls, turning squarely at each corner of the Romanesque turret. She reached the final flight. Shadows danced on the walls from a flickering candle in the tower above her.

Vincent was already there!

He sat on the floor illuminated by a single candle in front of him. His cheeks and eyes were sunken. She knew the look. She had seen it in the mirror often enough.

He rose when he saw her and smiled warmly.

She rushed to him and fell against his chest. His arms came around her and squeezed. She buried her face.

"Oh, Vincent."

"Sophie."

"I've been so worried."

"I know. I'm sorry."

They kissed, and then he motioned to the floor. "Will you join me?"

She wiped away her tears and looked down. That's when she saw the picnic. Atop a bedsheet were two strawberry garden salads on bark plates. Beside the plates lay two spoons (forks were unseen in the asylum) and metal mugs filled with juice. In the center of it all, a bouquet of sunflowers.

"Happy anniversary, Sophie," he said.

"We have an anniversary?"

"Our first kiss. It was on this date, May 23."

"Really?"

The thought delighted her. She looked down at the salads. "Is that…"

He nodded. "I picked the strawberries in Arles from the same spot you picked yours last year. There were so many of them, Sophie! You would not have believed it!"

"I wish I could have seen."

"I wished that, too. The whole time I was there. I wished you were with me."

"And the plates?"

"The same ones. We left them under the tree, remember? They were still there! I just needed to clean them up a bit."

She stared down at the picnic in wonder.

"Well?" he said. "Aren't you going to sit?"

They sat beside each other and began to eat their salads.

"Are you okay, Vincent?" she asked. "Peyron said you had a breakdown."

"Arles was too much," he said. "I thought I was ready."

"I'm sorry."

"But our anniversary gave me the motivation to get better," he said.

"And you're well now?"

He shrugged. "So how is the salad?"

"I'm sorry," she said. "It's delicious! It's all so wonderful!"

"Well, it's your recipe."

Sophie thought she would like to have heard more about Arles, but she kept her questions to herself. Vincent looked fragile, and she was aware that she had a way of overwhelming people.

When they finished eating, Vincent reached into the dark corner and pulled out a small box about the size and shape of a book. It was tied with a bow. He handed it to her.

"What's this?"

"Your anniversary gift."

She looked at it in wonder. The last time someone had given her a wrapped gift was her twelfth birthday. Oma had given her a book. It had been tied with a pink ribbon. Vincent's ribbon was yellow.

"Aren't you going to open it?"

She untied the bow slowly, savoring the experience of not knowing what lay inside. Vincent grinned at her. She set aside the bow and lifted off the cover. She looked in.

A map of the United States lay atop a stack of papers. The state of Missouri was outlined in yellow paint.

"What's this?"

"Keep looking."

She lifted out the map. Underneath was a collection of tickets, fares, timetables, and contact information with names and addresses.

"I don't understand."

"I'm giving you Missouri, Sophie. That's your gift. Missouri won't fit in an envelope, so you'll just have to go yourself. That box will get you to Missouri."

"Vincent—"

"No. Listen. One week from today, at this exact time, two o'clock in the morning, a coachman will be waiting for you outside the asylum gate. It's all arranged. He'll take you to Marseilles. You have a first-class ticket aboard *La Virginie*. It's a steamer. It sails for New York a week later. You have a private cabin on the top deck. You'll be able to live aboard until it sets sail. All meals are included. No one will look for you there, so you can use the week in Marseilles to buy some clothes. I imagine the dress code will be formal in the first-class dining room. When you get to New York, the port authorities will want to see documents. You won't have any, of course, but if you can prove sufficient means, the Americans will issue you a tourist visa. Just show them the purse."

"Purse?"

He pointed at the box. "Look."

She moved aside the papers. At the bottom of the box lay a velvet purse cinched with a string. She pulled it open. It was filled with the gold ingots, rubies, and emeralds from her necklace.

"How?"

He was beaming at her. "I found it, Soph."

Vincent's hunt for the purse had begun the day after Sophie's departure. That first pitiful attempt taught him that it would take more than luck to find it. He turned to his drawing skills. He sketched the river as accurately as he could, then marked an "X" where he estimated he had lost the purse. He drew grid lines around the "X" using landmarks on each bank—trees, rocks, a bridge, several buildings, and a crumbling wooden dock—as guides to fix a position on the water.

Vincent threw himself into the search with his usual fervor. It was easy to find the time because oil paints require drying periods. So each afternoon he would excuse himself from Paul Gauguin, who was living with him in the yellow house at the time, to go for a swim. Gauguin called these daily swims "Vincent's lunacy." Vincent knew that by then Gauguin had formed an opinion of Vincent's mental state that had nothing to do with swimming. Vincent never told him—or anyone—the true reason behind his trips to the river.

On the day Vincent found the purse, a bitter wind blew over the Rhône. It was six months earlier, and just a few weeks before the breakdown that caused Vincent to cut off his ear. The wind tossed up whitecaps that broke as waves on the shore at Vincent's feet.

Vincent stripped off his clothes and dove in.

The water was oddly warm. The Rhône was fed by snow melt in the Alps. Since snow does not melt in winter, the relative temperature between air and water was inverted. Vincent swam slowly at first to orient himself. He blinked against the reflected sunlight from the rippling surface. He located his landmarks on the bank and then swam toward his search point.

The river varied in depth from twelve feet to twenty feet within his search grid. That gave Vincent, who was a strong swimmer, thirty seconds of bottom time per dive. There was no visibility in the murky water, so he worked blind, keeping his eyes shut as he searched with his hands.

"Except for this day," Vincent told Sophie. "Because of the catfish."

"Catfish?" Sophie asked in wonder at the entry of this new character to the story.

Vincent smiled. He knew she would like this part. "That's right. I dove down, and I was feeling along the bottom as usual—"

"What did it feel like?"

"Oh, the softest mud you could imagine. So silty you can stick your hand up to your wrist before you realize you're on the bottom."

"It sounds disgusting."

"I got used to it."

"And that's when you met the catfish?"

He nodded. "I was about to surface when something brushed against my arm. As a reflex, I opened my eyes. To my amazement, I could see."

"Because the sun was so bright that day?"

"Exactly. And also because the current is weaker in winter, it kicks up less silt. So I saw this giant catfish pecking at something on the bottom. What was it? I swam closer and realized it was the tip of the drawstring on the purse. It was waving in the current. It must have looked like a worm to the catfish. I was nearly out of breath, so I grabbed the string and rose."

"Oh, Vincent!"

"When I got to shore and saw that everything was still in the purse, I screamed so loud my brother could have heard me in Paris!"

Sophie squeezed his hand.

"So... now you can go to Missouri, don't you see? Madame Giroux used her contact in Marseilles to arrange the whole trip. She didn't even ask for a fee. You might have been right that I misjudged her. Sophie, everything you need is in that box. When you get to New York, you'll have to see a man about selling your gemstones. Theo vouches for him. He's an honest fellow. And don't worry, my brother has no idea why I wanted his contact. From New York, there's a train called the *Southwestern Limited* that leaves for St. Louis once a week. It's called the Big Four Route. It stops in Cleveland, Chicago, and Cincinnati. Don't you just love Indian names? It's all written down. You'll be there by summer."

Sophie closed the box and set it on the floor. "Can we go together?"

"No."

"Why not?"

"I can't."

"You won't."

"I can't, Soph. I'm too sick. I feel it. Even now, at this moment, I feel it. I need to be in this place. It's helping me. Peyron is helping me."

"Then I'll wait."

"No. You have to go now. The sooner, the better. You were right about these walls. If you stay any longer, the spark will go out of you, my love, and then you'll never leave. I couldn't bear for that to happen."

Tears filled her eyes. "How can I go alone?"

Vincent took her hand. "Do you love me?"

She nodded.

"Then see the Mississippi for *both* of us. Write about it to me. Write about all your adventures. Write every day."

"Like you did for me," she said, seizing on the notion.

"That's right. This time, it will be *you* bringing life outside the walls to *me*. Don't you see?"

She nodded. "But... what if I have another episode?"

He nodded solemnly. "I don't know. I only know that you are dying here."

She swallowed hard and looked at her hands. "But... won't you miss me, Vincent?"

Vincent's lip began to tremble. Tears filled his eyes.

"I'm broken," he said. "I'm so sorry I can't take you to Missouri. I'm sorry I can't negotiate with that man in New York for your gems. I'm sorry I won't see buffalo or Indians or swim in the Mississippi with you."

Sophie sniffled. "I'm afraid, Vincent."

They fell into each other's arms. Sophie wrung Vincent's shirt in her fingers and looked past the tower rail to the distant hills. Her heart raced.

Could she do this? How could she do this?

She blew out the candle. In the darkness, they kissed and held each other until the distant creak of Sister Melanie opening the chapel door signaled it was time to go.

Twenty-Two

Vincent

Patient 166 scraped the mold off his bread and dunked it into a bowl of greasy porridge. He put it in his mouth, gagged, and then forced himself to swallow.

Breakfast.

He ate for the strength it promised; he had a busy day ahead. He used the last bit of the bread to mop up the bowl and then set it by the door.

Feeling revived, he looked across his little room with its cement walls, peeling plaster, and bars on the window. His eye fell on a pile of crates stacked haphazardly beneath the window. Among the books, art supplies, sketchbooks, and prints lay a brown paper tube. He slipped off the top and pulled out a rolled canvas. He spread it out on the floor in front of him.

It was his unfinished nude portrait of Sophie, the one he had begun the night of the storm when she had nearly drowned. It was water-stained with a scrape across one side. The paint was smeared around the edges. But the lines of Sophie survived. She was kneeling and gazing back over her shoulder with a playful expression. Her spark.

Her lips moved.

"How's this?" she asked.

He froze now, as he had then. My god. The pose was perfect. *She* was perfect.

A lump swelled in his throat, and suddenly he was aware of every molecule of Sophie, not just the usual things a man notices—lips, hips, breasts. It was her imperfections that spoke loudest. Her unruly hair was too long and always found its way into her face no matter how many ribbons she used. Her ears were too big. Her left eye opened a fraction of an inch less than her right eye. These were things a woman was sensitive about. But he could feel only joy at them. They were the building blocks of Sophie.

Patient 166 ironed the canvas flat with his hand. He pried nails from an old picture and then stretched the canvas onto a new frame. He got out his palette knife and began scraping away the parts of the painting that were unusable. When he finished, he stepped back.

Slowly, the canvas filled with a finished painting. He stared in awe. He saw the golden wheat of Sophie's hair when the light danced over it, the almond-blossom rose of her lips, the ruddy earth of her tanned skin, the wisteria of her femininity, and the swirling, cobalt-violet clouds of the storm in the window. These were the things he had seen on his first attempt at the portrait. But now something else was layered atop these superficial matters of craft. He saw Sophie's wicked humor. Her mystery. Her sadness. Her terrifying honesty. Her illness. Her joy for life.

My god, here was the portrait he had been unable to see a year ago!

He picked up his palette and went to work. His brush followed his emotions like never before, and he could feel how good he had become. What a long road it had been. He could never have imagined how hard it would be when he first picked up a brush a decade earlier.

Time stood still. It seemed to him that he was merely copying a painting that already existed. He floated.

Sister Beatrice arrived with his lunch tray. Beside the bread and cheese lay a letter from Sophie.

He removed his lunch from the tray and set his dirty breakfast bowl in its place.

"What about the letter?" asked the nun.

He couldn't bring himself to speak; the words withered in his throat. After a few seconds, the busy nun shrugged and left with the unopened letter still on the tray.

Poor Sophie, he thought. She won't understand this.

Sick with the knowledge of what he had just done to Sophie, he turned his attention to her portrait. He frowned.

What the hell?

For Patient 166, creation was always an act of destruction. To create a work of art was to destroy the perfection he had glimpsed the instant *before* he picked up his brush; to destroy the very thing that made him want to paint it in the first place. In his hand, a paintbrush was a sledgehammer, and every line he drew served only to tear down the edifice of his vision until, in the end, almost nothing of the original idea remained. And he supposed that's how it was for all artists, though some more than others. But for Patient 166, the failure was particularly hard to take. He had come to his calling late in life. He couldn't draw. His feverish temperament was unsuited to the work. Yet he had no other way to be useful to the world, which was all he had ever wanted. To justify his existence. So this *had* to be it. To paint. And so he labored, and he failed, again and again, until one day he found himself in a dingy room with peeling plaster and bars in the window.

But not this time. This time, his perfect vision was intact. It looked back at him from the canvas exactly as he had seen it in his mind.

How?

Then something *really* peculiar happened. The room seemed to swell outward and then collapse upon itself the way water does when it is disrupted by a pebble. For an instant, he imagined he saw a wave traveling outward from his painting. It caused the room to shimmer like heat on a summer road.

He blinked, and the vision was gone. All was as before. Cracked plaster. Bars. And a painting on his easel that, for once, wasn't half bad. Outside, a bird was singing; he didn't know what kind. Sophie would have known.

Still trembling from the vision, he walked to the window. Was this the start of another breakdown? He tried to look out through the bars onto the monastery lawn, but all he saw were the bars.

The awful thing about being crazy is that crazy ideas can look reasonable. Like cutting off your ear to keep Paul Gauguin from leaving Arles. The act made no sense. Vincent understood why it perplexed everyone. How would cutting off his ear accomplish anything other than to drive away his friend, the very opposite of what he intended? But at the time he did it, the choice had seemed sensible. When one's mind can bend reason into such absurd contortions, how can it be trusted? How does a person function when he can't trust his own thoughts? This is what he meant when he told Sophie he was broken.

He needed Dr. Peyron to fix whatever was happening to him. He was terrified of another breakdown and what he might do. He couldn't bear to think about what his death would do to Sophie. She was already fragile enough. Fear had transformed him into a war-weary soldier who interpreted every cracking twig as musket fire. It was exhausting.

The only thing that stood between him and madness, besides Dr. Peyron, was work. The act of painting kept the strange thoughts at bay. It was like swimming—stop, and you drown. The need to work imposed a focus on the ingenuity of God's creation. Standing before a blank canvas, Vincent was nine years old again, collecting birds' nests in the forests in southern Holland. He was twenty years old, working in London as a successful art dealer, smitten by a beautiful woman with delicate hands. He was twenty-seven, studying for the clergy, and awestruck by the privilege of bringing God's word to his fellow man. He was a missionary in Belgium living among the poorest of the poor, a modern-day Christ on the Via Dolorosa.

His mother had called these passions "Vincent's enthusiasms." Father dismissed them as "fevers." Art was Vincent's latest fever—until he met Sophie.

So, when Sister Beatrice had brought his lunch with a letter from Sophie, he had sent it back unread.

Vincent returned to his painting. He thought about his beloved Japanese Ukiyo-e prints and how they used symbolic backgrounds with literary and historical references.

Why not have some fun?

He picked up his brush. Working quickly, he added a background that contained the coliseum at Arles, the winding Rhône, crows on a wall, citril finches, and a magnificent lilac bush. And when that was done, he signed it—*Amant*.

That last bit made him smile. Private joke.

Patient 166 considered his work. He tended to work so quickly, he often couldn't remember having made the artistic decisions he had made—looking at one of his paintings was, at the end of a day, like looking at someone else's work. In the dim light of the cell, with his paint still wet and vulnerable, the painting seemed to dance like sunlight on a rippling river, and he saw something he had never seen before in any work of art. The painting didn't just express his love; it *contained* it.

In a flash of insight, Patient 166 understood that he was not the artist. Not this time. God, nature, or whatever divine spirit could take credit for having created Sophie was the true artist. Patient 166 was merely a craftsman trying to capture the echo of an echo of something perfect.

At least he was trying.

Twenty-Three

Sophie

Sophie stared down at the letter Sister Beatrice had delivered. She expected it to be a reply from Vincent. Instead, it was her own letter being returned.

"He said he didn't want it," said the nun.

"I don't understand. Is he sick?"

Sister Beatrice paused. Sophie knew that the nun equated mental illness with demonic possession. To her, no one at St. Paul de Mausole was sick—they were possessed. Vincent's missing ear was a mark of the Devil. He needed to be treated with exorcism and prayer, not science and compassion. Presumably, Sophie would benefit from the same treatment.

"He looked fine to me," said Sister Beatrice. "He was painting."

Sophie was aghast. "Painting? What was he painting?"

The nun sniffed and left. She walked down the long corridor with her chin high, and her hands clasped piously before her.

Sophie sat down immediately and dashed off another letter to Vincent. She demanded an explanation for refusing to read her letter. She insisted they meet face-to-face. This time, she gave the letter directly to Peyron.

The next morning, he returned it to her unopened.

"I'm sorry, Sophie. Perhaps he'll change his mind."

The following morning during her walk, Sophie spotted Vincent across the courtyard in the restricted males-only area. The irises were blooming, and he had set up his easel in front of them. She tried to catch his eye, but he was engrossed in his work. She longed to see the painting, to debate its merits with him. He behaved as though she were not there, but she knew that wasn't true. Why was he doing this to her?

She went to her room and retrieved the box from its hiding place in a sack beneath her bed. She had not looked at it since the night Vincent gave it to her. She carried it into the garden and sat down on the grass beneath her favorite lilac bush. The sun shone brightly, and the smell of lilac filled her nose. Butterflies flitted over the blossoms.

She removed the lid and sifted through the contents. She rolled the gemstones in her hand and watched them sparkle. She marveled at the weight of the gold ingots. She studied the rail schedule from New York and traced the route across the continent. Cleveland. Chicago. Cincinnati. Such alien-sounding names.

How could she go? She knew no one in America. Her English was poor. She had no identification papers, not even a name she could use officially. She could have a mental breakdown anytime. What was Vincent thinking?

She heard a familiar *caw-caw* and lifted her head toward the sound. It was the crows! They were lined up on the wall as they did every year. How she looked forward to this event! Her lips started to turn up into a smile. Then she heard Vincent's voice.

I thought you hated walls.

Her smile faded before it could take shape. Vincent's reproach came to her so vividly that she half-expected to see him beside her. Her gaze fell upon the wall beneath the birds. She looked at it in a way she never had before. It was ten feet high and made of heavy stone and mortar. It stretched in a long line from the main dormitory to a corner. There it turned and then disappeared behind bushes. A plaster parapet topped the wall. Sophie had always admired it as a lovely, Romanesque adornment. But now she saw that it was there to complicate any attempt to climb over it.

Tears filled her eyes. Damn you, Vincent!

He had ruined the arrival of the crows. How could she ever feel joy at birdsong while she lived in a cage?

Sophie waited until the last hour of the final night to pack her things. The only sound in the asylum was Sister Melanie's boots as the young nun made her rounds. Sophie didn't plan to take much anyway—a few clothes and toiletry items, a stack of letters from Vincent, and the gift box with her tickets, travel plans, and money. She stuffed it all into the sack and then sat down on the edge of her bed to wait.

This departure was different from her other escapes. Those were merely cries for help. Deep down, she'd known she'd be back. This time, she was leaving for good.

The hinges of the chapel creaked as Sister Melanie stole into the sanctuary and the waiting arms of her lover. A moment later, the night train blew its whistle at Gare de St. Remy.

It was time.

A quarter moon cut long shadows across the empty courtyard. Sophie was like a shadow herself as she crept to a corner of the back wall where she knew of gaps in the mortar that created footholds she could use to climb over. She swung her sack atop the wall and climbed.

She dropped to the ground. She reached for the sack, but someone else's hand got there first. She whirled around to see who was there.

It was Vincent.

Twenty-Four

Vincent

Sophie threw herself into his arms and peppered his face with kisses.
"You're here! You came!"

"Shh."

He grinned and let her go on kissing him frantically for several seconds before pulling her into a passionate kiss. She went limp, and he could feel her tears on his face.

"How did you get out of your room?" she asked.

He smiled at her guiltily.

"You mean... You stayed away on purpose?"

Her eyes glowed wide in the moonlight.

"I'm sorry."

Vincent knew meeting her here was a risk. Her nerve had carried her this far. What if it failed her now?

He ran his hand down the side of her face and said in wonder, "God, you're beautiful."

Her eyes glistened with tears.

"There has to be another way," she said.

"This is the way."

"What will happen to you? I'm worried about you, Vincent."

"You are all that matters, Soph. You are my life. As long as you live, I live. I want nothing. I expect nothing. It is enough for me to know that once upon a time, you saw the Mississippi. And that I helped make that happen."

"It's just a river."

"It's more than that. It's our happy ending. Maybe it's all we'll get."

She threw herself into his arms. "It's not enough."

"You have to prove them wrong, Sophie, the whole lot of them. These terrible nuns, who think we're less than human because we are sick. Your parents, who erased you from their portraits and took away your name. Your father, who pays blood money to Peyron to keep you locked away like a character in an Alexander Dumas novel. I can't do it. But you can."

"You really think so?"

"I know it. You are my star in the night sky, Sophie, swirling and powerful. You will prove them wrong."

"How?"

"By having a life."

He held her until the sound of hooves on the road caused them to turn.

"The coach," said Vincent. "It's time to go."

Sophie grabbed Vincent and pulled him to the ground on top of her.

"Take me, Vincent. Take me now!"

A fierce instinct swept over Vincent. His hands dove under her skirt, and in an instant, he was inside of her. The glorious sensation exploded in his head.

"Oh, my god," he groaned.

Beneath him, Sophie moaned and pulled him tighter. His weight pinned her. She wrapped her legs around him to draw him deeper.

In the moonlit darkness by the stone wall, Vincent and Sophie rocked like a single organism. Their mouths hovered an inch apart, inhaling each other's warm breath between kisses. Vincent's pleasure rose like water against a dam until he groaned and released himself. Sophie pulled him tighter and kept on holding him as the spasms faded.

Afterward, they stood up and straightened their clothes. Vincent was shocked by the suddenness of it. Sophie was quiet, too.

Vincent reached into the darkness and pulled out a brown paper tube. He put it in her hand.

"What's this?" she asked.

"A going-away present."

"But I have nothing for you!"

He grinned. "I think I just got mine."

She burst out laughing. They both laughed and giggled like young lovers until, from the road, they heard the coach come to a stop.

Vincent took a deep breath. "Now, you have everything? The tickets, the timetables..."

"... the maps, and the purse with the money, yes," said Sophie. "It's all in the sack."

"Good," he said. "Go now. Quick, before he leaves without you."

She nodded and took a step backward, not wanting to turn away.

Vincent grinned. "Say 'hi' to Mark Twain for me."

She chuckled, and he knew she was just trying to appear brave.

"I'll get him to sign a book," she said.

Vincent watched her walk down the path and then disappear behind the hill that hid this stretch of road from the asylum. It's the reason he chose this spot for the meeting. He heard a man's voice, followed by Sophie's, then the sound of hooves on the road moving away.

Vincent climbed back over the wall and then raced across the courtyard to the tower. He took the steps two at a time. He scampered onto the platform. He went to the rail and, panting, looked south.

Sophie's carriage moved silently over the rolling land on the ever-narrowing road. Overhead, a few bright stars seemed to dance and swirl in the purple sky, as if conscious of the carriage and its precious cargo. Vincent wrung his hands on the rail and watched until the coach crested a ridge and disappeared.

He sat down and put his back against the wall. He thought about their lovemaking and grinned into the darkness. He sat like that for a long time, savoring a feeling of perfect happiness. After a while, he fell asleep. He dreamed of Sophie von Tessen swimming in the Mississippi.

Twenty-Five

Sophie

Sophie stood in her stateroom aboard *La Virginie* looking at Vincent's canvas. It wasn't just a painting. It was a love letter.

In the painting, Sophie knelt in the nude as she had the night of the storm in the yellow house.

"How's this?" she had asked, and then watched him become paralyzed. She worried he would be unable to hold a brush!

In the portrait, she looked directly at Vincent with eyes that teased playfully. Her long neck, her teardrop breasts, the gentle curve of her waist, and the spread of her female buttocks were painted so sensually she blushed. In those powerful brush strokes, Vincent showed her how beautiful she was in his eyes.

The composition was an homage to their affair. He had placed her not in the yellow house, but in front of the lilac bush she loved. Behind her head was the coliseum in Arles, where he had been painting on the day they met. On the grass before her was a picnic with strawberry salads on plates made of tree bark. An orange lay beside the salads, recalling the game they played with the children in the farmhouse. His color choices—greens, pinks, yellows, and purples—arose from the palette of Provence in May, the month in which they had their affair. In a tree branch, two citril finches were perched. On the wall of St. Paul's stood a line of crows.

A lump formed in her throat. My god, Vincent was fearless! It was so intimate! As usual, he had gone all in. There were no half-measures with him. His courage inspired her. If Vincent could expose himself to ridicule by laying bare his deepest feelings in a painting, then surely she could find the courage to make the journey that would redeem the happy ending to their fairy tale. Perhaps that's what Vincent intended when he gave her the painting.

Through her tears, she read his signature and smiled. Even that recalled their affair. He used the silly alias she had flippantly given him after their first kiss.

Amant.

Part 3

Wheatfield with Crows

Twenty-Six

Jacques

The stranger was already fishing when Reverend Jacques Barbeau arrived at the spot. As far as he knew, no one else knew about it. There was a horseshoe-shaped rock just below the surface and a secret pool where trout fed. A ferocious storm the previous day had swept away most of the usual places. Jacques rose early and walked thirty minutes to arrive at his secret spot. He felt a moment of disorientation to find an intruder fishing there.

Jacques stood in his waders and a wide-brimmed hat, pondering what to do next. The man had his back to him and wore a camouflage bandana over his face. That's when he noticed that the stranger was casting a spotted spoon. He smiled with relief. The interloper wouldn't last long.

Jacques set down his gear basket a few feet away and began the ritual of preparing his equipment. He loved this moment when the morning stretched before him with promise and mystery.

"*Bonjour!*" Jacques called out to the man.

"*Bonjour.*"

"*Ça mord?*" Jacques asked. "Are they biting?"

"Not for me," the man replied. His French had a German accent. Probably from Zurich.

Jacques began to tie on a fly. He had been having good luck lately with a lightning bug fly and a single yellow thread.

"Maybe you can say a little prayer for me, Reverend?"

Jacques stopped tying. "Do we know each other?"

"I was at your service Sunday. 'This is the day that the Lord has made; let us rejoice and be glad in it.' Very nice."

"Thank you."

"Not hard on a day like this."

Jacques looked around. It was indeed idyllic. The storm had blown through, leaving behind piercing blue skies and the air heavy with honeysuckle. It smelled a bit like church, Jacques thought. And in a way, this place was his church. From where he stood, the only evidence of civilization was Chalet von Tessen, a thousand feet above where he stood. He and the stranger were completely alone in one of the most beautiful places on Earth.

"You are so right."

"So, Reverend, how about that prayer?"

"It's not a prayer you need, my friend," Jacques said. "You need the right lure."

"Huh?"

"You'll never catch anything on that spoon."

"Really? The guy at the store in Geneva said the trout would love it."

"In Lac Léman, maybe. Not here. Here, they're eating insects. They've never seen a minnow in their life. That spoon is probably going to give them nightmares."

"I guess I should have mentioned that to him, huh? Damn. So I'm just out of luck?"

"I'm afraid so. A spinner might work for you."

"A spinner?"

"I have some at the house. Stop by later this afternoon, and I'll set you up."

"That's very kind."

"You're from Zurich?"

"How'd you know?"

"The accent. And, I have to say, you seem familiar. Do I know you?"

"From church, maybe."

"Right."

The man cast his spoon in the direction of Jacques's horseshoe rock.

Jacques cringed. The fool wouldn't catch anything, but he might succeed in scaring away his fish.

The man began to reel the lure slowly through the water. "So you do a lot of fishing here, Reverend?"

"You could say that."

"Don't you mean 'guilty as sin'?" the man said with a chuckle.

The remark didn't strike Jacques as funny, but he smiled anyway.

"I'm blessed."

"You are, indeed. That's a gorgeous rod."

"Thank you."

"Oyster bamboo?"

Jacques raised his eyebrows. "You have a good eye."

"What's a rod like that go for, if you don't mind me asking?"

"They're not cheap."

"I know it's a rude question, but I'm just curious. Maybe I'll pick one up in Geneva."

"It's a lot."

"Five thousand euros?"

Jacques finished tying on his fly. "Could be."

"And that reel—what's that? An Abel lightweight? That's got to be, what, another fifteen hundred?"

Jacques frowned. He wished he could see the stranger's face, but he kept his back turned and the bandana pulled up.

"And those waders... very nice. That basket. That hat. Jesus Christ, Reverend, you must be walking around with ten thousand euros in fishing gear!"

"What's your point?"

"I'm just saying that's a lot of high-end gear for someone getting by on a church salary. I mean, that gear's got to be a couple months' salary."

Jacques scowled. "That is a very peculiar thing to say, sir."

"You don't think I have a right to know? I paid for it."

"Excuse me?"

"Francis Firth," said the stranger.

Jacques froze.

"Francis Firth," the man said again. "I believe that name means something to you, does it not?"

"No."

"Liar."

The man pulled down his bandana. It was Tomas Firth.

"So you see, I am not lying when I say I paid for everything you've got here, right down to that ridiculous fucking hat."

Tomas reeled his lure out of the water and cast it again. It landed near Jacques's rock with a *plunk*.

"You shouldn't be here," said Jacques. "This is not how we do things."

"How we do things doesn't work for me. We're going to do things my way from now on."

"What do you want? I got you the two paintings you requested. And it wasn't easy. I had to sit through a little girl's tea party to get it."

"I want the rest. All of them. I want to know where you're getting them from. I want to know how many are left."

"Those were the last two."

Tomas sighed deeply and put down his fishing pole. "The last two?"

"That's right."

"Swear to God? Swear to God, Reverend, and I'll believe you."

"I swear to God," said Jacques.

"Okay," said Tomas jovially. "You know, I think you're right about this lure. I'm not going to catch any fish this way. You can have your spot to yourself."

"Okay."

Jacques knelt to get his basket. He stood up and looked directly down the barrel of a gun.

"You won't be doing any fishing today, Reverend," said Tomas. "Here, or anywhere. Now sit down. We are going to have a little talk."

Jacques sat down on the grass beside his rod and basket, staring numbly at Tomas and his gun.

"This system you got worked out with my grandfather—it doesn't work anymore. We need to make some changes."

Jacques stared up at him.

"It's okay, Reverend. We have all day. No one will bother us. We're all alone out here."

"What do you want to know?" asked Jacques. His voice sounded far away.

"Let's start at the beginning. It was your father, I believe, who found the first painting."

Jacques nodded.

"I want to hear about that. And take your time, Reverend." Tomas grinned. "This is the day that the Lord hath made. Let us rejoice in it!"

The story did not take long. Jacques repeated it as it had been told to him by his father forty years ago when he took over as summer chaplain in Burgen. Jacques spoke, not to Tomas, but to the stone giants who had watched over the valley since before the first people arrived. Jacques would accept them as his jury. He would abide by their decision.

He finished, and Tomas chuckled.

"So you've been stealing from the church all this time. *Tsk-tsk*, Reverend. A man of the cloth."

Jacques glared at him.

"So, tell me about the paintings," said Tomas, his eyes brimming with lust. "How many more are there?"

"I told you. They're gone. I gave you the last two—"

Jacques never saw the blow. His cheek exploded in pain, and he was thrown onto his side on the grass. He gasped through the stalks and tried to fathom what was happening. Violence was an alien concept to him. He had no experience with it. Even as a boy, he had never been in a fight. He lay there listening to the birds. He could hear the water of the brook rushing past the bank beside him. In the distance, a hawk screeched.

"Sit up!" Tomas barked.

He sat up again and looked at Tomas. Jacques could feel his eye swelling.

"You want to try that answer again?" Tomas said.

"I don't understand. Why are you doing this?"

"I ask the questions here. Where are the rest of the paintings?"

With sudden clarity, Jacques understood that Tomas was to be his executioner. The stone giants, in their wisdom, had rendered judgment. Nothing Jacques could say or do would change the fact that he was going to die today.

Jacques closed his hand around the handle of his basket and hurled it at the pistol in Tomas's hand. Tomas used his elbow to fend off the basket, and for an instant, the barrel was pointed skyward. Jacques used that opportunity to dive headfirst into the stream.

"Forgive me, Father!" he cried out.

But he had miscalculated. In his haste, Jacques forgot about the horseshoe rock just below the surface.

His head hit the rock. His chin buckled to an extreme angle, and a sickening sensation of something snapping echoed through him. In the last moment before his death, Reverend Jacques Barbeau felt no pain, for his neck was broken and his spinal cord was severed. As a veil of darkness fell over him, he felt only sadness, regret, and, finally, gratitude that of all places to die, he would die here, in his favorite place on Earth.

Twenty-Seven

Jane

News of Jacques's death blew through the Valley of the Giants with the fury of the storm that had preceded it.

Jacques had failed to show up for his regular Bible study meeting that night. Parishioners went to his cottage and found it empty. He was last seen heading upstream with his fishing gear. The gear was not in his cottage.

The next morning, a search party was mounted. Geneva police arrived to help. But by then, the search was over. Max had already found him. He knew right where to look.

Jacques's body was tangled up in a tree that had fallen across the stream near one of his favorite fishing holes. It made sense that he had come there. The storm had flushed the fish from the upper holes. He needed to go downstream. It was the logic of a fisherman.

It would be weeks before the coroner made an official report, but the first responders believed his neck was broken. The circumstances appeared as simple as they were horrifying. The river was swollen from rain, and the banks were slippery. He had likely been trying to wade into the rushing water, slipped, and hit his head on the horseshoe rock. It was a tragic fly-fishing accident.

Klaus suggested that Jacques be buried in Burgen's cemetery, and the locals agreed. It was an honor Jacques would not have anticipated. Jacques had once told Jane that, even after forty years, he was not considered a true Burgener. Jane thought how pleased he would be to find himself resting among his flock near his beloved river.

She had been surprised to learn about the existence of the cemetery. It was located downstream from Burgen on a slope in the pastures, not far from the generator Max had installed to power the hotel. There was a fence and a gate and a view of the winding river. The reverend would have loved it. At a future date, Jane planned to return—cemeteries could be great storytellers for people who knew how to listen.

Klaus seemed to come to life. His valley needed him, and he discovered a vitality Jane had not yet seen. He arranged the funeral, picked the plot, and found a guest pastor to preside. He and Ursula spent one whole day tracking down and inviting former Burgeners to pay their respects at the funeral. The cottages in Burgen were fully booked, so Ursula and Agatha made up rooms in the guest wing for the visitors. Max rented a transport van with a wheelchair lift to bring them all to and from the valley.

The day of the funeral broke overcast with light fog. Nearly fifty people stood on the hillside. Shepherds that Jane had never seen before came down from the mountains to pay their respects. For the first time, Jane saw many of the women paired with their husbands. It was the first time she had seen Bernadette and Rochelle more than ten feet apart. Many of Max's building contractors showed up, too.

"The only residents of Burgen who will not mourn our beloved reverend are the fish in the river," Klaus observed in his eulogy. It was met with smiles and nods from the mourners. "Today, the stone giants weep."

He stepped aside, and the guest pastor knelt to scoop up a clod of earth.

"We therefore commit this body to the ground, earth to earth, ashes to ashes, dust to dust; in sure and certain hope of the resurrection to eternal life."

One by one, the mourners took turns casting dirt into the grave.

Afterward, Jane walked alone up the slope to the church for the reception. She thought back to that "glorious day" when Jacques prayed to his fish, and she felt the weight of Burgen's loss. She looked past the valley to the high peaks.

The stone giants had never seemed more alive. The tall one behind Chalet von Tessen seemed to lean toward her, as though preparing to speak—

The bells of the church began to toll. The reception was starting.

About fifty people were scattered in the small chapel. Klaus and Hannah were talking with a frail-looking woman in a wheelchair. Hannah's resemblance to Sophie took Jane's breath away. Jane's face-blindness had never extended to Sophie's face, and since Hannah looked so like Sophie, oddly, Jane could recognize Hannah without the usual visual cues. At the buffet, Ursula and Agatha were supervising Sydney's intake of sweets. Max stood a few feet away talking to a woman.

Collette.

Jane looked away. Her gaze fell on Ted Banks. He stood in the corner between Rochelle and Bernadette, who were no doubt regaling him with stories of the ways of Old Burgen. He looked up and their eyes met. She smiled at his predicament. She could not have found a better partner. If there was something in Burgen to be found, then Ted Banks would find it.

At the altar, a boom box played organ hymns. Beside it, on an easel, someone had placed a collage of photographs of Jacques. Jane went forward to investigate.

She floated down the aisle, carried by her memories of Jacques. She had not known him long, but he left an impression she would carry forever—cheery, committed, and filled with an infectious gratitude he expressed through fly-fishing. Jane continued along the aisle. She passed people seated in little groups in the pews. They ate finger food and talked softly. A few greeted Jane with an implied invitation to join them, but they didn't wear name tags, so Jane was shy about approaching. She just nodded and floated on.

She stopped at the collage of Jacques. The pictures seemed to be of another person. Like all Burgeners, Jane knew Jacques Barbeau as the jolly reverend in hip waders. But here was his other life, the one outside Burgen. Jacques on a beach in the Mediterranean. Jacques in a tux at the opera. Jacques atop the Eiffel Tower. Jacques at a castle in Scotland. In many of the pictures, he was accompanied by a tall man with a goatee.

Jane became aware of a man beside her. She turned. It was the same man—same goatee, only grayer. In a flash of insight, Jane understood that this man had been Jacques's longtime partner—he had been gay.

The man introduced himself as Pavel. He was from Poland.

"Did you make this?" Jane asked.

He nodded.

They stood side by side, looking at it for a while. Several photographs showed Jacques with large groups of children. She asked Pavel about it.

"That's SOS Children."

"What's that?"

"It's like the American Make-a-Wish Foundation, only it focuses on making dreams come true for orphans. Jacques put most of his free time into it—and all of his money. He was quite wealthy from his investments. SOS Children was his life's work. And his legacy."

"How wonderful."

She examined the photos of his travels.

"He sure got around," she said.

"He was not a natural traveler," said Pavel. "He never traveled anywhere that wasn't having some important exhibition."

"Exhibition? You mean, like, an art exhibition?"

He nodded. "Jacques had a great interest in painting. He read all the journals, went to the museums, and kept up on the big sales. He chased art all over the world."

Jane felt the hairs rise on the back of her neck. "Did he like any artist in particular?"

"As a matter of fact, he did. Every year we had to go to his latest exhibition. His name was Francis Firth. He's dead now..."

Jane's mind was spinning. She tried to think. That day by the river, she had asked him if the name Firth meant anything to him, and he'd replied that it didn't.

Why did he lie?

She squinted at a black-and-white photograph of two men and a ten-year-old boy standing in front of the church in Burgen. The man in the middle wore the collar of a Protestant pastor.

"Who's this?" she asked.

"That's Jacques with his father. It's the only picture of him I could find. It was in a box of his things. Funny he never hung it. I don't know who the other man is."

Jane knew. It was Eduard von Tessen.

She thought about the von Tessen curse and what she had read in the news clippings.

... a dark figure, all in black, moving through the English Garden at night.

Jane excused herself and raced to Ted. She pulled him away from Bernadette and Rosaline.

"Thank you," he said. "I thought I was going to have to—"

"Jacques was mixed up with the Firth Gallery," Jane blurted.

Ted recoiled. "What? How?"

She told him what she had learned. The money. The travels. The interest in Francis Firth.

She told him what Jacques had told her by the river on their first meeting.

They set up a trust for the pastor, but not for the upkeep. Do you have any idea what a new roof costs?

"In Gunther's book," she said, "you remember what he says about the first sale?"

"It was to raise money for the church. It needed a new roof."

"What if that part were true? Only it wasn't St. Séverine Parish's church, it was Burgen's? And it wasn't Gunther who made the sale, it was the church's pastor? Jacques's father! We've been going round and round about the same question: Why would Gunther lie about the location? What difference does it make whether Francis Firth painted in Burgen or St. Séverine? This could explain it."

"How?"

"He's protecting the vault. It's not in Geneva. The paintings are here in Burgen!"

Ted's jaw dropped. "Oh, my god."

The words were still hanging in the air when a voice came from behind them. "You must be Jane."

She turned. It was Collette.

Ted excused himself and slipped away, shooting her a "to-be-continued" look.

Jane nodded.

Collette put out her hand.

"I'm Collette. Sydney's mom."

Jane shook her hand, but she was already looking past her, plotting her escape. She and Ted needed to figure out their next steps...

Collette was going on. "I was hoping I'd get a chance to talk to you. We missed each other the last time."

Max would need to be told. Klaus and Ursula, too. They might have something to add...

"Such a tragic thing," said Collette. "He was such a dear man."

"Yes, he was."

"Max called me as soon as it happened. He thought I should be here. Something like this... Sydney will have a *lot* of questions."

Why was the woman still talking? Jane was being as rude as she dared, looking past her shoulder, answering in monosyllables.

"Sydney talks about you all the time," said Collette.

"Does she?"

"She has decided you are a suitable match for her father."

"What?" Jane exclaimed. "God, no. It's nothing like that."

"Relax. I know my daughter. She's fanciful. It's good to be fanciful at seven. Don't you think?"

Now, Jane allowed herself to look at Sydney's mom. Pauli, in one of his monologues, had once repeated Burgener gossip that portrayed Collette as a gold-digging man-trap. But that's not at all what Jane saw before her. Collette was taller than Jane, and every bit as beautiful as she appeared in the picture in the portrait room, wearing her big hat the same shade as the sea. But if Jane expected an aloof, high-maintenance sort of woman, she was mistaken. Collette wore a simple black dress for the funeral, and no jewelry aside from a wedding ring and minimal makeup. Her hair was styled in a short, practical bob. She looked more like a mom than a beauty queen.

"Did you know Jacques?" asked Collette.

"A little. He was teaching me to fly-fish."

"He must have liked you."

"The feeling was mutual."

From across the room, Sydney's giggle reached them. They both turned in that direction. Max was holding a cupcake for his daughter.

"Look at that man, will you," said Collette. "He wasn't supposed to be in the picture, you know? But how could I get in the way of that, even if I wanted to?"

"I don't understand. I thought you were married?"

"Heavens no. Max is just a friend. Who told you we were married?"

Jane's mind raced to find a suitable reply, but then Collette shook her head. "Damn Burgen gossip. Max couldn't be bothered to correct it, of course. He just doesn't care. He can be so infuriating."

"So how..."

"Is he the father? He's the sperm donor."

"Oh."

"Max and I have known each other since we were children. We practically grew up together. Our families' business affairs are all tangled up. We lived in the same neighborhood, vacationed at the same resorts, moored our yachts at the same marinas, shared jets... you know, rich people stuff. Like a secret society. I guess because Max and I were the same age and both 'oopses,' we sort of bonded."

She smiled faintly. "Sure, there was a time when we were more than friends, but that was just youthful experimentation. After graduation, we went our separate ways. I went to med school; he turned his back on the family business and went into construction. When I decided I wanted to have a baby, I was still single. I'm married now, but I wasn't then. So I asked for his help. Max was just supposed to be the sperm donor, you know. The end of his contribution. His sister wrote up a lengthy contract to that effect before we ever shared a bed."

"Oh, I see," said Jane. She cleared her throat. "I mean, of course she did. That's why she's 'The Viper,' right?" She gave a little forced laugh.

"But then along came Sydney," said Collette. "For Max, it was love at first sight. He comes to Paris four times a year. Did you know that? Positively showers her with gifts and attention. And that pony! That was dirty!" She laughed. "How am I supposed to compete with that?"

"But you're married now?" said Jane.

Collette held up her finger to show her wedding ring.

"As of last year, to a professional sailboat captain." She rolled her eyes. "I know. Completely impractical. He's traveling all the time, but god he's beautiful at the helm! If you ask Sydney, she'll tell you she has two dads—a water dad, and a mountain dad. She assumes it's perfectly normal."

They watched Sydney take a bite of a cupcake. A dot of frosting clung to her nose. Max wiped it away and licked his finger.

"Do you have children?" Collette asked.

"God, no!"

Collette frowned. "You don't like children?"

Jane could think of no way to explain her reaction, so she found herself telling Collette about her accident. When Jane finished, Collette stared at her the way the doctors always did. Like a specimen. Collette asked a few questions about the initial injuries, medications, therapies, and so on—questions that only a doctor would know to ask.

"Does Max know?"

Jane nodded.

Collette studied her for a long time. Jane squirmed; she was aware that her medical history didn't explain her reaction to the notion of having children. But Collette didn't press the issue. Her face softened, and it occurred to Jane that Collette might have gleaned more from the conversation than she had intended to reveal.

"Tell me, Jane, do you know how to ride?" Collette asked.

"Ride? Like horses, you mean?"

"Yes."

"No."

"Would you like to learn?"

After the reception, there was an informal reunion of Burgeners at Elsa's Kitchen. While several dozen munched on *zopf* and Swiss rolls, Jane listened to stories of a time when Burgen had a general store, a school, a post office, and a physician it shared with a neighboring village. Jane recalled Jacques's warning about the tenuous state of Burgen's existence.

This place is one defeat from death.

He had been thinking about Klaus, of course. But that night at Elsa's Kitchen, Klaus was very much alive, and Burgen had never felt more vibrant. Jane caught Klaus's face in the crowd. He stood with Ursula, the two of them laughing at the shared memories of the reunited Burgeners. His eyes glowed in the light of the lanterns strung across the café.

Who would fill their shoes? Who could possibly?

Not one for subtlety, Hannah halted the reminiscences to ask point-blank if anyone had ever heard of a goat-herder named Francis Firth. She didn't even bother to offer context. It was jarring.

The gathering murmured among themselves in a way that was generally negative. Then Rochelle's husband spoke up.

"Firth, ya say? The only Firths I know'd was a clan of damn Welschers over in St. Séverine Parish."

Jane leaned to Max and whispered, "Welschers?"

"German-speakers."

"He t'weren't no goat-herder, though," Rochelle's husband went on. "He was a Catholic. Worked for the Church."

Jane found Ted's face in the crowd. They exchanged grins. Ted had a new lead.

The gathering broke up, leaving Max with the herculean task of transporting a dozen elderly men and women up the mountain to the chalet. Jane helped by pushing people in wheelchairs as far as the parking lot. From there, Max carried them to the shuttle.

When they got to the chalet, the same operation was carried out in reverse until, after an hour, everyone was settled in their rooms.

Jane retreated to her room and was about to open a book when a knock came at her door. She got up to see. It was Max.

"I think you should come downstairs," he said mysteriously. "There's someone you're going to want to meet."

He led her into the den, where Klaus and Ursula sat beside a woman in a wheelchair. This was the same frail woman Jane had seen at the funeral.

"Jane, may I present Dorina Dubois," said Klaus.

"Oh, my god!" said Jane. She rushed to kneel before her. "Madame Dubois, I am so happy to finally meet you."

She stared blankly at Jane.

"This is my friend," said Klaus. "The one I was telling you about."

"The swift with the gold feather," said Dorina in a surprisingly strong voice.

Jane smiled. "That's me."

Klaus said, "Dorina was tired from the funeral, so I brought her back here."

"So you weren't at Elsa's Kitchen?" asked Jane.

"Whose kitchen?"

Dorina's eyes darted around, and she appeared disoriented. Jane put her hand on Dorina's hand to reassure her.

"I saw you at the reception," said Jane.

"At the church."

"Yes."

"I was married there, you know," she said.

"Really?"

"To my Jasper."

Dorina looked past Jane to the fireplace with a toothless smile so sweet it was as though the ceremony were taking place before her eyes.

"Reverend Barbeau performed the ceremony, I suppose," said Jane.

She nodded. "The dad, not the boy."

"Rolf?"

"That's right. Rolf. I was just happy it was not the other one."

"You mean Jacques?"

"No. The first chaplain. He was such an unpleasant man. Mama used to say, 'Who'd ya expect them to send? John Calvin? Of *course* they're going to give us the worst pastor in all of Switzerland.'" She chuckled at her attempt to imitate her mother. "I never believed the rumors about him and the pious woman, though."

"Pious woman?"

She nodded. "That woman went round Burgen every Wednesday eve and Sunday morn making sure the pews were full in the church, as if the bells ringing weren't enough. I must have been five years old at the time. I thought she was damn annoying."

Dorina's eyes wandered. Jane felt Dorina's train of thought leave the tracks.

Jane massaged the back of her hand and said gently, "Madame Dubois? You were talking about the pious woman."

"Who?"

"The woman who made sure people went to church."

"Why was I talking about her?"

"You were telling me that you never believed the rumors."

"No, of course not."

Jane and Max exchanged glances. Max shrugged.

Jane decided to try to coax her. "You mean the rumor that she was Eduard von Tessen's mistress?"

"Oh, everyone knew *that*. I was five, and even I knew it. Didn't think much of it. Good for her, you know, living up there in the big house like a princess."

"What rumors, then?"

"That she was carrying on with the chaplain. I heard about that years later, after he was gone. But I never believed that part. Why would anyone carry on with the likes of *him*? He was such an unpleasant man. And such a terrible orator! My god, how he put us all to sleep! And those paintings of his were awful things."

Jane's heart stopped.

"Paintings? He was a painter?"

"Not in Mama's opinion, he wasn't. 'He weren't fit to paint fences,' she used to say. That didn't stop him, though. Mama said he wandered the valley far and wide lugging his painting equipment. Eduard's mistress liked to walk with him after the church service, and I suppose that's what started the rumors."

"What was his name, do you recall?"

Dorina didn't answer. She was staring at the fireplace.

"What happened to him? What happened to the pious woman?"

"I was married in Burgen's church, you know," Dorina said.

"Yes."

"To my Jasper."

Jane stood up.

"I don't think you'll get anything more out of her," said Max.

"With your permission, I'd like to try something," said Jane.

Jane pushed Dorina down the back hallway to the portrait room while the others followed. Greta was working away as usual. She had already finished one portrait and was now working on the next. As usual, the room reeked of acetone.

Jane pushed Dorina to the first of the restored family portraits. It was the one with the spaniel and the mysterious floating drapery. Gone was the burgundy curtain, and in its place was a thirteen-year-old Sophie with her parents and younger siblings. The reason for the spaniel's happiness was now apparent. While the other members of her family posed stiffly, Sophie amused herself by rubbing the dog's belly. It was looking directly into her eyes. A ridiculously elaborate bow was tied on one side of Sophie's head, and her impatience with the portrait was palpable.

Jane could almost hear Old Rudy's voice in her head—*Fine, play with the damn dog if you must, but you will* sit*!*

Sophie's hair was cut short unlike the twins', who had long ringlets. She wore a high-necked lacy dress with a pearl pin on one shoulder. Her skin shone like polished marble. It was the same Sophie as in *The Lover*. Jane did not doubt it. Sophie von Tessen was Sophie du Burgen.

Jane pushed Dorina's wheelchair directly in front of the portrait. Dorina frowned at the painting. "What's this?"

"The von Tessens. That's Rudolph with Eduard—"

"I know who they are. What's *she* doing there?"

"Who?"

"Her."

She pointed at Sophie.

"You know her?"

"Of course I do. That's the pious woman."

That night, Jane couldn't sleep. After hours of tossing and turning, she slipped on a robe and went downstairs to the portrait room. For once, Greta wasn't there, though the odor of her work was very much present.

She walked to the restored portrait. Thanks to Dorina Dubois, Jane could now draw a line from Rudolph von Tessen III to a young Sophie von Tessen to Sophie du Burgen of *The Lover* to the "pious woman" living out her days in the Valley of the Giants.

Where had it gone wrong for Sophie? The sight of the preoccupied little girl in the portrait brought home the tragedy of her fate. Here, Sophie was so full of promise. She would become the beautiful siren of Granny Jo's painting. She would ride horses with Shawnee in Missouri and handle dock lines for riverboats on the Mississippi. How did she end her days alone in a drafty, windowless room, taking the name of her village as her last name and allowing the world to believe she was her brother's mistress? It was outrageous! Jane trembled with anger over the injustice of it.

For the first time since coming to Burgen, she doubted her enterprise. What if she discovered something terrible had happened to Sophie? Maybe it would be better to walk away now and let her live forever in her imagination as the playful ingénue of *The Lover*.

But Jane knew she had come too far to turn back.

Oh, my dear Sophie. What happened to you?

Twenty-Eight

Sophie

Aboard **La Virginie**
June 6, 1889

The Mediterranean Sea was calm that morning, and the motion of the ship was like a rocking cradle. Sophie walked easily along the upper deck to the dining room. She found her seat assignment from the chart on the wall and took her place.

This was Sophie's first formal dinner aboard *La Virginie*, and it would be her first test of life outside the confines of walls.

For the occasion, she chose her favorite gown of those she had purchased from the shop in Marseilles. It was light blue with a frilly bustle that would make sitting down a challenge. There was a contraption that allowed her to move the bustle aside when seated. She practiced until she could do it naturally. She tied a matching blue ribbon around her neck and a bow in her hair. The saleswoman had assured her that she would be expected to wear gloves that went nearly to her elbow, so Sophie put them on, too. Beneath it all, she was expected to wear a corset. She had bought one and even put it on, setting the clips to the loosest position. But then she changed her mind and took it off again. She dumped it in a corner. She vowed never to wear one again.

She was seated at the captain's table. *La Virginie* was not the most luxurious ship making the crossing to America. It was small, with only a dozen first-class berths and three six-person tables in the dining room. They would all get to know each other very well by the end of the journey, Sophie surmised. The crossing would take ten days, give or take.

At Sophie's table were two married couples in their thirties, a boyish physician traveling alone, plus Captain François Lambert, a white-bearded icon of a sailor who had fought with the French Navy during the Crimean War. The physician's name was Dr. Jean Duplantier. He had recently graduated from medical school and was traveling to San Francisco to open a medical practice. He seemed a serious sort and content to listen.

Soon after introductions, the first course arrived: Soup.

Sophie stared at the porcelain bowl and the labyrinth of silver utensils that surrounded it. The voice of her governess entered her head. It guided her to the proper soup spoon. She straightened her back and raised her chin, as she had been taught. She dipped the spoon into the soup, ladling front to back.

First test passed.

The conversation started with the captain answering questions about the ship, weather forecasts, sea state, timetable, and so on. The men were greatly interested in the ship's engines, fuel consumption rates, horsepower, reliability, backups, spare parts, and so on. The two wives carried on a private conversation about shops in New York they planned to visit. Dr. Duplantier ate his soup, content with his private thoughts.

The soups were whisked away, and the next course arrived: Salad.

Sophie was already full. The soup alone would have sufficed as dinner at St. Paul's.

She pushed her salad around with her fork, pretending to eat.

"Seasick?" asked the captain.

"No, sir," she said. "Homesick, maybe."

"You're traveling alone, dear?" asked one of the wives. Her name was Althea. She wore a stunning burgundy dress with a matching necklace of rubies and diamonds.

Sophie nodded.

"You poor thing," she clucked.

"Where are you heading to?" asked the captain.

"Missouri."

"Missouri!" the captain exclaimed. "My god, you're going to the Wild West!"

"You have a man waiting there, I suppose?" asked Althea.

"No. No man."

"But why, then? I mean, whatever possessed you?"

"Mark Twain," said Sophie with a smile.

"Is he a politician?" Althea asked.

Sophie laughed.

Althea scowled, and a pall fell over the table.

"Mark Twain is a writer!" Sophie said. "My favorite writer! He was a steamship captain on the Mississippi. Now he writes the most wonderful stories. I've read everything he's ever written, even the essays and travelogues."

She began to talk excitedly about Twain's books. "Of course everyone loves *Tom Sawyer*, but I think my favorite is *The Adventures of Huckleberry Finn*. When I read about that journey, of the wild freedom of the river, I knew I had to see it for myself..."

Suddenly, Sophie realized that no one was looking at her. The women had lowered their faces to their plates.

The voice of Sophie's governess came to her.

Books are not suitable for dinner conversation, except for certain classics under special circumstances. It's safest to steer clear of literature altogether.

Dr. Duplantier came to her rescue. "I met him."

"Who?" asked Althea, suddenly curious that the mute physician should speak.

"You met Mark Twain?" Sophie asked.

Duplantier nodded. "He gave a lecture in Paris. Afterward, we talked for a few minutes. His real name is Samuel Clemens, you know? Do you know how he got his *nom de plume*?"

Sophie knew, but she wanted to hear Dr. Duplantier tell it.

"You'll like this, Captain," said Dr. Duplantier. "It's a nautical term."

"Really?"

"'Mark' means position. 'Twain' means two."

"Two fathoms," said the captain. "Of course. How wonderful!"

"What was he like?" asked Sophie.

"He speaks plainly. It made me realize how rare that is. He just says what's on his mind."

"He sounds vulgar," said Althea.

Sophie lit up. "See, that's it! That's what I admire. He speaks his mind, and no one judges him for it. For me, that's what America is. A fresh start."

Althea was scowling.

Dr. Duplantier raised his glass. "To fresh starts!"

The others raised their glasses, even Althea, although reluctantly.

"To fresh starts!"

"To America!"

That night, as Sophie lay in bed, the gentle rocking motion of the ship stirred her imagination. She was on her way to America! For the first time since Vincent Van Gogh gave her his gift of "Missouri in a Box," she believed she could do this.

Her thoughts turned to Vincent. A week had passed since they made love by moonlight outside the asylum's south wall, and she could still feel the stubble of his beard on her neck as they made love. A sense of well-being swelled in her, and she was struck with a premonition. It landed with such force that she jumped out of bed and sat down to write a letter to Vincent.

Vincent, my love, tonight I had a vision. Two ladybugs are crawling across an enormous tapestry. And then I realized—we're the ladybugs! Not just you and I but everyone. We cannot see the design beneath us, but we must have faith that the design is there. And that it is beautiful. I am certain that it is. It must be, for we have found each other! Our parting at the south wall cannot be permanent. We are meant to be together, and we will be again. I hate that we are apart for now, but you were right to send me away. I see that it is not our place to know the whys of things, only to have faith and do our best at all times. I promise you, I will. And I know you are doing the same in your little room at St. Paul's.

The next day, Sophie sat in a lounge chair on the deck, attempting to read. The seas were flat enough that she could consider opening a book without feeling seasick. The voice came from above her.

"*Bonjour*, Mademoiselle."

She looked up to find Dr. Duplantier looking down at her. He wore a three-piece suit with suspenders, a tie, and a bowler hat. No top hat. Very modern.

"*Bonjour*, Dr. Duplantier."

"You can call me Jean, if that's not too forward."

"*Bonjour*, Jean. And please call me Sophie."

"Lovely day for reading on the deck," he observed.

"It certainly is."

"What's the book that has you so engrossed?"

"It's just something I picked up in the ship's library. I'm thinking of putting it back. I can't seem to get into it. It's called *Nana*."

"Émile Zola," said Jean.

"You know him? He's my husband's favorite writer. I thought I'd see why."

The idea of referring to Vincent as her "husband" came to Sophie in an instant. Jean showed no reaction to the revelation.

"Zola is excellent. And that's a wonderful book. But you can't begin with *Nana*. That's the ninth book in the series."

"That explains it!" she laughed. "I'm so confused!"

He pointed at the chair beside her. "May I?"

She set the book on her lap. "Of course."

He sat down and said, "You have to begin with *La Fortune des Rougon*. That's the first book. Almost all the characters are introduced there. I don't have a copy, or I'd loan it to you. Perhaps the library does."

"I'll look. Thank you. I loved your Mark Twain story last night. I'd love to hear more about that."

"And I'd be happy to oblige if there was more to tell. But that's all there is to it, I'm afraid. But as for you..." he said with a wink, "your adventure has set tongues wagging."

"Is that so?"

"Oh, quite. A lovely lady traveling alone to see the American frontier? I can't say I've ever heard of anything like it. No one has."

"My husband and I had planned to travel together," said Sophie. "But then he fell ill."

"I'm very sorry to hear that."

"He insisted that I go ahead anyway. It has always been my dream."

"May I ask, what does your husband do?"

"He's an artist."

"How fascinating! And he makes a living from this?"

"Not yet. But he will. Someday, he will be the most famous artist in the world."

Jean smiled. "He certainly has a great fan in you. Tell me about his work."

She told him all about Vincent and his new way of painting, about his frantic work pace, the obstacles he faced in the art world, and his total, uncompromising commitment to his vision.

"It all sounds fascinating," said Jean when she finished. "Perhaps I'll get to see one of his paintings someday." He winked. "In the Louvre, perhaps?"

"I have one in my cabin," said Sophie. "I can get it if you like."

"That would be marvelous!"

She hurried to fetch the painting and then set it in front of his chair. He looked for a moment, then his face turned as red as a ripe tomato.

"Oh, my god," he said and looked away.

"What? You don't like it?"

"Is that... you?"

"Yes."

"Oh, my god."

"What?"

"You must put that back in your cabin."

"You haven't even looked at it—"

"This instant!"

She carried it back to her cabin. When she returned, Jean was leaning on the railing, looking out to sea. She stood beside him, waiting for him to speak.

"Have I offended you?" she asked finally.

He turned to her, frowning. He spoke in a tone that reminded her of Dr. Peyron. "Sophie, what possessed you to show me that painting?"

"You said you wanted to see it."

"But..."

"But... what?"

"But... do I have to say it?" he asked.

"I guess you do."

"You're *nude*!"

"I realize that. But it's so beautiful! What other reason do you need?"

Jean eyed her with wonder. He tugged at his beard. "You amaze me."

"Do I?"

He laughed. "Definitely. Completely and profoundly."

"Okay," she said, unsure of what to make of that. Was she really such a mystery? She had always believed her problem was the exact opposite.

"Now, let's go to the library and see if we can find that book," he said.

Mon Cher,

I made a friend! His name is Jean. He is a doctor. He's younger than me, and a very serious fellow, but not stern like a stuffy old minister. He's a good listener, and I think that's why we get along so well. We talk about books and the places we're going. Since I've been nowhere, I talked about birds. I hope I didn't bore him. He didn't seem bored. He loves Émile Zola and recommended a few other books from the library. He's quite knowledgeable about art. I told him all about you and your paintings. I referred to you as "my husband," I hope that's okay. I didn't want him to get the wrong idea. He said he'd like to see one of your paintings, so I showed him your painting of me. Jean was so embarrassed when he realized it was me! You should have seen him blush! You'd think a doctor would be immune to that, but I guess even a doctor is foremost a man.

Two days later, *La Virginie* sailed into the teeth of a North Atlantic storm.

The storm arrived in stages, and Sophie watched the spectacle from her deck. First, a line of clouds appeared on the horizon, so low it appeared to be rising out of the water. It looked like a black wall. Next, the temperature plummeted. A rising wind whipped her hair. Then came freezing rain, which drove Sophie off the deck. Within hours, waves built until they were breaking in a terrifying waterscape of slate and white foam. *La Virginie* rolled in slow arcs that left half the passengers and many of the crew seasick. Captain Lambert declared the decks unsafe and ordered passengers to remain in their cabins. Three times per day, a crewman brought cold food and tepid tea to Sophie's door. Sophie was nauseous from the motion and couldn't eat. Making matters worse, there was nothing to do. Reading was out of the question. She lay in bed dozing and praying for the misery to end.

Jean was immune to seasickness and came several times each day to check on her. He was a welcome distraction. Each time, he would lead her to the railing, where he told her to fix her gaze on the horizon. It seemed to help a little. But the freezing rain soon forced them back to the private hell of her cabin. The entire ship had begun to take on a sickly smell as it absorbed a disgusting spectrum of odors produced by its wretched human occupants.

On the third day of the storm, Sophie lay on her back, watching the curtains sway to the ceaseless rhythm of the rolling ship. Suddenly, a shadow fell over her vision...

... like a bird passing in front of the sun.

She knew what it foretold.

"No," she begged. "Please, no."

Five days later, as the ship crept toward the coast of North America, Sophie wrote a letter to Vincent. Her penmanship was noticeably shaky.

Mon Cher,

You'll see from the date on this letter that it has been over a week since my last letter. I realize you'll get these all at once, but I really wanted to write one per day as you did for me so you could travel along with me.

I had one of my episodes. It was so bad! There was a storm and the seas got rough, and suddenly I was sure the ship was going to sink. They say I tried to throw myself over the railing into the sea. One of the other crew had to pull me back. They locked me in my cabin. It was quite the scandal!

Thank god for Jean! It turns out one of his interests is mental illness! So I told him all about my medical condition, going back to my childhood. He said he believed I had "recurrent mania" and prescribed a drug called lithium salts. It's new. He said he had read about positive results with patients with symptoms like mine. And now I feel so much better! I've never had an episode pass so quickly. Usually, they go on for weeks. Please tell Dr. Peyron about lithium salts. Maybe it could help you, too...

The sight of the Statue of Liberty guarding New York Harbor was something Sophie would never forget. Four years earlier, the statue had traveled to America in hundreds of pieces along an identical route from France. A year after that, President Grover Cleveland dedicated it at the mouth of the harbor.

Aboard *La Virginie*, passengers crowded shoulder-to-shoulder along the rail. The ship began to list to that side, and the crew had to frantically move people to the opposite rail to keep it from capsizing.

Sophie marveled at the sight. She was still weak from her breakdown, but the negativity of her episode had passed. Beside her on the rail, a man was sobbing at the sight of the statue.

She made it! She was in America!

The ship docked at Ellis Island for several hours to allow prospective immigrants to disembark. From there, the ship steamed across the harbor toward the main docks on the lower east side of the peninsula called Manhattan. The harbor was filled with so many steamships and sailing vessels that Sophie wondered how the captain could find a course.

When they reached the long quay, ropes were tossed to men on the wharf who slipped them over enormous iron bollards. The passage was over.

First-class passengers had a special disembarkment lane, and before she knew it, Sophie was standing at the top of a gangplank that sloped down to the wharf. Captain Lambert stood at the top of the gangplank, saying farewell to the passengers one by one. When Althea passed, he kissed her hand and then her cheeks. When Sophie reached the captain, his smile faded.

She offered her hand, and he bowed to kiss it.

"Thank you, Captain," said Sophie. "I'm sorry I was so much trouble."

"Not at all," he said. "Have a safe trip to Missouri, Sophie."

Still, he was unable to hide his relief to be rid of her.

A half-hour later, Sophie stood on the wharf beside two steamer trunks and Vincent's painting. The customs agents hadn't even asked for her papers. They had simply waved through all first-class passengers!

The bustle of the wharf left her feeling breathless. Horse-drawn carts were piled high with cargo and luggage. Men shouted in English, French, Portuguese, and other languages she could not identify. She watched a boy race to greet his father and then leap, squealing, into his arms. Every sound, color, and smell was present, and all at the same time.

The riot of activity left Sophie feeling dizzy. She sat down on one of her trunks to regain her strength. Suddenly, Jean was beside her.

"Welcome to America!" he said in English.

"Jean! This is so exciting!" she replied in French.

"English now, remember?"

She repeated it carefully in English.

"It certainly is," he replied.

"The Statue of Liberty—wasn't that the most perfect thing you've ever seen? I looked for you."

"I saw it," he said. "How are you feeling?"

"I'm not sure. Is the Earth moving?"

He laughed. "That's normal. It will take a few days to get your land legs back."

He handed her a bottle with a white powder and a slip of paper.

"This is the last of my lithium salts," he said. "It's enough for another eight days. You understand about the dosage?"

"Yes."

"You must take it every day, Sophie. Not just when you feel bad. That's extremely important."

"I understand."

"You're still determined to make this trip?"

"I am."

He sighed heavily. "This paper is a prescription for a one-year supply of the drug. I suggest you fill the entire amount here in New York. Who knows if they'll have it in St. Louis?"

"Thank you, Jean. This is so thoughtful."

"I have a coach waiting," he said. "Can I drop you somewhere?"

Sophie dug into her bag for the paper with the address of Theo Van Gogh's jeweler. She handed it to Jean, who gave it to the coachman.

"It's not far," said the coachman in English.

Jean looked up and down the wharf and said, "Let's get these trunks aboard before a cart runs us both over."

Mon Cher,

I made it! I'm in America! Oh, I wish you could see! New York is even more spectacular than I imagined. I will write more about it later when I get my thoughts straight.

I said farewell to Jean today. He gave me a one-year prescription for lithium, which I will fill before I leave for Missouri. He was such a good friend on the ship, and he dearly wants to meet you. I know you'll love talking about Zola with him!

Theo's jeweler gave me all your letters. It was wonderful to hear from you. Your paintings of the cypresses sound beautiful. I'm sorry you had another breakdown. Have you asked Peyron about lithium?

The jeweler was extremely helpful. I exchanged half the gems, and he gave me a fair price. He is also converting some of my gold into U.S. currency. It will all be ready in a week. Then I can catch a train west.

Apparently, I'm rich—or at least that's what the jeweler must believe. He sent me to stay in a hotel called the Astor House. You would not believe it! I counted eighteen chandeliers in the lobby! My room is like a royal bed chamber. I don't begrudge the delay in getting my gems converted to cash. There is so much to see here, a week is not nearly enough. There's a new museum called the Metropolitan. They have an Édouard Manet on display. Can you believe it? I thought I'd like to see that. I know you're an admirer. Imagine our French art finding its way across the ocean. Someday, I know your art will hang on those same walls.

I think about you all the time, Vincent. It's like you're traveling with me. I even talk to you. Thankfully, you don't talk back! That would be a bad sign.

I finished reading Émile Zola's The Ladies' Paradise. *It was in the ship's library. I know how much you admire that book. It was wonderful, but there's a quote in there that I am afraid spoke to you: "I would rather die of passion than boredom."*

Promise me you won't die of either, Vincent. When we do pass, as we all must, let the cause of death be extreme old age. And let us be together when it comes. You must promise me that. Okay?

Sophie took that letter, along with the stack from her voyage, to the post office, and mailed them all together to Vincent at St. Paul du Mausole.

Ten days later, she boarded the *Southwestern Limited* on the Big Four Route to St. Louis. She was unpacking her suitcase and settling into her first-class cabin when a familiar voice came from the doorway.

"May I borrow one of your books, Madame? I hear it's a long trip."

She looked up. Jean Duplantier stood in the doorway in a bowler hat. The mustache he had begun during the voyage was now well-developed with a slight upturn at the tips. It made him look older and, she thought, more handsome. He was grinning at her.

"Jean!" she cried.

He wagged his finger. "It's John now. I'm John Planter."

Sophie laughed. "I love it. It sounds perfectly American."

"That's what I thought. Do you have a *nom Américain*?"

"I went with Sophie du Burgen."

"du Burgen?"

"It's a little Swiss village. My family has a house there. What are you *doing* here?"

He grinned. "It turns out that St. Louis is on the way to San Francisco. So I was thinking, would you like some company?"

"Oh, Jean... I mean, John!" she exclaimed. She was so happy, she flew at him and kissed his cheeks.

When she stepped back, the young doctor was glowing red.

He cleared his throat and, for no apparent reason, took off his hat.

"I'll take that as a 'yes,'" he said.

Twenty-Nine

Vincent

Nine months later
St. Remy, France

Vincent Van Gogh walked the path that hugged the steep, open hillside. The mistral was blowing, and he had to lean into the wind to keep from being blown down the grassy slope. He arrived at a grove of cypress trees and stopped. His blue eyes shone in the morning light as he watched the trees bow under the force of the mistral. He pictured the roots gripping the soil like the talons of a hawk. A painting took shape before his eyes. The trees became two-dimensional. Branches swirled in unnatural directions, both bowed and straight at the same time. The sky was cast as the villain. It wielded the mistral as a weapon against the trees. Verdant Green opposed Prussian Blue on a battlefield of Sophie Gold that was cut by a Burnt Red dirt path that gaped like an open wound.

Yes, this would do.

Vincent set up his easel and fixed its legs deep into the ground. He clamped the blank canvas to the easel. After more than two years of painting en plein air in Provence, he was adept with the mechanics of working in the wind. He dabbed turpentine on a stained rag. He resisted the urge to breathe in the fumes, and, instead, he scrubbed the handle of his Number Three brush.

Vincent felt strong. His red beard was full, and his hair had returned after shaving it when he first entered the asylum. His straw hat concealed his missing ear, and to anyone who knew him, Vincent Van Gogh looked much as he had a decade earlier when he first took up his paintbrush. His seizures were arriving at three-month intervals, so if that cycle were reliable, he was safe for now. Peyron allowed him to leave the asylum and walk the outer fields in search of scenes to paint. A local gardener usually accompanied him, but not so today. Vincent's only requirement was that he be back inside the asylum by dinner. Of course, his very presence at St. Paul de Mausole was voluntary. Lately, he had begun to entertain the idea of leaving the asylum. Theo had learned of a doctor specializing in mental illness in artists. He was even a friend of Camille Pissarro! He lived in an idyllic suburb of Paris called Auvers-sur-Oise. Vincent longed to escape the misery of hydrotherapy baths and the haunting night cries of The Corporal and dozens of other inmates like him. It would be wrong to say he was cured, but perhaps he had accomplished all he could in this place. It sickened him to think that Sophie had spent a decade behind these walls. A year was all he could bear.

In her letters, Sophie was less supportive of his plan to leave. The doctor in Auvers was homeopathic, she pointed out, and she'd continued to tout a new drug called lithium salts. She claimed it had diminished the severity of her episodes until now they were mere "downtimes" when she stayed in bed. They never lasted longer than a few days. When Vincent mentioned lithium to Peyron, he dismissed it as "untested snake oil." Vincent could not tell Peyron that lithium had helped Sophie. That would have revealed his relationship with Sophie. Vincent kept his promise.

As he cleaned another brush, Vincent noticed a man approaching from the direction of the asylum. He wore thick-soled dress shoes and a suit with a tie. He carried a top hat in his hand.

"You are Monsieur Vincent Van Gogh?" he asked in a thick German accent.

"Yes."

"Phew!" he said, out of breath. "That is quite a hike."

Vincent waited. He was impatient to get on with his painting. It hovered before his eyes, demanding to be brought to life. He was in no mood for company.

"Dr. Peyron said I would find you here. My name is Eduard. My sister was a patient here for many years."

Vincent stared.

"Her name is Sophie. Dr. Peyron said you knew her."

"You speak of Sophie Alt?"

"Alt? Yes, that's right. Alt."

"We met in Arles a couple of years ago."

"He said you might have had a... uh, *relationship* with her."

"I don't see how that's any of your business," Vincent snapped.

"I'm sorry. I meant no offense. I only meant to say that you knew her well."

Vincent waited for him to go on.

"You may have heard that she escaped from St. Paul's nearly a year ago."

"Yes, I heard about that. Has she been found?"

"No. That's why I'm here. I'm looking for information on her whereabouts. I'm worried."

The image of the painting evaporated. Vincent put down his brush and turned to face Sophie's brother.

"I'm surprised you care," he said.

Eduard recoiled. "Oh, my! Why would you say that? What did she tell you?"

Vincent shrugged. "That her family had disowned her. That they sent her to live in one asylum after another. They paid for her care, but never sent her so much as a note at Christmas."

Eduard paled. "She said that?"

"So it's true?"

"Poor Sophie," said Eduard. "Yes, it's true. But it was not her entire family—just our father. His family was merely a tool to be wielded for his ambition—like everything else in his life."

"Was? You mean..."

"Yes. He passed away three weeks ago. He fell off his horse, took ill, and slipped away."

"I'm sorry."

"Thank you. But now that he is gone, I am looking for her. It weighs on our mother. It weighs on all of us."

"And you thought I could help?"

"Dr. Peyron said you receive a great deal of mail, some from America. He thought you might have heard from her. He said Sophie had this crazy idea about seeing the Wild West."

"I haven't seen or heard from her since her escape."

Eduard nodded grimly. "I see. Sorry to have bothered you. If you do hear from her, can you give her a message?"

"What?"

"Come home. The family has a *Jagdschloss*, a hunting lodge in the Swiss Alps. It's just outside Geneva in a little place called Burgen. It's hers if she wants it. She always loved it, and I think she'd be happy there." His gaze grew distant. "The mountains are beautiful. There's a stream and a little village. Lots of animals to delight her. The citril finches roost there, you know. She loves them."

"Citril finches? She mentioned citril finches to you?"

"Of course," said Eduard. "Why? Does that mean something to you?"

"And they roost at this hunting lodge?"

"Every year."

Eduard left, and Vincent packed up his equipment. The painting was long forgotten. He hurried to his room. On his wall, he slid aside a painting of Sophie's lilac bush to retrieve a thick stack of letters he kept hidden. He fanned them with his thumb. Two hundred and seventy-four letters, all from Sophie. Nearly one per day, just as she had promised.

And such letters! She described a magnificent journey across frontier America. The sights, the sounds, and the smells of the Wild West arrived each day to transport Vincent far from the walls of the asylum. St. Louis, she said, was "a boomtown," whatever that was. English crept into some of her letters. From St. Louis, she joined a riverboat that retraced much of the voyage of Huckleberry

Finn on the Mississippi. Each night she swam in the river, though everyone thought she was crazy for doing so.

I wore a bathing costume, of course. But I was thinking about when we skinny-dipped in the Rhône. Do you ever think about those times? I do. Every day.

From there, she traveled by train southwest to a place called "Oklahoma." It was there she fulfilled her dream to see buffalo and meet Indians. She traded a scarf with a Sioux squaw for a bird-feather necklace and an arrowhead.

They are my most precious possessions—except for your painting, of course.

After Oklahoma came Texas, then Sacramento, where she spent a week panning unsuccessfully for gold.

You would not recognize me, Vincent. In Oklahoma, I started wearing pantaloons like some of the rancher girls. It is so much more practical than a dress. In Texas, I bought a straw hat and a leather vest. I look like a girl in a rodeo show! Today when I was out panning, a man came to pan beside me. He spoke for several minutes using the foulest language I have ever heard. He thought I was a man! When he realized I was a woman, he slunk away! I never saw him after that.

After Sacramento, Sophie returned to St. Louis, where she got an apartment over a shop. In one letter, she included a genuine Shawnee warrior feather and a few strands of buffalo mane. He kept them beside his bed. Her letters were filled with praise for Dr. John Planter, whom she had met aboard *La Virginie* nearly a year earlier. He continued to prescribe her medication and seemed to be looking out for her well-being. Vincent was relieved. Sophie was stronger than she knew, but when she stumbled, it was best if there was someone nearby to catch her.

Vincent took out a pencil and began to write.

My Dearest Soph,

Today I was thinking about something you once wrote about God's plan being like a tapestry we cannot see entirely. We must have faith that there is a design and that the design is beautiful.

Well, my love, I had a visitor this morning...

Vincent never received a reply to that letter, nor to any of the next several letters he sent after that.

The next time he heard from Sophie was four months later when he was looking up at her from his deathbed with a bullet in his gut. Her skin was brown from sun exposure, her hair was braided strangely, and she wore a long bandana like a cowgirl. He thought he was hallucinating.

She kissed his mangled ear. He knew then that it was her. Who else would do that?

"Sophie?"

"Oh, my love," she said. "What have you done?"

Thirty

Jane

Jane Ward looked out her bedroom window at the Valley of the Giants. It was a clear August morning, and wildflowers painted the hillsides with delicate brush strokes of purple, red, and rich cream. Jane saw them all.

Dr. Ravi Das had been fascinated by her progress in her latest report. "Your brain is rewiring itself in ways that go beyond the original markers. Now it is learning from its learning. I'm so happy for you!"

"But is it really seeing?"

"Of course. You don't see with your eyes, Jane. No one does. We see with our brains."

In the distance, Jane spied four tents on a nearby ledge—two green, one orange, and one yellow. They were backpackers on the Alpina. The famous trail crossed the road not far from the turnoff to Chalet von Tessen. Jane liked watching the hikers in their heavy boots and broad-brimmed hats pitch their tents on stone ledges and then kneel beside miniature stoves to cook. They were emissaries from the outside world. Jane supposed it was like the bird migrations that had meant so much to Granny Jo. It reminded her that, though she lived in a remote place, she was still a part of the greater world.

Jane made a mental note to call Granny Jo and then slipped on her clothes and dashed downstairs for coffee. She had hoped to cross paths with Max and Sydney, but the kitchen was empty. Jane was antsy and didn't feel like being alone. She could have taken her coffee to the portrait room, but Greta made poor company. Jane strolled through the chalet looking for someone to talk to. She found Ursula under a big hat in the English Garden, trimming the rose bushes beside the chapel.

"*Bon matin.*"

"*Mm,*" Ursula said without looking up.

"Where is everybody?" Jane asked.

Ursula stretched her back. "Let's see. Collette left this morning for the airport. Agatha took Klaus to Geneva for a doctor's appointment."

"Is he alright?"

Ursula shrugged.

"What about Max and Sydney?"

"They left early. Hitched up the horse trailer and took off."

"Where?"

Ursula scoffed and went back to work.

Jane wandered back into the house. Of all the people in the chalet, Ursula had been the hardest to win over.

"She hates me," Jane had complained one day to Max in the barn.

"She doesn't hate you," said Max, filling a trough from a water hose. "She's protective of Klaus. She's afraid you're going to hurt him."

"I would never hurt him!"

"I know that," said Max. "But it's different for her. From the moment Klaus saw that common swift, he accepted you. It's a matter of faith with him. To him, the valley is one gigantic organism made up of thousands and thousands of critical parts. Everything is interconnected. No one part is more critical than another. Is the heart more important than the liver? Or the lungs?"

"Or the gyrus?"

"Exactly."

Jane dumped a bucket of feed into Lela's stall. Jane was slow to retreat, and the horse pushed her aside to get to the food. Lela began slurping at the trough.

"Ursula doesn't see it that way?" asked Jane.

"I think she does. She believes her part is to protect Klaus."

"She's good at it."

Max nodded. "She'll come around."

Jane left Ursula to her roses and walked back through the library to the den. She sat down on the sofa and called Ted. They spent a half-hour discussing his latest discoveries. He had finished a long interview with Reverend Jacques Barbeau's partner, Pavel. Ted was now able to link Burgen's chaplain to the Firth Gallery. Ted had also traveled to a village called St. Séverine Parish in the German-speaking portion of Switzerland.

"There are still some Firths living there," he said. "In the church cemetery, I found twenty-six headstones with the last name Firth. I took pictures of them all."

"Good. Send them to me."

"Done. I gotta say, this thing is stacking up."

"It sure is." Jane absorbed this new information and went on. "So, somehow Gunther Firth of St. Séverine Parish got ahold of paintings by our mysterious pastor in Burgen, and he has been passing them off as his grandfather's ever since."

"That's how it looks."

"Francis F. on all the paintings," she mused. "Why the dot? Why not 'Firth'?"

"No idea."

"Why two per year?" she asked. "Does that make any sense?"

"It would really help if you could find that vault," he said.

"Ya think?" Jane groaned.

"It's gotta be somewhere in Burgen."

"I'll keep looking."

"Oh, one other thing," said Ted. "Blueprints for the church. They weren't in the church archives or with the diocese. Perhaps they're in the chalet. They would have the name of the architect. That could give me a money trail that would lead to the von Tessens."

"Good idea. I'll have a look now."

"Oh, I have a title for the book," Ted said. "*No-Talent Hacks.*"

Jane laughed. "Perfect."

Jane descended into the basement and began to search for blueprints. She didn't find the church's, but she did find the original blueprints for the chalet and the East Wing addition. It was a spectacular find. They were faded and unreadable, but she knew of techniques for restoring them. She would discuss the cost with Hannah.

Suddenly, Sydney appeared at the basement doorway, out of breath.

"Jane. There you are! Boy, it's so scary down here."

"It's just a basement, Sydney. What are you doing here? Is everything alright?"

Her face lit up. "Oh, Jane, it was so much fun!"

"What was?"

"You have to see! Come on!"

Sydney dragged Jane upstairs by the hand and then outside toward the barn. Max's black truck was parked by the barn door still hitched to the horse trailer. Beside it, Max stood next to a red-brown horse. Max held the lead line and watched Jane approach.

"What's this?" asked Jane. "You got a new horse?"

"We went to this big farm outside Geneva," said Sydney breathlessly. "There were sooo many horses. Millions of horses! Tabitha was in the pasture. We just walked up to her and put on the halter. She went right into the trailer, too. Most horses don't like the trailer. I think she wanted to come. She was so bored out there just eating grass all day. Isn't she pretty?"

"She's beautiful," said Jane.

"She was in their riding lessons program," said Max. "They had to stop it for liability reasons. I called them looking for a good horse for a novice rider, and they said if I would come to get her then I could have her. She's as gentle as they come, Jane. She'll be perfect."

"For what?"

"Lessons. Collette said you wanted to learn to ride."

Jane recoiled. "What?"

He frowned. "She said you told her at the funeral that you'd always wanted to learn to ride. You needed some kind of leisure activity while you were here, something to get you out of the basement once in a while, and wouldn't riding be perfect?"

"Collette said that?"

"Did I misunderstand?"

Jane walked to the horse and petted its face.

"Her name's Tabitha," said Sydney.

"Hello, Tabitha. It's very nice to meet you."

Tabitha blinked sleepily.

"She likes you."

"I like her," said Jane. She turned to Max. "I love her."

He smiled. "Good. When do you want to start?"

"I really must get back to work," said Jane. "I'm so behind. Dr. Schmidt is expecting a report, and I'm still sorting."

"Of course," he said. "And I have some check-ins today. Sydney, don't you have some chores with Oma?"

Sydney groaned.

"Six o'clock?" he said.

"Six o'clock."

The following weeks passed in a glorious procession of clear skies and pastures humming with the cries of sheep. The air was so crisp Jane's clothes crackled with static electricity when she got dressed.

In the chalet, Jane filed her latest report to Dr. Schmidt in Leipzig. An hour later, she received a reply.

First-class. More on the banking investments, please. Keep going.

Jane read the praise several times. It was a heady thing for Jane Ward of Ontario Hills to be exchanging emails with the curator of the formidable Leipzig Archives. It held one of the most important archival collections in the world, with ancient scrolls, papyri, and monastic texts going back a thousand years.

The highlight of each day was Jane's riding lesson. After work, Jane would meet Max and Sydney on the lawn outside the chalet. Atop Tabitha, Jane learned to ride with her heels down, shorten her reins, and keep her back straight. She learned how to mount and dismount without a step stool. She learned to walk and trot and how to communicate these commands to Tabitha. She learned when to use her knees and when to use her stirrups. As her balance improved, the sensation that she was about to fall receded. Before each lesson, Max instructed her on how to tack up the horse and, afterward, how to rinse down Tabitha with the hose, and then, finally, how to brush her. The riding was exhilarating, but these little moments of grooming were satisfying in their own right.

At the end of the first week, Jane stepped outside for lunch to find Max and Sydney with Tabitha. The horses were saddled up and ready to go. Sydney was on her pony. Lela was tied to a post.

"What's going on?" Jane asked.

"It's your graduation day," said Max.

"My what?" she laughed.

"We're riding down to Turtle Rock," said Sydney. "All of us. You remember Turtle Rock?"

Jane nodded. She thought about the steep trail they would have to descend to get there, and the stream to be crossed. She gulped.

"Are you sure?" she asked Max.

"You're a natural, Jane."

He held out an oversized cardboard box.

"What's this?" she asked.

"Open it."

She lifted the lid on the box. It contained a pair of knee-high black leather riding boots.

"You can't keep riding in those jogging shoes," he said. "You'll lose your stirrup on the hill."

The thought of the steep hill brought butterflies to her stomach.

"It's okay, Jane. You're ready. Trust me."

She sat down beside the chicken coop, slipped off her sneakers, and pulled on the boots. She stood up and wiggled her toes.

"How do they fit?" he asked.

"They're perfect."

"Whoo-hoo!" said Sydney. "Turtle Rock, here we come!"

Max led the way on Lela, with Jane second and Sydney in the rear.

"The first part is the steepest," Max said. "Just use your stirrups and ease your reins. Let Tabitha do the work."

They started down. Jane sunk her new boots into her stirrups and leaned back in her saddle. The trail was wider than it had seemed that day in the fog, and in no time they cleared the slope and were on a gentler part of the trail. They still had a long way to go to reach Burgen, but the worst was over.

Max reined in Lela and turned in his saddle to check on her. He grinned like a boy filled with joy and mischief. Beyond him lay the stark beauty of the Valley of the Giants. Jane drank in the dry air, the feel of Tabitha beneath her, and the whistle of the wind against the rock. A sense of perfect joy filled her like a narcotic.

"How are you doing, Jane?" Max asked. "You want to turn back?"

"Heck, no!" Jane cried.

A half-hour later, they reached Turtle Rock. They dismounted and let the horses drink, while Sydney went off to find a monkeyflower.

Max knelt and spooned water into his mouth, slurping from his palm. He filled his canteen and passed it to Jane. He watched her drink in a way that made her self-conscious.

Suddenly, a scream from Sydney brought them both running.

She was pointing at the ground beneath a bush. Max got there first.

"Is it a snake?" Jane asked.

Max shook his head. "Bird."

Jane came beside them. On the ground was a fledgling, its feathers still waxy and unformed. It looked like a mouse with a beak. It was chirping frantically.

"Back away!" said Jane. "Slowly."

They went back. One, two, three steps.

"Further," said Jane.

When they were thirty feet away, Jane said, "That's enough."

"We have to help it!" said Sydney.

Max knelt in front of Sydney. "If we touch the bird, its parents will reject it. The best thing we can do is leave it. It may still learn to fly. Sometimes, Sydney, we have to let nature take its course—"

"Sydney's right," said Jane.

Max recoiled. "Excuse me?"

"Listen," said Jane.

Almost immediately, they heard a high-pitched medley of chirps and trills.

"It's the parents!" said Sydney.

"If we leave it, an animal will get it for sure," said Jane. "We have to put it back in the nest. I've saved many a fledgling, and the parents never once rejected them. But you have to do it in a way that doesn't alarm the parents. If they abandon the nest, then the baby won't survive. Max, you stay with the horses. Sydney and I will put it back. Are you up for this, Sydney?"

Sydney nodded, wide-eyed.

"The key, Sydney, is to let the parents hear the baby chirping. That way, they know it's alive. You're not there to kill it. You're saving it. They won't leave unless they think it's dead."

Sydney put her hands to the ground beside the fledgling, and Jane nudged it in. Jane pulled back the branches while Sydney raised it to the nest. Two other fledglings chirped from the nest. Sydney opened her palms and laid the fledgling among its siblings.

They backed away until they stood with Max and the horses.

"What now?" Max asked.

"Shh."

Seconds later, two birds appeared. Garden warblers. They flew to the top of the bush and scanned the surroundings.

"Look!" Sydney whispered. "They're coming back."

One of the warblers chirped. The fledglings began to squeak in reply, and then it flew into the nest. It sang to its mate and then he, too, flew to the nest.

Sydney was holding her hands over her mouth. "We did it! We saved the baby bird! We saved the baby bird!"

Sydney hugged Jane, who held her in her arms while they listened to the warblers sing to each other. Jane glanced in Max's direction. He was not looking at the birds. He was looking at her.

Jane turned away, and for an instant, she caught sight of a small bird on a tree limb above the warblers. It flew to a higher branch, and for an instant, she caught a flash of what looked like a gold feather.

"I think we should go," said Jane.

A half-hour later, as they climbed the trail that led to the chalet, they heard the whir of a helicopter approaching from Geneva. Max reined Lela. They stopped and looked up.

It passed overhead in the direction of the chalet and then disappeared behind the ledge.

"Why is there a helicopter, Papa?" Sydney asked. She began to cry. "Is it... Opa?"

"It's okay, Sydney."

"But... but..."

"I need you to focus, Sydney," said Max. "Yara needs you to focus. She's depending on you."

Max was right. They were in a particularly treacherous place. One false step could be fatal.

Sydney nodded and wiped her eyes.

Max looked at Jane. "Just stay in line, okay? Follow me."

Max led them forward. Every few minutes, he turned in his saddle to check on them.

"All good?" he asked.

They nodded in reply, but the specter of the news that awaited them at the chalet hovered like a dark cloud.

A few minutes later, they reached the trail's final steep section. With a kick, they climbed onto the broad, flat lawn and stopped. The helicopter idled on the grass. They dismounted and led their horses toward it.

Ursula appeared from behind the helicopter and hurried toward them. She looked stricken.

"What's going on?" Max asked. "Why the helicopter?"

"It's for Jane."

Jane recoiled. "Me?"

"You weren't answering your phone, so your brother called the chalet. It's your Granny Jo."

Jane staggered and leaned against Tabitha.

"She had a heart attack. She's in surgery now. The helicopter will take you to the airport. Hannah has the jet waiting. I packed your bag. It's in the helicopter. Now *go*!"

When Jane arrived in Ontario Hills, Davis was waiting on the tarmac. It was surreal. Ten hours earlier, she had been riding Tabitha in the Valley of the Giants.

Davis said nothing about the improbability of his sister arriving in a twenty-million-dollar jet.

"She's going to be okay," he said.

Jane fell into his arms. They hugged for a long time.

When they parted, Jane wiped her eyes.

"Yeah, the surgery went well," Davis said. "The doctors are pleased. Would you like to see her?"

Granny Jo was asleep in the ICU when she and Davis arrived at the hospital. Her mouth lay open unnaturally from a large breathing tube that snaked back to a ventilator machine. Three smaller catheter tubes looped and swirled around her. One was filled with blood. Amid the clutter, Granny Jo looked like an afterthought. It was horrifying. Jane realized she had never seriously considered a world without Granny Jo.

"She's a fighter, Jane," said Davis.

"I know."

For the next three days, Granny Jo was unable to speak because of the ventilator tube, but even when she was awake, Jane sensed her grandmother was only just there. Doctors said she was not completely out of the woods yet; it would take several more days to know for sure.

When Jane wasn't at the hospital, she spent her time haunting her former life. Being home was not what she expected. People were happy to see her, and they had kind wishes for Granny Jo. But the newspaper had not put out an issue since she left. Did anyone miss it? At the library, her mother had replaced her with a pair of interns. Her mother seemed particularly taken by one young man who was able to wipe viruses from the library's computers, a skill Jane had never mastered.

One afternoon, Jane drove her car to the site of the disputed shopping center. Not a blade of grass had moved since the last time she was there. At least the tree was still standing.

Jane stood a while, looking up at the old oak, thinking about everything it had seen. She looked forward to telling Klaus about it. There were no oaks in the valley.

It occurred to Jane that, months earlier, she had nearly turned her back on her quest for the truth about the Firths. Why? So she could rejoin her life in Ontario Hills? What life? She resolved that whatever future awaited her after she finished her book, it would not be in Ontario Hills.

On the fourth day after her return, Jane came into Granny Jo's room to find her awake and alert. The ventilator tube was gone, and she was watching a pair of robins hopping among the branches of a tree.

"Knock-knock," said Jane.

Granny Jo turned. "Janey-girl!"

Jane rushed to her side. "Oh, Gran!"

"There, there. I'm sorry for all the fuss."

Jane wiped her eyes.

After they dispensed with Jane's health questions and Granny Jo's dismissive replies, they proceeded to talk for an hour about everything that had happened since they last spoke.

"I'm selling the farm," Granny Jo blurted out.

"Uh, okay."

"Davis found a developer offering twelve million."

Jane laughed. "Twelve million! That'll certainly pay for your nursing home."

"No," said Granny Jo. "I'm leaving it all to the Iroquois."

Her farm was built on Iroquois land, and Granny Jo often spoke of feeling "the blood of the Iroquois" in the ground.

"What? Really?"

"For Aponi."

"Whoa. Does Dad know?"

"He'll find out after I'm gone."

"He'll flip."

Granny Jo shrugged. "I'm going to transfer *The Lover* to you now. I think that's important. I had Davis draw up a document."

"Gran, I don't even have it back yet!"

"You will, I have no doubt. And if what you suspect about the painting is true, then you're the only person I trust to take care of our girl. Promise you will."

"I promise."

"So," she said in a way that signaled a change of subject, "you've learned to horseback ride."

"Yes."

"With Max von Tessen?"

Jane laughed. "Stop, Gran. I see what you're doing. It's not like that."

"You sure?"

"Positive."

"Well, we'll see, won't we?"

Granny Jo smiled faintly. "Your grandfather hated birds. Did you know that?"

"Really?"

"Of course. All farmers do. They peck holes in the house, crap all over everything, and eat the seeds right out of the ground. Terrible nuisances. But he knew I loved them, so he made all those birdhouses. You never saw them in their prime. They were such elaborate things, with shutters and little doors. One for each wedding anniversary. Do you understand what I'm saying?"

Jane shook her head.

"Love is not always like in the books, Jane. I suppose sometimes it is. But sometimes a woman just decides, 'Yes, this is the person I'm going to love.' And then she does. With all her heart and conviction. That's how it was for me and your grandpa. I think he knew that, and that is why he worked so hard to make me all those birdhouses. How could I not choose to love such a man?"

"Love is a choice," Jane said.

"Exactly."

"But is that real love?"

"It was for me."

"What about for Grandpa? Did he just *decide* to love you?"

"Oh, heavens no!" she said laughing. "Poor man, I bewitched him."

The next day, *ArtNet* published a teaser article about Ted Banks's forthcoming book on the Firth Gallery. *ArtNet* paired the article with a picture of *Sunset on Lone Aspen*, the Firth painting that had just sold for ten million dollars. The headline read "Francis Firth Did Not Paint This."

Martina Delgato called from Geneva to ask that Jane remain in the United States until things blew over.

"Gunther won't be able to ignore this," said Martina.

"I agree."

"What is that charming expression you Americans use?" Martina asked. "The shit's about to hit the ventilator?"

"The fan," said Jane and hung up.

She booked a flight to Geneva for the next day.

On the trip back, Jane was stranded for eleven hours in Paris's Charles de Gaulle Airport due to a mechanical problem with her plane. Seated in an unused gate, as far from the bustle as she could get, Jane called Ted Banks.

"Cancelled flight, huh?" he said when he heard about her complications. "Traveling commercial must be a real bitch for you jet-setters. Couldn't get Max to send his jet?"

Jane chuckled nervously. "I'm ready to tell you about my book, Ted. You got a minute?"

"Absolutely."

"I need your honest opinion."

"And you shall have it."

Jane sighed heavily and looked around the airport lounge. She'd been rehearsing this moment during her entire time in Ontario Hills. She finally summoned her courage.

"It's called *Van Gogh's Lover*," she said.

"Huh?"

He listened quietly while she laid out her research, pausing only to wait for airport announcements. She told him about Arles and Alan Silver. She told him about the walled garden at St. Paul's being identical to the one in *The Lover*. She told him about the coliseum in Arles, which was also in *The Lover*. She told him about the love letters she had found—"My Dearest Soph"—and the conclusion of the FBI's handwriting expert that the letters "were most likely by the same man." She told him about a news clipping she had found in Arles from *L'Arlésien* in 1888 about a search for an asylum escapee, Sophie Alt. Alt was Sophie's mother's maiden name. The article contained a sketch that looked a lot like Sophie du Burgen. She told him about records she had obtained from Dr. Pierre Dupont at St. Paul de Mausole that showed Sophie Alt had been a patient there at the same time as Vincent Van Gogh. The last record of her was a few months after the arrival of Vincent Van Gogh in May 1889, the month he painted *Lilac Bush*. This was about the time a young Jean Duplantier met Sophie aboard *La Virginie* and one year before her departure from St. Louis in a thundersnow storm—a storm which, coincidentally, was just four months before Van Gogh's suicide. Jane told him about a memoir of a Mississippi riverboat captain in the 1880s who wrote of a woman in St. Louis who "handled dock lines with the competence of a proper seaman." Jane told him about the Mark Twain book in the library dedicated to Sophie. She pointed out that Mark Twain loved Vienna, and often traveled there. It was just over the mountain from Burgen. Jane concluded by laying out a continuous timeline that followed Sophie from Chalet von Tessen to St. Paul de Mausole, to Arles, then back to the asylum at St. Paul de Mausole, to St. Louis, and finally back to Chalet von Tessen.

When she finished, Ted asked, "Is that it?"

"Yes."

"And who have you told about this?"

"No one."

"Good. Keep it that way."

"Why?"

"Because it's fucking crazy, Jane."

"Ted..."

"No, I mean it. It didn't happen."

"But the handwriting alone—"

"Jane, listen to me carefully. If you ever hope to be taken seriously about anything ever again, you will never repeat this to anyone. You once asked me why I had never written a book on Van Gogh. It's because I value my career. The scholarship borders on a religion. Every minute of his life from Belgium onward is documented in exacting detail. You want to know what Van Gogh had for breakfast on July 7, 1888? Some guy will tell you! There's literally a hardbound cookbook of his cuisine from Auvers-sur-Oise. I'm not joking. And then there's the Goghpies."

"Yeah, I met one."

"So you know. They will fucking crucify you. If you magically produced a videotape that showed Vincent Van Gogh in 1889 painting *The Lover* and then signing it '*Amant*,' they'd still never accept it. They're zealots. Give this up, Jane. Plus, it can't be true."

"Why?"

"You're asking me to believe that Sophie, having had a romantic relationship with one of the most brilliant painters of her time, retreated to Burgen where she started a new relationship with the local chaplain who, coincidentally, was also a world-class painter."

"Perhaps she acted more as a teacher? A muse?"

"Stop this, Jane! Vincent Van Gogh would never have kept such a huge secret from his brother. Never. Vincent wrote volumes about sunflowers, and they're just fucking flowers! A nude portrait? My god, he'd be over the moon. It would be the most significant work of his entire career. It would probably be the most valuable, too. More valuable even than *Starry Night*, and that went for over a hundred million dollars. It's ludicrous."

Jane fell silent. She had expected some pushback, but not this.

"Jane?" Ted said.

"They erased her," Jane said softly. "They called her crazy and erased her."

"Maybe she was crazy."

"Or maybe she was just a free spirit at a time when women were not allowed to be free spirits—especially not a baroness."

"You're making this out to be a *feminist* cause?"

"Maybe it is. Would a son have been erased like that? People would have rolled their eyes and said, 'Boys will be boys.' Whatever mental issues Sophie may have had, who's to say they weren't caused by the trauma of having been rejected so utterly by the very people who were supposed to love her? And for what? For simply being who she was! They made her believe she was sick, and so she went willingly to a string of asylums, which were nothing more than polite prisons, places with no one to love her, just a bunch of well-meaning doctors being paid by her father. Who wouldn't have scars?"

"Maybe."

"You've seen *The Lover*, Ted. Is it really so ludicrous?"

For the first time, Ted hesitated. A thought struck her.

"You're worried my book will discredit yours."

"You're damn right I am! Who's going to believe a word of it when the principal source is running around telling everyone, 'Oh, by the way, I found a Bigfoot'?"

Jane sighed. "You might have a point."

"Thank you!"

"So remove me from your book," said Jane.

"What? No!"

"Write me out of it."

"I can't do that! This is your work as much as it is mine. You're baked into every chapter. You deserve credit."

"I don't care about credit, Ted. Call me 'an anonymous source.' Change my name, my hometown. Say I wanted my identity kept secret. I'll write up a nice little fake backstory if you like."

Ted was silent. "You're sure about this?"

"Positive. Oh, and Ted?"

"Yes?"

"Thanks for your honesty."

Thirty-One

John

St. Louis, Missouri
The day of the night of the storm

John Planter drew a cloth over the boy's wound and then wrung it clean in the water basin.

"It's just a scrape, Doc," said the mother. "I don't see what all the fuss is about."

"Scrapes can become infected," said John.

They were in John's clinic on Market Street in central St. Louis. A privacy curtain covered the window, but the bustle of the city still found its way inside—the *clip-clop* of horses, whistles from the lumber mill, carpenters hammering from rooftops, men shouting from the waterfront. John's clinic was just one half of a storefront he shared with the telegraph office. It was tight quarters, but he was able to cram it full of the latest equipment—a complete set of surgical instruments, a stethoscope, a wall of medicines, and his latest acquisition, a gas autoclave for sterilization. It was all very modern, and already he had established a reputation as a physician on the leading edge. His medical books and journals filled a bookshelf. And thanks to the telegraph office next door, he had the luxury of a gas connection for lights and his new autoclave. At night, he slept on his examination table.

Out front, a shingle hung from a bracket: "Dr. John Planter, M.D."

St. Louis was booming, and the clinic was flourishing. Fresh immigrants arrived almost daily. Some days, there weren't enough chairs in his waiting room. If things kept going the way they were, he would be able to take over the telegraph office and then build a second floor for an apartment. There would be space for a wife and children.

John got a clean rag and soaked it in alcohol. He dabbed it on the clean wound.

The boy winced.

"I know it stings," said John. "I'm sorry."

"Serves him right," said his mother. "I just hope he learned his lesson."

"Why? How did this happen?"

She whacked the boy on the back of his head. "Tell him, Tony."

The boy stared at the scrape on his leg.

His mother went on. "He was down in Gaslight Square watching them whores. They was swimming nude."

She clucked her disapproval.

"That's a steep bank, Will," said John. "You slipped?"

The boy nodded.

John wrung the bloody bandage in his basin and thought for a moment. "Gaslight Square, you say?"

"That's right," said the woman. "'Twas three of them whores from Darlene's Silver Palace. Plus that German girl hangs with 'em."

John's heart sank. "Is that right?"

"Yeah, the one they call 'Sophie the Squaw'—'Sophie the Slut' 'tis more like."

John gave no reaction. He finished wrapping the wound and sat back to admire his work. Even in a task as simple as this, he could take satisfaction in a job well done. His skills were improving. The previous month, he had done a leg amputation of a poor miner whose initial wound had been no worse than this one. It was gratifying to know this boy would be spared that fate.

"It might itch a little, young man, but that just means it's healing. You must not scratch it. Come back tomorrow and I'll redress it for you."

"And stay off Gaslight Square," said the mother, hitting the back of the boy's head again.

She paid John two dollars and left. He put the money into his cashbox and sat down heavily.

Sophie the Squaw? That was a new one. Lately, Sophie was spending more and more time with the Shawnee. She had begun to wear her hair in a Shawnee braid, and John had seen her around town riding bareback on a dappled mare. Bareback!

Sophie was infuriating, but he could not regret his decision to settle in St. Louis instead of San Francisco. It was the best decision he ever made. After an enchanting week on the train with Sophie from New York, he got off with her in St. Louis to make sure she got settled. He saw at once the opportunities for a young doctor. They were limitless! Everyone was bound for San Francisco. Competition for patients would be fierce. Meanwhile, St. Louis was doubling in size every decade. Half the physicians were alcoholics and morphine addicts driven from their practices in the East. Unscrupulous veterinarians were doubling as doctors.

And then there was Sophie to consider. She was as fragile as a butterfly in a gale. The lithium he prescribed was not a magic elixir. Her dosage required constant tweaking. Her moods were volatile, and her impulsive behavior was troubling. But her fascination with riverboats was harmless, and if she wanted to handle the dock lines from time to time when no man was around, what was the harm? Still, swimming nude with the whores of Sin City and parading about as a Shawnee squaw... it couldn't go on. Something had to be done. But what?

The door to John's clinic opened, and a rancher came limping in. He knew at once he would be treating yet another case of foot fungus. It was rampant. He could build a practice on that malady alone.

He told the man to sit while he went to fetch his forceps, cotton balls, and cleaning solution.

Suddenly, the door flew open of its own accord and crashed against the wall.

"Sorry, Doc," said the man, who went to close it. "Wind's gone north."

"North, you say?" asked John, suddenly wary.

The rancher nodded soberly. "There's a storm a-comin', Doc, as sure as there's shit in a goat."

John could see that Sophie was unimpressed by his account of the boy's accident on the riverbank.

"What was he doing there?" she asked.

"What do you think?"

"I think boys shouldn't be spying on girls when they bathe," she said.

"I agree."

"Then I don't see how that's my fault."

He sighed. "Of course you don't."

They stood in Sophie's apartment. After the foot fungus case, he had put up a sign in his clinic window saying he'd be back soon, and made the short walk across town to her apartment. He noted that it looked exactly as it had on the day Sophie moved in. She was certainly no homemaker, he thought. The chairs, the bed, the little table—she hadn't even thought to rearrange them. Everything stood exactly as it had on that first day, as though nailed to the floor. The only thing she had done to personalize the apartment was to hang her painting on the wall *opposite the window*.

"Can you at least cover that up while I'm here?" he asked, pointing but not actually looking at the offending object.

"Why?"

"Oh, my god," he exclaimed. "You're impossible to talk to."

"I'm sorry, John, are you mad at me about something?" she asked.

"People are talking. Today, I heard someone call you..."

"Call me what?"

"Sophie the Squaw."

She laughed. "But that's a compliment!"

"It's not. It's really not."

Sophie frowned and considered this. "Then they're small-minded."

"People *are* small-minded, Sophie. And you can't keep swimming with Darlene's whores. That has to stop."

"Because of that *boy*? No! They're my sisters, John, and I love them all. It makes me happy to swim with them."

"Sophie, stop this nonsense! I treat their ailments, remember? I'd list them for you, but it's too depressing for words. You can guess. They're whores."

"Don't be cruel, John. And I know all about their ailments. We talk about *everything*. The reason you treat them at all is because I tell them to go to you, the best doctor in Missouri."

John sighed in defeat. He could never win an argument with her. Outwardly, he had all the power—money, position, standing in the community. But somehow, it never worked out that way. As she waited for him to speak, she drew her tongue across her lips, her beautiful lips. Oh, god. He was in a state of perpetual misery when it came to her.

He took her hands. "Sophie, I'm worried about you, that's all I'm saying."

"I'm fine."

"You need someone to take care of you. Let me be that person."

"You already take care of me."

"I don't mean just as your doctor."

Sophie pulled back her hands. "Not this again."

"Marry me."

"I'm already married."

"No, you're not, Sophie. I know you made that up."

She stepped back. "John, stop it."

"Why won't you marry me?"

She considered the question for a moment and then said, "Look at my painting."

He didn't move.

"You can't, can you?"

"It's indecent, Sophie."

She shook her head in sympathy. "The answer's there, John. The man who painted it put it there. But you can't even look at it."

She was right. He couldn't. To stand and gawk at his beloved butterfly posed as a modern Aphrodite was just not something he could ever do. He had the urge to snatch the damn thing off the wall and throw it in the Mississippi.

"I think you should leave, John," Sophie said.

Thirty-Two

Sophie

The storm arrived with a flash and a crash. Snow fell amid flashes of lightning and rolling thunder. It was unlike any storm Sophie had seen or even heard about. She went downstairs to the general store, where she was told by the proprietor it was called "thundersnow." He had not seen thundersnow in St. Louis for over a decade.

She heard a whimpering from the corner.

"What's that?"

"That's just Dexter," he said. "He's scared of thunder."

"Poor baby," said Sophie.

She followed the sound of whimpering to a barrel, where the beagle lay trembling. She knelt to pet him. He looked up at her. His eyes glowed like red embers. Sophie stood up quickly and, backing away, collided with a stack of canned beef. It crashed to the floor.

"Devil!" exclaimed the shopkeeper.

"Sorry," she said and fled upstairs to her room.

She lit a candle from the one she carried and then got into bed. She listened with mounting terror as the thunder grew nearer. She pulled the blanket over her nose. Her heart raced. Darkness descended over her mind like a curtain. On the opposite wall, *The Lover* flickered in candlelight. It brought her no comfort. It was, after all, born in a storm.

No! Please!

John's gentle voice came to her—*Refocus, Sophie. You can do it.*

John's medical treatment for Sophie was more involved than simply prescribing lithium salts. Together, they worked on what he called "strategies." The idea was that Sophie would learn to recognize the early signs of a coming episode—the shadow of a bird passing in front of the sun, the darkness of a descending curtain, unusual negativity, and so on. Then she was to deliberately drag her cascading dark thoughts back out into the light, where they would wither under the exposure.

She was supposed to avoid triggers—high walls, stray dogs, and enclosed spaces. Storms were also a trigger, but Sophie had never told John about storms. What was the point? How do you avoid a storm? But now she wished she had told him. If she had, he would be here already.

"How, John?" she asked the empty room. "How do I refocus?"

His voice came to her once more—*Drive out the bad thoughts with good thoughts.*

"I can't think of any good thoughts!"

And then she remembered the list. *The list!*

In their sessions, they made lists of images that were powerful enough to drive out the bad thoughts. She kept the list in a notepad by the bed. She opened the drawer to get it. She read.

The way he bobs his head.

Right. She pictured the funny way Vincent bobbed his head before launching his brush at the canvas. He was like a human pendulum.

She read on.

He can't build a fire.

She remembered their first picnic when Vincent tried to build a campfire for her. He was going to use his last match until she suggested he save it for his pipe. Afterward, he smoked as though he hadn't a care in the world. God, he was beautiful that day.

Her heart rate slowed. It was working. She read on.

Oranges.

She thought about the game with Vincent and the children in Arles.

"Did an angel send you?" he had asked afterward.

Sophie kissed him that day. And the way he kissed her back, she knew she would always be his.

She thought about something he had written in one of his letters from the asylum.

We are terribly flawed.

We are perfectly flawed.

The curtain lifted. Her heart beat normally. Dexter was not a demon. He was just a scared little beagle. The thunder was not coming to get her. It was just a storm.

John's strategy worked!

She threw back the blankets, grabbed her painting off the wall, wrapped it in a blanket, and plunged out into the thundersnow.

Thirty-Three

John

John was lying on his exam table trying to read a novel when the knock came on his door.

He put down the book, not that he would miss it—he had been stuck on the same page for a half-hour. Ever since his talk with Sophie, he had been unable to focus on anything. The knock was a welcome distraction from his misery. The way he was feeling now, he looked forward to an impressive case of foot fungus—the more extreme, the better.

"One minute!" he called out.

He got up and slipped on his clothes. He pulled open the door.

Sophie stood in the darkness, snow falling around her. She held a large object under her arm.

"Oh, my god!" he said and pulled her inside. "Are you alright? What are you doing out? You shouldn't—"

She kissed him. It was a brief kiss, but she let her lips remain on his lips for an instant longer than she needed to. That extra moment was pregnant with meaning.

She had his attention.

"I do love you, John."

"You do?"

She smiled and kissed him again. This time he pulled her close, and the kiss became more than a kiss.

They made love for hours on the floor, surrounded by his instruments, his exam table, his medical journals, and his shiny new autoclave. John laid out a blanket and brought a candle nearby. Outside the storm raged, but it only made their love nest that much cozier. It was John and Sophie versus the universe, and they were winning.

When they finished, John lay back, grinning at the ceiling.

"We will be so happy," he said. "You will see. I will build that upper floor, and we will live and work together, right here. When there are no patients to see, I can watch the kids so you can have a break. You will be our receptionist—"

She put her fingers on his lips. "*Shh*, John."

"Sorry," he laughed.

"I am leaving."

"What?"

"It's true. Tomorrow morning. On the Big Four."

"But you just... We just..."

"I know. I'm sorry, John, I truly am. You saved me, and I will always be grateful. But my heart belongs to someone else. He needs me now. I have just received a letter—"

"So what was this then?" he asked bitterly. "Your '*bon voyage*' fuck?"

John shocked himself by using such coarse language. She didn't flinch.

"John, don't ruin this," she said gently. "This has been... special."

While he sulked, she got up and walked naked to the corner where she had set her package. Even in his grief, he watched her every movement with fierce attention. He observed the way the muscles of her round bottom flexed from cheek to cheek as she walked; the glimpse of her womanhood between her legs as she knelt to pick up her package; the way her breasts became teardrops on her chest when she stood to walk toward him; the way her nipples stood erect in the cold room...

John Planter knew that, no matter what happened for the rest of his life, the sight of Sophie crossing that room would be with him forever.

She knelt beside him and removed the blanket from her package. It was her painting.

"I want you to have this," she said.

He made no move to take it. He wasn't sure he even wanted it.

"You know what this means to me," she said.

"Yes."

"But it is nothing compared to what you mean to me, John Planter. Do you believe that?"

"No."

She sighed and looked at her gift. "Maybe someday you will be able to look at it. And when you do, then you'll understand why I had to go."

She got up and began to dress. He lay naked on the floor, watching her. He didn't even try to cover himself. At last, she pulled on her boots and then came beside him.

She knelt and kissed him.

"Goodbye, John Planter."

She turned and went out the door.

For a long time, John stared at the door hoping it would fly open again.

Sophie changed her mind! She was back for good!

But the door stayed shut.

John's mind raced. The whole thing had been so sudden. He should have been angry. In the end, she rejected him. But he wasn't angry. Hurt, but not angry. Why wasn't he angry?

It took months for him to realize the reason. Deep down, he recognized that his love would have killed everything he loved about Sophie. John's love came with conditions—no more skinny-dipping with whores; no more riding bareback with the Shawnee; raise his children; work in the clinic. For Sophie, those conditions would have looked like walls.

It would take a special man to love Sophie without such conditions, John thought. John was not that special—he knew that even before she walked out the door.

Still, as time passed and no letter came, the memory of Sophie haunted him. He mulled over the things he might have done or said that would have made her stay. She came to him in dreams—dreams that often included her naked walk across his clinic.

It was intolerable! He decided the continued presence of her portrait was not helping him get over her. He carried it upstairs to his attic and set it against a back wall. For the first time, he allowed himself to look at it properly, and he saw that Sophie was right about the portrait. The painting did explain her decision to leave. The man who painted it—Vincent was his name—loved Sophie as she deserved to be loved. It dripped from every brush stroke.

He sat a long time looking at it until the bell downstairs jingled. A patient had entered the clinic.

He threw a sheet over the painting and went downstairs.

Part 4

Bombfire Night

Thirty-Four

Tomas

Fuck.

Tomas Firth slammed the brakes on his Aston Martin DBS. His car skidded, and two puffs of smoke rose into the mountain air.

In the passenger seat, Gunther's forehead hit the dash.

"Jesus! Are you trying to kill me? I told you, *slow down*!"

Ahead of them stood a wall of fleece. Hundreds of sheep packed the road from the cliff to the guardrail as far as he could see. The convertible's top was down, which allowed the wind to deliver a powerful whiff of damp wool and manure.

Fuck!

Gunther was rubbing his forehead. "This car's such a piece of shit."

"I paid over three hundred grand for this 'piece of shit,' so I suggest you show Asti some respect!"

"*Asti?*"

"That's right."

"You're daft, boy."

At the back of the herd, Tomas spotted a bearded man. He wore a tweed Alpine hat, complete with a feather. His age was somewhere between sixty and Moses.

"Hey, you there!" Tomas shouted in German.

The shepherd glanced up with dull eyes that registered no threat.

"They speak French here," said Gunther.

Tomas laid on his horn. "HEY!"

The shepherd gave him the finger.

Gunther was laughing.

"What's so funny?"

"Your horn," he laughed. "It sounds like someone's strangling a baby duck."

Tomas unclipped his seatbelt and got out.

Three weeks had passed since he made this same drive to confront Jacques Barbeau. It was shocking how much the scene had changed. A dusting of snow now covered the high Alps, and he sensed a crispness in the air. The setting was undeniably magnificent, like something from a desk calendar, but Tomas had no time to appreciate it. He had always looked upon himself as special by birthright. But ever since the American had shown up with her painting, dominoes had begun to fall. First, his father's suicide. Then the writer, Ted Banks, with his prying interviews. Then Martina Delgato and her suspicions. Then that idiot reverend leaping into the river and breaking his neck! It was unbelievable! Tomas had only meant to scare him into revealing the location of the vault. Gunther was furious; the courier was their only link to the vault, but how was any of this Tomas's fault?

And now the latest domino had fallen with Banks's article in *ArtNet*, "Francis Firth Did Not Paint This."

It was outrageous! Did the media have no ethics anymore?

The article was only a few paragraphs long, but it claimed that Gunther's book was essentially a work of fiction. Francis Firth had worked not as a goat-herder, but as a caretaker for the church. The article contained photographs showing the *actual* locations in Burgen of the artwork. It also showed a von Tessen family portrait of a woman named Sophie von Tessen, who bore a striking resemblance to Caroline Firth. The article alluded to another portrait of Sophie that was even more damning, clearly referring to the one Tomas had stolen while Jane was drugged. Tomas wondered if he should have destroyed it. But he thought it might be worth something—either as a work of art or as a bargaining chip with Jane Ward. Banks's article went on to say that the

Firth Gallery had no vault of paintings, as it claimed. It said they were acquiring them from a "third-party supplier." The article concluded with quotes from Burgeners, making it seem laughable that Francis Firth could have been the artist Gunther claimed in his book. At the bottom of this hatchet-job was a plug for Banks's forthcoming book to be published next year. The working title was *No-Talent Hacks*.

Fuck.

The gallery's phone had not stopped ringing ever since.

In Geneva, Martina Delgato was trying to get the gallery's bank records. Things were unraveling fast.

"Don't worry," his highly-paid lawyer assured him. "This is Switzerland. No one gets your bank records in Switzerland."

The next day, when Tomas spoke again to his highly-paid lawyer, his veneer of bravado was gone.

"You didn't tell me the von Tessens were involved."

"So?"

In a tone dripping with condescension, the lawyer explained that the von Tessens were one of Switzerland's most powerful banking families. There was a statue of Eduard von Tessen in Von Tessen Square! And apparently, their lawyer had a terrifying reputation—they called her The Viper.

Tomas didn't need his lawyer to tell him that if The Viper somehow got a hold of the gallery's bank records, then the gig was up. The records would show annual payments to the Barbeaus—father and son—going back sixty years, always on August 1. The last payment to Jacques was for a quarter of a million dollars. He and Gunther would go to jail. The police might even charge Tomas with Jacques's death!

But there was still a way out. It was a long shot, but if, somehow, the gallery's Geneva vault were to be filled with paintings by Francis Firth, then key art critics could be invited to take a vault tour and see the truth. They would write their own stories. Ted Banks could be discredited. His publisher would drop him. *ArtNet* would retract its story. The police would drop the case. The whole thing might even turn in Tomas's favor. Prices on the next two Firths would soar. Tomas could get a bigger boat.

Tomas went to Gunther with his idea. He expected to be shot down. But for once, his grandfather went along with him.

"Does that mean you know where the vault is?" Tomas asked.

"I have a pretty good idea."

"I don't understand. If you know, then why were you using the pastor?"

"Because I can't get to it. Only he can." His eyes narrowed. "Could."

Tomas ignored the jab.

"But isn't that still true?"

Gunther smiled. And what he said next gave Tomas hope that the dominoes that had been falling for weeks could be stopped before another one fell.

It was called Bonfire Night.

For as long as anyone remembered, Burgen Day was celebrated on the first fair weekend in September. There were traditional Swiss games and food, and the whole thing was capped off with a bonfire. The bonfire was everyone's favorite part, so they just called it Bonfire Night. After World War II, locals began using the English translation to avoid associations with the Nazi habit of burning books in the *lagerfeuer*.

As luck would have it, Bonfire Night this year was being used to promote the hard launch of the Valley of the Giants Hotel. Coaches were bringing in spectators from Geneva, including politicians, prominent former citizens, travel bloggers, and television crews. There would be crowds, live music, and fireworks. It was the perfect cover.

Tomas looked at his watch and shook his head. Fuck! He and Gunther had left early to beat the crowds and, in particular, Jane Ward. It was likely she would be attending, and she was the only person who knew Tomas and Gunther by sight. If they could avoid her, then the plan could work.

Tomas walked to the opposite shoulder of the road. The guardrail had been set back a few feet off the cliff ledge to accommodate hikers. The Alpina trail passed through this region, and this must have been one of the places where it joined the road. But the path was too narrow for a car, even Asti. How was he going to get around these sheep?

An idea came to him. He began to gather rocks, which he stacked at the base of the guardrail. After a few minutes, he had a short ramp rising to the top of the guardrail. He got back in the car.

"Get ready for a lesson in respect," said Tomas, and put the car in reverse.

He backed up and then drove toward the guardrail until his right front tire was at the bottom of his stone ramp, and his left tire was at the edge of the cliff. He eased out on the clutch and inched forward onto his stone ramp. Gunther fell against Tomas as the car angled toward the cliff.

"Are you crazy? Let me out!"

Asti's tires reached the top of the guardrail, and Tomas eased further off the clutch. The car leaned precariously now on just two tires. Using one eye, Tomas lined up the guardrail with the left edge of the rearview mirror. He reasoned that as long as he kept the guardrail on that line, his tires would remain atop the rail. Gravel crunched beneath the two tires still on the ground. He crept along, slipping the clutch to control his speed. Slowly, he passed the sheep, then the shepherd himself, who was looking at him wide-eyed.

Tomas flashed him the finger.

Tomas followed the guardrail along the long, slow curve. Ahead, the sheep were climbing off the road through a gate into a field. Dogs were guiding them into the pasture. Cars from the opposite direction idled behind the crossing.

Tomas neared the end of the guardrail. He gunned the engine. The car leaped off the rail, scraping metal on metal as the front tire struck the earth. His rear tires landed and spun a hailstorm of gravel into the abyss. The car fishtailed a moment toward the ledge. Tomas spun the wheel to correct the loss of control. The tires found asphalt and squealed. The car lurched forward, and suddenly he was speeding up the road past the astonished faces of the other drivers.

Tomas was laughing. He turned to Gunther, who was white as the fleece wall they had passed.

"Jason fucking Bourne!" said Tomas.

They raced up the road in the direction of Burgen.

Thirty-Five

Jane

Sydney was so excited she could talk about nothing else. Ursula had made the tactical mistake of presenting her traditional Swiss costume a week early, and now it was all she would wear. It had lace sleeves with a leather vest and ribbons up the chest. She speculated endlessly about who would win the Miss Burgen pageant and how unfair it was that she was too young to enter. Her new playmates from the next village were coming, and they were all going to try clogging and blowing on the ten-foot-long alphorn. Her father was doing fireworks, and there was a special firework just for her. It was a surprise.

Sydney called the festival "Bombfire Night."

For Sydney, it also marked the end of summer. Collette had arrived several days earlier to collect her daughter and help with the last-minute details. She was swept up instantly in Sydney's excitement. She made modifications to Sydney's costume and helped her braid Yara's mane with red and white bows that matched the bows in Sydney's hair, which, of course, matched the Swiss national flag. Collette declared that Sydney was the "perfect Swiss Miss," and the ladies in Elsa's Kitchen agreed.

Sydney's costume showed itself to Jane in full color, and Jane admired it as much for its color as for its lace and bows. The previous week, a rainbow had appeared over the valley, and Jane was transfixed by the sight of a complete spectrum, red to violet. No gaps interrupted the flow from one hue to the next. Her recovery was complete. But there was something else, too. She could no longer pretend that the colors were the way she remembered them. If she accepted Ravi's explanation that her brain had rewired itself based upon visual cues in *The Lover*, and if *Amant* was who she thought he was, then she was not just seeing color—she was seeing color the way *he* saw color. Jane hadn't seen any "spangled stars" yet, thank god, but the colors were strangely alive. She didn't just see them, she *felt* them. Red poppies made her toes tingle. Blue monkeyflowers made her anxious. But yellows gave the strongest reaction of all—they were like a breathless ride on a rollercoaster.

Max was using Burgen Day as the official launch for Klaus's *auberge diffuso*. Brigitte was handling marketing in the run-up to the event, and she was in a last-minute frenzy of activity. A famous travel blogger was staying in Jane's former cottage. Brigitte declared that the woman had the power "to make or break us." Max appeared unimpressed.

Everyone in Burgen—locals and guests alike—wore name tags. Max argued that it enhanced the authenticity of the nineteenth-century experience by putting everyone on a first-name basis, but Jane knew the real reason. Brigitte embraced the mandate by ordering elaborately engraved pins that identified permanent residents as "Burgener." They wore them with pride. At reception, guests were presented with a pre-printed name tag. Brigitte offered them a discount on a future visit if they posted a picture of their name tag on Instagram.

Max had all but vanished into the morass of logistics associated with the opening. There were last-minute repairs to the cottages, interviews with the media, temperamental musicians, street banners to print, better highway signage (long overdue), catering, and coaches to bring everyone to and from Geneva. Max had reserved blocks of rooms at a half-dozen downtown hotels for out-of-town guests. A campground sprung up along the riverbank, mostly of hikers arriving by the Alpina trail with their tents and cookstoves. Max installed a port-a-potty for their use. He spent a half-day overhauling the new generator to make sure it wouldn't fail at an embarrassing moment. The week before the event, he had disappeared for an entire day. When he returned, his SUV was filled with fireworks.

Two days before the event, Jane rode Tabitha into Burgen. It was the first time she had soloed from start to finish without any help, and she was feeling pleased with herself. She put Tabitha in Bernadette's barn and walked into town. The village, she marveled, was transformed from the last time she had seen it. The buildings and the stone walkways were freshly scrubbed, and banners hung across the walks proclaiming "Happy Burgen Day!"

Everywhere pictures displayed Brigitte's redesigned village mascot, a stone giant with a pointy Swiss hat. Jane thought it looked like a garden gnome.

Jane was walking in the direction of Elsa's Kitchen when she spotted Max working with several men on a rooftop. Hannah stood on the street below. She looked as though she had arrived by flying saucer. Her hair was ironed straight, and she wore a business suit with stiletto heels. She was holding her phone to the sky and grumbling.

She saw Jane approach and then grumbled, "Ach, no signal."

"You get used to it."

"I don't want to get used to it," she snapped.

On the roof, Max shouted something to one of the men.

"What the fuck is he doing up there?" Hannah asked.

As they watched, Max hoisted a heavy timber onto his shoulder and began walking across the steep roof toward the chimney while his helper held the other end. Even from the ground, Jane could see his legs tremble under the load.

"Max!" Hannah yelled. "Hey, watch out—"

Max turned toward her voice and slipped. He and the timber went down. It landed across his legs, and together they slid toward the edge of the roof.

Jane gasped.

Max pawed at the surface of the roof with his work boots as he slid closer to the ledge. At the last moment, he managed to dig his heel under a tile seam. It caught. He came to a stop.

"*Scheiße!*" Hannah breathed.

When it was clear he had a firm grip on the roof, he looked up. His gaze met theirs, and he broke into a grin.

"Phew!" Max said.

Hannah fumed. "He never listens."

They watched as Max and his helper prepared to repeat the maneuver that nearly killed him moments ago. He squatted and lifted the beam onto his shoulder.

Hannah raised her head, and Jane realized with horror she was about to shout a warning again. Jane put her hand over Hannah's mouth. Hannah stepped back, wide-eyed.

"What the fuck?" said Hannah.

"Maybe we shouldn't distract him this time," said Jane.

Hannah sulked in silence as Max and his helper laid the timber in place. The men took turns winding a long screw that ran through the center of the timber. Slowly, the stone walls of the structure, which had been leaning, were drawn together until they stood straight.

"That's got it!" Max shouted to his helper.

"He looks happy," said Jane.

"Happy?" Hannah snorted. "What do you know about it?"

"Just that he looks happy."

"That's Max von Tessen! He shouldn't be happy laying fucking roof tiles."

Max was climbing down the ladder. He came toward them. He was shirtless and holding a bottle of water, which he guzzled as he walked.

He winked at Jane. "Hey sis, what brings you to our little shindig?"

"I just thought I'd come up here to watch you kill yourself, that's all."

Max turned to Jane and grinned. "Did I dream it, or did I see you cover my sister's mouth with your hand?"

Jane winced.

"Wow," said Max. "You have no idea how badly I've wanted to do that my whole life. I never had the courage."

"Good thing," said Hannah.

"I was afraid I'd get bit."

"You would have."

Max took a swig from his water bottle and said to Hannah, "Seriously, why are you here, *mein Hase*?"

Jane smiled at the nickname. *My bunny-rabbit.* Hannah von Tessen was as far from a bunny rabbit as a rabbit was from a velociraptor.

Hannah ignored the dig. "Opa wants to see me."

"What about?"

Hannah scrunched her face. "Attorney-client privilege. Are you going to be ready here, or what?"

"We'll be ready. You're staying, I hope."

"Not much choice. Family obligations, and all that."

The whole von Tessen clan was coming to the chalet to support the launch. Max's parents would be there, as well as his older brother, plus everyone's wives and children. Sydney had confided to Jane that she was worried about an older cousin who had once pushed her off her pony.

Max swigged his water and turned to Jane. "Did you ride Tabitha down by yourself?"

"Yes."

"How'd she do on the big turn?"

"I tried to go outside the big rock, but she wanted to go inside. So I trusted her judgment."

He nodded. "You put her at Bernadette's barn?"

"South stall, out of the sun. She took a little water. She wanted feed, but I just threw in a little hay. She was overheated."

Max took another swig. "Good, Jane. Very good."

Hannah watched this interaction with interest. From the roof, a man called to Max. He took a last swig and excused himself.

Hannah watched him go.

"You're right, Jane, he does look happy. Damn it."

Jane left Hannah still searching for a cell phone signal, and started down the hill toward the church. Suddenly Sydney was beside her, out of breath from a long run. She had seen Jane ride in on Tabitha.

"Can I come with you? Oma and Agatha are sewing drapes for the stage, and it's *soooo* boring."

"If your oma says it's okay," said Jane.

Soon they were walking through the village down the long slope. Sydney was chattering on about yodeling and how funny it sounded. Jane smiled. She was happy for the company.

"So what are we doing?" asked Sydney.

"It's kind of a secret," Jane said. "We're looking for treasure."

Sydney wrinkled up her nose. "Treasure? Here?"

Jane laughed. Even a seven-year-old could be skeptical about finding treasure in a place like Burgen.

At that moment, Jane glanced over Sydney's shoulder toward a pudgy man standing at the corner of a cottage. Their eyes met. He turned away and slipped behind the wall.

Jane lowered her face to Sydney. "Once upon a time, a hundred years ago, a great painter worked in this valley. He hid his paintings here in Burgen. I'm trying to find them."

"You need a treasure map."

Jane laughed. "Wouldn't that be marvelous?"

"So where do we look first?"

"The church," said Jane.

She and Sydney arrived at the door. Jane hesitated. She had not been inside since Jacques's funeral. It was strange to think of him gone. It was as though one of the stone giants had gotten up and walked away.

"Come on!" said Sydney and pushed open the door.

The quest for treasure began. Jane tried to be methodical, but Sydney darted about like a hummingbird. They stomped on the floorboards. They pulled books off shelves. They moved Jacques's desk and chair. They even removed his trout trophies from the wall. Nothing.

They went into the basement and tapped the perimeter of the moldy walls until their hands were filthy. They climbed into the bell tower. More stomping and tapping. Still nothing.

Sydney's interest waned. It shifted to the bell tower's three bells and the mechanism of pulleys and levers that controlled them. She stuck her head inside the big bell and sang a song from school. Jane leaned on the belfry's railing and looked out over the village.

She went over all the clues again in her head. Why would Gunther lie about where his grandfather painted if not to conceal the vault?

Suddenly, Sydney was beside her, looking anxious. "I heard the ghost last night."

Jane nodded. She had heard it, too. At breakfast, everyone was talking about it. No one had heard the groaning from the East Wing since the night she and Max had found *Portrait in Winter*. Now it was back with a vengeance, groaning through most of the night.

"It's not a ghost, Sydney. It's just a draft whistling through the walls. There's no such thing as ghosts."

"My dad said you were named after a girl in a book called *Jane Eyre*. He said there was a ghost in *Jane Eyre*."

"And you thought because of that, I might know something about ghosts?" Sydney nodded.

Jane knelt before Sydney. "I think your father needs to re-read *Jane Eyre*. There was no ghost. The owner had his wife locked in an attic."

"Why?"

"She was sick. She kept trying to burn the house down. Does your father have someone locked in the attic?"

Sydney scoffed. "No."

"Are you sure?"

"Of course!"

"What about an animal? A coyote, perhaps? They like to howl."

"Yes… but no. That would be dumb."

"A hyena, then?"

Sydney laughed.

"Because it sure sounds like a hyena, doesn't it? Whining and carrying on at all hours of the night—"

"It's not a hyena."

"Are you sure?"

"There's nothing in the attic! I've been up there a million times."

"Right. So enough of this nonsense about a ghost, okay? There's no ghost in *Jane Eyre*, and there's no ghost in the East Wing."

Sydney nodded and wiped her eyes. "We didn't find your treasure."

"We'll just have to keep looking," said Jane. "You can help."

"I want to. What if I find it?"

Jane thought. "Then you would get the finder's fee, of course."

"What's that?"

"In this case, I'm sure your father would be so grateful he would let you pick out one of the paintings for yourself."

"Can we look tomorrow?" she asked.

"Tomorrow your cousins arrive."

"What about the next day?"

"That's Burgen Day."

"What about the *next* day?"

"You're going home, Sydney. Remember?"

Her shoulders sagged. "Oh, yeah."

Jane left Sydney with Ursula and then allowed herself to be led through Burgen by the smell of Elsa's ovens. It had been weeks since she had eaten in Elsa's Kitchen. With Ted in Paris and her work at the chalet, she had little reason to come down the mountain. She hadn't realized how much she missed the pulse of Burgen.

Max came beside her.

"Jane," he said, "I'm glad I caught you. I was going to have my lunch by the stream. I know a good spot. Care to join me?"

"Uh, sure. But can we grab a loaf of Elsa's bread? I've got such a craving for it."

Max's lunch spot was lovely. It was beside the stream where a large, irregular boulder doubled as a bench and table. There was a small beach for wading. A knee-high waterfall connected two water holes. They laid out their food and began to eat.

In the distance, someone was trying to blow the giant alphorn.

"I got a job offer," said Jane.

"Wow. Really? Where?"

"The Leipzig Archives. They were so happy with my work, they wanted me to keep doing it. Apparently, there are dozens of private archives like yours scattered across the great houses of Europe. It's not much money, but the travel will be nice. I've never been anywhere."

"Well, congratulations," he said.

"Thanks."

They sat in silence for a while, keeping to their own thoughts. A fish jumped in the waterfall.

"See that?" said Jane.

He nodded. "It's making its way upstream. It will find the same hole it was born in and there, and only there, will it spawn."

"Amazing," said Jane. "I wonder if it knows where it's going?"

"Of course it does."

"Really?"

"Is that so hard to believe? It's answering a craving. Earlier, you craved Elsa's bread. You went to buy some. Didn't you know what you were doing?"

"It sounds like you're saying a fish has free will."

"Why not?"

Jane considered this. "So in this theory of yours, the fish could choose *not* to go to its spawning hole?"

"It would be unhappy, but yes."

"You've made a study of this?"

He shrugged. "I don't know about that. But if you spend enough time watching animals, you see that's how it works. Cravings are like breadcrumbs."

"And where do these breadcrumbs lead?"

"To happiness."

Jane frowned and searched his face for a sign that he was trying to make a larger point. She saw none, so decided to play along. "And what do you crave, Max?"

He blinked and turned away.

"Max?"

When he looked back, she thought he looked flushed.

"We should get back," he said.

The air was crisp as Jane began her ride out of the valley to the chalet. The day hummed with possibility, just as it had on that fateful morning so long ago when she set out to walk to school. Something about this day reminded her of that other day, and not just because of the weather.

It had always seemed to Jane that by stepping off the curb in Ontario Hills, she had passed through a door—maybe because she had no memory of the impact of the truck, or the long flight to the car windshield, or the arrival of the emergency vehicles, or the ambulance ride, or any of the many surgeries that put her body back together. One moment she was at the curb, and the next she was in the hospital, looking at unfamiliar faces through a gray-tinted lens.

As she rode Tabitha higher along the trail, she felt as though another door had just opened in her path.

Max had blushed.

Tabitha halted unexpectedly, and Jane had to kick her harder than usual to get her moving again. At the midpoint of the climb, Tabitha stopped yet again, and it occurred to Jane that the horse had been jumpy almost since the start of the ride. Jane paused to scan the landscape. Was there a predator?

Jane patted Tabitha's neck.

"What's the matter, girl?"

And that's when Jane saw the cloud shelf. It appeared over the craggy stone giant they called Ulysses. The monolithic cloud was a menacing gray-black and was seemingly as impenetrable as concrete. It curled over the top of the peak and then descended into the Valley of the Giants like an avalanche. Even as Jane watched, Chalet von Tessen was gobbled up.

Oh, my god.

The air changed from crisp to damp. Jane shivered as the blast of cold air hit her. In seconds, she was in it.

The fog was as dense as the day Pauli had led her to the overlook. She looked down from her saddle. She couldn't see the ground. She was floating.

That day with Pauli, Max had been able to climb through the fog to reach the chalet. But he had been on Lela. Tabitha was not Lela. Lela knew the trail from hundreds of trips made over a decade, whereas Tabitha was a newcomer to the valley and had only made the trip a dozen times—and always with Lela guiding.

Tabitha snorted and stomped nervously on the ground. Jane didn't want the horse to spook and go plunging off the cliff, so she dismounted. With her boots on the ground and her hand on the reins, Jane stroked Tabitha's nose.

"I know, girl. Don't worry. It's okay."

A sense of responsibility for Tabitha pushed Jane's mind into survival mode. All thoughts receded until there was only the fog and the cliff and the awareness that one false step meant death.

Jane considered their plight. Fog is a peculiar blindness. Though light is reaching your eyes, the light carries no information. Your brain rejects it. Normal people might as well be in a cave.

Normal people.

In a very real way, Jane had spent the last twelve years training herself to see in a fog. But even armed with this unexpected superpower, the idea of continuing was terrifying. Thunder rumbled through the valley, and Jane was on the verge of panic. Tabitha gave a little tug at her reins as if to reassure herself that the human was still there.

As Jane stared helplessly into the white veil, a shape appeared.

"Max?" Jane called out.

But it wasn't Max. It wasn't even a person. It was a word. The word was written in block letters, and it said...

"*M-A-C-K.*"

It is emblazoned on the chrome grille of a truck that now fills her entire world. She reads it in wonder.

M-A-C-K.

Then comes the impact. Her book bag is torn from her grasp. Her phone is no longer in her hand.

"My phone," she thinks.

The air is expelled from her lungs. It feels like drowning. Her chest collapses like a tent in a storm. Ribs snap. She is flying. Soaring higher and higher. She sees the roof of her school. A blue Frisbee lies beside a pile of leaves.

Jane somersaults backward, in the opposite rotation of her flight. She is head-down when she hits the windshield of the postal truck. Her skull penetrates the glass like a diver piercing the surface of a pool. She comes to a stop with her body half-in, half-out of the windshield. She is looking down at the front seat. It is strewn with mail.

Darkness...

She wakes up in an ambulance. EMTs talk in medical shorthand.

"Motor vehicle accident, multiple injuries... Get blood type and crossmatch ready... Notify the surgeon... We'll need to assess for internal bleeding."

Darkness...

Now she is on a gurney in a hospital corridor. Ceiling lights race backward.

"Fluid in the stomach... Prep for intubation... Ortho is on standby for the fractures... Possible head injury..."

The prick of an IV, a shot of cold fluid entering her arm...

These dormant memories spilled into her mind like water into a cup. Because they had remained untouched by her conscious brain until that moment, they played out before her like a movie. The fog served as a movie screen. The memories should have shaken Jane, for they were horrifying, but strangely, they calmed her.

She had been wrong about her accident all along. She hadn't passed through a door. There wasn't a "successful Jane" living on the other side of this fanciful door. It was an accident. A stupid accident by a careless teenage girl. There was only one Jane, *this* Jane, her. How long had she indulged in the fantasy that this world was somehow not the real world? How long had it given her a convenient excuse to go through the motions of living without actually committing to it? It's why she had scoffed at Collette about having children. To have children was to commit to life and love. It's what Granny Jo was trying to tell her in the hospital.

Love is a choice.

The movie faded. But the memories of the accident remained. They were a part of her now. And this restored Jane looked at the white wall before her and watched with satisfaction as, slowly, it transformed into a landscape of color only she could see.

The color revealed a path.

Jane clucked to Tabitha, and together they started up the trail.

When Jane reached the barn, she found Max saddling Lela. Jane dismounted and led Tabitha toward her stall.

Max looked up, and his shoulders sagged. "Oh, thank god!"

His face was etched with worry.

Jane said nothing. She tied Tabitha's reins to a post and walked toward Max.

"I was about to go out after you," he said. "This storm... How on earth did you—"

He never got to finish. By then, Jane's lips were pressed firmly on his.

Thirty-Six

Jane

All through the next day, they arrived in their limousines—Max's parents in designer clothes with personal assistants and a private chef; Hannah with her impossibly tall husband and three impossibly tall boys; a squat uncle who held a high position at the bank, with his bejeweled wife and their three unhappy-looking daughters. Max's fifty-year-old brother, Rudd, arrived in a helicopter with a twenty-one-year-old supermodel who appeared to be seven months pregnant. Jane observed him from a safe distance. Rudd had Max's deep-set, intelligent eyes and the same square jaw. His posture was straighter, as though he had embraced the stature that embarrassed Max. Except for the salt-and-pepper hair, he was the spitting image of Max, twenty years older.

The chef worked in the kitchen under Agatha's disapproving eye. There was to be a family banquet that night in the dining hall. Jane didn't even know the chalet *had* a dining hall. It was accessed through one of the doors of the library. Ursula kept it closed for the rest of the year. Jane had thought it was a closet.

At the sound of the dinner gong, Jane went to the barn to visit Tabitha. A few minutes later, Max appeared.

"You didn't hear the bell?"

"It's for the family."

He took her hand and led her back inside.

In the dining room, two dozen people of every age were seated around an enormous table covered with plates of uneaten food. Sydney's chin rested on the table; she was barely visible behind her place setting. Everyone looked up when they entered.

"Maxi, what are you doing?" asked Rudd. "It's family only. I'm sorry, Mademoiselle—"

"Jane *is* family," thundered Klaus.

Rudd withered under Klaus's glare.

Max pulled out the empty chair beside his, and Jane sat.

"*Now* can we eat?" asked Sydney.

After dinner, Klaus asked everyone to fill their champagne flutes and then led them to the portrait room. One by one, he and Sydney took turns unveiling the restored portraits.

"Allow me to introduce Sophie von Tessen," said Klaus.

"Who?" asked Rudd.

"Jane, tell them," said Klaus.

Jane related her discoveries of that summer, culminating in the finding that Eduard had an older sister who returned as *la gardienne du maison* of the chalet. When she finished speaking, Klaus asked everyone to raise their glasses.

"To Aunt Sophie," he said. "Welcome home!"

That night, Jane sat alone in her room writing her fake identity for Ted's book. It was unnecessarily elaborate, but she was having fun. She was writing fiction again. A knock came at the door. She got up expecting to find Max. In all the commotion, they hadn't spoken about the kiss in the barn. Or tried to repeat it. She pulled open the door. Klaus stood alone in the corridor.

"Klaus?"

"Can you come with me?" he asked. "I want to show you something."

He led her downstairs and into the English Garden. They followed an overgrown path to the door of the Garden Chapel. They went inside.

A single candle burned beside the door. Klaus used it to light several more candles until the room glowed.

"I've never been in here," said Jane.

The chapel was barely larger than a walk-in closet. There were two pews on either side of the aisle. On the facing wall was a plain wooden cross. A small altar held a silk cloth and a candelabra. On the right wall was an icon of Mary and Jesus. To the left was the von Tessen family crest carved in wood—a common swift with a star on its chest. The chapel smelled of smoke and paraffin from the candles, but also of the roses that grew all along its outer walls. It was a heady mix.

"It's nice," said Jane.

"Let's sit," he said, sounding out of breath.

They sat side by side on a pew. He propped his cane beside him and turned to her.

"Are you religious, Jane?"

"I believe in God," she said.

"The valley is my church. I was fifteen when I came to the chalet to live. I was unsuited to the family business." He snorted. "You can probably guess why. It was obvious to everyone. Can you imagine me at a bank?"

Jane shook her head.

"So they sent me here."

"Max told me."

"I met Ursula in Burgen. Did you know that?"

"No!"

He grinned. "It's true. At Wednesday Evensong. She's a Burgener through and through. Who else could bear this life?"

"I see what you mean."

He pointed to the family crest that hung on the wall and grinned.

"The swift," said Jane.

"Everyone—even me—assumed the swift was in The Crags that day to save Eduard from the avalanche. After all, Eduard was an important man. But now—thanks to you—I know it wasn't there for Eduard. It was there for Sophie. I think Eduard knew that. That's why he changed the family crest. The swift chose Sophie to look over the valley, just as it chose me, just as it chose you."

"Klaus—"

"I want you to consider staying on as *la gardienne du maison* of the chalet."

Jane recoiled. "What?"

"I have spoken to Ursula and Hannah. I will transfer ownership of the chalet, its contents, and all its holdings in the Valley of the Giants to you. You'll own everything."

"Because of a *bird*? Klaus, I'm not even sure what I saw—"

He waved his hand. "It's not just that."

"Then why?"

"Because the swift was *right*. You fit here, Jane, more than anyone else I've ever met, even more than Max. I think you know that, too. But before you thank me, you need to know that this gift comes with certain conditions. For example, if you accept it, you can't just sell it."

"I would never do that!"

"I know you wouldn't."

"What about your family?" Jane asked. "Won't they be upset?"

He clucked. "There will be some trouble over this, I won't lie to you. But don't worry about it. Hannah will write an ironclad contract. They won't be able to touch the property, provided you keep up your part of the bargain."

"By being *gardien du maison*."

"It not a prison sentence, Jane. Travel when you want. Write your books. Find a husband—that's very important. No one should live up here alone. But the valley must be your home. And you need to run the *auberge diffuso*. I can't keep asking Max to help. He may not have gone into the family business, but he is an engineer with a construction company he's neglected long enough. I'm sure he will help you, just as he's helped me. But he can only do so much. It's up to you to make it succeed. And it must succeed, Jane. If it fails, Burgen will cease to exist. And someday you will have to find your replacement." He grinned and nudged her with his shoulder. "Perhaps the swift will help you."

"I already have a job offer," said Jane.

Klaus frowned. "What?"

She told him about the Leipzig Archives.

"They want me to start next month."

"Congratulations," said Klaus.

"Thanks."

"It's your decision, of course," said Klaus. "But don't wait too long. I don't want to sound overly dramatic, but tomorrow's Bonfire Night will be my last."

Burgen Day was a magnificent blur.

Max placed Brigitte at the center of the event, and the intern was like a flower blossoming in the sun. She looked radiant in her Swiss costume and blonde braids with bows at the tips. She flitted about between activities and guests, passing out smiles like candy from her pocket. Jane could only marvel. The girl had a future in tourism—if not politics. Jane checked to see if Max was as spellbound by Brigitte as everyone else. But every time Jane saw Max, he was looking at her.

Max went about with his walkie-talkie, handling the patchwork of issues—planned and unplanned—that cropped up. She marveled at his composure. At one point, Jane overheard a particularly snotty influencer complaining about her straw mattress. Jane wanted to punch her. But Max calmly recounted the history of straw mattresses, how they had once been only for royalty, but by the nineteenth century, they were within reach of even simple Burgeners. It was considered the height of comfort. While the woman absorbed these facts for her blog, he remarked on the tattoo sleeve that covered her right arm. He pulled back his shirt to show his tattoo. The influencer laughed and then touched Max's arm in a way that was completely unnecessary. Jane winced.

Klaus and Ursula held court in lawn chairs in front of the stage. Ursula wore a traditional peasant dress with a sunflower tucked into the vest. Klaus wore a black vest with red-and-white pinstriping. He, too, sported a sunflower.

At the start of the festival's events, Brigitte gave a short welcome speech and then called Klaus to the stage to officially begin the celebration.

"This is my seventy-second Burgen Day," he said. "I missed a few in my youth."

People applauded, but he held up his hand. "Don't be too impressed by that. There are people here who have seen more." He pointed to one of the villagers. "You know who I'm talking about, Anna. You too, Felix."

He went on. "This year, we introduce our *auberge diffuso*. I would like to take this moment to recognize the incredible work of Maximillian von Tessen, my grandson, in making it a reality. I would call him to the stage, but... but... I don't see him in the crowd."

He looked around for Max, and for an instant, he seemed to lose his composure. Brigitte came to his side and touched his arm. She whispered in his ear.

"Clogged port-a-potty, you say?" he said into the microphone. "I think we can agree that's more important."

His gaze found Jane. She smiled in encouragement. He straightened.

"Before I leave the stage, there's one question that keeps coming up again and again, so I thought I'd address it now, once and for all." He paused dramatically. "Why the straw mattresses?"

Everyone laughed.

"We want our guests to have a good time, of course, and we believe they will. It is also our goal that guests leave the Valley of the Giants with a positive impression of the Alpine way of life. But not an unrealistic one. This life may appear idyllic, but it was also hard. Men worked long days driving livestock to far-flung pastures."

"Still do!" someone shouted.

"Thank you, Harold," said Klaus. "Women washed clothes in the stream and hauled buckets of drinking water to their cottages. You should try that sometime. It's hard work! Perhaps the straw mattresses will remind our guests of that side of life, too."

"Or they can try coming in January!" a man shouted from the back.

Klaus shook his head. "I'll let Gaston have the last word. His wife Margaret always does."

The crowd burst into laughter as Gaston sank into his chair.

"I officially declare the start of Burgen Day!"

A man blew a note on the alphorn, and everyone cheered, "*Hourra!*"

There were a few hiccups to the day. A fog moved in for an hour after two o'clock, delaying the yodeling contest. A French beauty from Geneva won the

Miss Burgen pageant, only to have the crown and sash disappear during the presentation. (They found them later.)

To Jane's amazement, the von Tessens were more than mere spectators. They wore traditional costumes and participated in the various contests. The uncle won the yodeling contest. Rudd had to be coaxed by Klaus to the alphorn, but once he began to blow, the sound echoed over the valley like thunder. When he finally ran out of breath, the crowd broke into applause.

Max spoke publicly only once. It was during the fireworks when he took to the PA system to announce the forthcoming launch of "the Sydney-work."

"A very special firework for a very special daughter."

The crowd fell silent as the thump launched the firework. It rose grandly and then exploded in a constellation of falling purple trails—Sydney's favorite color.

"Way to go, Sydney!" someone shouted (Jane thought it sounded like Bernadette), and then everyone broke into applause.

Afterward, people moved to the clearing where the fire marshal lit the bonfire using a flare. As the flames grew, Jane settled back on the grass to watch people's faces glowing in the firelight. Sydney's friends had left after the fireworks, and now the little girl was sandwiched between her mother and her great-grandmother. She was pointing at something in the fire. Her face glowed in the firelight. Brigitte was circling the fire passing out blankets. Bernadette and Rochelle sat apart for once, each with their respective husbands.

At some point, the von Tessens broke away one by one, back to their limousines, back to Geneva and the world beyond. Jane didn't envy them. She was precisely where she wanted to be. She sat alone, staring into the flames, as Rudd's helicopter flew overhead.

Max appeared above her. "There he goes."

Jane nodded. "He couldn't stay one more night?"

"They never stay more than one night. May I join you?"

He slid in beside her and covered himself with her blanket.

He grinned at her.

"What?"

"Klaus told me."

"What?"

"You know."

"Aren't you upset?"

"Why would I be upset?"

"I'm not family!"

"In Klaus's mind you are. You heard him at dinner. What happened between John Planter and Sophie—that makes you family as far as he's concerned."

"Not really," she said doubtfully. "Besides, it's your inheritance."

"The chalet is not an 'inheritance,' Jane. It's not a gift, either. It's a call to duty. If you're even considering this, you need to understand that. It's a crumbling old firetrap at the end of an unmaintained road beside a dying village."

"And the *auberge diffuso*?"

"It'll never pay its own expenses, much less the chalet's. We've all tried to show the numbers to Klaus. But he's a dreamer."

Jane sighed. "I'm a sucker for dreamers."

"Me, too."

"But I'm not one," said Jane. "I have a wicked practical streak."

He nodded. "Maybe that's what the valley needs now."

His gaze went to her lips. Jane looked away before his stare could become a kiss. Bonfire Night was still crowded with Burgeners and guests—not to mention Sydney. Jane was not ready for a public display.

Time passed and log by log, the fire consumed itself. The night grew colder as the fire exuded less heat. People wandered off in search of warmth. The remaining von Tessen contingent rose and said their *bonne nuit*s to Jane and Max. Collette carried a sleeping Sydney.

"I need to get this one to bed," she said. "Are you coming?"

"I have to stay with the fire," said Max. "I promised the fire marshal."

Collette nodded.

"I'll stay too," said Jane.

Collette smirked at Jane and then disappeared in the direction of the parking lot. When they were out of sight, Max turned to Jane and kissed her. He started with a probing kiss to test the waters. He must have found them inviting, because he followed up with a long kiss that left Jane trembling.

"Whoa," said Max.

"Whoa," said Jane.

For the next hour, they sat beneath the blanket, kissing and talking and cuddling for warmth, until the fire became just a bed of embers pulsing beneath a crystal sky.

Max used buckets of water scooped from the river to extinguish the remaining coals. He waited fifteen minutes, per fire regulations. When he was satisfied the fire wouldn't re-ignite, he took Jane's hand and led her through the darkness to his car, to the chalet, to his room, and ultimately, to his bed.

That night, Jane was troubled by dreams of falling. She lay immobile at the edge of the chalet's East Cliff. Someone was preparing to roll her over the side. She wanted to fight, but she couldn't move. She was cold, so cold. Her teeth chattered, and she couldn't stop shivering. The man knelt to give her a final push. She clawed for something to hold on to, but her fingers found only air…

She awoke shivering in bed beside Max. She was about to snuggle against him when she heard a groaning sound. For an instant, she thought the sound had carried over from her dream. But the moans went on, and she realized it was just the chalet's "ghost." She checked her clock. 2:14 a.m. She wriggled closer to Max and went back to sleep.

The next morning, everyone rose early to say goodbye to Collette and Sydney who were returning to Paris. Jane and Max sat at the kitchen counter drinking coffee and shooting ridiculous grins at each other whenever no one else was looking.

Collette came in. "Hey, has anyone seen Sydney? She's not in her bed."

When no one answered, Max set down his cup. "She's probably out at the barn saying goodbye to Yara. I'll get her."

A few minutes later he returned, shaking his head. "Not there."

"What about the pony?" asked Jane.

"In her stall."

And so began the search. They split up and moved in ever-widening circles as a person does when searching for something. They started in all the obvious places, and when she wasn't there, they looked in the East Wing, the attic, the lawn, the equipment shed, and the barn again until they were looking in places she couldn't possibly be—trapped in the freezer, asleep in a closet.

They reassembled in the den.

"Where could she be?" asked Collette.

Ursula's gaze went to the French doors, where across the English Garden loomed the specter of the East Cliff.

"You don't think..." said Ursula.

Agatha gasped. "The curse."

Until that moment, the group had staved off panic. But now Collette lost it. "No. No. No."

Max threw open the door and charged across the garden, past the little chapel to the East Cliff.

The rest of the group trailed a few steps behind. Klaus, leaning heavily on his cane, brought up the rear. Max reached the ledge and peered down. Jane couldn't bear to look. The thought of seeing Sydney lying broken at the bottom of the cliff was too horrifying...

"It's clear," he said.

Jane sighed.

"Where is she, Max?" Collette sobbed.

"Perhaps she went for a farewell walk," said Agatha.

"Where?" exclaimed Ursula. "There's nowhere to go."

"Burgen?" Klaus suggested.

"She wouldn't," said Collette. "That trail, it's not safe..."

Max looked at his watch and turned to Collette. "Call Hannah. Tell her to send the police. Tell them to use the helicopter. And bring the dogs."

Collette's hand went to her mouth.

"I'm going to take Lela and check the trail," said Max.

Until that moment, Jane had remained silent. She had an escalating feeling that the answer was in front of her.

"Wait," she said.

They stopped and turned to her.

"What?" asked Max.

Images and snippets of her conversation with Sydney in the church tower flashed in front of her.

"She went looking for the picture vault," said Jane.

"What?" exclaimed Max and Collette together.

"Why would she?" asked Max. "I mean, how does she even know about that?"

"I told her," said Jane.

"You *what*?" Collette exclaimed.

"It was the other day when I was in Burgen, at the church," Jane said, speaking rapidly. "We were making it into a game. A treasure hunt. She wanted to be the one to find the treasure. I told her if she did, then she could have her own painting. She was disappointed she was leaving and wouldn't get to look for it."

"Oh, my god," said Collette.

"Where would she go?" asked Max.

More snippets bubbled up from her subconscious...

MAX: *It's not a ghost. It's a draft blowing through the planks.*

SYDNEY: *It's creepy down here.*

JANE: *There's nothing to be afraid of. There's no such thing as ghosts.*

MAX: *The house was built on a natural shelf, but the shelf was not perfectly level. There are voids...*

2:14 a.m.

"Jane?" said Max.

"She's under the house," said Jane.

"Under the house?" scoffed Max. "How do you know that?"

"Come with me," she said.

Jane led them back to the portrait room. She went to her computer and used her new catalog to access her archive. A few seconds later, she held two large rolls of paper.

"Are these the blueprints for the chalet?" asked Max.

Jane nodded.

"Where did you get them?" asked Max.

"The records vault, where else?"

Jane rolled them out. "I had them restored. It's like you said, the shelf under the house is uneven, which creates voids. But it's even more uneven than you thought. Some of the voids are more than just voids. There are whole rooms in some areas. In the East Wing addition especially. There's this one spot, very deep, into which every void flows. I'll bet it was once a pool. All the other passages were stream beds that fed it."

"What's this got to do with Sydney?" asked Collette.

"Cold air falls, just like water. It would accelerate down the passage just like the water used to before they covered it up. Down, and down to that spot. From there, it would have nowhere to go."

"Nowhere but up through the planks of the room above it," said Max. "Our ghost."

"Can we agree to stop calling it that?" said Jane.

"Absolutely," said Max. "But Jane, the catacombs are sealed. For there to be a draft, air would have to get in somewhere."

Jane nodded. "Like when someone opens a door."

"I heard the gho... er, draft last night," said Ursula.

"So did I," said Collette.

Jane was nodding soberly. "At two fourteen a.m." She swallowed. "I think it was Sydney entering the catacombs looking for treasure."

"My god," said Ursula.

"But Max, that area is huge!" said Collette. "And it's pitch dark down there. She could be anywhere! What if she's trapped or unconscious? She won't be able to answer!"

"Collette, call Hannah back," said Max. "Tell her to send an air ambulance to the chalet."

Collette raced outdoors to make the call.

"Oma, I'm going to need the good flashlights and also the headlamps," said Max. "They're in the equipment shed."

"I'll go with her," said Agatha, and they both left.

Klaus was studying the blueprints and mumbling, "I never knew. All this time."

Collette returned from making the phone call. "Hannah's going to make the calls. Now what?"

Max frowned at Jane. "How did you come up with all this?"

"I don't know. It just came to me. I've been neck-deep in this stuff for months. But it makes sense when you—"

"Stop. I believe you. How did she get in?"

Jane thought. "The kitchen entrance, maybe. That day you brought Tabitha, Sydney found me in the records vault. And at least there are some lights there."

"Okay, good. I'll start there."

"You mean 'we'!" Jane exclaimed. "I'm coming, too!"

"Yes, you are," he said. "We're going to need your knowledge of those blueprints. Collette's not kidding. The catacombs are huge. A maze. They weren't built by men. As you said, they were carved by water over millions of years."

"You've been down there?"

"A few times when I was a kid. It's not pleasant, I'll tell you that."

"What do I do?" asked Collette.

"Keep your phone on," said Max. "We won't have a signal down there, but the Wi-Fi should be good enough. We may want you to stomp from above, so we can orient ourselves below."

Collette nodded.

"Okay, Jane. Are you ready?"

She wasn't, at least not for the liquid darkness that lay beyond the records vault. She kept close to Max, sharing his light. As they moved through the maze, she was keenly aware that overhead was a structure built at a time before permits and certificates of occupancy. Old pipes, rusty and long retired from the workings of the chalet, dangled in their path. They had to move cautiously, since a cut from a pipe would surely bring a case of tetanus.

In a few places, tiny trails of light leaked from above between gaps in the flooring. They were like oases in the darkness. She and Max would pause beneath them to study the blueprints and discuss where to go next.

On and on they went, ever deeper into the catacombs. Max used his phone to communicate with Collette about where to stomp on the floor. Steadily, they made progress east.

Every minute or so, they would call Sydney's name and wait for a reply. But all they heard was the creaking and popping of the old house as it shifted above their heads.

Whatever misgiving Jane might have had about entering such a godforsaken place was driven away by the thought of Sydney sitting alone and frightened somewhere in this overpowering blackness.

They came to a three-way fork and paused to consult the blueprints.

"The middle one," said Jane.

Max agreed, and they forged on to the next fork and then the next. The passageways became higher and wider as they made their way from the original house to the East Wing. In places, Jane could almost stand.

After a half-hour of on-again-off-again progress in this manner, Max called out once again.

"Sydney! Are you here?"

A faint sound followed.

"Did you hear that?" asked Jane.

"We're coming, Sydney!" Max shouted. "We're coming!"

"It came from over here," said Jane, pointing to their right.

But it was a dead end.

"She must be on the parallel passage." He studied the blueprints. "There's no way we can get there from here. We'll have to circle back. Goddammit!"

"Wait," said Jane.

She traced her beam along the wall where it met the floor. A gap appeared between the rock and the underside of a floor joist.

Max started up the slope, but Jane stopped him.

"You'll never fit."

Before he could argue, she scrambled up the side of the passage to the floor joists. She considered the way ahead. She was pretty sure she could worm her way under the first gap, but the second looked even tighter. For an instant, the prospect of getting stuck between floor joists with the weight of the house above her paralyzed her mind.

"Here goes," she said.

She lay on her back and began wiggling through. The joist pressed against her breasts, and she used her hand to guide them out of the way.

"I'm through," she called back to him.

"What do you see?"

"Another gap. I think I can just make it."

A sound came to her from the other direction. Louder this time.

"Papa?"

"I hear her!" Jane cried. "It's Sydney!"

She called down the corridor. "Sydney, we're coming!"

"Help!"

"I'm coming, too," said Max.

"No! If you get stuck, no one is ever getting out of here. Just keep the light aimed at that slot so I can find my way back."

Jane scooted to the next joist and then wriggled her body under it. She slid down a slope into the next passageway, and suddenly, she was standing.

"I'm through," she called back.

"Do you see her?" came Max's voice.

"Sydney!" Jane called.

This time, the reply was loud and clear.

"Help!"

"I hear her!"

Jane rushed down the dark passage to a wooden door.

What is a door doing here?

Help!

Jane tried to push it open, but it was stuck. She worked her hands around the perimeter and then, suddenly, the door was free. She pushed it open and shone her flashlight into the room. It fell on the grimy face of Sydney. She was curled up in the corner of the room, coughing and shivering.

Jane ran to her and wrapped her in her jacket.

"You're okay now, Sydney. Your papa is just down the hall."

"A gu... gust... of w... wind blew the... the do... do... door shut," said Sydney. "I couldn't ge... get out."

"I know. It's okay, baby. You're safe now."

At that moment, Sydney closed her eyes and fainted.

"Sydney!" Jane said. She shook her gently. "Sydney, wake up."

The little girl groaned, but her eyes remained shut.

Jane scooped her up and carried her back down the corridor to the place where Max's light was shining through the slot.

"I've got her!" Jane shouted.

She pushed Sydney's limp body up the slope to the slot. She climbed behind her and then pushed her under the first joist. Sydney fit easily through the space. Jane wriggled to come beside her and then pushed her the rest of the way into the tunnel where Max was waiting.

Max pulled her into his arms. Jane continued to lie in the tiny gap between the joists.

"What's wrong with her?" he asked.

"I don't know. I picked her up and... and she just collapsed."

"Hurry, Jane!" said Max. "The air ambulance is here."

"Go! Don't wait. I can find my way out."

Max hesitated.

"GO!"

With that, Max disappeared into the darkness in the direction they had come. She could hear him shuffling away down the long passageway back toward the kitchen.

It took Jane a further ten minutes to reach the kitchen. By then, the air ambulance was idling on the lawn. Sydney was already strapped to a gurney in the helicopter. Collette was beside her, holding her hand. Ursula, Klaus, and

Agatha were inside, too. Max stood beside the helicopter door waiting for Jane. She raced to him.

"Is she okay?" Jane shouted over the roar of the rotors.

"She's in shock," he shouted. "We're taking her to the hospital in Geneva. Hop in!"

Jane shook her head. "No."

"No?"

"You go ahead. There's something I need to do."

Collette spoke from Sydney's side. "What's the problem here? We need to GO!"

"Do what?" Max demanded to Jane.

"Never mind. You don't need me at the hospital. Take care of Sydney. That's what matters."

"Max!" Collette called again.

"Go," said Jane. "I'll be fine."

Max climbed aboard the helicopter. The engine revved and the rotors began to whirl faster.

Jane leaned inside the cabin. She had to shout over the roar.

"Max, the day of Sydney's tea party—why did Jacques Barbeau come?"

"I don't—"

"Tell me."

"He wanted to service the Garden Chapel," said Max. "It's part of his contract with the diocese."

Jane nodded. *So there it was.*

The air nurse came to the door and said, "You need to step back now." She slid the door closed.

Jane lowered her head and backed away to a safe distance. The rotors accelerated, and the helicopter rose. It turned toward Geneva, sending with it a blast of air that caused Jane to stagger. She stood for a long time on the lawn, watching the helicopter shrink and shrink until it was just a dot flying far below her. And then the dot disappeared behind a mountain.

She took a deep breath. Now she was alone at Chalet von Tessen. After the noise of the helicopter, it felt unnaturally peaceful on the lawn. Down in Burgen, she could see the aftermath of Bonfire Night. Tents of a few campers still dotted the pasture beside the stream, but most had moved on. Near the parking area where the fire had blazed lay a black stain. She listened to the wind whistle through the rocks. The chill of looming winter seasoned the autumn air. She shivered, and realized Sydney still had her coat.

Jane hadn't told Max everything about the room where she found Sydney. If she had, he might not have left. And she knew he needed to be with his daughter.

Down in the catacombs, Jane had been unable to open the wooden door because it was locked.

From the outside.

Jane had been looking in the wrong church.

Eduard von Tessen built *two* churches for Sophie. The big one in Burgen, and the other small one in the English Garden. Reverend Jacques Barbeau—and his father before him—had been responsible for maintaining *both* churches.

Back in July, when the sound of the ghost led her and Max to the little room with the lock and *Portrait in Winter*, it had been because Jacques had entered the catacombs to retrieve a new pair of paintings. It must have been hard that summer for him to sneak in and out of the chapel undetected. Jane was always around, not to mention Sydney, who was now old enough to be a fresh obstacle to his larcenies. At the tea party, Jacques knew everyone would be busy. That was his chance. It's the reason he drove his own car. He loaded the two paintings into the trunk and then went back to Burgen to "write his sermon." Later, she found him fishing.

Jane circled the house. Near the back corner, standing against a wall, were four cans of gasoline. She lifted each one. Full. Beside them was a stack of rags.

She found footprints in the dirt and followed them up the hill behind the chalet. They led to the upper encampment where she had watched backpackers cook freeze-dried dinners on tiny camp stoves and then disappear into their colorful tents.

A white Mercedes Sprinter van was parked beside a silver Aston Martin. She opened the back of the van. Dozens of crates stood like books on a shelf. They looked specially made and appeared to be the right size for carrying multiple canvases in a single rack. She lifted the lid on the nearest crate and slid out the first painting. It was a Cubist rendering of a snowy landscape. She slid out another. Another Cubist experiment, this one of a view of the stone giants of the valley. She pulled out another. This one took her breath away. It was a spectacular portrait of Sophie von Tessen posed in a field of poppies. Jane checked the signature.

Francis.

Not Francis F.

No "F-dot."

She slid the paintings back into place and closed the crate. She shut the door and walked back down the hill toward the chalet.

Thirty-Seven

Tomas

In the vault room, Tomas Firth carried the latest crate of paintings along the dark passageway toward the stairs that led out. His headlamp bobbed as he moved, and the motion of the beam on the stone wall was making him sick. He would be glad to be done with this. The crates weren't heavy, but they were as awkward as fuck. There were so many paintings, more than either of them expected, and they had been forced to double up the crates. He was exhausted. They had been at this all night.

"Hey, Opa, how many more?"

"This is the last of it," said Gunther.

"Thank god. I'm sick of this place."

"You'll never see it again."

Fuck, yeah.

Tomas was giddy. His idea had worked! Even Gunther, the old prick, was impressed. They would put these paintings in their vault back in Geneva and then invite a few friendly critics to view them—after they added the "F-dot" signatures, of course.

Ted Banks would be ruined.

"There must be a thousand paintings here," said Tomas.

"Nine hundred and twelve by my count," said Gunther.

"Jesus, didn't this guy ever take a break?"

Tomas hauled the crate up the stairs toward the trapdoor in the ceiling.

The secret entrance to the vault had been a cinch to find. It was under a rug behind the altar of the Garden Chapel; Gunther had guessed long ago that the vault was accessed from there. It was a good thing he had insisted on bringing the Sprinter van to Burgen the previous week. Parked among the other work vans and coaches for the festival, no one had noticed. And they sure needed the cargo space! Asti was not up for the job. While the Burgeners celebrated, he and Gunther found the vault and began emptying it into the van. They had expected to be long gone by now, but who knew there would be so many paintings?

Nine hundred and twelve! He was rich!

He reached the top of the stairs and stopped.

What the hell?

The door must have fallen shut. He pushed. It didn't open. He set the crate at the bottom of the stairs and pushed with both hands, then with his shoulder. He walked to the top step and put his back against the underside of the door. He pressed up with his legs. It didn't budge.

"Hey, Opa. The fucking door's stuck."

Gunther stopped loading his crate.

"What?"

"It won't open."

"Why did you close it?"

"I didn't. It must have fallen shut."

"Let me try."

Gunther climbed the stairs and pushed.

"It's really stuck," he said. "Let's try together."

Still nothing.

"Hey, Opa, is there another way out of here?"

A voice came from behind them.

"No."

Tomas whirled in the direction of the voice. He flashed his light around the catacombs, but he found only bare stone walls and dangling pipes. God, what a creepy place!

"Who's there?" he called out.

"Over here," said the voice. It was a woman.

And then his beam found her in a narrow gap between the floor and the passage wall.

How the hell did she get up there?

"You!" said Tomas.

Thirty-Eight

Jane

Jane looked down from the narrow gap into the passageway. The two men were illuminated by an array of flashlights and headlamps scattered over the floor from their long night of work. An old-fashioned gas lantern glowed from a nail in a joist.

"The door didn't 'fall shut,'" said Jane. "I closed it. And it's not stuck. It's got about four hundred pounds sitting on top of it."

After inspecting the van, Jane had gone to the Garden Chapel where she found a trap door behind the altar standing open. A rug had been moved aside. The trap door was on hinges and springs, like one of those attic pull-downs. From below, she could hear men's voices. She closed the door and then dragged the altar on top. For good measure, she stacked two pews against the altar. They weren't getting out through there. Only one other way out remained.

Jane went through the house to the kitchen, down the stairs, past her records vault, and then along the labyrinth of passages leading in the direction of the East Wing. She arrived at the same gap she had slipped through to save Sydney an hour earlier. She wriggled through in time to hear Tomas and Gunther wrapping up their work.

She was safe in the gap. They couldn't reach her. They couldn't follow her through, either—Tomas was too pudgy, and Gunther too frail.

"The police are on their way," said Jane.

"Bullshit," said Tomas.

"I called Lieutenant Delgato an hour ago. You remember her, right, Tomas?"

"Let us out of here," said Tomas.

"You locked a little girl in a room, and you were going to burn the house down on top of her," said Jane. "You're not going anywhere."

"That's a lie!" said Tomas. "We heard her creeping around. But then we scared her off. Tell her, Opa."

Gunther said nothing.

"I found the gasoline cans and the rags. The police probably would have blamed sparks from the bonfire, or maybe the fireworks. I gotta hand it to you—burning down the house was a nice touch. It would remove all evidence that there ever was a vault."

"Opa?" said Tomas.

"She would have told," said Gunther.

"Wait," said Tomas. "You mean it's *true*?"

"People might have even chalked up her death to the von Tessen curse," said Jane. "But you were counting on that, weren't you, Gunther? The curse was your invention."

"What's she talking about?" asked Tomas.

"Poor Tomas," said Jane. "He thinks the curse is just some silly superstition. He doesn't know his grandfather planted it decades ago with the help of Reverend Rolf Barbeau—right after he killed the first maid. A vault protected by a phony curse. It was very *Scooby-Doo* of you."

"It was before *Scooby-Doo*."

"That's true," said Jane. "So, I assume the maids found the vault. Did they try to blackmail the reverend?"

"Greedy little bitches," said Gunther.

"Oh, my god," said Tomas. "You *killed* them?"

"Your son Otto knew," said Jane. "And that's why he was trying to expand the gallery business beyond dealing only in Francis Firths. He was looking for a way out of the lie. Then I showed up with *The Lover*, and he knew the truth was going to come out."

"It's a tragedy what happened to him," said Gunther.

"And to Jacques," said Jane. "Both men were heirs to their fathers' crimes. Why did you kill Jacques?"

"I didn't kill him," said Tomas. "I swear. He just jumped! I was trying to scare him into telling me where the vault was located. And he shouted 'Forgive me, Father,' and jumped into the river!"

"Maybe," said Jane. "But the maids—that was not an accident. The newspaper reports I read said the police found no sign of a struggle. There were no drugs in their system. And the time of death was fixed at a time when they would have been alone. No one could have pushed them. They just seemed to have gone inexplicably mad and jumped. That was the essence of the curse legend. I spent a lot of time wondering how you did that, then it hit me—the apple barrel."

Gunther smiled. In the stark shadows of the catacombs, the smile looked like it belonged to a monster.

"I thought so," said Jane. "The old photographs I found showed what they called an 'apple barrel' near the East Cliff. Why? No apples grow in the Valley of the Giants. Not at this elevation. Believe me, we know a thing or two about apples in Upstate New York! It was a strange choice for a bench. Then I realized—you used it for the murders. You bound the women and put them in cold water in the apple barrel and then waited for hypothermia to set in. After they passed out, you untied them and just rolled them over the side of the cliff. No struggle. No drugs. And the hypothermia caused the coroners to fix the wrong time for the death. Did you sit there watching while their life slowly drained out of them? They must have pleaded for mercy. That was some sick shit, Gunther, even for you."

"Do you have any idea how hard it is to throw someone over a cliff?" he said coldly.

"Not really."

"Like trying to put a cat in a bathtub."

"Let me out here!" cried Tomas. "This man is crazy! I knew nothing about any of this! I swear to God! Is this about your painting, Jane? Because I'll give it back to you. It's in the vault at the gallery. You can have it tomorrow."

"So you *did* drug me."

"I had to. My father was frantic about your painting. I could see he was at the end of his rope. I had to do something." He cleared his throat. "And just so you know, I didn't..."

"Didn't what?"

"You know."

"Rape me?"

"I could've."

"Well, thank you, Tomas, for not raping me after you drugged me and stole my painting."

Tomas sat down on the floor and buried his head in his hands.

Jane turned her attention to Gunther.

"I have some questions for you, if you don't mind."

"Why not? Fire away."

"About the paintings—I'm guessing Reverend Rolf Barbeau found them in the forties or so."

"He didn't *find* them," said Gunther. "Eduard von Tessen suggested he sell a few to raise money for a new roof for the church. The war was on, and he had fallen on hard times like the rest of us. The fundraiser was in Geneva, and my father—the real Francis Firth—happened to see them. They were signed "Francis," the same as his name. He bought all four of them for one franc each. Can you imagine? One franc for an authentic Firth!"

"So he was in on the deception as well?"

"Francis? God, no. He was a simpleton who did odd jobs around the church. After he died, I inherited his four paintings. Francis was an amateur artist, though. I didn't make that part up. Unfortunately, he had no talent. I have a few in the vault. Awful things. I should have destroyed them long ago, but..."

"Your father made them."

Gunther shrugged. "After he died, I decided to see if the four paintings were worth anything. I figured it would help if I put an "F-dot" after "Francis" so I could claim provenance. I used some of my father's old paints to do it, which was harder than you might think. That turned out to have been a stroke of luck because his old paints were of the right vintage. The chemistry supported my story."

"So you sold them for a profit?"

"Twenty-four francs *per painting*. A fortune at the time! A gallery owner in Geneva promised to buy anything I could get my hands on. Eduard von Tessen was dead by then, so I tracked down Rolf in Burgen. It took him a few months, but eventually, he found the vault. We struck a deal. Two paintings per year."

"Why so few?"

"They weren't the easiest things to steal. Plus, we weren't thinking big back then. We just wanted a few hundred francs a year to improve our lives a little. Maintain the church. Buy some nice things for our wives, for once. Then it just went crazy."

"So you wrote your little fictional biography about your father being a goat-herder and then opened your little gallery. When Rolf died, Jacques picked up where his father left off?"

"That part was tricky," said Gunther. "It was fortunate that young Jacques had followed his father into the family profession, but he knew nothing about the source of his father's money. He was horrified when he found out. But ultimately, he was persuaded by the chance to use the money for his favorite causes."

Jane thought about the photographs of Jacques with the orphans. It was a devil's bargain. He must have known it. That's why he had been so quick to jump in the river when Tomas threatened him.

Forgive me, Father.

She shook her head. So here it was. A timeline of chance and greed passed down through generations like a genetic disease. It made her sick. A couple of no-talent hacks raided a stash of paintings and conspired to build an art empire off another man's unheralded work. Everything else—the murders, the curse, the ghost—it was all just part of their snowballing greed.

But there was one more question.

"So who did paint them?" Jane asked. "Really?"

"Does it matter?"

"Of course it matters!"

Gunther shrugged. "It was before my time. Eduard never said. I asked him once."

"And?"

"He just got this funny look. 'You wouldn't believe me if I told you,' he said."

Jane's phone buzzed with a text. It was from Lieutenant Delgato.

Passing Burgen now.

Jane attached the voice-note recording of Gunther's confession and hit SEND. She slipped back through the gap, dropping down into the passageway.

"Hey! Where the fuck are you going?" Tomas shouted.

She started along the passageway toward the kitchen.

"Come back here, you bitch!"

As she moved through the darkness, Tomas's pleas grew ever-fainter until they sounded less like the cries of a man and more like the moans of a ghost.

Twenty minutes later, Martina Delgato arrived with four other police cars and an ambulance. Jane met them on the driveway. Their blue and red lights danced wildly in a fog that had descended while Jane was under the house. By then, the detective had listened to the recording of the pair's confessions in the catacombs.

Gunther and Tomas were hauled out of the vault like dogs from a well. The police handcuffed them and sat them on the same pew Jane had used to trap them in the catacombs.

"I want my lawyer," said Tomas.

Jane went outside to wait in the garden. After a while, Lieutenant Delgato came beside her.

"That was good work. Remind me never to piss you off."

"Not funny, Martina."

"Well then, maybe this will cheer you up. We've got Gunther Firth on multiple homicides, plus the attempted murder of Sydney von Tessen. Tomas looks like second-degree homicide, but that's for a jury to decide. Plus the theft of your painting, the drugging, and all the other fraud stuff with the gallery... it's a lot. I think it's safe to say there will be no more riding around in speedboats for Tomas Firth. The boaters of Lac Léman will be safe once again."

Jane laughed. "Now that *is* funny."

Four uniformed officers came through the chapel door with Tomas and Gunther in cuffs. Tomas's eyes were swollen from crying. Gunther's face was hard to read. It occurred to Jane that he had been living most of his life atop a massive lie—a not particularly well-constructed one at that—and the threat of imminent collapse must have been exhausting. The skyrocketing value of the paintings was a mixed blessing. As prices rose, so did the likelihood that the lie would be exposed. The appearance of Jane's painting had been a wild card, but he had to know that, sooner or later, a Ted Banks was going to come along and knock the whole thing down.

His expression was closer to eagerness than relief. She thought about Gunther's long confession in the catacombs.

Why not? Fire away.

Why had he been so forthcoming? He had to know she was recording the whole thing. He seemed almost anxious to get it off his chest before...

And then the reason hit her.

She looked at Gunther. Their eyes locked.

"Wait!" said Jane.

But it was too late. At that instant, Gunther pushed Tomas, who tumbled into the other police officer. They both landed in a pile on the ground. As the officer scrambled to help Tomas to his feet, Gunther broke free and sprinted toward the East Cliff. He ran awkwardly with his hands cuffed behind his back. The police jogged after him but with no great urgency. He had nowhere to go.

They were wrong about that.

Gunther never slowed down. He reached the ledge and leaped into the abyss as though he were jumping into a swimming pool. He seemed to hover a moment as the arc of his leap reached its apex. Then gravity took hold. In a blink, he disappeared behind the ledge.

"Goddammit!" Lieutenant Delgato shouted.

Jane waited in horror for a cry, or, worse, the sound of Gunther's body exploding on the sharp rocks below. But there was no sound. The Valley of the Giants had simply swallowed him whole.

Thirty-Nine

Jane

That night, everyone returned by car to the chalet, including Sydney. There was no reason to keep her in the hospital. She was shaken but fine, and she'd recover better in her own bed. Ursula stayed with her, while everyone else gathered in the parlor with Detective Delgato and a half-dozen police from Geneva. They spent several hours going over the events. This was how the others learned about the Firths, the vault, and all that had happened in their absence. After a while, Martina announced they had enough information for now. She informed them that portions of the property had been cordoned off to preserve the crime scene. She would return in the morning with a team to recover Gunther's body and continue their investigation.

Max offered for them to stay in his cottages, which were now empty following the Burgen Day festival, and they agreed. Throughout the evening, Collette clung to Max. Jane managed to make eye contact a few times, but she couldn't read his expression—perhaps because of her face-blindness, or perhaps because Max was trying to make up his mind about her. Did he blame her for Sydney's ordeal?

The police left and everyone scattered to their rooms. Max went to Burgen to get the police settled for the night. Jane didn't even get a chance to say good night. She went alone to her room and stripped off her mud-caked clothes. She lay down and stared at the ceiling, not even trying to sleep.

The knock came an hour later. Jane slipped on a robe and got up to see. It was Max.

He held his finger to his lips. "Get dressed."

She pulled on fresh clothes, while he went to her closet. He found her coat and handed it to her.

They crept downstairs, through the foyer to the library.

"Where are we going?"

"The vault," he said.

"I thought the police taped it off."

"They did. If we're going to get answers, it has to be now."

They went out the French doors into the English Garden. By moonlight, they followed the narrow path through the overgrown rose bushes toward the chapel.

It occurred to Jane they were following the same route Jacques Barbeau and his father had used to reach the vault and grab their annual allotment of two paintings. Eighty years of larceny. The ghost. The curse. Sheesh!

The entrance to the chapel was cordoned off with police tape. Max lifted it so that Jane could pass under, and together they went into the chapel.

The chapel was strangely undisturbed by the events of the day. Seven candles stood in a candelabra beside a silver cup on the altar Jane had moved to trap the Firths. It was mere inches from the open trap door.

Her eye went to the cross over the altar. To her surprise, she bowed. It just felt right. Max watched her, and then he did the same.

"Come on," he said, taking her hand.

He led her to the trap door, and then slowly they descended the creaking stairs.

The vault was a large square room, barely high enough for Max to stand in. He held his light to the walls, and ran his hand over the rock.

"Chiseled," he said.

Jane nodded. This was not like the catacomb walls, which were smooth from millennia of running water.

Max consulted the blueprints, and walked toward a shelf.

"There should be a passage here," he said.

He pushed the shelf. It moved slightly.

"Let me help," said Jane.

Together they slid the shelf to expose an opening in the wall. Max held up his light, but the darkness closed around it after a few feet. It was a passageway.

"Let's go," said Jane.

Jane pressed tightly against Max to stay within the sphere of his light. After several minutes, the passage ended abruptly. Overhead was another trap door. Max handed her the lantern while he pulled down the stairs. They climbed up into the house and looked around. Jane knew exactly where they were. She knew it before they even pulled down the trap door—the little room in the East Wing with the lock on the door.

Sophie's room.

"Now we know the source of the draft," said Jane.

"This wasn't built as a vault," said Max. "It was a secret passage."

They went back down into the tunnel and then made their way to the vault. Ten minutes later, beneath the steps, Max found a metal box.

"Look at this," he said.

Jane held the lantern, while Max brushed away the dust.

He lifted the latch. Inside lay a folded sheet of paper. He opened it.

"It's a letter," he said "from Eduard von Tessen."

It was dated 1968, the year of his death. Jane huddled beside Max as he read aloud, translating from German into French as he went.

To whom it may concern,

Regrets are funny things. In my middle age, I had so many regrets I could not count them all. Now, from the vantage point of my ninth decade, I have almost n one.

Almost.

For my entire life, I was part of a grotesque deception in which I allowed myself to be presented to the world as the firstborn child of Rudolph and Madeline von Tessen. It is a lie. I have an older sister, Sophie.

One of my earliest childhood memories is of my big sister sneaking into my room when I was supposed to be asleep. I can still see her face through the bars of my crib. She would read to me and play games. I would wait up for her. As a toddler, I was often in trouble. When I was sent to my room as punishment, she would sneak me food and toys. I think she took those deprivations harder than I ever did. As I grew, she taught me how to avoid Rudolph's wrath, and when I failed, she would deflect my punishments onto herself. She protected me, and I adored her.

And then one day she was gone. Papa sent her to various institutions to be "cured." Cured of what, I did not know, though I did recognize that there was something different about Sophie. I did not have a word for it then. I suppose today we would call it mental illness. From time to time, she would return from the asylums only to be sent away yet again—until that time she went away and never came back. After that, her name went unspoken. Her existence was ripped (literally) from the family bible. She was erased from the family portraits.

At the time, I accepted this abominable deception. We all did, even Mama, who, like her children, lived in terror of the bully she had married. Later, after Papa's death, we all tried to make amends. Sophie said she would be satisfied with the arrangement that allowed her to live as gardien du maison *in our family's Swiss chalet. I am not.*

I must interject here that my sister, for all her gifts, did not always make the best decisions. The servants would catch her walking barefoot in the snow and have to drag her to the hearth before she lost her toes. She had long conversations with birds and animals. She swam naked in the river. She allowed herself to be preyed upon by men and then made light of it as though she were a willing participant. There were regular visits to doctors. New medicines. Relapses.

Don't get me wrong, I resented none of this. Keeping her safe and alive was not my penance—it was my privilege.

After my father's death, I begged Sophie to let me restore her name to House von Tessen, but she had no interest in it. Instead, I altered the family crest to reflect her secret existence—a magical swift that watches over the Valley of the Giants. She seemed to like that.

Enclosed herein you will find the missing records of Sophie's existence, as well as the paintings she treasured more than anything.

Do with them as you see fit. In this matter, I appeal to your judgment. If you think charity can come of restoring her to our family, then I urge you to do so. If you see harm in it, then, as we say, "Lass schlafende Hunde liegen."

Sincerely,

Eduard von Tessen

"'*Lass schlafende Hunde liegen*'?" Jane asked; he had neglected to translate it.

"Let sleeping dogs lie."

Forty

Jane

Overnight, Chalet von Tessen became a crime scene. Police swarmed every inch of the estate. Miles of police tape with "*Zone Interdite*" went up. The police took thousands of photographs, tagged evidence, and gathered witness statements. They towed Gunther's Sprinter van along with every painting by Francis to an evidence room in Geneva.

Max helped a forensic team recover Gunther's body from the base of the East Cliff. There was no way to reach the spot from the chalet, even with climbing gear, and no place to land a helicopter. It could only be reached by foot via Burgen, and only he and Klaus knew the way.

During Klaus's witness statement, Martina questioned him about how Rolf and Jacques had used their duties to access the Garden Chapel. Jane listened from a nearby chair.

"So you just allowed them onto the property?" Martina asked.

"It was their job," said Klaus weakly.

"For eighty years?"

"They polished the silver. They cleaned the icons. They brought new candles."

"And in all this time you never suspected anything?" Martina asked.

Klaus grabbed his chest and hunched over.

Ursula ended the interview. Klaus spent the next week in bed. The betrayal of his trusted friends was a grave blow.

Later, Ursula asked Jane to take over temporarily as *gardien du maison*. She needed to look after Klaus. Sydney had recovered from her ordeal, and now she and Collette were back in Paris for the start of the school year. Hannah and Max were occupied with the police investigation, which also spanned much of Burgen. That left only Agatha to handle everything else.

"It will be easier on Klaus if he knows you are looking after things," said Ursula.

Jane, who had never been able to do anything right by Ursula, could have wept at the acceptance the favor implied.

Her first order of business was to deal with the journalists and curiosity-seekers that had begun to appear at the chalet's front door. Jane hired a security firm suggested by Hannah. The next day, four ex-military men arrived in black suits and sunglasses, looking like the bad guys in *The Matrix*. They briefed Jane on their plans using phrases like "secure perimeter," "incident reporting," and "visual surveillance."

There were no trespassers after that.

One morning, at the end of the first week, Jane was in the barn feeding Tabitha when Detective Delgato called.

"Tomas Firth wants to cut a deal," she said.

"I don't know how to respond to that."

"It means he's cooperating," said Martina. "He just gave us the combination to the vault. I'm heading to the gallery shortly with a team. Wanna come?"

Three hours later, Jane walked into the Firth Gallery in Geneva. It looked much the same as it had that spring when she met the Firths for the first time.

Martina greeted Jane at the door. "Are you ready?"

"I think so. What if it's not there?"

"It's there," said Martina.

She led her to a hallway with a steel door. It had an enormous spinning handle that looked like a ship's wheel. A man in police uniform was waiting for them.

"Okay, Sergeant," said Martina. "She's here. Open it up."

"In all my years, I've never seen a private vault like this," he said as he dialed the combination. "We got the blueprints from the contractor who built it. The walls are foot-thick cement. Even the floor is reinforced in case someone tries to tunnel in. It must have cost at least ten million francs to build. It's the most secure vault I've ever seen. And this is Switzerland!"

The lock clicked, and he spun the big wheel. They stepped back as he pulled open the heavy steel door.

Years later, Jane would write about the moment in *Van Gogh's Lover*.

I stood in the doorway, aghast. The contents of the vault was one of the most cherished secrets of the art world, and now I didn't know whether to laugh or cry. What I beheld could have been any suburban storage unit in America. Cardboard boxes with old clothes. A pair of moldy golf bags. A set of rims for a sports car. A mountain bike caked in mud. The Lover *stood against the far wall, the rear wheel of the bike resting against the back of the canvas. I pushed past the police to roll the bike safely away from the painting.*

"Is that your painting?" Martina asked.

Jane smiled and nodded.

Martina burst out laughing. The sergeant stared at her as though she'd gone mad.

"What's so funny?" he asked. "There's nothing here! I wouldn't have bothered with a fucking padlock!"

"It's a prop!" Martina cried. "Don't you see? Their fraud was pure theater. The vault is a ten-million-franc prop!"

Jane picked up *The Lover* and said to Martina, "So can I just take it?"

It seemed too good to be true.

"It's your painting," said Martina. "Case closed."

Martina and the sergeant began discussing how they would inventory the vault's meager contents and then transport it to the evidence locker, and if that was even necessary...

Jane held *The Lover* in front of her with both hands and gazed at it for the first time since she removed it from Granny Jo's wall. A lump came to her throat. She had become so accustomed to the image on her phone, she had forgotten how powerful the real thing was.

There's no substitute for standing before the actual painting.

"Hey, Martina," said Jane. "Can I ask a favor?"

A half-hour later, Jane stood in the evidence room of the Geneva Police Department where the full inventory of paintings by Francis occupied a closet with its own guard.

"Stay as long as you like," said Martina and left.

For the next four hours, Jane sat on the floor and paged through the paintings. She wondered who was the last person to ever do this. Eduard? Probably not. She would have to go back to Sophie herself.

The paintings weren't all masterpieces. Quite a few were experiments that didn't quite succeed. There was a comical attempt to marry Cubism with Japanese woodblock etchings. Religious themes popped up rather too often for Jane's tastes. But even in these failings, Jane was impressed by Francis's courage. Painters tended to find a style and cling to it, especially professional painters who had an audience of buyers and critics with specific expectations. In their later years, they painted defensively, more in fear of a negative review than desire for a positive one. Not Francis. He was an amateur who had only one buyer and one critic—Sophie. And based on what Jane saw in that evidence room, Francis was fearless. Jane imagined Francis showing Sophie a finished work and asking, "How's this?" They might spend hours discussing its merits and failings. Then he would pick up his brush and go to work again. There was something intimate about it.

But among the failed experiments and outright misses were hundreds upon hundreds of magnificent paintings. Landscapes you wanted to crawl into. Modern works with ideas that asked you to engage your brain as well as your eyes. But of all these, the portraits of Sophie stood in a class of their own. Francis was born to paint portraits of Sophie.

At one point, Jane came across a portrait of her sitting beside a stream with her feet in the water. Jane grinned. She knew the spot. She had cooled her feet there in much the same way.

Jane set the painting in front of her and studied it for a long time. An idea took shape. She pulled out her phone and called Alan Silver.

"Jane Ward? What a wonderful surprise! I hope St. Remy was all you hoped."

"It certainly was. I'm calling because..." She laughed at herself. "Because, well, I need to speak to a Goghpie."

"You called the right number," he said.

The sound of children and a television set rumbled in the background.

"I can call back if you're busy."

"No. Now's good." There came shuffling, then the sound of a door closing. "Okay, go ahead."

"Alan, did you just shut yourself in a closet?"

He laughed. "The kids are watching some shark movie. I should have come here long ago. How can I be of service?"

"I have a question: How did Van Gogh become Van Gogh? I mean, he died a pauper with almost no following, and then within a decade, bam, he's one of the most famous painters in the world. How?"

"Joanna Bonger."

"Who?"

"Vincent's sister-in-law. As you no doubt know, Vincent Van Gogh died in July 1890. His brother Theo died six months after that. Suddenly Theo's wife, Joanna, was a widow with a young child. She was educated, but she had no income and no money to speak of. She couldn't even afford to keep her Paris apartment. All she had from her marriage to Theo was a massive collection of weird, unsellable paintings from her crazy brother-in-law, Vincent. Everyone told her to get rid of them. Well-meaning friends told her to burn them and go back to Holland to be with her parents. The paintings weren't worth the cost of transport. Then, for some reason, she read Vincent's letters, which Theo had thoughtfully saved. Joanna was moved by how Vincent had literally worked himself to death in the service of his art. She knew nothing about art, but her husband had, and he had believed in the paintings. Joanna, it turned out, was a very smart lady. And one hell of a marketer. It's no exaggeration to say that without Joanna Bonger, there would be no Vincent Van Gogh."

"Tell me how she did it," said Jane.

Jane set the meeting for ten o'clock in the den of Chalet von Tessen.

Klaus was feeling better, and he sat with Ursula on the long couch. Max, Hannah, Agatha, and Jane sat on chairs they had pulled into a circle.

Jane began by handing a piece of paper to Hannah.

"That is a list of one hundred sixty-eight Franciscans—that's what we're going to call these paintings from now on—in circulation. Every single one of them was stolen from Chalet von Tessen. The laws on stolen art are very clear. They're ours, and I want every last one of them returned."

Hannah scanned the list.

"This will take years," she said.

"Every last one," said Jane.

Hannah smiled faintly, and slid the list into her handbag.

Jane went on. "The only way anyone is going to be able to stand in front of a Franciscan will be at the Franciscan Museum. We'll build it on the banks of Lake Geneva. Perhaps Max's construction firm will build it."

Max raised his eyebrows thoughtfully.

"People will come from all over the world to the museum, and while they're there we'll cross-market side trips—pilgrimages—to Burgen. We'll shuttle people up for the day, or they can stay overnight at one of our cottages. We'll have an art walk that takes them to actual locations in the Valley of the Giants that inspired the paintings. I saw this in Arles with Van Gogh; it's very effective. We don't know who Francis was—we may never know—but we do know where he took his inspiration from: the Valley of the Giants."

Klaus said, "Does this mean—"

Jane raised her hand. "Let me finish. You may change your mind after you hear my conditions on your offer. First off, I'm going to raze the East Wing."

Ursula gasped.

"It's completely impractical, and we simply can't afford it. It's a fire trap that risks the entire structure. Seriously, who needs twenty thousand feet of living space? Servants' quarters? A ballroom? A formal dining hall? Even unused, it has to be cleaned and maintained. It's a shame about Sophie's old room, but it has to go too. Instead, we'll expand the barn, and add horses for our art tours."

Max chuckled.

"Is that it?" asked Hannah.

"No. The 'My Dearest Soph' letters—I need you to keep their existence secret for now."

"What? Why?" asked Hannah.

"Granny Jo wants to enjoy her picture for the few years she has left. More money is not going to make her any happier. Having *The Lover* on display in Paris or New York or Tokyo is not going to do her any good, either."

"She can't just hang it on her wall!" Hannah exclaimed.

"That's exactly what she's going to do. As it stands now, nobody outside this room—except Ted Banks and Granny Jo—knows the truth about those letters and that painting. As long as that's true, Granny Jo can hang her picture in her little room in the nursing home and no one's the wiser. Meanwhile, I'll finish my research and write my book. But I'll sit on all of it until Granny Jo is no longer with us. That's a condition. Non-negotiable. I want it in the contract."

Klaus rose. "And so it shall be." He went to Jane and pulled her into a bear hug. When they parted, his eyes glowed. "Welcome."

Ursula gave her a quick hug and stepped back, followed by Agatha.

Hannah shook Jane's hand. "You'll have the contract tomorrow."

Lastly came Max.

"You've given this a lot of thought," he said.

"Yeah."

"Good."

"I was kinda hoping I'd get some help, though," she said.

His eyes danced over her face.

"The museum should look like a Swiss chalet," he said.

Le Musée Des Franciscains opened in Geneva four years later on September 1—Burgen Day.

Klaus didn't live to see the opening. He died in his sleep three weeks after signing the agreement with Jane Ward. It was as though he had clung to life long enough to secure a successor. Ursula passed the following year. They were buried together in Burgen's cemetery, not far from Jacques Barbeau. Some had wanted to remove the chaplain's body from the cemetery—Jane among them—but Klaus wouldn't hear of it.

As time passed, Jane realized Klaus was right. Whenever Jane visited the cemetery, she would pause to tell Jacques the news of the valley, which always included a report on the state of the fishing.

One day, not long after the museum's opening, Jane stood near in the lobby waiting for one of her private guests to emerge. A voice came from beside her.

"Whoever he was," a stranger whispered.

Jane smiled. The phrase was engraved over the museum's exit so that everyone leaving was encouraged to read it. She heard it dozens of times every day. The idea had come from Ted Banks.

His book *No-Talent Hacks: The Shocking True Story of Murder, Lies, and Greed in the Art World* had been a bestseller that spawned a blockbuster movie. The book told the story of the Firth fraud chronologically, beginning with the mysterious chaplain, Francis, painting in the high Alps. It ended with the conviction of Tomas Firth for second-degree murder, along with a laundry list of other crimes.

Three years after *No-Talent Hacks*, Ted Banks followed up with *Whoever He Was*. Readers seeking a solution to the mystery of Francis of Burgen were disappointed. The book was a deep dive into Francis's art. As for the mystery of the identity of its creator, Ted suggested that it should never be solved. He made his case in an essay in *The New Yorker*.

Francis's anonymity was part of his gift to us. What we have in him is something utterly unique in the history of art—a large body of work that stands apart from its creator. Today, artists must have social media accounts and interactive websites. Art is not asked to stand on merit alone. Imagine if Francis turned out to be a Nazi sympathizer or a bigot? Could we ever look at his paintings the same way again?

I believe the "not knowing" is part of Francis's legacy. After studying this question for the last five years, I have concluded that Francis, whoever he was, deliberately concealed his identity. Since that was his wish, I have no desire to learn who he was. Knowing could only diminish the work. To those who would seek to solve the mystery, I say with all due respect, "I hope you fail."

Jane read the essay and immediately called Ted. He answered on the first ring. They talked for an hour. It was during that conversation that he suggested the slogan above the door.

In the lobby, Jane watched Dr. Ravi Das come through the gallery exit. He looked befuddled.

"So," said Jane, "what did you think?"

"Amazing turnout," he replied.

Jane smiled and reminded herself that art was not for everyone.

"You wanted to see me?" she asked.

"Yes. Interesting developments at the lab now that we have those high-resolution scans of *The Lover*. We have a patient, a fifty-five-year-old male, with injuries similar to yours. We tethered him up to an interface with the AI models from your amygdala."

"Like with a helmet?" Jane asked, alarmed by the image of a man wearing a helmet with a bunch of wires snaking back to a computer. She had, after all, seen Ravi's lab.

"Not exactly, but okay, something like that. Anyway, he's seeing color. The markers your amygdala is using from *The Lover* are repeatable."

"That's fantastic! And he can really see the way I see?"

"Yes, but..."

"But what?"

"He's describing some peculiar side effects. When you see red, Jane, do your toes tingle?"

Jane laughed. "Only with poppies."

He frowned. "I was thinking, maybe we could get you back into the lab—"

"No, Ravi. We're done. I'm grateful for a scientific explanation for my recovery. But there's a part of me that's never going to believe it."

He frowned. "Okay, so what's your explanation?"

Jane grinned. "Breadcrumbs."

"Huh?"

At that moment, Max emerged from the gallery and walked to Jane. They kissed.

"Ravi, I'd like you to meet my husband, Max von Tessen."

Max proposed to Jane during her second year at the chalet. It was after a heavy snowfall that had closed the roads. The public snowplows stopped short of Burgen, so after each snowfall, Max would come up from Geneva to clear the roads. He kept an enormous snowcat beside the barn at the chalet. He would drive his truck as far as the conditions allowed, then switch to a snowmobile to reach the chalet. Jane loved riding shotgun in the snowcat—the chalet could get claustrophobic in a winter storm. Afterward, Max spent the night. He called these conjugal visits "a snow-removal fee."

On the day of his marriage proposal, Max packed a lunch for them to eat in the cab. Max was not one for grand gestures, and neither was Jane, but he used the moment to have a little fun.

Jane laid out the contents of the lunch bag between them on the seat. Her hand found something hard among the sandwiches, and she took it out. Her jaw fell. It was a gold ring with four rubies around a delicate diamond.

"This is Ursula's ring!" Jane exclaimed. "Oh, my god! What's it doing in here?"

"I can't imagine."

"That's crazy! Could it have fallen in?"

"I don't see how," he said.

"We could have lost it," she said, aghast.

He cleared his throat. "Why don't you try it on?"

"Oh, I couldn't."

"Why not?"

"It wouldn't be right."

"It should fit. I had it sized."

"Sized? Why would…"

He was grinning, and then it hit her.

"Oh, Max."

"So, is that a 'yes'?"

Jane slid the ring onto her finger and then looked into Max's eyes.

"A perfect fit," she said.

Jane wanted a simple ceremony at the courthouse, but Max wouldn't hear of it. The *gardien du maison* of Chalet von Tessen would be married in Burgen's church on Burgen Day. And so it was.

In her wedding dress, Jane was invited to blow the festival's opening note on the giant alphorn. Their first dance was to a *mazurka*. Sydney was still too young for the beauty contest, but she was perfect as Jane's maid of honor.

Granny Jo arrived by private jet. It would be her only trip to the Valley of the Giants. Ten months later, she would fall in her bathroom at the nursing home and never wake up.

But on the day of the wedding, Granny Jo was very much herself. After the wedding, Jane drove her back to the airport. Max had offered to drive, but Jane wanted the time alone with her.

"Max seems like a good man," said Granny Jo.

"He is."

"I'm glad you decided to love him."

"Oh, Gran, I didn't 'decide to love him' any more than you 'decided' to love Grandpa Matthew."

Granny Jo's eyes went wide, and she was quiet for a moment.

"I think we should keep that between ourselves, dear."

Jane helped her up the stairs into the plane. While the jet waited for a fuel truck, they sat talking about *The Lover* the way they used to, inventing stories as though Jane hadn't already found out the truth. As they laughed and spun out their tales, they looked at the bulkhead wall of the jet as though the painting was in the cabin with them. And in a way, Jane thought, it was.

Jane Ward had grown up in a loveless home, but the heart still thirsts for love. So young Jane sought to learn about it from the few sources available to her—her grandmother and her grandmother's painting, which in Jane's mind were never entirely separate things. Young Jane had spent thousands of hours looking at *The Lover* and experiencing the artist's passion for his subject. Sometimes, it seemed to Jane that *Amant*'s love wasn't simply rendered on the canvas, it was *contained* there, like a bottled elixir—and simply by looking at it, she could drink. It was a fanciful notion that Jane had never revealed to anyone—not to Max, not even to Granny Jo. There was a chance they would dispute it, belittle it even, and she couldn't have borne that. So Jane guarded her secret the way Granny Jo had once guarded John Planter's secret. And Jane's secret was this: *The Lover* hadn't just taught her to see color again, it had also taught her how to love.

With her eighty-five-year-old grandmother beside her, and the smell of her lavender perfume hovering like a cloud, Jane was six years old again. Her chest swelled with love the way it did when she saw Max heading off to work with his tool belt slung over his shoulder, or sitting in a chair reading a magazine, or cursing at some bit of plumbing that was infuriating him, or in bed snoring beside her. It was love indistinguishable from gratitude. Who would she be without these people? They lived in her body like donor organs.

Which reminded her of something.

"You know what Van Gogh once said about love?" Jane asked Granny Jo.

"What, dear?"

It was in a letter to his brother, written in September 1888, which, it occurred to Jane, would have been a few months after Sophie's brief stay as a fugitive in Arles.

"'There's nothing more truly artistic than to love people.'"

Granny Jo considered this a moment and then smiled. "I'll bet Sophie taught him that."

Jane laughed. "I'll bet she did."

Davis called Jane with news of Granny Jo's death. The previous year, her parents had divorced (about time!), and they were now even less able to think of others than they had been when they were married. Jane was six months pregnant when she flew home for the service. She knew she would have to run interference with her father when the terms of Granny Jo's will were read out. As Jane had once predicted, he flipped.

"This will not stand," he kept saying.

Jane could only nod and appear sympathetic. He would not win. The previous year, Hannah had turned Granny Jo's will into an airtight document. It set up a college scholarship fund for the Iroquois Indians called the Aponi Planter Scholarship Fund.

Her father had no chance against The Viper.

Jane left the reception while her father was still mid-rant and drove to the nursing home. Granny Jo's things were still in the room, including *The Lover* and Davis's cuckoo clock. Jane removed *The Lover* from the wall and drove to the airport. It would be the last time she was ever in Ontario Hills.

Over the years, Jane's mother would visit the chalet to spend time with her three grandsons. Though she'd never been much interested in mothering, she was an enthusiastic grandmother. She always arrived with a new batch of books for the chalet's library and would read them as many times as her grandsons asked. Davis also came every year with his family. Jane taught them to ride, while Davis and Max fished.

On one of those visits, Davis arrived with Granny Jo's cuckoo clock.

"Why?" she asked.

"Rachel thinks it's obnoxious," he said. "*Coo-coo-coo* all day long. I thought you might consider a trade? My clock for your painting."

"Ha ha."

With *The Lover* in hand, Jane could now begin the daunting task of getting the painting authenticated as a genuine Van Gogh. By this time, she had some clout in the art world as curator of Le Musée Des Franciscains. She called the curator in Amsterdam and told him she was sending over a file "regarding the possible discovery of a new Van Gogh."

A decade earlier, Ted Banks had made a prediction: "They will crucify you."

They certainly tried. But by then, the evidence was irrefutable, and Jane knew it was only a matter of time. It was like when Albert Einstein introduced his theory of relativity—even the greatest physicists in the world needed to take a beat to adjust to the new reality.

The letters and the handwriting analysis had been persuasive, but the X-ray scan was the clincher. Jane would never forget the phone call from Hannah von Tessen when the results came back.

"Are you sitting down?" asked Hannah. Before Jane could answer, Hannah said, "There's another painting *behind* the painting!"

Jane recalled that Otto Firth had said the same thing when he examined it, mentioning a "*pentimento.*"

"The cheapskate reused a damaged canvas!" Hannah said, laughing. "He kept parts of the original portrait, but then he scraped off the background."

"What did he scrape off?"

"The original painting showed a small bedroom with a single bed, a window, a wicker chair, and a painting of sunflowers on the wall."

"Oh, my god."

"Yep. It's Van Gogh's bedroom in the yellow house of Arles, no question about it. I was with the curators when the scans came through." She laughed. "I thought those crusty old fuckers were going to have heart attacks! Jane, there's no doubt about it now. They're going to authenticate *The Lover.* It's a Van Gogh. Hell, it's two Van Goghs!"

"Thank you, Hannah," Jane gushed. "I couldn't have done it without you. You know, I'm starting to think this whole 'Viper' thing is nothing but an act."

The line went silent.

"Hello?" said Jane.

Hannah's voice came through with measured indignation. "That may be the first cruel thing you've ever said to me."

Van Gogh's Lover by Jane Ward was published five years after Granny Jo's death, and ten years after Gunther Firth jumped from the East Cliff. It was an excruciating wait that drove her publisher mad, but Jane wanted the painting to be authenticated without public pressure from her book. Jane used the time to hone the manuscript, which documented Sophie's life before, during, and after meeting Vincent Van Gogh. For Jane, Van Gogh's *Lover* was never a painting. It was always Sophie.

The book was well-received by readers who gobbled it up through successive printings. At age forty, Jane was an overnight sensation. Reviews were mostly positive, except when it came to the ending in which Sophie settled down in the Valley of the Giants with the mysterious chaplain named Francis. The harsher critics found it anti-climactic, and "not up to the standards of the rest of the book."

Jane sent *The Lover* on a world tour that would last two decades. It drew crowds at museums wherever it went. Jane always appeared on opening day to make a short speech, sign books, and pose for selfies. She savored those all-too-infrequent moments when she was reunited with *The Lover*.

Years later, in a foreword to a twenty-fifth-anniversary collector's edition of *Van Gogh's Lover*, she would write about those precious reunions.

Before it was Van Gogh's Lover, *it was Granny Jo's painting.*

So you might see me standing beside the painting in a museum in New York City or Paris or Amsterdam but know this: I am not really there. I am in Ontario Hills, New York, in a little farmhouse with a dozen birdhouses standing like skyscrapers atop high poles. Rose bushes cling to the picket fence and cookies sweeten the air.

If you ask me a question and I don't answer, it's not because I'm ignoring you. I am listening across time for the gentle soprano of my grandmother's voice calling from the kitchen.

"Would you like another cookie, dear? They're still warm."

The painting is, for me, a time machine, and in those moments when we are reunited by some event, my heart lifts. I half-expect to see Granny Jo in the crowd. Then I remember that the farmhouse is gone. So is Granny Jo. And all that remains of that time and place is Van Gogh's Lover, *me, and a love story that is not my own.*

Jane celebrated her sixty-fifth birthday that year. By then, her two oldest boys were living abroad. Only the youngest, Jean—named after John Planter—still lived with them in the chalet. Jean loved everything about the valley and was miserable anywhere else, including at college. Eventually, Jane and Max gave up fighting it. Jean was blessed with his father's engineering inclinations and preferred to work as a maintenance man for the *auberge diffuso*. In his free time, he fished, hunted, rode horses, and devoured books in the library. He never returned from an outing without some bit of garbage he had picked up from the trail or the stream.

Jane thought about Max's description of Klaus long ago: "He's on a first-name basis with every chipmunk that ever buried a nut in the Valley of the Giants." That was Jean. Jane didn't need a swift with a gold feather to tell her who her successor would be.

On July 7 of that year, Jane awoke thinking about the rose bushes in the chalet's English Garden. It would have been Granny Jo's one hundred and twenty-fifth birthday, and Jane always pictured her grandmother outside her farmhouse beneath a floppy hat, trimming her beloved rose bushes.

"I think I'll have breakfast in the garden by the roses," said Jane.

Max stood beside the bed, buttoning his shirt. He was always the first one out of bed. Even after all these years, his energy still astounded her. Just the previous day, she had caught him crawling on the roof of the chalet to caulk a leak. When she objected, he argued that he had tied a safety rope to his waist, as if that made it okay. Jane could only roll her eyes.

"I'll make the eggs," he said.

Jane and Max carried their breakfast trays to a small wrought-iron table in the garden and sat eating and reading their electronic tablets. Jane was checking her email when she noticed one from Ted.

"Max!" she exclaimed. "Email from Ted!"

"What does it say?" he asked eagerly.

She read quickly and then summarized it.

"Good news! The tests are clear. It looks like he beat the cancer."

"Oh, thank god," said Max.

Ted Banks never wrote another book after *Whoever He Was*. He and Philippe moved to Geneva, where he took over from Jane as curator of the Franciscan Museum. She could not have asked for a better replacement. For her part, Jane needed to refocus her attention on the Valley of the Giants, which faced a new threat: Runaway growth. Burgen was now a must-see destination for travelers. The *auberge diffuso* had added forty-seven new cottages. There were two restaurants, a gift shop, an art museum, a history museum, three travel offices, a power plant, and a grocery store. Some of the heirs of Burgen's former residents had resold their cottages to investors who didn't share Jane's vision for the village. They built multi-family dwellings, and in one case, a small hotel. Garbage was showing up in the river and along the trails. Taxes skyrocketed. One and one no longer equaled two.

It was the flip side of the crisis Klaus had faced thirty years earlier, but it was a crisis all the same. At first, Jane tried to float prices, thinking the market would regulate attendance. But costs soared until only millionaires could afford a stay. Next, she introduced a ticketing system, but scalpers exploited it, making no one happy other than the scalpers themselves. The latest strategy was a lottery—but bloggers, bitter that they could not secure a pass, smeared the system as "rigged."

That morning, Jane and Max went round and round about the problem until Max finally called a halt and suggested they go riding.

Jane shook her head. Granny Jo's birthday had caused her to think about the roses.

"I think I'll work on these rose bushes," she said. "They've grown right up to the Garden Chapel wall. See?"

Max nodded. "I'll help. Did I ever tell you that when Granny Jo was here for our wedding, I showed her our rose bushes?"

"No!" Jane exclaimed. "What did she say?"

He chuckled. "She was not impressed. She told me rose bushes only live for fifty years. Did you know that? These scrawny things we have in our garden probably date back to the beginning of the garden itself..."

Jane's coffee cup crashed onto the table.

"Jane?" Max asked in alarm.

In that instant, Jane knew. She knew everything. She knew what happened to Sophie. She knew who painted the Franciscans. She knew why she had seen color in the Franciscans when she saw it nowhere else. And she knew what she would find beneath those rose bushes.

The world shimmered and faded like a transition between scenes in a movie. Max dissolved into a green pasture, and her nose filled up with a strange smell like...

Forty-One

Sophie

Burgen, Switzerland
August 12, 1924

... turpentine.

Sophie von Tessen wrinkled up her nose as the breeze carried the smell to her. She sat back in the grass watching her husband prepare his paintbrushes for an afternoon of painting. He dabbed a little turpentine on a rag and began wiping the brush handles one by one. It was a ritual, and its movements filled her with anticipation. With each new painting, they embarked on a journey together, and neither had any idea where it would end.

He passed the cloth near to his nose, trying to make it look accidental, but Sophie knew better. She had never been able to break his turpentine addiction, and now he was too old for it to matter anyway. He was a man with so many flaws, she had to pick the few that might be mended and then abide the rest.

They had come straight to the pasture after his nine o'clock service. This was their favorite picnic spot. She had a basket filled with bread and sausage she had brought from the chalet. They would eat it later while he waited for the first application of paint to dry.

His fierce focus meant she could study him freely, so she did. Over the years, he had taken on the look of a seasoned sailor. The broad-shouldered, brutish strength of his youth gave way to a subtle power he was unaware he had. In her eyes, it was more attractive. A few months earlier, he had abruptly thrown her over his shoulder to carry her across a stream. As he made his way through the water, she pounded on his back and scolded him for risking an injury. But when he finally put her down, he was barely out of breath and merely grinned at her with that mischievous look of his. His hair and beard had gone gray, but it only added to the ruggedness she had admired the first time she had seen him a lifetime ago. He no longer walked for many miles in search of the perfect spot to paint, thank god, but when the opportunity presented itself to work outdoors—as it did today—he seized it.

He wore his clerical clothes—black trousers, vest, and collar. He looked handsome in his uniform, she thought. For her part, she wore a floral sundress she had made from fabric her brother brought from Paris during one of his visits, and a broad-brimmed hat decorated with poppies she picked that morning from the church garden. It was one of those rare days that, as she grew older, she treasured more than ever—for she knew any one could be the last.

"In your sermon, what did Isaiah mean by 'they shall mount up with wings as eagles'?" she asked.

He stopped cleaning his palette knife and looked down at her in the grass. He tried to appear cross like a stern schoolmaster, but she knew he was pleased with the question. This was their private game. Knowing she loved birds, he made a point of inserting them into every sermon. It kept her alert. He was not a great orator.

From the grass, she watched him consider her question. His blue eyes twinkled, and he said, "In Hebrew lore, there is a story about the eagle."

Sophie sat up.

"They say that every ten years, the eagle tries to fly up to Heaven. But the poor eagle... he never gets there. The sun is too hot. It burns his feathers, and he falls to the sea. But there, in the water, he is revived. He grows new feathers. And so he is renewed and lives for another ten years when he tries again."

He smiled, and for an instant, she glimpsed him as he had been when they first met, so determined in his cause, painting as though every brush stroke bore a fresh atom into the universe.

He went on. "This pattern goes on until his tenth attempt. Now the eagle is ten times ten years old. This time he falls and is not renewed."

"He *drowns*?" she asked, aghast.

He nodded solemnly. "We may be renewed, *mon amour*, for a time. But we are not eternal. That is for God."

Sophie thought about that and then threw back her head dramatically. She leaned into a sultry pose on the grass. Her dress opened slightly, exposing the inside of her thigh. She felt his gaze go there.

"Well then, oh master," she cooed, "renew me now."

He looked confused.

"Paint me, silly," she said. "I'm asking you to paint me."

His thick eyebrows rose with interest.

"A portrait?"

She knew he liked portraits and would have painted her every day if it were up to him. But sitting still was torture for Sophie. It always had been. Her husband was a landscape painter out of necessity.

"But don't paint me as I am today," she said. "Give me fresh feathers. Like the eagle."

He laughed.

An idea exploded in her head, as ideas tended to do. "Paint me as I was on our first date. Can you remember that day?"

She watched him consider her request—not as a painter now, but as her husband. A shadow passed over his face, and he began to mumble as he did when he was vanishing into an idea. This, she knew from experience, could be dangerous.

"I can pick something else," she said.

"No, I'll do it."

He closed his eyes and stood still a long time behind the easel. She knew he was imagining what the final painting would look like. He opened his eyes, picked up his brush, and went to work.

Sophie rolled onto her stomach and opened her book. It was *Life on the Mississippi* by Mark Twain. It was her special, signed copy. Many years ago, they had gone to Vienna to hear him speak at the press club. It was one of their rare trips out of the valley. After his talk, Sophie found him and told him about her trip to St. Louis, seeing his hometown of Hannibal, handling dock lines for the riverboats, learning a few words of Shawnee, and skinny-dipping in the Mississippi.

When Twain heard all this, he abandoned the journalists clamoring for interviews and found a corner of the club where the three of them spent an hour in the most delightful conversation. Sophie had never laughed so much in one afternoon.

Sophie had read *Life on the Mississippi* three times since that day in Vienna, a fact confirmed by the three forget-me-not petals pressed into the pages. But that morning, while browsing the library for a new book, she decided impulsively to embark upon a fourth reading. The book always brought back memories of her adventure to America. John Planter. Happy memories.

Sophie began to read. She fell instantly under the spell of Twain's prose. Time passed.

Suddenly, her husband was beside her, brushing her arm. It was so unexpected that she dropped her book. As a rule, he never left his easel without Sophie insisting that he take a break to eat or, at the very least, to let the paint dry. What was he doing?

He rolled her onto her back and kissed her. She responded by pulling him on top of her. He tore off his clerical collar and began kissing her neck. She lay back, offering herself to him. She pretended she was Eve in the Garden, giving herself to the only man on Earth.

Afterward, they straightened their clothes and giggled at what they had done. They ate lunch quietly, and he went back to work. Sophie tried to read, but she was distracted by the *rat-tat-tat* of a woodpecker on a tree by the stream. From the slow tempo, she knew it was a pileated woodpecker. She would have liked to see it. Perhaps they could take a walk later.

She laid her book across her chest and fell asleep to the tapping of the bird's beak on the tree.

Forty-Two

Jane

Tearing out the rose bushes was harder than Jane would have expected.

"Like wading into barbed wire," Max complained.

While they worked, Jane marveled at the explanation she had glimpsed. Of *course* she had seen color in the paintings of *Amant* and Francis. The markers her brain had learned from *The Lover* were also in the Franciscans. Why? Because they were *painted by the same man*!

Van Gogh *was* Francis!

Long ago, Dr. Ravi Das had even suggested it, and while at the time Jane had dismissed the idea, now she saw her mistake.

After leaving John Planter in the thundersnow in St. Louis, Sophie had managed to arrive at Vincent's deathbed in France. With Eduard's help, they saved him. His "death" in Auvers-sur-Oise was a ruse invented so that the daughter of a baron could marry a penniless Dutch painter. With Eduard's money, connections, and personal physician, it wouldn't have been hard to pull off. Theo would have been in on it, of course. Following the theater of Vincent's hastily arranged, closed-casket funeral, they went to recuperate in the Valley of the Giants. Sophie cultivated a rumor that she was Eduard's mistress while Vincent Van Gogh returned to his former profession—the clergy. It explained the mystery of why Eduard, who had never been particularly religious, had commissioned such a fine church for Burgen. He built it for Vincent!

He also built the Garden Chapel complete with a secret passage to his sister's room so that Vincent could come and go undetected. Later, he converted it to a vault.

After an hour, Max's shovel struck something hard.

Jane and Max began working like archeologists to clear away the debris without disturbing the ground. Gradually, they were rewarded with the appearance of two identical rocks that stood against the wall of the chapel. It was obvious from their spacing and placement that they were headstones. But whose?

Any possible markings were made illegible by a thick coating of fungus and mud. Max got some water and brushes. They each went to work scrubbing the stones.

After a while, Max said, "I've got something."

"Me, too."

They polished a little longer until they were satisfied they had found all there was to find. The stones contained no names. No dates. Just two pictures.

One of a finch. The other of a sunflower.

Forty-Three

Sophie

A voice brought Sophie awake. Her eyes blinked open. Her copy of Mark Twain still lay across her chest. Vincent Van Gogh stood over her.

"It's time to go," he said.

She sat up and rubbed her eyes. The shadows were long. How long had she slept?

"Is it finished?" she asked.

He nodded. "Have a look."

She walked around the easel and looked at the finished painting. Her hand came to her mouth, and tears filled her eyes.

The painting showed a young Sophie, barely thirty years old, in the middle of a golden field. In the lower right-hand corner, a broad-shouldered Vincent stood with his back to the viewer. He wore a straw hat. You couldn't see his face, but you could see the half-finished work on his easel. He was painting the almond blossoms behind her, as he had been doing on the day of their picnic. What a clever man!

He signed it "*Amant*," as he had done on the painting she had given to John Planter three decades earlier. It was a private joke. Vincent loved that sort of thing. The signature was a departure from the usual "Francis" that he used since coming to the Valley of the Giants. Sophie had suggested the alias in honor of her favorite saint, and Vincent agreed. He had no interest in competing with the painter he had been in France.

"I'm not him anymore," he told her once. "Back then, I believed the work would redeem me. Then you wandered into the coliseum in Arles."

For ten years after coming to the valley, Vincent didn't paint. He returned to the Van Gogh family business, the ministry, and threw himself into it with his usual gusto. He wove complex sermons that stupefied the puzzled Burgeners, who wanted nothing more from the pulpit than to be reassured of their righteousness. Sophie had to go door-to-door before every service to shame them into attending.

Then one day, Vincent saw some pictures in a magazine by a young painter named Pablo Picasso. And just like that, Vincent was painting again. His work was different after that. He wasn't aiming for a "new kind of painting." He was painting for the joy of it, unconstrained by dreams of success—not looking for a sale, simply presenting every painting to Sophie as payment for having saved his life. Vincent was right; as a painter, he wasn't Van Gogh anymore. He was Francis now.

Outside the valley, Vincent Van Gogh's fame grew, and the notion of ever leaving their happy bubble became unthinkable. They both kept up with their medications and had regular visits from Eduard's physician. Even the doctor agreed—the scrutiny of the outside world would surely kill them both.

"Why would we leave?" Vincent asked during one of their many talks on the subject. "Theo's gone. I was never close to my other siblings. And Joanna seems to be doing a fine job with the paintings. They're hers by rights, anyway. Theo sacrificed as much as I did."

In the field, Sophie continued to admire Vincent's painting. Young Sophie's hair was messy, as it was so often in those days. She wore a yellow summer dress, one that was extremely low cut. Sophie had forgotten all about that dress. She had bought it from Marie at Madame Giroux's using the money she got from Vincent's reward. She wore it every day that summer. She had to. It was the only dress she owned.

Vincent had rendered the dress precisely, in every detail, right down to the pale blue bows on each shoulder. She had forgotten about the bows.

"You always paint me young," she said.

"Do I?"

"I never age. Do my wrinkles offend you?"

He shrugged. "I paint what I see."

Sophie accepted this. Over the years, she had watched him struggle to paint from his imagination. He wasn't that kind of painter. And it was nice to think that he still saw her this way. In truth, she had never been as beautiful as his portraits of her.

Still studying the painting, Sophie realized that it wasn't just a portrait of her—it was a portrait of *how she had looked to him* on that day so long ago. She blushed to see it now, across the decades. Oh, how he loved her!

Sophie's gaze went to the contents of the picnic, and tears slid down her weathered cheeks.

On the ground lay two strawberry salads on plates made from tree bark.

THE END

There is nothing more truly artistic than to love people.

—Vincent Van Gogh

Acknowledgments

This novel has gone through countless drafts, more than anything I have ever written. I must, therefore, acknowledge my indefatigable, long-suffering beta readers—Tamara, Stephanie, Beth, Carla, Fred, Wendy, Steve, and Janice—who got to see how the sausage is made, whether they liked it or not.

Questions for Discussion

1. Do you think Jane should reveal to the world that Francis Firth is Vincent Van Gogh? What would be gained? What would be lost?

2. The novel returns twice to a quote by Van Gogh: "There is nothing more artistic than to love people." How is this idea explored in the novel?

3. What is the significance of the common swift with the gold feather?

4. Rudolph von Tessen IIII made the swift his family crest after it saved Eduard from the avalanche. In Eduard's letter from the vault, he writes that he believed the bird was there to save Sophie, not him. Who do you think is right?

5. What parallels do you see between Sophie and Jane?

6. Jane muses that *Van Gogh's Lover* doesn't just depict the artist's love for Sophie but *contains* it. Do you think this is possible?

7. Granny Jo tells Jane that she "chose" to love her husband and that Jane can do the same with Max. Do you think this is true? How does this idea conflict with Max's view that we are driven by "urges" that show us the path to happiness?

8. In *The New Yorker*, Ted Banks makes the case that works of art should stand solely on their merit. Do you agree? Or do you think an artist's ethnicity, religion, politics, and gender should affect how we view a work of art?

9. For all the time that Dr. John Planter knew Sophie, he could not look at *The Lover*. Sophie used this failing to explain why a marriage between them could not work. What did she mean by this? When John finally did look at the painting, he agreed with her. What do you think he saw?

10. In the asylum, Sophie told Vincent that—unlike everyone else—she didn't need to ask him why he cut off his ear. She knew the reason. What do you think she meant by this? Why do you think this understanding is significant to their relationship?

Michael Hetzer is a former foreign correspondent and founding editor of *The Moscow Times*. His novel, *The Forbidden Zone*, was featured in *The New York Times* and was named one of the top five debut thriller novels of the year by *The Boston Globe*. His other novels include *Van Gogh's Lover* and the forthcoming *One Year in Eden*. When he's not out sailing his boat, he sets anchor on the Carolina coast.

Printed in Dunstable, United Kingdom